# TRINITY

# BOOKS
## by DAVE BARA

*Trinity*

### The Lightship Chronicles
*Impulse*
*Starbound*
*Defiant*

### Standalone Novels
*Speedwing*

# TRINITY

## DAVE BARA

Trinity

Copyright © 2021 by Dave Bara

All rights reserved, including the right to reproduce this book or portions thereof in any form.

A Baen Books Original

Baen Publishing Enterprises
P.O. Box 1403
Riverdale, NY 10471
www.baen.com

ISBN: 978-1-9821-2566-0

Cover art by Kurt Miller

First printing, October 2021

Distributed by Simon & Schuster
1230 Avenue of the Americas
New York, NY 10020

Library of Congress Cataloging-in-Publication Data

Names: Bara, Dave, author.
Title: Trinity / Dave Bara.
Description: Riverdale, NY : Baen Publishing Enterprises, [2021] | "A Baen
  Books Original"—Title page verso.
Identifiers: LCCN 2021036344 | ISBN 9781982125660 (trade paperback)
Subjects: GSAFD: Science fiction.
Classification: LCC PS3602.A735 T75 2021 | DDC 813/.6—dc23
LC record available at https://lccn.loc.gov/2021036344

Printed in the United States of America

10 9 8 7 6 5 4 3 2 1

# Acknowledgments

I'd like to thank my editor at Baen, Tony Daniel, and his publisher, Toni Weisskopf, for their faith in me and in *Trinity*. It is always gratifying to see your work and your career given a second chance, another bite at the apple, as it were. Writing is a hard business, and I encourage all of you out there working to break in to keep writing, keep taking your shot at the stars.

I would also like to acknowledge the hard work of my agent, Paul Stevens of The Donald Maas Literary Agency, (and all the people there) in making *Trinity* a reality.

Onward and upward,

Dave

# ☆ PROLOGUE ☆

Captain Jared Clement of the Rim Confederation Navy gunship *Beauregard* contemplated his tactical screen. He was alone in his cabin, as was his habit before battle, concentrating and formulating his upcoming strategy.

The tactical screen showed him no love. The fleet of 5 Suns Alliance Navy ships approaching his position over the planet Argyle, and its space station of the same name, had left their positions around the planet Shenghai in the nearby Kemmerine system over thirty-eight light-hours ago. The ships had accelerated impossibly fast, well over twenty-five *g*s, and had reached a velocity so close to light speed as to be insignificant in its difference in just thirty minutes. Normally acceleration at that speed could only be accomplished by unmanned vessels or weapons. Any human crew would be left as bloody splatters against the walls of the ships, unless there was some mitigating technology perhaps, he suspected, a new propulsion system aboard the 5 Suns Navy vessels.

Clement had heard rumors of inertial dampening technology being developed by the 5 Suns, some sort of projectors that literally distorted space in front of an accelerating ship by pushing out leading gravity waves. Humankind had been pushing at the limits of light speed for decades, and this "rumored" technology was extremely promising. So much so that Clement was fairly sure he was watching it in action for the first time on the tactical screen right in front of him.

Just a light-hour earlier the attacking formation had split into three groups, one each setting course for the three inhabited planets, Helios, Ceta, and Argyle, of the weak orange dwarf Rim star. They were close enough now that Clement could count their numbers: five light cruisers for each of Ceta and Helios, but fifteen reserved for him at Argyle. He'd made no secret of where he was stationed. Now he regretted that decision.

He'd beaten the 5 Suns Navy enough times in the ongoing conflict that it was clear they were going out of their way to finish him and the *Beauregard* off as quickly and efficiently as they could. As a former 5 Suns Navy officer himself, he was undoubtedly high on their hit list, as was his crew, he reminded himself. And he wasn't willing to sacrifice them, especially not his XO, who happened to be his former lover, and a native of the planet Helios. Commander Elara DeVore had broken off their relationship when he'd been named captain of the *Beauregard*, a move he had agreed with from a professional standpoint, if not a personal one. She in turn had agreed to follow him to his new command, but only if they broke off the relationship. It was a high price to pay, but he knew he needed her on his ship. She was still, for him, the most extraordinary woman he had ever met, but the rules were the rules, and Clement had reluctantly accepted her decision more than two years ago. Oh, there had been women since then, but none like Elara DeVore, not even close.

He fingered the rim of his whiskey glass as he tried to work out some kind of tactical strategy that gave them a fighting chance. He could find none. He wanted a drink now, badly, but he repressed the impulse. Alcohol was his personal demon, one he had learned to accept, but he didn't have to like it.

In response to the approaching flotilla, the Rim Confederation Navy had only their famous gunships. Clement had four here at Argyle, and there were three each at the other planetary defense stations. It wasn't enough. But it was all they had left. Clement himself had been in charge of the development plans on the gunships, so they were practically designed for him and his style of fighting. The Rim Navy had lost many ships in the last two years, including all of their capital ships in a mistaken attempt to take the space station at the nearby Kemmerine star. For the record, Clement had been against that move, thinking it was likely to sharpen the 5 Suns Navy's fighting edge. Regrettably, he'd been right. But the "Admirals" in charge of the Rim Navy (former commanders and captains with the 5 Suns Navy before the war) had made their plans and as a good soldier Clement had done his best during the attack.

The only ships to escape Kemmerine that day had been his

gunships and a pair of battered destroyers, both of which had to be scuttled on the return trip. It had been a bad day for the Rim, if not a personal victory for him and his tactics. They'd made him Fleet Captain then (he had turned down the offered rank of Admiral) and he'd spent most of the last year preparing the Rim Navy for the inevitable, a full-scale invasion by the 5 Suns. It now appeared this was the day they had dreaded.

This had all the signs of an end-game maneuver by the 5 Suns Navy, and looking at his tac board, it seemed likely it would succeed despite his best efforts. He contemplated the situation, and briefly considered surrender, but his orders had been clear from Fleet headquarters: fight until you could fight no more. The order was tinted with the likelihood that those admirals were facing the noose for treason soon, but Clement was too good a sailor to do other than what he was ordered to do.

Just then he got the com chime from his bridge and he responded quickly. "Report, XO," he said.

"Enemy flotilla is decelerating rapidly, estimate eleven minutes until they are able to engage us on the battlefield," she said. He was amazed at the rapid deceleration he was witnessing, but not surprised. The rumored inertial dampening tech was on full display.

"Eleven minutes? Christ, I find myself longing for the old days when you had a couple of hours to prep for the battlefield," he said.

"Those days are gone, sir," she replied, the alarming tone of her voice indicating her desire for him to take control of the situation and start giving orders. He decided he should heed her. He shut down his display and got up to take the nine steps from his cabin to the bridge, a path he might be taking for the last time.

"Order the fleet to accelerate to 0.25 $g$, maneuvering thrusters only, 0.000086 inclined to the ecliptic. Get us some distance from Argyle Station. Hopefully, that will make them have to adjust their course," he said as he hit the mechanism and the doors to his cabin parted.

"What about the station? Are we leaving it undefended?" He paused to reconsider.

"No. Tell Captain Cormack to hold back the *Antietam*, but his orders are not to fight if he is outnumbered. If we don't give them multiple targets with our gunships they *might* leave the station intact. Might," he said.

"Understood, sir."

A few short steps later and he was on his bridge. The main tactical display showed the glowing dots of the incoming 5 Suns flotilla. The screen was rimmed with a pulsating red light, indicating danger, something Clement already knew.

"Status," he ordered, standing in front of his tactical station. Each of his bridge crew in turn gave their updates.

"Fifteen 5 Suns Navy light cruisers coming in hot, sir. They're still decelerating, but estimate they will be at zero within two minutes. Then they will have to shift their flight path to intercept us," reported DeVore. "It will take about five minutes more for them to catch us on our current course, using conventional thrusters."

"I don't think we can count on that, XO, based on what I saw of their crossing speed."

"The gravity wave technology?"

"Possibly. I just don't know if they can use it effectively on a short-range battlefield."

"How long do we continue our burn, sir?" The question came from Mika Ori, the *Beauregard*'s pilot.

"We don't, Lieutenant. As soon as they reach zero acceleration I want us moving at forty-five degrees to their position. If they precalculated our course based on our current burn they'll have to reconfigure. Give them something to think about," Clement said.

"Looking for the best ground to fight on, sir?" asked Ivan Massif, Ori's husband and the *Beauregard*'s navigator. Clement eyed the tall, lanky man.

"Regrettably, there is no 'best ground' in this area of space, Ivan. We'll make two of the forty-five-degree pivots, three minutes apart, then we take our chances."

"We're going to attack?" said DeVore. Clement gave her an annoyed look.

"This is most likely our last battle, Commander. I wouldn't want it any other way, giving them one last bloody nose."

"But—"

"Commander," he said, beckoning her to come to his station. She did, reluctantly. He looked into her dark brown eyes, searching for understanding in them, but finding only confusion. He was always an enigma to her, he knew, and that's what had probably made their relationship work for as long as it did. "XO," he started in a whispered voice, "if they come after us, then perhaps they'll go easier on the other ships. I'm hoping this maneuver will save lives."

"But not ours," she replied, equally quiet. He looked away from her.

"I'm the Fleet Captain," he said. "I'm the prize they want."

"What about the rest of us?"

He gave her a silent nod of affirmation. "I'll do the best I can," he whispered. And the conversation was over. She returned to her console, and he continued taking reports.

Thirty seconds from the 5 Suns fleet reaching zero point, he sent out a private com to his navigator and pilot, giving them specific time and instructions on the two burns and the attack vector. Each pinged him with confirmations. They understood. He wouldn't have to give the orders verbally.

The 5 Suns fleet reached zero deceleration, just one hundred kilometers from Argyle Station in a precision maneuver his ships could never emulate. Three light cruisers immediately broke off from the main fleet and accelerated toward the station and the *Antietam*.

The rest, twelve ships, started burning their thrusters toward the stationary Rim gunships. He was outnumbered four to one—not bad odds, considering. He looked down at his tac board.

*Now*, he thought, just as Mika Ori gunned the engines.

Perfect.

They'd been engaged with the 5 Suns Navy cruisers for more than fifteen minutes, and so far, so good. Clement had them scrambling to defend their positions, but he still had one surprise left in his hand of cards. One his crew had practiced, but never executed in battle.

"Inverted C dive, now!" demanded Clement of his pilot.

"Full C dive, aye, sir!" said Mika Ori. She slammed the *Beauregard's* chemical infusion drive to the wall, accelerating the ship to over six gravities as they started their dive, pulling them away from the 5 Suns Navy cruiser formation. At this speed, on a crowded battlefield, it had never been tried. The chances of hitting a slice of metal or even colliding with a full ship were high, but Clement believed his ship could carry out the maneuver—and after all, he was her designer. He knew how much she could take, beyond what the specs said.

Some would have called a max-thruster inverted "C" in battle a suicide move. Not Clement. He'd built his ship for just this kind of off-the-books performance. The burn took the *Beauregard* away from the battlefield in a tight curve, from under the main plane of battle and then up through the battlefield again before his ship dropped back "down" on the enemy from above. No enemy commander would have tried it in one of the clunky 5 Suns Navy cruisers. Hell, no enemy ship could have likely carried it out.

He strained against his acceleration couch, his body squirming inside his g-force dampening suit. The suit at least partially compensated against the forces of inertial gravity. Clement and the rest of his suited bridge crew could still move, just not nimbly or quickly.

He watched on his tactical board as the 5 Suns Navy ships hardly reacted at all. Certainly, no one dared to chase the *Beauregard*, and most probably thought he was trying to escape. The Rim Confederation Navy was outgunned in this particular encounter, but the *Beauregard* had a way of evening things up. She was faster, better shielded, and carried enough ordnance to make any 5 Suns Alliance Navy cruiser's day miserable. And the 5SN relied almost exclusively on their midsized light cruisers to fight the RCN.

The *Beauregard* reached the apex of its dive (relative to the ecliptic of the Argyle system and the battlefield) and kept burning, powering through the lower arc of the inverted C-curve maneuver. "Cut the engines," ordered Clement as they reached their max speed of one hundred seventy-five kilometers per second, completing their acceleration and driving back down to the battlefield, nearly ten thousand kilometers distant now. At that speed, they would be back on the invading fleet in slightly less than a minute.

"Prep the scatter mines," ordered Clement through his pressure suit's com system.

"We're ready," came the response from his engineer, Hassan Nobli, via the com from his engine room. What they were ready with was more than two hundred mobile metal mines armed with .10 kiloton charges that would be released over the battlefield as the *Beauregard* swept through the multitiered 5 Suns fleet formation. The result would be potentially devastating to the 5 Suns light cruisers, a cloud of death unleashed on the battlefield, enveloping everything in its path. Clement had used these weapons only once before, at the Battle of Kemmerine as a means for his gunships to escape the 5 Suns fleet. But in that case the scatter mines had been used as a rear-guard action while his deployed gunships sped away from the battlefield. They'd never been used in such a high-speed maneuver before.

"I'm detecting unusual EM activity from four of the 5 Suns Alliance cruisers," came a warning from DeVore.

"Specify, XO," said Clement.

"I can't, sir. I'm reading heightened electromagnetic activity on four ships, as I said, sir. Uncertain as to what it means. We still have time to break off the attack and reform with the other gunships," she said.

Clement thought for a moment, looked up at his tactical board one last time and said, "No. Maintain course and speed."

No one said anything, least of all DeVore. They had all learned to trust their captain, his instincts and intuitions. They had been fighting together in a civil war for autonomy from the 5 Suns Alliance for the most distant planets in 5 Suns space, the Rim Confederation. But this battle was the biggest of the entire war, a game-ending play by the 5 Suns Navy to finish the costly four-year-old conflict which had seen both sides pushed to their limits.

They had seconds now before the *Beauregard* pierced the positions of the 5 Suns Navy cruisers at blinding speed. Clement watched on his tactical board as the 5SN ships finally began to scramble, looking to get out of range of the gunship's suicide dive. Near Argyle Station itself, Clement watched the desperate battle between the Rim Navy's remaining gunships and the 5SN cruisers, a battle the Rim Confederation Navy was losing. This was his biggest play ever, and it *had* to work.

"Captain!" came DeVore's warning, a second after Clement saw it. Four 5SN cruisers had formed up in a flat square, a full kilometer on each side, right in the *Beauregard's* descending path. They were sacrificing those cruisers . . . but to what end?

At the speed the *Beauregard* was traveling the metal from the mines would rip through the hulls of the cruisers on kinetic energy alone. But these weapons, which Clement had a hand in creating, were designed to be more powerful than anything else that had been used in the war to date, containing their own propulsion systems and the exploding ordnance.

At ten seconds to contact he ordered the scatter mines released. They swarmed out and accelerated away from the *Beauregard*, as they were designed to do, seeking out their targets. The four 5 Suns Alliance Navy cruisers didn't stand a chance against them.

At five seconds to contact he saw their play. An orange-tinted EM field, looking like a waving, beaded carpet, extended between the four ships, forming a perfect one-kilometer-square blanket of electron-charged plasma. The *Beauregard* had no chance to evade it, no hope of changing course or decelerating to avoid contact.

The scatter mines slammed into the four battle cruisers with devastating effect, sending showers of sparks and flame out into the eternal night of space. For a moment Clement thought they were delivered, but then he saw the awful truth: four probes that were detached from the cruisers had kept the plasma blanket as a fully charged closed circuit.

The *Beauregard* impacted the plasma, and Clement's world exploded. The bridge arced and flamed with static energy. It seemed like everything was on fire, including some of the crew. He opened his mouth to give orders but nothing came out, nothing comprehensible at least. His ship rattled and rocked, rolling uncontrollably through space, spinning and decelerating at a frightening clip. The crew were pinned to their acceleration couches again, some of them burning in place. His com filled with their screams of agony and shouts for help. It was an eternity until Clement was strong enough to escape his couch and grab a fire extinguisher. He put out three fires, two of them on members of his crew, charred bodies now, while the rest of the survivors did the same. It was true Hell.

He pulled off his helmet and his lungs filled with the acrid smell of burned flesh and burning equipment. Only a few systems were left operating on the ship, one of them the tactical board. He looked around the bridge. Of his nine bridge officers only himself, DeVore, Mika Ori and Ivan Massif, had survived.

"Show me," he said to DeVore. She brought up the tactical board.

The four 5SN cruisers spreading the plasma blanket had been destroyed, cut to pieces. Two others were damaged to less than fifty percent tactical efficiency. The rest of the flotilla, six operating cruisers, was intact and closing in on the *Beauregard*. The remaining

Rim gunships had fled, trying to protect Argyle Station. The *Antietam* was adrift, with heavy damage, knocked out of the battle and sinking into the gravity well of the planet Argyle itself, where she would no doubt burn up. There were nine active cruisers now against just three working gunships, a three-to-one advantage for the 5 Suns Navy, and the *Beauregard* itself was finished, that much was obvious.

"What did they hit us with?" asked DeVore.

"Some kind of electron-charged plasma weapon. Our own speed through the battlefield displaced enough energy to magnify the blanket's effect a hundredfold. We're done," Clement said.

"If they'd kept to standard tactics we should have gotten half their fleet, at least," said Ori.

"Yes, we should have," said Clement. "But they anticipated our move."

"How?" asked Ori. Clement shook his head.

"Only one way I can think of. They knew what our plan was and how we were going to execute it." Clement promised himself he would find out who had betrayed him and his crew, and one day enact revenge.

He went to the tactical board again and checked his ship's course and speed, and the status of the remainder of the Rim Confederation fleet. The *Beauregard* was rapidly decelerating. The remaining gunships protecting Argyle itself were in the process of surrendering. Argyle Station had already fallen. If this scene was being repeated at Ceta and Helios then not only was the battle over, the war was too.

"We should consider surrendering," stated DeVore.

"Should we?" said Clement, then he turned to Ori. "Mika, can you give me one-quarter speed on the chemical thrusters?" She nodded.

"I'll try, sir."

The *Beauregard*'s thrusters groaned and moaned but eventually she started moving again at the pilot's command. They had been drifting in the general direction of Argyle 4, a twenty-kilometer-wide rock that passed as a moon of Argyle. Clement set his direction there.

"What are you doing?" asked DeVore.

"We may be beaten but we're still Rim Confederation Navy. They want my ship for a trophy. The *Beauregard* has kicked more 5 Suns

Navy ass in this system than any other ship we've had in the entire war. They'll want her so they can scrape her insides for every bloody secret she has. But I'm not going to let them," he said, defiant.

"You're scuttling her?" said DeVore.

"I am," he replied without looking up from his board.

"But sir—"

"They're not getting their grubby hands on my ship, Elara!" he snapped. "All of you to the rescue pods, that's an order," Clement said, then he sounded the general alarm, and called down to Hassan Nobli, his closest friend on the ship, besides DeVore, of course. "Get off the ship, Nobli. I'm going to scuttle her."

"If you're going down with her I am too!" insisted Nobli through the com.

"Evac now, Hassan. That's an order. That alarm is for you too." There was a moment's silence, then Nobli said, "Aye, sir. It's been a pleasure serving with you."

"It damn well hasn't, and you know it. We were never close. You were only my friend for the drinking," he said.

"Understood, sir," came Nobli's reluctant reply, indicating he had absorbed his cover story for the 5 Suns Navy interrogations that would likely follow their capture.

Clement cut the line.

The evacuations aboard the rest of the ship started almost immediately. When he was satisfied the bulk of the surviving crew was free of the ship and the rest would surely be gone in the next few minutes, he personally fired the thrusters a second time on a collision vector toward Argyle 4.

"Mika, Ivan, off with you," he said. "I don't need anyone to help me fly my ship into an asteroid."

"I want to stay with you, sir," Ori protested. Clement shook his head.

"Not possible. Now get to a pod and get off my ship, both of you. That's an order." *And probably my last as captain of this ship*, he thought. Ori and Massif saluted sharply and then they were off to one of the three bridge escape pods. One of them was damaged beyond repair, but Clement watched as they boarded another pod and a second later they were gone. There was one rescue pod left with a capacity of two people.

Alarms blared as the emergency lights flickered amongst the still burning fires and system circuit overloads. Clement looked around his smashed bridge. DeVore came up and wrapped her arm in his, taking hold of his hand.

"I don't know what you're thinking, but you are *not* going to go down with this ship," she said to him. He looked at her. A loyal comrade, his most trusted advisor, his lost love, and his friend. He smiled weakly.

"No, I'm not," he admitted. He checked the vector of the *Beauregard* one more time, satisfied she would meet her end on Argyle 4 and not fall into the hands of the 5SN, then he let DeVore lead him by the hand to the last escape pod. He unlocked it and pushed her through, then, after a moment's hesitation, he stepped off of his Rim Confederation Navy command for the last time and into the rescue pod. This, he was sure, would be his last commission, in any navy.

They both strapped in and Clement donned his helmet again before he switched on the IFF beacon that would identify them to the enemy. In his final act as captain, he hit the activation button and the rescue pod explosively accelerated away from the *Beauregard*. He felt the pain of loss, of losing his ship, but also a sense of relief that the long, uphill climb was finally over. He was embarrassed that he felt that way.

Six minutes of silence later he watched his ship crash onto the surface of Argyle 4, scraping a scar across its already ugly face. Four minutes after that and they were in the shadow of a 5 Suns Alliance Navy light cruiser.

"So what happens now?" asked DeVore. Clement shook his head.

"It doesn't matter," he said. "We've lost. And I'll become a ghost. We'll all become ghosts of this war." DeVore squeezed his hand.

"No," she said, "some of us won't."

# ✵ 1 ✵

*11 Years Later*

Jared Clement held up his normal end of the bar, just like every night, drinking his Irish whiskey, straight, and watching the propaganda that passed for "news" on the Argyle Station monitors. According to the 5 Suns Alliance News Network, crop yields had just broken records on the planet below the orbiting space station, but Clement knew better. That was one of the reasons he preferred to stay aboard a well-stocked space station instead of on the bleak landscape of the planet Argyle itself. The people below, almost two million of them, were mostly starving, and everyone around here knew it. Hell, more than a decade ago, Clement had fought, and lost, a war over it. Not that any of that mattered now.

The real truth was that the relatively well-off world of Ceta, where he was born, had upped their food shipments to Argyle just to stave off the starvation of a handful of the colonists below. Crop yields on Argyle were lower than at any time in the last two decades, and even though the 5 Suns Alliance had promised increased food aid to the three worlds of the former Rim Confederation as a promise made for ending their civil war with an armistice, that support had never come. What aid that did get sent was skimmed and sold on the black market by 5 Suns Alliance administrators, with a sizeable kickback to the Rim Worlds Governor-General to look the other way. It was the same kind of issue that had started the uprising, but nowadays people in the Rim just seemed to have no belly for the fight anymore. They were too busy trying to survive.

As a war veteran though, Clement had a better deal than most. He hadn't been forced by conscription back into the 5 Suns Alliance Navy, nor exiled on Ceta or Argyle itself. And he used his vet status

13

and a meager pension (really, just a buyoff from the 5SA to keep the peace) as a means to stay in space and serve in the merchant marine. He'd managed to squeak out a pretty good subsistence as a reliable ship captain and sometimes pilot. It wasn't much, but despite the drinking he'd proven reliable enough to keep an apartment on the station, and most merchant sailors had stopped giving him stick for being a "dirty rebel" years ago. Most, in fact, rarely even recognized him anymore. He had become a nobody to the 5 Suns, and that's the way he wanted to keep it. He'd lost enough in the goddamned war, his ship, friends, and even a lover. Rebellion wasn't even a word in his vocabulary anymore.

He'd chosen Argyle as his base because it was the best of the Rim stations, and the main port where the 5 Suns Navy offloaded all of their best contraband for reselling. In retrospect, it had been a wise choice. There was (almost) always good booze and even some delicacies from the Core Planets that came through the station, like oysters and shellfish and even the occasional blue lobster. It made life a bit more interesting anyway.

He flipped his index finger at the barkeep, another grizzled veteran of the war whose name he'd forgotten, as a signal to hit him with another shot of the whiskey. The barkeep did as instructed, then said, "one more," and held up his own index finger just to emphasize the point. Clement had set himself a drink limit at the bar to keep from falling into financial chaos. Six shots a night was all he would allow himself. Tonight though, that limit was looking dubious. These days, since the war, drinking was his only solace and alcohol usually his only companion.

The 5 Suns Alliance news had now turned to sports, specifically the Super-Rugby Final between Voyagers and Holy Sacrament from the Core Worlds of the two main-sequence inner suns, those being Colonus A and B. The planets Santos, Carribea, and Freehold orbited Colonus A, with Atlas and Columbia orbiting B. Clement forgot which planet which team was from, but he was pretty sure he used to be a Voyagers fan when he was a kid. Either that or he hated them. He couldn't actually remember.

Clement downed his fifth shot. It was now nearly certain the barkeep was watering down the whiskey. He barely had a buzz on, and it was getting near midnight.

Word was he might have a job coming up as a Class VI freighter pilot, but that wasn't for two more weeks. Plenty more shots to go between now and then, and that was fine with Clement. The war had taken all of the ambition out of his system, in more ways than one.

The 5 Suns shipping syndicates liked hiring him because of his reputation for being fast and efficient, and also his ability to avoid troublesome Tax Compliance patrols. He was a good pilot, using a combination of speed, stealth and sometimes just brute power to avoid trouble with the authorities. Everything he'd learned had been from watching his pilot in the war, Mika Ori. She was magnitudes of scale better than he was. Absently, he thought about contacting her and her husband, Ivan Massif. It had been over three years since their last communication. Heck, maybe they were divorced. He let that thought slide out of his mind with the whiskey . . .

"Captain Clement," came the voice from over his shoulder. It was female, and pleasant, but still, Clement had to decide if he wanted to turn around. Ultimately, he decided he didn't.

"There is no 'Captain Clement,' lady, hasn't been for many years. My name's Jared, and I can tell from your voice that whatever you came here to ask me, the answer is no." He signaled the barkeep one last time, and was dutifully rewarded with his final shot glass. The woman came around his shoulder and leaned in on the bar, looking toward him and getting in his personal space to the point where he had to pay attention to her. Unable to avoid her further, Clement relented and looked at her.

She was a pretty woman of Asian descent, in her late twenties he guessed, and all made up in a 5 Suns Alliance Navy commander's rank uniform. Her hair hung short and straight with a full run of bangs across her forehead with no part. He decided *she* looked serious enough, even if *he* wasn't.

"By the rules of the Treaty of Argyle you're still allowed the honoraria of your Rim Confederation Captain's rank, even if you're retired, Mr. Clement," she said, pointedly avoiding using his rank this time. For his part, Clement looked away and contemplated ordering his last shot.

"You know, I think you're the highest-ranking navy officer I've seen since my war parole ended," he deadpanned. She humored him.

"And how long ago was that?"

"About nine years," Clement said. "I did nine months in navy confinement after the armistice, forced to give up my tactical secrets to your navy, was separated from my crew after the war ended, then had supervised parole for another two years to make sure I was firmly compliant and not thinking about restarting an old conflict. Not the best of times. And you're reminding me of them now."

"I really don't know that much about the war, or its aftermath, Mr. Clement. All of that was over well before I joined the 5 Suns Alliance Navy." She leaned in a bit closer, as if she were examining his face. It still had some of the glow of youth. The short-cropped and buzzed hair had a hint of gray at the temples and he had his share of weathered wrinkles on his forehead and crow's feet, though not in abundance. It certainly was the face of a man who had been through some difficult times in life.

Clement made a squinty face of disapproval at her. "Don't you have to study navy history anymore? Hell, I did when I was in the 5SN."

She nodded, humoring him. "We do. But now we have peace again, and everyone gets along like they're supposed to," she said.

Clement twirled his empty shot glass on the bar and eyeballed the commander, then signaled for the barkeep to fill his last shot. She watched as Clement's shot glass was filled.

"You're new to the Rim, aren't you, Commander?" he said sarcastically. She smiled before continuing, and it looked pleasant on her face.

"As a matter of fact, yes. This is my first time in the Rim Sector. I've spent most of my career in the Kemmerine Sector apart from a short stint at Colonus Sector on Atlas," she said. Colonus Sector was the richest part of 5 Suns Alliance space, where the two main-sequence G-type stars that formed the core of exo-Sol human civilization revolved around each other in an eighty-year dance. The three outlying orange K-type stars that completed the 5 Suns Alliance all had habitable planets, but the three outlier worlds of the Rim were by far the poorest, not being blessed with nearly the natural resources that the five worlds that spun around Colonus A and B had. Clement smiled.

"You're practically wet behind the ears, Commander. What did you say your name was?"

"I didn't, but if you must know it's Tanitha Yan. Commander Tanitha Yan."

"Tanitha? Odd name for a Chinese girl from New Hong Kong on Shenghai," commented Clement. She blushed just a bit and then sat down on the empty stool next to him.

"How did you know what city I was from?" she asked. He smiled.

"I'm pretty good with my colonial accents. Yours is very slight, but I was still able to make it out," he said. "From what I know of the culture on your world, I'm guessing that most of your friends were no doubt more interested in being socialites, but you joined the 5 Suns Navy, Tanitha. I wonder why?"

She shrugged. "My father was a professor," Commander Yan offered. "My mother stayed at home. I guess you could say I was privileged. Compared to almost anyone on the Rim worlds I'm sure you'd think me rich and spoiled. But I wanted to do something on my own, away from my surroundings and my parent's protection. When the navy needed recruits, I agreed to join the officer corps right out of college, but I wasn't given anything. I got where I am on merit, Mr. Clement."

He nodded. "Fair enough. Now tell me how you got that name again, Tanitha?"

Again the shrug. "It's just a westernized name I took over my given name when I went to school. My parents thought it would be easier for me growing up on a split colony," she said.

"Well, the French and Chinese have gotten along so well over the centuries," Clement deadpanned, referring to the early colonial wars that broke out on her home planet. "So now you have to tell me because I must know. What was your given name?"

She blushed again and her face took on a lovely pink tone. "Xiu Mei," she said. Now Clement laughed openly and loudly.

"Xiu Mei? Do you know what that means?" he said. She gave a nod of her head as she turned even more pink.

"Yes."

"Beautiful Plum!" He looked at her, laughing as she smiled, embarrassed. "Well you certainly are all that, Miss Yan. But now that I've had my fun with you, why don't you tell me why you're here talking to me?"

"I would prefer that to be done in private, Mr. Clement," Yan said. Clement downed his last shot.

"Well, I'm a very private man, Miss Yan; I don't open my door to just anyone." Now she got a serious look on her face. "The proposal I have for you will be well worth your time, I would think. And it comes from the highest of authorities."

"I'm not much on authority these days, especially when it comes from the 5 Suns Alliance Navy," he said.

"You're going to want to hear this proposal, believe me," she replied. The look on her face was firm and serious.

He shrugged. "My time isn't free," Clement said flatly.

"Name your price," she said quickly.

Clement looked to the barkeep. "Argyle Select Scotch, single malt," he said, "and unopened." The last was to verify that it wasn't watered down.

"You're over your limit," protested the bartender, not wanting to give up a bottle of his highest-quality booze at any price. Clement looked to Yan and back.

"I'll have the bottle," he said. "She's buying." The bartender looked to Yan, who nodded. Reluctantly he pressed a key on his register and a biometric scanner flashed across her eyes and debited the listed amount for the scotch, which was much higher than its real commercial value. The bartender took the bottle off his rack and slid it across the bar to Clement, who took it with a practiced ease and a nod, and then slid a two-crown tip the other way. Then he stood to leave.

"You'll have fifteen minutes to convince me in my cabin, Miss Yan. Then I kick you out," he said.

"Fair enough," she replied, standing as well, "but I hope you don't think my 'convincing' will be with anything but words."

"Oh, I have no doubt of that. Besides, I would never dream of asking such a thing of an obvious lady like yourself. Now, if you'd like to follow me . . . " He gestured toward the door of the bar with a broad sweep of his hand. Yan said nothing, but stepped past him and into the adjoining corridor, which was full of general station riffraff.

They both went silent as they walked, Yan observing in her staid, military way and Clement walking casually, cradling the unopened bottle of scotch. They arrived at his cabin on C deck and he keyed in the door code, the security system scanning Yan for weapons as she passed the threshold.

"You're not the trusting type, are you, Mr. Clement?" she commented.

"Just something I learned from your kind during the war," he said.

"I was fifteen," she replied, "during your war."

Yan entered and surveyed the room. It was small, barely more than a studio, but he had a porthole view of the station's stem and the dusty planet Argyle below. There was a small desk, entertainment complex, separate bathroom and a divider for his bed, a small sofa, and a reclining chair which Clement promptly sat down in, likely his favorite spot, she decided. It was neat and clean, and showed the care of a former military man who was deep on discipline if not entirely flowing in crowns and luxury.

"So what's your assessment of my lifetime of accomplishments?" he said, capping the scotch and pouring into two drinking glasses. Yan looked around one more time, then started in.

"Despite your rather shaggy outward appearance, which I suspect is a false front, underneath you are disciplined and thoughtful. You don't need for much, and you don't want much, but you seem to be a man who is ready at any time to take advantage of an opportunity if it comes your way, and I would guess you've been expecting it to come your way for a while now," she said.

He contemplated her from over the rim of his glass. "And now, coincidentally, you're here. Thanks for the psychoanalysis, by the way," he said.

Yan sat down on the sofa facing him and picked up her glass of the scotch. She looked to a bookcase in the entertainment complex. One display panel had his military medals, some 5SN and some Rim Confederation, a pair of old conventional field glasses in a glass box, and . . . a photo of his former command crew on the *Beauregard*. She pointed to the photo.

"You feel like you let them down." It was a simple statement, followed by a simple answer.

"I did, which is why I can't imagine why anyone in the 5 Suns Navy would want to talk to me," he said.

"And yet here I am, representing that very same navy, and

someone of special importance in it. Someone who knows your military record very well."

Clement sat deeper into his chair, crossing his legs and resting them on the table in a show of disinterest. "So tell me your proposal, Miss Yan," he said as he took a small drink of his scotch, which was damn good compared to the swill in the station bar.

"Aren't you curious who it's from?" she asked. He shook his head.

"If it's a shit job I won't care to know, so you'd best be out with it," he said.

Yan settled in a bit, then addressed him in an almost formal way. "The Fleet Admiral of the 5 Suns Alliance Navy for the Kemmerine Sector wants to offer you a command," she said simply. Kemmerine was the nearest 5 Suns Alliance sector to the Rim. Its single star was one of the orange K types, but much more powerful than Argyle, with six planets in the system, two habitable, one of which was Yan's home world of Shenghai. The other was called New Paris.

"Why?" he said, skeptical and taking another drink.

"Because the mission is dangerous. Because it requires a ship commander of exceptional ability and experience, and the Fleet Admiral doesn't feel she has anyone who fits that description under her command," Yan said.

"*Her* command?" said Clement, intrigued. "I can't think of too many women who have that kind of respect for me."

Yan looked at him, eyes unwavering. A smile crossed her face. "Elara DeVore does," she said.

That shocked him. Hearing her name was like a bolt of lightning through his nervous system. It took all of his efforts to control himself, to try and not show Yan the very tender button she had just pushed. He thought long and hard before he spoke again.

"I haven't seen or heard from Elara DeVore since the war ended, and that was eleven years ago. We were split up, all of my crew, into different POW camps while the peace treaties were being negotiated. And now you're telling me that she's a 5 Suns Alliance Navy *Fleet Admiral*?" he finally said, his voice raising more than he wanted it too.

"Yes," said Yan, "in command over the entire Kemmerine Sector. And she wants you to undertake a very special mission. That's why I'm here."

Clement said nothing. After another long silence between them, Yan stood to leave. "I see you're a bit stunned by this news. I understand. But I'll need to give her an answer. Shall I tell her it's a no?" Clement looked to the bottle, then up at Yan.

"Not yet," he said.

Yan got a look of frustration on her face. "I leave Argyle station at 1000 hours tomorrow, Mr. Clement. I'll come by here in the morning at 0800. If you're going with me to Kemmerine, you'll be ready. If you aren't ready, then I'll know your answer," she said.

Clement poured into his glass again, saying nothing.

Yan went to the door, but turned back one last time. "They said you were the best captain in the Rim Confederation fleet. They must be wrong, because I don't see that man here now. I just see someone who's lost inside of a bottle," she said.

Clement glared at her, holding back his rising anger. "Maybe you're right," he said. "Maybe that man doesn't exist anymore. Maybe the man that Elara DeVore wants never existed. Maybe, he's a myth."

Yan's face gave away nothing. "Perhaps he is. At any rate, what I see now is just useless Rim Confederation trash," she said, using a nearly forgotten war slur. "But I want you to know, if you don't take this job, then it falls to me, and I can't wait to go on this mission for my commanding officer." At that she opened the door to leave. Clement's voice stopped her.

"And what happens to you if I do take the mission?"

"Then I will be your executive officer," Yan said.

Clement looked at her with disdain. "The hell you will," he said.

"Well, you've made your position clear. I hope you enjoy holding up your end of the bar here on Argyle. See you at 0800. Or not." Then she stepped through the door and it shut swiftly behind her.

And Clement was left alone with his bottle of scotch.

# ✤2✤

Yan buzzed in at Clement's door at precisely 0800. To her surprise the door slid open immediately. She stepped in and looked around the room. It was completely cleaned, almost spotless, in fact. The bed had been made up in military cut and a single open duffel bag sat at the foot of it. She turned again and noticed that the bottle of scotch was still on the table from the night before. It looked like it hadn't been touched since she'd left. The drinking glasses were cleaned and put back in their cabinet. Water was running in the bathroom.

"Just give me one more minute," said Clement from behind the partly open bathroom door. Yan just stood in place waiting. After a few seconds Clement emerged from the bathroom in attire that could only be described as military in fashion, separate pants and a jacket cut tightly around his body. He was in fine shape for a man of his age, which Yan realized she didn't actually know.

The jacket and pant cuffs were rimmed with black, while the main material was a dark heather gray. After a moment Yan realized what she was looking at: it was Clement's Rim Confederation Navy captain's uniform with all the rank and adornments removed.

Clement was rubbing his freshly shaven face with a towel. His hair was clean and swept back. In short, to Yan, he looked like a million bucks.

"I doubt that outfit will be warmly received at Kemmerine Station," she said.

Clement put the towel back in his bathroom and took one last look in the mirror. "It's all I have," he said.

"I doubt that," she replied. And she was right. Clement was clearly making a statement. He looked at her and shrugged.

"Once a navy man, always a navy man," he said.

"Yes, but, wrong navy," said Yan.

"Depends on how you look at it, I guess," he replied, smiling sarcastically at her. With that he picked up his duffel, zipped it up and slung it over his shoulder. "Ready when you are, Commander."

Yan eyed him, doubtful of his quick turnaround from the station drunk to spritely military man, but for lack of any other evidence, she was forced to accept the man before her at face value. She turned to leave. She had to admit to herself that he cleaned up very nicely. As they walked out the door of his cabin Yan glanced one more time at the wall. Although his navy medals were still there, the photo of his crew was gone. No doubt he was taking it with him. She made a mental note of that.

After he had locked his cabin door with a security code they made the trek to the military docks together mostly in silence, just the necessary chatting between them. When they arrived in the military section of the station almost all personnel were in 5 Suns Navy uniforms. Clement's choice of attire certainly stood out and got more than a few second looks and glares from the 5 Suns sailors.

They approached a security checkpoint and the young ensign behind the podium asked for identity cards. Yan produced hers and was quickly processed through. The ensign took a lot more time with Clement, looking at him and his clothing with disdain.

Clement's card identified him as a commercial spacer and pilot, and the red rim around the card identified him as former combatant and possible security risk. The security officer took full advantage of this, having Clement remove all the contents from his duffel bag and even take off his jacket so they could check the lining. Yan stood by watching this impatiently as they waved a variety of detection devices over him. Finally, after ten minutes of exams, she stepped in.

"I think that's enough, Ensign. I know security is your job but this man is under my jurisdiction for the duration of the flight to Kemmerine and at the station after we arrive. I'm convinced he'll be no trouble," she said.

"I'm glad to hear that, *Commander*, but I still have my job to do and the trash here is even wearing the colors of the RCN," the ensign protested. The 5 Suns Alliance Navy favored navy blues with red trim and gold adornments, an ugly color combination in Clement's mind, colors he had come to hate over the years for what they represented. Colors he himself had once worn.

"I'd like you to pass him through now, *Ensign*, and that's an order," said Yan.

"But Commander, I am well within my rights—"

"Yes you are, Ensign. But my orders override your rights in this matter. Now clear him." The threat in her voice was obvious. Reluctantly the young officer did as she requested. Clement took back his ID and then gathered up his belongings, strewn all over the deck, and went to a nearby bench to repack.

Yan took the opportunity to lean in and speak with the security officer privately.

"One last thing," she said. "You may want to watch who you call trash around here. I know it's a popular name to call the old rebels, but I feel I should tell you that if all goes as planned, that 'trash' may be someone you'll have to salute soon. Very soon."

The ensign nodded, gave her a "yes, sir," and then resumed his duties without another word.

Yan went over to Clement, who was just zipping the duffel bag back up. "Everything in order?" she asked.

Clement nodded as he threw the duffel back over his shoulder. "Of course."

The two of them started walking down the corridor together toward their waiting ship.

"You enjoyed that, didn't you?" she asked.

Clement smiled. "Oh, Commander Yan, you have no idea," he said.

Their transport was a fast frigate called the *Bosworth*. They both locked down in acceleration couches for a five-*g* acceleration that lasted forty minutes, after which the couches disconnected and the cabin assumed a smooth and comfortable one *g* cruising attitude. Kemmerine Station was nine hours away at their current speed.

It was Yan that started in on the conversation.

"So how close were you and Fleet Admiral DeVore?" she asked casually.

The answer was anything but casual for Clement. "I'm not sure you want to know that answer, Commander," he said back, casually shuffling through a navy travel brochure, hoping to warn her off.

"But what if I do?"

Clement stopped his paper-shuffling and looked at her. For all the world she seemed like a naive girl thrust into a position above her skill level by the benefit of having a wealthy or influential family. It would never have happened in the old days of the 5 Suns Navy, when Clement was a green middie. He had to earn his way to the top of the ladder, and he did that, getting his own command in just six years. But inopportune timing on a trip home from his station in the Virginis Sector had caught him on the wrong side of the line when the war started. It only took a couple of days of seeing what was really happening on Ceta—the starvation, the exploitation—for him to give up his 5SN blues for Rim Confederation Navy grays.

Yan waited patiently for Clement to answer.

He stared at her, uncertain that he would answer, when suddenly the words were coming out of his mouth, almost as if it was against his own will. "Elara DeVore was the love of my life," he said. "We fought side by side for four years. I lost two other ships in battle and she still followed me to the *Beauregard*."

"That was your last command? The one where you scuttled your ship rather than let the 5SN have her?"

Clement nodded. "We were betrayed, by someone close, someone inside. I've never figured out who. But I'll have a special dagger for him if I ever figure it out."

"That's a long time to carry a grudge," said Yan.

He looked at her again, trying to determine whether she was the simple girl she appeared to be, or something more. Clement smiled, as a cover for his emotions.

"The dagger is only metaphorical," he said, more casual. "I'm not sure I could ever use it even if I found out who the traitor was. War makes for strange bedfellows, Yan. I wouldn't put it past the Confederation Council for giving us up. We were going to lose anyway, that was obvious by the winter of 2504, but the 5 Suns Alliance and their Navy wanted my hide."

"Because you had beat all of their best rising stars, in every battle. And you left them all alive to spread the word about how badly they were beaten by the rube gray coat from the backwater planet," she said.

Clement nodded.

"And Elara DeVore?"

Again Clement smiled. "A dark and comely girl from Helios," he said, "full of brash ideas and seething anger at the 5 Suns Alliance. A great tactician, a leader, a combat fighter, tall, lithe . . . everything a soldier boy dreamed of."

"But after the war—" Clement's look made her stop mid-sentence. Then just as quickly, he continued with the story.

"After I scuttled the *Beauregard* I never saw Elara again. I don't blame her, I would have stayed away from me too. But now, to find out she's a 5 Suns Navy Fleet Admiral . . . " He trailed off.

Yan stayed silent, then Clement looked at her and said, "You never forget a woman like that." And with that he turned away from her, and Yan knew the conversation was over.

Clement tried his best to snooze through the trip to Kemmerine, but it would only come in fits and starts. Yan, for her part, just took a sleeping pill and nodded off for five hours of timed rest. There was really nothing more for them to talk about until they met with Fleet Admiral DeVore.

Thoughts of Elara DeVore were enough to keep him from fully resting, but that didn't matter to Clement. His body clock was on Argyle time and it was the middle of the day for him anyway. Yan was almost certainly on a different sleeping schedule, Shenghai having a twenty-six-hour (and change) planetary rotation, and Kemmerine Station kept the same clock, at least it had when Clement was in the 5SN. He reset his watch to Kemmerine time and saw that it would be 2130 hours local time when they arrived, just enough time to catch dinner and hit the station pubs before bed.

Clement gently shook Yan awake when the twenty-minute docking toll chimed.

"What? What time is it?" she asked. Clement looked at his watch. "Almost 2100."

She sat up quickly. "Argyle time or Kemmerine time?"

"Kemmerine," he said. "Just early enough to get unpacked and catch some dinner. You know a good restaurant on the station?"

Yan smiled. "I know about ten," she said.

Clement nodded. "Impressive."

"What's your pleasure? New Hong Kong cuisine or French Colonial?"

They both made Clement's mouth water. There was nothing like that cuisine on Argyle Station, something he had often lamented. "Let's try New Hong Kong," he said.

"All right. Always a favorite of mine."

"And a navy pub for a drink after."

Yan eyed him skeptically. "Now, wait a minute. You're going to mix with navy sailors? In *that* uniform? That sounds like trouble to me."

"You of all people should know that I'm trouble by now, Yan," he said. She started to say something else, but he cut in. "I promise I'll be good and not start any fights."

"Can I trust you?" she said.

He shrugged. "You'll have to, unless you want to put a guard on me," he teased.

"That's an option," she replied, smiling back at his charm despite herself. Then the *Bosworth*'s captain came on the com and asked them to activate their coaches again for deceleration.

"Don't let me down, Clement," said Yan.

Clement smiled as the couch safety glass closed over him. "I wouldn't dream of it."

After arriving at Kemmerine Yan followed Clement to his room, an outside berth with a large view window of Shenghai. The view was spectacular; the green glow of the planet was nothing like looking at the poor, dull beige worlds of the Rim. The cabin, or rather stateroom, was much more than Clement had expected, a full suite with a large bedroom and, of all things, a bathtub. It was clear that Fleet Admiral DeVore was using her power and influence to put a full high press on him. Once he got his duffel contents stowed he came back into the living area to find Yan had a gift for him. It was a 5 Suns Navy commander's uniform with rank stripes but no bars and stars to identify him as a full member of the navy.

"I thought after yesterday's fun that you might be done with your little protest about a war that's been over for a decade," she said.

Clement looked at the navy blue uniform with gold and red piping and crinkled up his nose in a distasteful look. "I'd still prefer to wear my Rim grays," he said. Yan laid the uniform over a chair.

"Not to meet the Fleet Admiral you won't. I want to avoid any more conflicts like that security guard yesterday."

"You see, that's the difference between you and me, Yan. I don't consider yesterday to be a conflict in any way."

Yan picked up the uniform and gently pushed it at him. "Please?" she said sarcastically, dipping her head slightly but keeping her eyes on him, like a young girl trying influence her boyfriend.

"Maybe," Clement said, "as long as I get to pick where we eat."

"That would be fine."

He looked disdainfully at the uniform one more time. "All right then, Commander, you win. We'll play it your way." Then he took the uniform from her and made his way to the bathroom to dress in private.

They got dinner at what Clement would definitely call a restaurant, not a pub. Linen tablecloths were not prevalent in Argyle Station pubs. Kemmerine was huge, more than twice the size he remembered it from his navy days. There were at least fifty navy ships and maybe twice as many tourist ships, merchants and private yachts docked at its many spider-webbed ports. The deck they were on had a view of Shenghai below and seemed exclusively for leisure, with shops, restaurants, and even a film theater. No doubt the sailor's pubs were somewhere less savory, but at least on this deck the 5 Suns Alliance was showing off for the tourist classes.

Clement gently swirled his tea in his cup before taking a last sip. On the expansive table was the scattered remains of their meal. Clement couldn't remember the last time he ate so well. An automated busboy swung by and cleaned their table of dishes while Clement contemplated the view of the planet below.

"You seem satisfied with your dinner," said Yan.

He smiled. "I am. We have nothing like this on Argyle. Blue crab and lobster . . ."

"Well, you didn't have to pick up the check, you know. The navy has been quite generous with my expense account."

"I know, Yan, but the fact is there isn't much to spend your money on at Argyle. And besides, you've been a gracious host so far. It's the least I could do."

She smiled at that. "You're a man of contradictions, Clement."

He shrugged. "It's been a while since I've been out with a proper lady. Why don't we just say I needed the practice?"

Yan shifted in her chair. "Practice for meeting Elara DeVore again?" she probed.

"Maybe," he said, then put down his teacup and stretched. "Time for a walk to see the sights?" he suggested.

"You seriously mean to go get a drink at a navy pub? And cause a ruckus?"

"Me?" he demurred. "I wouldn't dare. I'm here at the behest of Fleet Admiral DeVore. No ruckusing for me."

"I'm sure."

He stood and pulled her chair out for her, like a gentleman would. His attitude toward her had certainly warmed since Argyle. Yan wondered if it was because of his proximity to Elara DeVore, or for other reasons.

They made their way through the atrium, glancing in at both formal and casual diners as they shared a meal, a bottle of wine, or something stronger.

"I wonder," started Clement.

"Yes?"

"I wonder how many of these patrons, no doubt on their way to or from someplace exciting, are having an illicit tryst, or hiding some secret from their wives or husbands, perhaps meeting a beau on a secret rendezvous," he said.

"That's fairly melodramatic, don't you think? This is a military station after all. Constant observation. I doubt too many get away with things like that here."

Clement acted surprised. "You think so? I find the thought kind of romantic, personally."

Yan smiled at that, thinking it over. "One drink, Clement." Then she held up her finger to him. "One."

"Lead the way," he said.

They made their way down the escalator, and after a few minutes of sticking their heads in several crowded bars full of 5 Suns Navy sailors, they settled on a dark but warm looking place called The Battered Hull. Appropriately named, Clement thought.

They came in and sat down at an open table, Clement ordering them both a glass of the local sailor's ale from the bartender. You could always tell the quality of a place by its basics. It was a good sign if they took care of their sailors. An auto waiter served them their glasses of a dark brown ale and they clinked glasses, with Clement taking a deep drink of his. It was damn good.

"My compliments to The Battered Hull," he said.

"Mine too," said Yan, then she looked around the bar. "I don't think I've ever been in here." The crowd was a mix of noncoms and middies, and occasionally their significant others in civilian dress. Yan was the only officer in the place, and Clement stood out because of his 5 Suns officer's uniform and accompanying lack of rank. They were getting plenty of steely-eyed glances from the crowd.

"Are we sticking out like a sore thumb?" he inquired.

"Yes. I'm beginning to think this was a bad idea," she said. Clement shrugged.

"Just finish your ale and we can get out of here, then," he said. Looking around the bar he noticed a group of four middies at a booth that were giving him more than the occasional light glance. One in particular, a blond male, was motioning quite vigorously to his companions.

"Uh oh," said Clement, smiling at Yan.

"What?"

"I may have been outed." He nodded toward the booth.

Yan observed them for a moment. "Does trouble *always* have a way of finding you?" she said.

He shrugged again. "Just comes with the territory, I guess."

Then the game was up. All four middies, three men and one young woman, vacated their booth and made their way toward Clement and Yan. They gathered around the high table, standing and resting their ales with him and Yan. It was the blond one who spoke first.

"I have a bet with my friends here," he started. "I think I know you. I saw your pictures in my military history classes."

"And just who *do* you think I am?" said Clement to the middie, not backing down.

"I'm betting you're Captain Jared Clement of the Rim Confederation Navy. You fought in the War of the 5 Suns. You were the Scourge of the 5 Suns Alliance fleet," he said, as if it were a matter of fact, or a title.

Clement took another drink of his ale. "And what did you bet?"

"Pardon, sir?" said the middie.

"What did you bet on me being this 'Scourge of the Fleet' character?"

"I have to pick up the tab if I'm wrong, or Tsu here does if I'm right," he said, nodding toward a tall Asian middie.

"And what if you're only half right?" said Clement, taking another drink. Yan watched the interplay closely.

"I don't understand, sir," the middie said. Clement looked at the four young faces, all of them wore a determined look; they were going to succeed, none of them doubted it. He went from one to the other to the next until he had their full attention.

"You're half right, Middie, because I am Jared Clement, but I'm not a captain, and there's no such thing as the Rim Confederation Navy anymore."

"I knew it!" said the middie, then turned to his friends, demanding that they pay up in navy silver crowns. This caused quite a reaction in the bar, and Yan leaned in close.

"Now you've done it," she said.

"Started a ruckus? Maybe," he whispered back.

When the horse trading in silver was over, the middies turned back to Clement, and many other patrons of The Battered Hull were watching their table intently.

"Would you tell us a war story?" asked the blond middie.

Clement hesitated. "War is nothing to trifle about, son. People live and die every day, and some never heal from losing their friends. If I start bragging in here about how I got the better of the 5 Suns Alliance and their navy I might find myself spaced out the nearest garbage port," he said.

"Well done," whispered Yan in his ear, then she assumed her disinterested commanding-officer pose.

"Please, sir?" asked the middie again, and then there were nods all around.

"Well . . ." started Clement, leaning back and catching Yan's eye. She was not amused. "Maybe just one story."

Again the nods. Yan covered her face with her hand. Clement started in.

"The first thing you lads and lasses have to understand about the war was that it was over before it began," he said in a loud enough voice to be heard by several nearby tables. Yan assumed that was what he wanted. "And by that I mean there was never any doubt about the outcome. The 5 Suns Alliance had far too many resources and far too many navy ships for the Rim planets to have a chance at winning, so the war strategy from the beginning was one of pure defense. You have to remember the seeds of the war were that the Rim planets are poor, and that's still true. They're the furthest from the Colonus core twins—they don't get much light, so it's hard to grow food—and the soil on those planets is shit anyway. Livestock doesn't take much to the climates on Ceta or Argyle; Helios is a bit warmer, but try living in the warm glow of an orange K-type star for a while... it's not easy."

"So if the war was not winnable then why did you fight it?" asked the young female middie, an African girl by complexion.

"That's a good question, Middie. When I signed up for the navy, the 5 Suns Alliance Navy mind you, I was helping fill a quota for my home planet of Ceta. The navy needed recruits constantly, just like now, to fulfill their end of the bargain, which was food, tech, and industrial assistance for the Rim colonies. Unlucky for me, one day I found myself on leave visiting my parents on Ceta. The conditions at home were horrible, food was scarce, and so was everything else—medicine, fuel, electrical power. I was sending back half my paycheck every month to my family but the fact was there was nothing to buy with it. Most of the food assistance was being hijacked by the Governor-General and his lackeys and sold for a profit on the black market, and the 5 Suns Alliance government was looking the other way. Unfortunately, the navy was the government's enforcement arm. I wasn't home for two days when there was a riot in Ceta City and the Governor- General was run out of town and into hiding in a secret bunker. I was called back to my command, but when I got to the spaceport my shuttle was already gone—hell, the whole 5 Suns Navy had bugged out. There were some merchants and local navy personnel that stayed and tried to form a navy for defense of the Rim. After two weeks of laying low back at home they finally contacted me and asked if I'd join the cause. On my way back to the city I saw why the revolution had come; people were starving in the streets. I gave away all my rations on the way in, and when I got to the base, I decided to join up with the Rim. I had to do something.

"Within a week they had me in command of a forty-year-old destroyer named *Benfold* that the 5 Suns had left behind in the

Argyle docks. I had half a crew, thirty sailors instead of sixty. We trained for a few days, expecting the 5SN to be back and end the rebellion any time. Then I got called to a meeting where men who had been commanders in the 5SN were calling themselves Admirals, and they told me they had a plan but no ship captain to carry it out. They wanted to attack first, give the 5 Suns Alliance government a bloody nose, and they wanted to know how well I knew the Virginis sector. Since I'd been stationed there I really couldn't lie to them, so they armed up that old destroyer and put me in charge of a stealth mission, a rearguard maneuver, to knock out 5SN supply lines and communications. So I went, and when we got there the 5 Suns Navy was not expecting us."

The middies were entranced now, and Clement held their attention in the palm of his hand. He continued, "We coasted in for seven hours after our deceleration burn. Without a heat signature from our engines we were practically invisible to their scans. One by one we started to knock out the local ansible network, taking down random satellites as we went on an approach vector. It made it look like they were experiencing a system failure rather than a pending assault. They had no idea a Rim Navy ship could get to them as deep into space as the Virginis sector.

"The station was only guarded by three corvettes. Their primary ships had been sent off to Kemmerine or were out on patrol, looking for the Rim Navy. I used conventional tactical missiles to knock out the first two of the corvettes, taking them completely by surprise, but the third one got its only energy cannon locked on to us. I had just enough momentum left for a thruster burn to make for the station. The corvette commander must have been very young, because he used his thrusters to keep spinning his ship and keep me in firing range the whole way in. He splattered volley after volley at us, missing by a few hundred yards every time, but we had the advantage of speed and that kept him from hitting us. Eventually we passed behind the station itself, which in those days had no defenses of its own, and started our turn back toward him. His next three volleys hit the station instead of us. Again he used his thrusters to try and turn, but by then we had him in our sights. One missile finished the job. We docked, raided the food storage section of Virginis Station, and stole their best booze. The station personnel were terrified of us.

They thought the war would stay very far away, but we brought it home to them, and that concept scared the shit out of them."

Clement shrugged then. "Looking back at it now, it wasn't much of a tactical victory, but it had the effect of diminishing 5 Suns Navy morale, which was almost better than taking the station would have been. We snuck out of there as fast as we could, avoiding 5SN patrols the whole way home. When I got back to Argyle, I was the first hero of the Rim Confederation Navy and the war, like it or not."

"And how many 5 Suns Alliance Navy sailors did you kill in your sneak attack?" asked the female middie, pointedly. All eyes turned to Clement then, measuring how he would react.

"I have no way of knowing. Corvettes used to carry a crew of eighteen in those days. The one thing I will say in my defense is that in those early days of the war we never sought to destroy the enemy ships. Hell, the 5 Suns Navy wasn't our enemy, the corrupt 5 Suns Alliance government was. We targeted the propulsion sections of the corvettes only, to knock them out, not destroy them, but they were too small and they were destroyed. The war was fought that way all the way up to the Battle of Columbia," Clement said, then he took another drink of his ale.

"What changed the rules of engagement at Columbia?" asked the Asian middie, Tsu.

Clement thought about that before answering. "We started making our own ships, better ships than before, better than the 5 Suns Navy even had. I got the gunship *Beauregard* and she was almost untouchable. But our leaders forgot they were fighting for survival, not victory. We got too close to winning, we became a real threat to the 5 Suns Alliance government, and then one of our ships took out an unarmed troop transport with two thousand 5 Suns Alliance soldiers on board. After that, it was mayhem. No quarter, and our little war of independence turned into a war of attrition we had no chance to win."

"They say you personally extended the war for two years with your tactics," said the blond middie.

"Well, I don't know about *that*," replied Clement, "but I do know we fought hard to win every engagement, and we had more than our share of successes. Hell, the Virginis sector government surrendered to us after our surprise attack, but we never had any intention of taking it over. It was just a hit and run. It was just our three little worlds, fighting to survive. We thought the 5 Suns government might leave us alone. We weren't really offering much to the other worlds in the 5 Suns Alliance, and we took more than we gave. My parents relied on subsidies to grow wheat and corn but it was all we could do to survive eating our own food and never shipping anything to the Core worlds. But they came after us anyway, and that was that." Clement downed the rest of his ale, and Yan followed suit.

"Thank you, gentlemen," Clement said to the middies, then started to leave.

The blond one piped up one last time. "Sir, if I may ask, why are you here on Kemmerine? And why are you wearing a navy uniform with no rank?"

Yan leaned in at this. "No, you may not ask, Middie, now off with the lot of you," she said forcefully, like an angry mother, with a wave of her hand. And at that they were all gone back to their booth. Clement turned to walk out of The Battered Hull, and all eyes were on him as casual conversation resumed around them.

"Satisfied?" asked Yan as they made their way back to the escalator. Clement shrugged.

"No," he said, and they walked on in silence.

A few minutes later they were back at Clement's cabin door. He turned to Yan. "Want to come in?"

"Why?" she said.

"You look a little 'peaked,'" he said.

"What does 'peekt' mean?"

"Peek-ed." Clement smiled as he unlocked his cabin door. "It's just something my mother used to say to me when I was sick. It means you look a bit pale, that's all."

"I'm not sick," protested Yan. Then her hand went to her forehead. Clement's smile got a bit bigger.

"Are you sure?" Clement asked.

"Goddamn sailor's ale," said Yan, then she wobbled just a bit. Clement took her by the waist, to steady her at first, then pulled her in close. "I think I'm gonna—" At that Clement hustled her into his room and got her to the toilet just in time. He left her alone with the bathroom door shut for a few minutes until she reemerged, still unsteady but with a bit more color in her face.

"Thank you," she said, then sat down on the couch, far apart from him.

"You're welcome. I called down to the navy concierge, and they're sending up a female MP to escort you back to your room," he said.

Yan glanced at him from under the hand covering her eyes. "Thank you again."

The MP arrived and Yan departed without another word. As Clement shut the door behind her, he turned back, contemplating his empty stateroom.

# ✦ 3 ✦

Clement was up by 0730, showered, ate, and was ready to go by 0815. Yan showed up right on time at 0830. Their meeting with Admiral DeVore was on the military side of the station, a good twenty-minute tram ride from the cabin decks to the Admiral's office.

Yan was pleased that Clement was ready, smiling at him as he left his cabin, and walked side by side with him to the tram station, just a few hundred meters away. She said nothing about the previous night, and Clement was gentleman enough not to bring it up.

Once on the tram with the bustling uniformed crowd heading to their morning stations though, things changed.

"About last night," Yan started as they sat together as the high-speed tram accelerated toward the navy wing of Kemmerine Station, tugging gently against the artificial gravity generated by the station. Clement held up a hand.

"No need to bring it up, Commander. It was my fault."

Yan hesitated, then, "I don't remember much, goddamned sailor's ale, but I'd like to know if I . . . if we . . . I remember being inside your cabin?"

"Just to puke. Nothing happened, Yan."

Yan laughed uncomfortably. "I really can't remember."

Clement brooded, then decided he owed her more. "You seemed to warm to me after our dinner and the storytelling at The Battered Hull, and despite my best efforts, you were very attractive to me in that moment. A proper soldier, but also a woman. But I realized I was being influenced by the ale and a memory from my past, not by anything you said or did."

Yan looked at him. "Elara DeVore?"

Clement did not reply. He didn't have to.

The tram hummed to a stop a few minutes later and about half the car emptied out, going to the main service section of the navy stockyards. Mostly they appeared to be technicians and professionals, no doubt higher ranking staff and the like. The tram continued on to the next stop and the emptying process repeated itself. There were only a handful of officers left on the tram now, some of whom glanced at the 5 Suns Navy commander and her unranked companion in curiosity. Clement, for his part, kept his eyes focused straight ahead, only pausing to glance out at the docks when he saw an interesting ship or some repair work going on. Kemmerine Station was a very big and busy place.

Finally, the tram made its final stop at what could only be the station's main administration complex. Clement and Yan made their way out of the tram and onto a broad and wide deck. A large office tower took up most of the far end of the complex, with huge view windows to either side looking down on the ships below. Clement imagined that the top office in the tower would have a panoramic view of the whole shipyards. That would be the office, undoubtedly, of Fleet Admiral Elara DeVore.

Yan led him through a promenade where fleet officers were chatting and conferring in groups, large and small. Clement wondered what kind of work would justify this bustle of activity. It was almost what you would expect during the preparation for a large military operation. They made their way through the busy crowd and inside the tower to an elevator, which took them up five stories.

The elevator opened onto a bright office area with two large hardwood doors, undoubtedly the Fleet Admiral's office. It was the only office on the entire top floor of the tower. Yan made her way to a long reception desk where a man with the 5 Suns Navy rank of lieutenant sat behind a full security station. Clement, for his part, held back while Yan checked them in. The lieutenant called him over and handed him a security badge, which he attached to his uniform. They were both pointed to a waiting area where they sat down, presumably to wait on the Admiral. Clement checked his watch: 0900 on the dot. It wasn't like the Elara DeVore he knew to be late.

He and Yan sat together in silence for what seemed a long time, but when Clement looked at his watch again, only five minutes had passed. His heart was beating faster and he was twitching his leg in nervous activity. Yan noticed, but said nothing. Finally the door to the Admiral's office opened up and a short and small man in captain's rank uniform came through from the other side and went straight to Yan, who stood.

"The Admiral is ready now," he said. Clement glanced at his watch, which said 0908 hours. Then the captain turned to Clement and extended his hand. "I'm Captain Craig Wilcock," he said formally. Clement stood and shook his hand.

"Jared Clement." Wilcock nodded and then turned quickly as Clement and Yan followed the captain through the reception doors. A long way down the office toward the windows there was a desk, and Clement could see there was someone sitting at it, but he couldn't make out the face well. They walked across the office past a large conference sitting area, a small kitchen, and some cubicles for technicians and the staff, before arriving at the Admiral's desk.

Elara DeVore was busy dictating notes on a pad, her head turned partly away from her guests, saying nothing to them for a few moments as she spoke quietly into the com. Captain Wilcock waited with what seemed unending patience. Clement just felt annoyed as they all stood, waiting, Yan and Wilcock at attention. Clement had his hands clasped behind his back, taking a more casual stance. He reminded himself he wasn't in the military anymore, least of all the 5 Suns Alliance Navy.

He looked at Elara. From the side her hair was cut shorter than she used to wear it, in a regulation style, and although her uniform was well-adorned, it wasn't overly garish for a high-ranking Fleet Admiral. Her skin was still a gentle olive, but lighter than he remembered, indicating perhaps that she spent much of her time now in space, and not on any planet like her hot home world of Helios. That planet's proximity to the Rim's sun had darkened her skin in her youth when he knew her the first time. Her face seemed free of wrinkles, and she looked every bit of ten years younger than what Clement knew her age to be, forty-two standard years. Eventually she finished her pad entries, and looked up.

They say the eyes are the window to the soul, and when Clement looked into the eyes of his former lover for the first time in eleven years, he saw why. The brightness, the enthusiasm of her youth was still there, every bit of it.

Clement exhaled as Fleet Admiral DeVore stood and came around the desk, a deep and warm smile on her face. He held out his hand to her.

"Don't be ridiculous," she said, and waved his hand away as she gave him a firm hug that lingered a bit, like old friends that had been apart too long. Still in Clement's arms, DeVore looked over to Yan.

"Thank you for bringing him here, Tanitha," she said. Yan nodded.

"Of course, Admiral."

"Have you been well, Jared?" DeVore asked.

"Well, I'm not an Admiral, if that's what you mean," he deadpanned. DeVore stepped away and made her way back around to her side of the desk.

"Was he hard to convince?" she asked Yan.

Now Yan smiled. "Not once I mentioned your name, ma'am."

DeVore laughed and gestured to two chairs. "Please sit," she said. He and Yan both did, and then she just looked at Clement, smiling. She turned to their escort. "That will be all for now, Captain Wilcock." He nodded and left the office without another word. DeVore turned back to him and Yan. "Jared Clement. I swear, the years have just made you even more handsome," she said.

"Yan has already tried flattery on me, Admiral. It didn't work," said Clement in mock seriousness.

"I'll keep that in mind. I don't suppose Yan here has shared why I asked you to come today?"

Clement shook his head. "No, Admiral, she hasn't," he said. Despite the warm hug, Clement was still all business. At that, DeVore got up again and went toward the conference area.

"Follow me, please," she said. Clement did so, watching every tug on her uniform as she walked. Her body was certainly more mature than he remembered, but every bit as enticing. Yan, a step behind him, gently nudged him to get his attention back on business. Presently DeVore motioned to a set of conference chairs and Yan and Clement sat down.

"What I'm about to show you now is classified, and even if you don't accept my offer, I do expect you to keep this presentation secret, on your honor as a former navy sailor and as a gentleman," DeVore said.

Clement nodded his assent and DeVore fired up the viewing screen. After a few seconds the panel lit up, revealing a 3D map of 5 Suns Alliance space. Before she started speaking though, she slid a thin electronic pad across the desk to Clement.

"What's this?" he asked.

"A military NDA. Just a written guarantee of your honor as a gentleman," she said. Clement slid it back.

"I'm not in the military," he said.

DeVore sent it back to him a second time as Yan watched the interchange, noting the undoubted chemistry between them, and the underlying competition.

"It will only be relevant if you choose to re-enlist," she said. Clement at least looked at it this time, then pulled up an attached pen and signed without really reading it. A glowing red sensor lit up next to his signature and he pressed his left thumb to it. The print stayed on the pad. "Thank you," said DeVore, then put the paper to one side before continuing.

"What I'm sure you know as a matter of course is that the planets of the 5 Suns Alliance have been in an uneasy peace since the War of the 5 Suns. Oh, there's no imminent danger of violence breaking out again, and there are no more war criminals, but the dangers that faced humanity during that war face us again today. Essentially, we have two billion people on eleven planets, facing much the same population problem as Earth faced before the Exodus, three hundred years ago. The problem here in the Alliance is that our worlds are not nearly so fertile as Mother Earth," she started. "Our projections are that within a decade the Rim worlds, where you and I were born, will face starvation on a widespread scale."

"They already do in many places on Ceta and Argyle," interrupted Clement. "I'm not as sure about Helios."

"Oh, there are food shortages there as well," said DeVore. "Scattered, but becoming more systemic. The Rim worlds should probably never have been colonized, but you can't stop pioneers and libertarian free thinkers from trying to make a paradise of their own."

"Yes, well, this is all very good information, Admiral, but it's planetary economics, and I'm a spaceship captain," said Clement. "Or at least I was." Yan gave him a concerned look at his tone, but said nothing.

"I understand. If you'll allow me to continue?"

"Of course."

"We expect the Rim economies to collapse in the next few years, and there won't be enough aid available from the other worlds to save them. Our models indicate the Kemmerine worlds will soon follow with their own collapse within a decade, brought down by millions of refugees from the Rim planets. Then Virginis within another decade, and so on, so that within thirty years the five central worlds of Colonus Sector will be in danger themselves, both from a starving populous seeking to emigrate and the possibility of wars over resources. It's a cascading-failure event just waiting to happen," she said.

"If you'd been home in the last eleven years you'd see that it's already started," said Clement. DeVore gave him an impatient look.

"What makes you think I haven't?"

"With all due respect, Admiral, the woman I commanded aboard the *Beauregard* had a deep olive complexion, like a native of Helios would. You don't look like you've been in the sun, of any planet, much in the last eleven years."

Now impatience turned to anger on DeVore's face. "So, you're judging me now?"

Clement shook his head. "No, Admiral. I'm merely stating that if you'd been home recently, you would probably have found that your cascading-failure event has already begun," said Clement in an even tone.

"Ever the rebel, aren't you, Clement?" said DeVore.

"Better than being a sellout," he snapped in reply.

DeVore opened her mouth to retaliate when Yan stepped in before any more damage could be done. "Perhaps now would be a good time to focus on the proposed mission," she said.

"I'm not sure the captain here is up to it anymore," said DeVore in an angry tone. "Maybe I've made a mistake."

"Perhaps you're right, Admiral. And maybe I was never going to accept your proposal anyway." He stood to leave and Yan stood with him. "Maybe all I ever wanted was to have my curiosity about where you disappeared to for eleven years sated, and maybe that's already been done. You sold out to the enemy."

"There is no enemy anymore, Clement, that's what you fail to see.

It's fine with me if you want to back out," said DeVore. "You always took too many chances for my taste. You were bound to hit rock bottom at some point, and now I see that you're there."

Yan jumped in again, trying to save the mission. "Wait. Clement, you've come all this way, and you're going to leave before you even hear what the mission is? And with respect to the Admiral, how many times in the last six months have I heard you say there was only one commander for this mission, and that's Jared Clement? I can leave the room now if you two want to hash out your personal anger at each other, but I'd much rather stay and hear the rest of the mission briefing," she said. DeVore looked to Yan, surprised at her take-charge tone, and then glared at Clement, who finally relented and sat back down. Yan followed suit. The tension between them was obvious, as was the connection that had brought them together. After a few tense moments of silence, DeVore sat down and continued on with the briefing.

"So we've stated the problem. And now it's time to discuss the proposed solution," she said. "Four years ago we started a program using unmanned probes, a program to develop a high-speed interstellar drive that could get us to new star systems much faster than the old-generation ships that we used to found our colonies. As part of that program we sent out probes to a number of nearby star systems using different kinds of experimental FTL technologies. Most of them we lost contact with almost instantly, others kept sending us data but never made it to their destinations. But one of those probes went out, completed its survey, and came back within a very quick, and very surprising, time frame. In short, Clement, we think we've broken the light-speed barrier," DeVore said.

Now Clement was intrigued. He sat forward in his chair. "You *think* you've broken the light-speed barrier? What does that actually mean?"

DeVore nodded to Yan, who took over the briefing for the technical details. "It's called LEAP, Liquid Energy Absorption Propulsion. Essentially, it's a quantum-fluid drive," she started.

"Well that just rolls right off the old tongue," said Clement.

"Please listen," replied Yan, perturbed at his sarcasm. "LEAP is based on a centuries-old concept called an Alcubierre drive. Basically, when the drive is activated, a ship or probe creates a bubble of warped space around the vessel that contracts in front of the ship and expands behind the ship. The ship itself doesn't actually move within the bubble, but rather 'surfs' on a 'wave' of 'liquefied' space generated by the LEAP drive within the bubble. The bubble moves, but the ship doesn't. Normal space-time is warped around the ship. Essentially, it creates a quantum-fluid environment that allows for movement through normal space at faster-than-light speed."

"To warp space as you describe would take an enormous amount of power," stated Clement, skeptical. "What do you use to power the thing?"

DeVore cut in here. "An antimatter annihilation reactor."

"A what?" said Clement.

Yan took over again. "Basically, the power we need is created by containing a matter/antimatter interaction within a closed vacuum. We accelerate quantum particles until they become unstable enough to create a singularity, which in turn generates an antimatter particle. That particle is then dropped into the reactor vacuum chamber where it is bombarded by an equal particle of normal matter. The resulting collision annihilates both particles inside the chamber and releases tremendous amounts of energy that takes on a quantum-liquid state. The energy is then channeled from the reactor and through the LEAP drive components to provide the power we need for creating and maintaining the bubble and running the drive."

"So essentially you're creating an antimatter micro-universe and then destroying that same universe every second to drive your ship?" asked Clement.

"Essentially," said Yan. "Only it happens a lot more often than once a second."

"How often?" Clement asked.

"About one hundred fifty million times per second, we estimate."

Clement looked at the two women. "That's insane," he said.

DeVore shrugged. "It works, and we can control it. As to the specifics of it, I leave that to the scientists. The navy just does the sailing, Clement."

"You said that this probe went out, completed its survey, and came back quickly. How quick are we talking here, and how far did it go?"

"It went to a star system 11.5 light-years from here, completed a full survey of the system for five days, and then returned to the station in seventy-three total days, roundtrip," said Yan. "That's about one hundred ten times the speed of light, if you were wondering."

"I was," said Clement. He leaned back in his chair again. "Has this LEAP drive ever been tested with humans on board? I mean what about radiation, g-forces, acceleration, and the like? I wouldn't want to just be a blood spatter on the wall once it starts accelerating."

"Again," said Yan, "the ship itself wouldn't actually be accelerating, just the bubble around the ship, therefore no corresponding g-forces or inertia."

"So it would be like accelerating at one $g$ the whole way?"

"Like sitting in your living room, or the local bar," said Yan.

"I have to admit I'm intrigued," said Clement. "But—"

"We've refitted a prototype ship with the LEAP drive. It has successfully made the round trip, unmanned, three times with no discernable effects that could be harmful to humans. Now the time has come for a human crew to make the journey," said DeVore.

"So you need a new captain and a crew," said Clement.

DeVore nodded. "And now you know why you're here."

Clement thought about it.

"So only one more question: How does all this relate to the planetary-economics lesson earlier?"

"And that's the real question," said DeVore, warming to the interchange now that she had engaged Clement's curiosity. "This new system is a red dwarf, not unlike the dim K-type stars of Argyle or even Virginis. There are five rocky planets and two dwarf gas planets, and three of the rocky worlds are habitable with abundant water, gentle temperatures, and comfortable oxygen/nitrogen atmospheres. However, in addition to those beneficial conditions, each habitable world has more natural resources than all of 5 Suns Alliance space put together. Minerals like platinum, gold, silver, chromium, natural gas, petroleum, and so on. In short, all three planets are like a paradise, just waiting for us to colonize them."

"And solve your overpopulation problems with conscripts from the Rim planets," said Clement.

DeVore nodded. "They would be the first colonists. Others would follow, trained professionals from throughout the 5 Suns Alliance. You have to admit, Clement, it's better to move the Rim populations than to let them die and bring down our whole civilization."

"You realize you're talking about forcibly moving nearly 4.4 million people."

"No one will be forced, Clement," DeVore said. "The lure of these new worlds should far outweigh the prospects of starvation on the Rim. And eventually we'll open up these worlds for general migration. The 5 Suns planets will survive and flourish, and so will the new colonies."

"Plus, you'll need workers," he replied.

DeVore nodded, and the conversation stopped.

"We call the system Trinity," interjected Yan after a few moments. "In many ways, it's like the divine has intervened for us. These three planets are the jewels in the crown. They will save humanity."

DeVore put up a representation of the Trinity system. There were two inner rocky worlds that were uninhabitable, one with atmosphere, one without; three blue/green middle worlds with water and atmosphere; and two outer planets, both gas "giants," at least in comparison to the inner five worlds. The three habitable planets on the visual display all had names: Alphus, Bellus, and Camus, going from the inside out. The fourth planet in the system, Bellus, was the largest of the three and had a notable moon.

DeVore looked at Clement. "So you've seen the mission. What do you think?"

Clement took in a deep breath and exhaled. "I think I'm going to have to see this miracle ship of yours, Admiral."

DeVore smiled.

Twenty minutes later the three of them plus Captain Wilcock were on their way down an elevator to the station dockyards.

"You can see it from here," said DeVore, pointing out the glass windows of the elevator to a specific ship. What Clement could see was a small section of the hull and a large ring around the rear third of the ship. It was obviously a prototype; it looked nothing like the standard navy ships in dock, nor any of the commercial vessels. It did, however, have a main fuselage that was a familiar shape, but modified by several attached cylindrical tubes and the ring.

"Is that ring the LEAP drive emanator?" Clement asked.

"It is," said Yan. "You have a sharp eye."

"For spaceships I do, yes."

"The ring is connected by four tubular pylons that translate the reactor power to the drive components, making it go."

"How long does it take for the bubble to form once you activate the drive?"

"About thirty seconds," said Yan.

"And when it's fully formed?"

"Then off you go, instantly."

The elevator moved out of visual range of the prototype and they descended into a large, wide hallway that was filled with dock personnel scurrying to and from their assignments. There were two oversized beltways that carried large components, such as engine drive components, to either side of a pair of sliding sidewalks. The sidewalks were also full of people in work coveralls moving and connecting to other walkways leading throughout the dock. It was an impressive sight.

"I see the 5 Suns Navy has spared no expense on these dockyards," said Clement.

"I am a bit proud of it myself, I have to admit," said DeVore. She was clearly gauging his reaction to everything she was showing him, and liking what she saw.

The elevator settled and they stepped out into the scurry and bustle, making their way straight forward toward the far end of the station. There was little talk among their party of four, but DeVore had to deal with plenty of salutes from uniformed officers heading the other way. The utility and technical workers were apparently exempt from this protocol, especially if they were moving some sort of equipment. Clement surmised they were probably civilian contractors.

Eventually they turned right onto a new slideway that had large metal doors, emblazoned with the identifier "DOCK 19" in exceptionally large lettering looming over it. The scene was enhanced by two fully armed station security guards with cobra rifles at the ready. At their arrival at the dock they stepped off the slideway and then went in through a side door after being scanned by the security team. Wilcock pulled open the door and said, "This way." Clement let the two ladies go in first and then followed them through.

He was far more impressed by the sight of the prototype than he thought he would be. It was big, as big as an old 5 Suns Alliance Navy light cruiser or even a Rim Navy gunship. She looked like she could carry over a hundred crew, easily. She had the look of gleaming silver chrome about her, which gave her a certain grace as she hung above them in her antigravity dry dock.

Her fuselage caught his attention most though. Forward of the drive ring and support pylons she had very similar lines to a Rim Confederation gunship, much like the one he'd commanded at the end of the war. Aft of the ring and pylons, though, she was much bulkier, seeming to carry a great deal of her mass to the rear. The constructs there looked like boat pontoons, six of them, attached to the main body of the ship. DeVore gestured for them to go up an inclined gantry walkway and into the ship, and Clement did so.

Once inside they were in a broad cargo hold, but it reminded Clement of where the enlisted crew's quarters would be on a Rim gunship. In fact, the layout, to his naked eye, was almost exact.

"Is there a problem, Jared?" asked DeVore.

He looked around some more. "No, Admiral, just a bit of déjà vu," he said.

She said nothing to that and they continued upward a couple more decks via a central gangway and stairs, Clement looking right and left as they went. The Admiral had to stop multiple times to return salutes from uniformed officers who were overseeing maintenance and installations on the prototype. It had all the look of a rush job for an imminent departure.

As DeVore and Wilcock led the way ahead, Yan caught up to Clement and spoke softly as he scanned the ship's innards. "You're looking squirrely, Clement. Something bothering you?" she said.

He nodded. "This just all seems so familiar. I'd swear this was a Rim Confederation gunship, at least the main fuselage is."

"I've never been on a Rim Confederation gunship, so I wouldn't know. I did hear that the main hull was salvage, refurbished and repurposed for this mission," said Yan.

"Salvage? Hmm, as I recall we surrendered a half dozen fully functioning gunships at the end of the war. Well, as far as I know they were still functioning."

"But not your ship. That was scuttled, correct?"

Clement nodded, not really wanting to recall his most ignominious moment of the war. "Correct," he said. "Onto the surface of Argyle 4, a satellite of the main planet."

"Do you think this could be—"

"The purpose of scuttling a ship, Yan, is so that it can't be used in the future by your enemy."

"So then this could be another of the surrendered gunships. You said there were half a dozen."

"Yes, six." Clement went silent then as they made their way up the walkway and on to Deck 2, senior crew quarters. There was no doubt in Clement's mind now, they were on a Rim gunship.

"Looking familiar yet?" asked DeVore as she stopped one small flight of stairs short of what was undoubtedly the bridge.

"This is a Rim Confederation gunship, isn't it, Admiral? I can tell that this used to be part of the bridge area," Clement said.

DeVore smiled. "Indeed it is, or was. There have been so many changes, but the primary hull is a Rim gunship, yes. When we were proposing this mission the Admiralty wanted to risk as little 5 Suns Alliance materiel as possible because of the experimental nature of the missions, so I used a design that I was familiar with as a basis. Plus, the gunships had been in surplus for more than a decade. I also had a captain in mind for the mission, and I thought he might benefit from familiar surroundings," DeVore admitted. Clement just nodded and then went to the captain's cabin and opened the door. It was a wide and spacious stateroom inside, with a full bed, conference table for four, working area, and a private bath.

"This is nicer than my apartment on Argyle Station," commented Clement, "and a distinct upgrade over the original design."

"We went for a more spacious layout, seeing as we had free reign to refit her. The old gunships had crews of eighty, but this prototype can be run with a quarter of that, thanks to systems improvements and automation. There are five cabins here on Deck 2 plus a galley, and fourteen double berths below on Deck 5," DeVore said.

"That's why the cargo hold was so spacious. No need to cram sixty techs into the free space."

"Exactly." She looked at him expectantly as he stared up the last five steps of the gangway to the bridge.

"Lead on, Admiral," he said. She gestured for him to pass her by and Clement did so. He entered the bridge and looked around. The whole room was lit from below by blue glowing lights which gave off a steady luminosity about the bridge. The room was long and curved with a ceiling that inclined downward, and the station displays were lit with a mellow pink-maroon color. The front wall was a blank; there were no windows like in the original design, and besides the captain's couch there were just four other stations, likely for the helm, navigation, XO and engineer.

"Take a seat, Captain. Try her out," tempted DeVore. Clement looked at the captain's nest, an acceleration couch and console combination that fully dripped with the latest technology. Some of the systems were familiar, others not so much. He looked hard at the seat, something he'd sworn never to get into again.

"I'm not your captain yet, Admiral," he said.

DeVore waved off Wilcock and Yan, and they went a few feet away to check out the other stations and give DeVore and Clement some semblance of privacy.

For the first time in eleven years, DeVore reached out and touched Clement with genuine warmth. Her hand went to his shoulder and he turned to face her.

"I know what this represents to you, Clement. Betraying so many promises of things you swore you would never do again. But please look at the opportunity this represents. There's no one in the Rim or the 5 Suns Alliance that I want commanding this ship more than you. There's no one who deserves it more, and no one else I can trust with this mission. Please Jared, take the seat."

He turned away from her, then stepped up and sat in the captain's chair. Damned if it didn't just feel *right* sitting in it.

DeVore smiled as Clement sat uncomfortably, wondering if he had just made a bargain with the Devil.

# ✵ 4 ✵

An hour later they were all back in the Admiral's office, sitting around the conference table.

"I have not officially said yes yet," insisted Clement as Captain Wilcock swept a series of papers in front of him, papers that would enlist him in the 5 Suns Alliance Navy again for the first time in over a decade.

DeVore sighed. "Just sign the goddamned paperwork, Jared. If you want out we'll tear it up later," she said.

"I have that option?" Clement asked. She nodded.

"Everyone enlisting in the 5 Suns Navy has three days to back out, the same as when you enlisted originally."

Clement looked at the first set of papers. It promised him the full rank of captain, serving at the pleasure of the Supreme Admiral of the 5 Suns Navy and his fleet-level designates (that meant DeVore); he would have to take the oath again, etc. He scribbled his signature at the bottom of the page, imprinted his thumb for authentication, then flipped over to the next. At the top of the page it had his full name, rank, and assignment. The salary was substantial, one hundred sixty-thousand 5 Suns crowns per year, nearly four times what he was making as an independent pilot. The commission was for five years, and officially designated as the 5 Suns Alliance Navy Exploratory Gunship *Beauregard*.

"Wait," he said, looking at DeVore. "You said this ship was one of the surrendered gunships—"

"I said it was a *Rim* gunship, not which one," said DeVore. Clement got up from the table and started pacing.

"We scuttled the *Beauregard*," he said plainly. "You were there."

DeVore stood with him. "Yes, we did. But what I needed for this mission was an intact hull. Not the engines, not the gun batteries or

53

the missile complement, and I needed a very specific captain. So I ordered the *Beauregard* to be recovered, and when we got her, we found she could do the job more than adequately. The repairs and refit took two years. Now, do you want her back, or not?"

Clement looked to DeVore, then over to Yan, and back again.

"I need to sleep on it," he said.

"You have that option," DeVore replied.

"Then I will take my leave of you, Admiral. You'll have my decision at 0900 tomorrow." With that Clement started for the door and Yan started to follow. Clement stopped her with his outstretched hand and looked to DeVore. "I would prefer to have this time to myself, Admiral. Certainly Miss Yan here can find something to occupy her time besides me?"

DeVore nodded to Yan, who returned to her seat at the table.

"Until 0900 then," said DeVore.

"Until then." At that Clement was out the door of the Admiral's office, headed for The Battered Hull as fast as he could go.

The door chime buzzed incessantly for several minutes before Clement roused from his sleep. He'd been dreaming it was going off and remembered cursing it several times, though whether he did that in real life or just in the dream world he wasn't really sure of. He sat up and felt surprisingly good considering how much he'd drunk at The Battered Hull. He hit the privacy call button and said "Just a moment" in what sounded to his ears to be a very gravelly voice. He got no response but the buzzing stopped.

He checked his watch, just past midnight, and wondered who would be visiting him at such an hour. He supposed it was Yan, trying to influence him to take the mission command. He unzipped his uniform tunic, checked his breath, which was foul, and quickly went to freshen up in the bathroom. Two minutes later he was at the door and hit the privacy com.

"Who is it?" he asked pleasantly enough.

"Just open the goddamned door. I've been out here for twenty minutes," came a low, brusque voice. It *sounded* like Yan, but he couldn't be sure, so he opened the door. A woman brushed past him quickly, her face shrouded in a hooded cloak, then turned to face him as he closed the door behind him.

She pulled the hood off of her head. It was Elara DeVore.

The cloak was definitely not duty standard, and she unzipped it to reveal a black unibody suit underneath. She filled the suit, as always, with a firm and fit body. The sight startled him more than a bit.

"Admiral—"

"Cut the bullshit, Clement. We're not on duty and this is not happening."

He opened his mouth for a second, but couldn't think of anything to say until "I wasn't expecting you" came out.

"Obviously," she said. "I came here to give you something." He looked her up and down, the cloak draping off of her shoulders . . . "Not *that*," she said, frustrated with him.

He was confused now, a product of both his earlier drinking and the unexpected visit from the Admiral. "Then what?" he said.

She looked around and to his surprise she went to his bed and sat down at the foot of it. He went over and sat next to her, close, but not too close. She pulled a square, flat case out of a pocket in the cloak and handed it to him. It was padded, and he opened it from the top.

It was the commissioning plaque from the *Beauregard*. Not a new one from the 5 Suns Alliance Navy, but the original one from the Rim Confederation. He held it in his hands. It was battered and bruised, burnt from the obvious wear and tear it had endured: battles, fire damage, and finally the scuttling Clement had put it through when he thought he was destroying her forever. To Clement, it was a gift of unmeasurable kindness.

"I . . . I don't know what to say," he said, emotions welling up inside him.

"You don't have to say anything, Jared. And I'm not giving you this to try and influence your decision in any way. I just wanted you to have it, to keep it with you if you take the mission, or to take home to Argyle if you don't. You deserve to have it, and people deserve to know who you really are, not what they think you are now." Then she kissed him quickly on the cheek and got up, zipping up the cloak again and heading for the door.

He followed.

"Elara, wait," he said.

"No," she replied. "If I stay we both know what will happen, and I can't allow that. What was, was, and it can never happen again."

He hung his head. "Is there someone else in your life?" he asked.

She shook her head. "No, and there never has been, really. Bedmates, for sure, some short-term relationships that may have benefitted me in some way in my career, but no one like you, and there never will be again, I know that. Now I've got to *go*, Clement. What passed between us all those years ago is gone from my heart forever, and that's just the hard truth of it," she said with finality.

Clement watched her go, a mixture of emotions, gratefulness, and pain at her confession of their love and her gift to him roiling through his emotions. He set the plaque down on his coffee table and poured himself a drink from the bar, Argyle Scotch, the good stuff, and sat down to contemplate what had just happened.

More than a decade ago they had been intense lovers. She was a dominant woman, one that was hard to tame, in or out of bed. But Clement had never given in to her impulses to control things between them, until the last day they had been together. She had come over to his apartment, he thought to celebrate his new promotion to captain, but that wasn't the case. She had paced around the room, explaining her reasoning, telling him how she would always treasure what they had, etc. He hardly heard her words and just watched her prowl the room like a caged cat that wanted to run free. In that moment, he had truly regretted taking the captaincy of the *Beauregard* if it would cost him DeVore. Once she was finished, telling him of her decision to end their relationship, he had accepted what had to be, the only time he had ever given in to her. Once done, she had leapt on him like a hungry predator, and they'd made love for hours on end. Precisely at midnight, she had left his bed without another word. And then today, at midnight, she had returned.

On his second taste of the scotch the door chime buzzed again. He got up and went to the door, hesitated a second, then opened it.

DeVore came through again, pulling him in with one hand and shutting the door behind her with the other. With a quick motion she unzipped the cloak again and let it fall from her shoulders to the floor. She pulled him in close and then took his hands, running them over every curve of her body. She kissed him passionately, their tongues flicking in and out together. After a long kiss he pulled back.

"But I thought—" he started. She put a finger over his mouth, shaking her head.

"I lied," she said, "about everything," then she kissed him again, pulling him quickly over to the bed.

# ☆ 5 ☆

Clement was awake by 0600, but Elara was long gone. She'd left quietly in the night and he'd let her, pretending to be asleep. Their sex had been frantic, and everything he'd ever wanted from her she had given to him, but she was gone now, Elara was gone, and he was sure from here on out he would be dealing with her only as Fleet Admiral DeVore.

He got ready and dressed in his undecorated 5 Suns Navy captain's uniform, then made his way out to The Battered Hull for a leisurely early breakfast. He ordered the Sailor's Ale Special, which promised a quick hangover recovery from any antics the night before. He'd already had his pills, but if he was being truthful he'd admit they weren't as effective now as they used to be when he was younger. Or maybe it was just *him* that wasn't as effective. He sat back with a cup of mocha coffee from New Paris, which also claimed to have anti-hangover properties. It wasn't bad, not at all, and as he sat there nursing his cup, he was interrupted by a group of midshipmen, the same four middies he'd told old war stories to on his first night at the station.

"You're interrupting my breakfast, Middies," he said disdainfully, looking away, as if he was not giving them a second glance, or a second of his time.

"We apologize for that, sir," said the lead one, the sandy-haired leader of the quartet from their previous engagement. Clement didn't really want company, but he decided to humor them, if only for a moment.

"What are your names, Middies?" he asked.

The leader answered for them all. "I'm Caleb Daniel, from New Paris, Huang Tsu is from Shenghai, Kayla Adebayor is from Carribea, and the big quiet one is Frank Telco, from Columbia," he said.

Clement gave them nods of acknowledgement all around. "And what is it that you *middies* want?"

They all looked at Daniel eagerly.

"Sir, we've all just completed our final school exams, and we're due to get our commissions after another semester of post-grad service training," Daniel stated.

"And what's that to me?"

"Well, sir," Daniel said, then hesitated. "To be honest, the rumors are that you're about to get a command, sir. And being as straightforward as we can be, we'd like to volunteer for that mission. Each of us have to serve a three-month-minimum internship to get our graduation plaques, and we'd like to serve that time with you. Sir."

Clement looked from each one of the middies to the other. They were all very young, and obviously very eager. "Are you serious?" he asked. They all nodded yes. Clement laughed, then started in on them.

"First of all, I don't have a ship yet. In fact, I'm not even sure I want the mission I'm being offered. Second, this mission has a crew complement of only twenty, so you'll have to prove to me your worth taking over an experienced space tech at your position. So tell me what your specialties are and your class rank, one by one, and I'll decide if this goes forward," he said.

Daniel started. "Command track, sir. Top five in a class of fifty."

"Well I don't need a command officer, but I'm sure we can find something for you to do. Next."

Tsu stepped up. "Propulsion sciences, sir. Eighth out of fifty."

Clement rubbed at his chin in an affected manner. "Ever heard of a LEAP drive, Mr. Tsu?"

Tsu looked confused. "No, sir."

"Good. It's Top Secret. And you didn't hear that term from me." Clement looked to Kayla. "Miss Adebayor?"

"Star Navigation, sir. Third out of twenty."

"Hmm," said Clement. "Why only twenty in the class?"

"The other thirty dropped out, sir," she said. "Including Tsu." Tsu looked embarrassed at the revelation. Clement thought about that.

"Tell me why you only came third in your class, Middie," said Clement.

Adebayor looked at her friends. "Because I spent the first

semester tutoring Middie Tsu, sir," she said. All the rest laughed except Tsu, who at least managed a smile.

"Very good, Navigator," he said, then he looked to Frank Telco. He was a big kid, even bigger than Tsu. "Mr. Telco?"

Telco stiffened as if at attention. "Weapons systems and security, sir," he said with confidence. "Top of my class, sir."

"I bet you could kill me with your dog tags," said Clement.

"Yes, sir!" replied Telco.

"Brains and brawn. You all make for a good mix of skills. I'll tell you what I'll do, I will put in a good word for you, but if you get on board my mission you'll have no rank status as middies. You'll do the least important tasks on board and you'll take orders from everyone, including the noncommissioned techs. I make no promises though, gentlemen. Is that good enough for you?"

They all smiled. "Good enough, sir!" said Daniel, the obvious leader.

"Great. Now make yourselves scarce. My breakfast is here." They all did as they were told, scattering out the door as the waitress laid out his breakfast plates.

"They seem like nice kids," said the waitress.

"They won't be nice when I'm done with them," said Clement, smiling. Then he dug into his food, suddenly finding himself very hungry.

Clement took the tram ride back to the Admiral's office, his belly full and his heart at peace for the first time in a long time. He knew what he was going to do.

On arrival he was quickly ushered into the meeting room with DeVore, Yan, and Wilcock. They all sat facing him on one side of the conference table while he sat alone on the other. Wilcock pushed the paperwork across the table to him again without a word. Clement found he didn't like Wilcock much. Too quiet and he looked like he'd never fired a weapon in his life.

It was Fleet Admiral DeVore who spoke first. "You've seen our offer, Mr. Clement. I've done all I can to convince you how important this mission is. The question now is if you'll take the offer or not. Will you be captain of the *Beauregard* again, or will that honor fall to Commander Yan?"

Clement wasn't making eye contact with her, but he answered anyway. "All things considered, and I do mean *all* things, Admiral, I'd be lying if I didn't say I wanted this mission, and this command. But, given that, there are still certain conditions."

DeVore sighed, no doubt a bit annoyed at his "all things considered" comment, an obvious reference to their late-night tryst, which she much preferred to keep secret from her staff. "Of course you have conditions. Name them before I change my mind about offering you this job." To her surprise Clement reached in to the middle of the pile of paper and pulled out a single sheet.

"This clause limiting my right to consume alcohol has to go," he said.

"That clause is based on your behavior over the last decade. There have been several reported incidents while working, and we'd be negligent if we didn't indemnify ourselves against any 'unexpected' surprises," the Admiral said.

"Yet I never lost my flying license, and I think it's you, Admiral, not the 5 Suns Navy, who want some indemnification on this mission," Clement said. Devore stared at him, not giving a centimeter. Clement drew a big red X through the sheet and then turned it over and started writing (in blue) on the back. When he was done, he slid the sheet across the table to DeVore. She picked it up and began reading out loud.

"Six bottles of Argyle Scotch to be kept aboard at all times for the captain's personal use and pleasure, and to share with the crew at his discretion," she said aloud. Then she got out her pen, switching to red, and began marking up the paper herself, then slid it back to Clement to read.

"Three bottles of Argyle Scotch, to be kept in the possession of Commander Yan and distributed at her discretion," he read aloud. He was annoyed, but decided not to press the point. "Should I initial this?"

"Yes," DeVore said, and he did so.

"Item two, captain's choice of key bridge personnel and technicians. I have to be able to trust my command crew," he said.

"Understood. So who would you choose?" DeVore asked.

"Hassan Nobli for one, as my chief engineer. Mika Ori and Ivan Massif at helm and navigation, if you can find them and I can convince them," he said.

DeVore smiled. "Nobli signed on to the LEAP project two months ago. Mika and Ivan have been my guests here on Kemmerine Station for the last eight days, waiting for you. They'll join up as soon as you sign your papers and take the oath," she said.

Clement smiled at that. "Well played, Admiral," he said. She nodded as Clement signed off on the staff sheet.

"Anything else, Clement?"

"One more request. There are four middies that want to join this mission as part of their intern semester. I want to add them to the crew. We can bunk them in the cargo hold," he said.

DeVore shook her head strongly no. "This mission is Top Secret, Clement. It's no place for unseasoned middies. You've got the finest techs I could find for you. Why do you want four greenhorns in the way?"

"Because they asked, and that shows initiative and bravery, something I had once, and maybe, just a little bit, I've lost."

"So, they remind you of a younger you? That seems like slim reasoning to me."

"A chance to mold young minds, Admiral," he said. She crossed her arms and leaned back in her chair, shaking her head at his boldness.

"Yan, see to the bunks and extra rations. Captain Wilcock, run a background check on these four middies. If even one of them doesn't have a spotless record, none of them go. Clear, Clement?"

"Yes, Admiral. I'll forward the names to Captain Wilcock," he said, nodding toward the staff officer.

"And now I want something back from you," said DeVore. Clement nodded once to her, waiting to hear her conditions.

"Captain Wilcock here will go on the mission with you."

"What? Why would I need a staff officer?"

"Protocol."

"Protocol? You mean a spy. And besides, you've already got Yan for that," Clement said. Yan gave him a withering stare from across the table. Wilcock, for his part, said nothing.

"Take it or leave it," said DeVore. Clement looked Wilcock over. Beady, shifty eyes. Clement was reminded that he'd had sweaty palms when they first shook. He didn't like him at all, but . . .

"Done, Admiral," Clement said.

"Good," said DeVore, slapping her palms on the table and then standing. "Finish your paperwork with Captain Wilcock here. We will get you proper rank adornments, and then you'll take the oath."

"How long until I can take her out for test runs?" asked Clement as he busily started signing papers.

"Oh, there's no test runs, Captain. The *Beauregard* leaves dock in slightly less than forty-eight hours. Now if you'll excuse me, I have a fleet to run." And with that she was off to her office desk, Clement staring after her.

"Can we just get the goddamn thing running?" The angry voice belonged to Captain Jared Clement of the *Beauregard*, less than twelve hours after he'd taken the 5 Suns Alliance Navy oath as her commander.

"This is precision work, Captain. One wrong move and we could disintegrate this ship in a microsecond. Antimatter is powerful stuff." The second voice belonged to Hassan Nobli, chief engineer of the *Beauregard*, and caretaker of the LEAP drive. Nobli was a disheveled-looking man with curly, unkempt hair and rounded wire-rim glasses, which Clement took for an affectation rather than a necessity. Nobli always seemed to be wearing a pair of coveralls soaked in grease of some kind, even when there wasn't any around, and this situation was no exception.

The two men were standing face to face in front of the antimatter annihilation chamber. It was spherical, no bigger than a small steam boiler Clement had seen used on his home world of Ceta, and surprisingly simple in its design. The only sense of sophistication came from the eight exit pipes that would channel the antimatter material to the LEAP drive components on the ship's outer-perimeter drive ring.

"Look, Mika and Ivan haven't even so much as taken this thing for a drive around the block, let alone fire it up and take on the first faster-than-light interstellar mission in the history of mankind. Now how much longer will it be?" demanded Clement.

"The station scientists are monitoring the fluid outflow now, Captain. They say we should be ready to fire her up in about two hours, and I won't argue that point with them," said Nobli.

"Fine then," said Clement. "But I want you and your techs on this until we have the right mix. There won't be any second chances to get it right out in the wild."

"Understood sir."

"In the meantime why don't you get that propulsion middie, Tsu, to warm up the conventional drives. I want Mika and Ivan to at least get a chance to handle the controls before we start surfing the universe."

"I'll get Middie Tsu on it right away," Nobli said. Secretly, he'd already had the conventional drives, ion plasma, and chemical thrusters fired up and ready to go, but giving the middie something to do would keep him out of Nobli's way, at least for a while. And it had the added effect of placating the annoyed captain of the *Beauregard*.

Clement pointed at Nobli. "I want hourly reports on this thing," he said.

"Of course, sir."

Clement started to walk away.

"Sir," Nobli called after him. Clement turned. "It's good to see you back, sir."

"It's good to be back. I think," said Clement. Then he was off to his next stop.

Down inside the cargo bay, Clement stopped to check in on his four middies. He had passed Tsu in the corridor on his way to assist Nobli, but Daniel, Adebayor and Telco were all at their bunks. They stood and saluted as he came up. He saluted back.

"That's enough of that; we don't salute onboard. At ease, Middies," he said. They all relaxed, but just a bit. They were clearly nervous. "I hope you've settled in because we won't have much time to get you up to speed and I don't have time to babysit you, so you each have to find a sponsor and stick to them like glue, which means you do whatever they tell you to do, even if it's sweeping the floors.

"Now, Miss Adebayor, you'll be up first. I want you to meet with my navigator, Lieutenant Massif, at your first possible convenience. He's a top navigator and when you're plotting an interstellar mission, well, whatever he knows you should try to glom off of him. And also check in with the com and engineering techs. I may have a console for you on the bridge as Mr. Nobli likes running things from the bowels of the ship."

"Yes, sir," she said, with way too much enthusiasm.

"Daniel, there isn't much you'll be able to learn from me and I don't want you following me around like a puppy dog anyway. Commander Yan is an accomplished officer and on the command fast track so please communicate with her about your assignments. She probably won't like it but tell her that I insist. Oh, and stay away from Captain Wilcock. That's one career path you don't want to emulate, understood?"

"Aye, sir," said Daniel.

Clement turned to the last middie, Telco. "Mr. Telco, I have a special job for you. Inventory our weapons systems—missiles, torpedoes, energy weapons, and stashes of small arms. I want a complete accounting in two hours and I want you to familiarize yourself with all the ship's weapons systems. Understood?"

"Aye, Captain," said Telco, then added, "will do."

Clement eyed him, annoyed. "Cut out that last part, Middie. It will get annoying real fast."

Telco stiffened at that. "Yes, sir," he said.

"And one more thing I want you to do. Clear out some of these cargo boxes and set up a shooting range down here. God knows it's big enough with only a small crew. Once that's done I want you to find some of the techs when they're off rotation and make them shoot some rounds, once we're underway. I want as many as we can to get in shooting practice during the journey out."

Telco looked at his friends and they exchanged surprised looks.

Daniel, ever the leader, stepped in again. "Are you expecting that we may have to go into combat, sir?" he said.

"Gentlemen," Clement said, looking at the three of them, "we're heading to an unexplored star system aboard an experimental faster-than-light-speed prototype ship. I expect nothing, but I want us to be prepared for anything at all times, understood?"

"Yes, sir," came a chorus in reply.

Clement looked at his watch. "Then get to it. Admiral DeVore wants us gone inside thirty-six hours from now. Let's not disappoint her. Now off with you."

And with that they all scattered, and Clement made his way back toward his bridge.

# �֎ 6 ֎

Clement called together his first staff meeting in the tiny officer's galley on Deck 2 for 1930 hours. There were only six rooms on the deck: the captain's cabin on the port side, which was the most spacious, obviously; Commander Yan's across the hall starboard from him; then Mika Ori and Ivan Massif one door down from Yan; then the galley. On Clement's side of the aisle there was a cabin for Hassan Nobli that he hardly ever used, preferring to bunk with the crew closer to his engine room, and Captain Wilcock got the small room at the end of the hallway, which was really just a guest berth with no bathroom, and across from the officer's galley. Clement got some small satisfaction knowing that Wilcock would have to use the technician's shared bathroom two decks down every time he had to use the head.

They gathered quietly after a long day, most looking worn out but shunning coffee. It had been a full day and there was still work to do before their scheduled departure at 1200 hours tomorrow. They shuffled in, Yan sitting next to him, the gangly Massif and the tiny Ori sitting together, then Nobli and finally Wilcock filling out the table. Before he started, Clement flipped through a series of reports on his com pad and frowned. He looked up at Yan.

"This ship is severely under-armed," he said to her. "Midshipman Telco reports to me that we have only a half dozen cobra rifles on board, a smattering of handguns, and no grenades of any kind."

"There are only twenty crew," said Yan calmly. "Are you expecting to fight an army?"

"First of all, there are twenty-four crew with the middies, and no I'm not 'expecting' a fight, but this is a military vessel and as such we should be properly armed. I expect a full complement of rifles and pistols loaded aboard before we depart and plenty of extra ammo as well."

"How much 'ammo,' sir?" she replied sarcastically, with a smirk. This time Clement suspected he was being played with by Yan. He decided to double down.

"Two crates worth, of each," he said.

"But that would be—" started Yan.

"One hundred forty-four packs of each style," finished Wilcock.

"Thank you, Mr. Wilcock," said Clement. "And a crate of RPG rounds."

"Are you serious? That will take up half the cargo hold," protested Yan.

"Hardly. And may I remind you, Commander, this *is* a military mission, and I expect everyone to behave accordingly. This is not some show cruise and we are not explorers. So we follow the rules. We may not be expecting any trouble, but if my navy career is any indication, it often finds me," Clement noted before continuing. "And that reminds me again, this ship has literally no advanced armaments for protection. I want a full complement of missiles, conventional and atomic, brought on board."

This time it was Wilcock who spoke up. "I'm not sure the Admiral will authorize that," he said.

Clement looked up at him sharply. "This is a gunship, Captain. A gunship with no weapons is pretty useless. And may I remind you that you're on this ship as a favor to the Admiral, Mr. Wilcock. If I don't have a full missile room of sixty conventional missiles in my launch bays with at least a half dozen ten-kiloton nuke warheads on board by the time we head out, I'm leaving you on the loading dock."

"Is that *all*, sir?" said Wilcock, perturbed. "We don't even have a weapons tech on board." He had a soft, high voice, the kind that would annoy any crew, and it was annoying Clement already.

"We have Middie Telco. He'll have to do for now and I expect to have him properly trained on all types of missiles and warheads, by you."

"Do you think you'll need more missiles than just the nukes?" asked Yan, feigning surprise.

Clement looked at her, very seriously. "Commander Yan, the

solution to almost any problem in space is more missiles," he deadpanned.

Yan sighed. "Boys and their toys," she said.

Clement ignored her and looked down the table. "Mr. Nobli, a report on the LEAP drive if you please," he said.

"Well," started Nobli, adjusting his glasses. He looked for all the world like a misplaced university professor, not a spaceship engineer, as he scanned his hand-pad readouts. "I've got her humming pretty good, Captain. The nuclear accelerator seems to run as smoothly as promised, and I've no doubt once we release the hold on the two chambers of the LEAP reactor that everything will work smoothly and we can start annihilating antimatter universes."

Clement nodded. "That's . . . that's good, I guess?" he said. "What about the conventional drive?"

"Well, we've got a state of the art Xenon thruster system and an Ion plasma drive that will push us along at a clip we would have loved to have had during the war, but just like the LEAP system, they're both untested with humans on board," said Nobli.

"What about acceleration?"

"We can easily achieve six *g*s of acceleration inside two minutes. Enough speed to get us out of any pickle, I'd say."

"Thank you, Nobli. Fleet Admiral DeVore expects us to be half an AU from the station before we light up the LEAP reactor. Let's make sure we give the Ion plasma drive a good test on that run. It will be our primary means of travel inside the Trinity system," said Clement.

"Aye, sir."

Next Clement looked down the table to Mika Ori and Ivan Massif, his pilot and navigator. "I regret we won't be able to give you a chance to bust the seams on this baby before first flight, Mika," he said.

She nodded. "I understand the circumstances, sir. I'm looking forward to getting her under power." She'd been his pilot, and a damn good one, for three years on the original incarnation of the *Beauregard*.

"How's your station checking out?" asked Clement.

Ori shrugged. "It's state of the art, but I've spent most of the last decade on similar systems in the private sector, in fact, some of them I like better than this one. But I should be able to fly her, sir, if the Admiral ever lets us leave the dock."

"Oh, she will," smiled Clement. "Ivan?" he continued, pronouncing it the navigator's preferred way, *E-vaan*. Massif was a tall and lanky man, and a great navigator, but the LEAP drive would make him less relevant on this mission.

"I'm also familiar with this type of navigation system from our years running luxury yachts and the like. It's different though, in that it's really a 'point and shoot' system. Since we'll be traveling at FTL speeds in a quantum-fluid bubble the normal types of flight plans don't really come into the equation, as long as there aren't any uncharted rogue planets on our path that I don't know about," he said.

Clement smiled. "Sorry if you'll be bored, Ivan. We'll take the same path as the last LEAP probe, which should be clear of potential hazards. Once we're in the Trinity system though, we'll need you to be full up and ready to chart our path inwards toward the three habitable planets. I guess you'll just have to wait a couple of weeks to become important."

"Aye, sir, I'll be ready. I've already plotted us to follow the LEAP probe's course, sir. You just have to say the word."

"Good enough," said Clement, turning back to Yan. "Do we have a medical officer aboard, Commander?" he asked. She scanned her own pad for personnel profiles.

"Lieutenant Pomeroy is the dedicated medic. She also doubles as a science tech," said Yan.

Clement nodded. "Good enough. Have her run you through the med bay equipment as a pre-req, and I want her to have a backup. Let's give Mr. Daniel a shot at that."

"Yes, sir," said Yan.

Clement looked around the room. "Anything else?" Everyone stayed silent. "Good. I want you all in bed by 2400 hours but I want my ordnance and equipment aboard and stored before 0800 tomorrow, so that duty falls to you, Mr. Wilcock."

"Understood, Captain."

"Then I'll leave you all to it," he said as the meeting broke up. Before they could all exit though, he added, "We're all clear for departure at 1200 hours tomorrow. I want us to be ready two hours prior to that." There were groans and acknowledgements as the command crew shuffled out. Clement reached out to Yan indicating she should stay.

"Do you think we'll be ready in time for the launch?" he asked when they were alone.

"I don't know, sir. You're a much different commander than this crew is used to, excepting your friends, of course. The 5 Suns Alliance Navy is a different kind of animal; they're more used to formality and protocol. They may fall in line with your style, or they may resist. It's up to you to find the right combination," she said.

"As long as I have your loyalty, Yan," he stated.

She looked at him, hesitating before answering. "You do, Captain. For now," she said, and then went down the hall to her cabin.

Yan was surprised when she got a knock on her cabin door fifteen minutes later. She hit her visual monitor and found it was Captain Wilcock standing in the hallway. She could see over Wilcock's shoulder that Captain Clement's door was closed. She buzzed Wilcock in and he came in quickly and quietly. Yan looked at him. "What can I do for you, Mr. Wilcock?"

He quickly went over to her desk com system and started it up. "Message incoming from Fleet Admiral DeVore," he said.

"Shouldn't Clement—" Yan started.

"It's just for us, Commander," he replied as Admiral DeVore's image came up on the screen.

"Hello, Yan," she said.

"Hello, Admiral."

DeVore looked dead serious.

"Look, I want to make this quick and I want us all to be on the same page, is that clear?" Yan looked to Wilcock, who said nothing, and then back to the Admiral.

"Clear, Admiral."

"Good. I'm going to approve Clement's request for the conventional missiles and the small arms. The way I know him, he's looking to pick a fight and if I say no to his request he'll just sit on the dock until I give in. I want this mission off on time tomorrow—in fact, timing is critical for the *Beauregard* to reach Trinity."

This intrigued Yan, as to why timing was so critical, but she decided to say nothing for the moment.

DeVore continued. "But this request for atomic warheads, that's different. I can see no reason why he might need them, but I'm going to give him six warheads anyway, under certain conditions. The most important of these conditions, Yan, is that you and Wilcock have to be in agreement that use of the warheads is justified. To safeguard this condition, you're both going to have to wear security keys around your necks for the duration of the mission. You will both have to be in agreement to unlock the safe to access the warheads and you'll both have to agree the situation is dire enough to use them. The keys must be used simultaneously to both unlock the safe and release the missile controls for Clement to launch them. Do you understand, Yan?"

"I do, Admiral," she said. At that Wilcock handed her a small clear case with a nuclear key inside. Yan broke the seal and placed it around her neck, slipping it under her uniform tunic, then zipped back up. All command-level officers had taken atomic level protocol classes as a condition of their promotion, but this was the first time Yan had ever been issued one of the keys. When that was done DeVore looked to Wilcock.

"Your shipment of atomic warheads will arrive in a case at the loading dock in fifteen minutes. I expect you to be there and to secure the warheads personally. Understood, Captain Wilcock?"

"Understood, sir," he replied.

"Good. Then that's that. The rest of the conventional missiles and small arms will be aboard by 0600. Who's going to be in charge of loading them into the launch bays?"

"Middie Telco, ma'am," said Yan.

DeVore nodded. "Oversee his work, Yan. I don't want a middie blowing up my prototype in the dry dock."

"Aye, Admiral."

"Then off with the two of you," she said with a wave of her hand. "And good luck."

"Thank you, ma'am," said Yan as Wilcock mumbled some other reply. Yan found she didn't care much for his speaking voice, too soft and indistinguishable. She found she didn't trust him much either.

With that the com to DeVore's office severed and Wilcock made for the door. With his hand on the door control he stopped and looked back at her. "I appreciate your support on this, Yan," he said. She merely nodded in reply. A few seconds later and she watched him on her monitor as he went down the deck ladder and out of sight, heading toward the loading dock, there to presumably await the arrival of the atomic warheads. She waited a few moments more before heading across the hallway to Clement's cabin. She buzzed in. The door slid open silently.

Clement was at his office desk, rifling through various pads as he checked to see if his orders were being complied with and if the ship was ready for her manned maiden voyage.

"Can I help you, Yan?" he said, not looking up from his pile of pads and floating monitor displays.

"I just wanted you to know that your atomic warheads are coming on board presently, sir," she said.

"I assume that's what Captain Wilcock wanted from you in your quarters?" Clement replied.

It bothered Yan that her cabin was being monitored by him, but, "Yes, sir," she said without hesitation.

Clement continued to work, seeming to ignore her. "You realize not having the warheads already loaded onto a ship-to-ship missile will slow our response time, possibly to a very dangerous level?" he said.

"That's Captain Wilcock's purview, sir, not mine," she defended.

Now Clement looked up. "I don't trust Wilcock," he said.

"Neither do I, sir."

"Really? That's good to hear. But then I'm not entirely sure I trust you either, Yan."

She bristled inside at that, but she didn't back down from Clement's steel gaze on her. He had a way of making her feel like he could see right through her. "I hope I can change that opinion with time, sir," she said.

Clement leaned back from his displays. "Do you, Yan? I hope that's true," he said, then he got out of his chair and paced the cabin while Yan watched him. "Admiral DeVore—" he started. She cut him off before he could finish the thought.

"She's my primary report, sir. But you're my commanding officer on this mission," she offered, unsolicited. Clement took that in stride.

"Please understand, Yan, I have a long history with Mika, Ivan, and even Nobli. I don't have much history with you. I may make decisions you disagree with. I just need to know I won't find a cobra pistol round in my back if I do."

Now Yan got very serious. "Captain Clement, please don't question my loyalty to you or this mission."

"But you undoubtedly have private orders from Admiral DeVore, don't you?" he accused.

She nodded once. "I do, sir. But they are to protect the ship, protect the mission, and protect the crew. She wanted you for this command very badly, and I'll admit I don't know why. But beyond those general protocols, sir, you are my commanding officer, and I want you to know you can trust me," she said.

"Even with that atomic key hanging around your neck?"

Suddenly Yan became conscious of the cold metal between her breasts, set against her skin. Despite Clement pushing her to her limits, Yan didn't waver. "Yes, Captain, even with the key."

Now it was his turn to nod once, then he returned to his desk. "When will the missiles be loaded?" he asked.

"0600, sir."

"Make sure Middie Telco has a full set them packed and ready for the launch tubes well before we leave."

"I was just on my way to take care of that, sir."

"Good. And Yan, thank you."

"Aye, sir," she said, then turned on her heels and made her way out of his cabin. She went down toward the cargo hold, there to make sure the middie got his instructions as early as possible.

"Do you understand your orders, Middie?" said Yan to the strapping young middie Telco.

"Aye, ma'am," he said, bright-eyed and eager to please despite the ever-later hour.

"Good," she said. "Make sure you validate that the ordnance in those missiles is primed and ready to go. We don't want any surprises in the middle of a battle."

"Understood, ma'am."

"What about all the small arms?"

He stiffened. "As requested, ma'am. I've already tested the cobra rifles and pistols. The kinetic rounds work just fine, and the burner rounds have passed all the test marks. I haven't tested the RPGs for obvious reasons, but I have to say these are some of the finest guns I've ever seen. The workmanship is fantastic."

She smiled again at his youthful enthusiasm. "I imagine what you used in the academy weren't top-of-the-line materiel. The navy doesn't skimp on the real thing." Yan gestured to a bunk and Telco hopped up to the top of one of them. "Set your alarm early, Middie. The captain will want those missiles stored and ready to go as soon as they get here. In fact, I imagine he'll be checking in with you every few minutes after 0600. You shouldn't disappoint him. Now get some sleep, and when you see your friends tell them the same. Today has been a big day; tomorrow will be bigger," she said, then turned down the light in the middie's tiny berth, feeling all the world like a mother putting one of her children to bed. A very handsome young child at that.

"Do you think we'll see battle, ma'am?" said Telco with way too much enthusiasm.

Despite herself, Yan smiled at him. "I highly doubt it, Middie, but you never know," she said. "Now go lights out. We have a lot to do yet to get this bucket rolling."

He nodded. "Goodnight, ma'am," he said.

"Good night, Middie," she said, then shut the door behind her.

# ⟡ 7 ⟡

Clement was up and prowling the decks well before the missiles were scheduled to arrive at 0600. When he arrived at the loading dock Middie Telco was already there. He checked his watch. 0540. Not bad for a rookie.

After exchanging pleasantries, the two went silent, both anticipating the same thing. Ten minutes later at 0550 the missiles started arriving. Clement jumped right in with directions for the dock techs and Telco.

The ship-to-ship missiles were five meters long and came in crates of two, with the warheads stored separately. The cargo bay had an automated racking system which pulled the missiles from their crates and then shipped them via a gantry loader up two decks and forward to the missile room where they were re-racked, waiting for their warheads to be installed. Telco had arranged for Middie Daniel to take care of the warheads, and he had them all loaded onto an open lift for travel. In Clement's experience, it took about two hours to turn a load of crated missiles and a full complement of warheads into ready-racked missiles. Telco and Daniel had a lot of work ahead of them.

Once he was satisfied that the process was moving efficiently, Clement clicked the com to Daniel's channel and gave the middies final instructions. "It's 0615, Middies. My expectation is that you'll have these missiles racked and loaded in the forward missile center by 0830 hours. I hope you don't plan on disappointing me?"

"No, sir," they both said in unison. Clement turned to address Telco directly. "As of this moment, Middie, you are my missile-room tech. That's your station full time. Daniel, you will be his relief, covering the position while he eats, sleeps and pisses. Am I clear?"

There was a round of "aye, sirs" from the two middies.

Clement looked at Telco one more time. "I'm holding you personally responsible for making sure those nuke warheads are stored within a hand's reach of the missiles at all times."

Telco looked concerned. "Sir, Captain Wilcock has insisted that the nuke warheads stay in the ordnance hold under lock and key. Sir," Telco said nervously.

"Unfortunately, Middie, Captain Wilcock is an idiot who has never had a ship command. You store them right where I said. If he wants to protest you come and get me. I'll be coming by before we shove off to check your work, you can count on that," Clement warned.

"Yes, sir. I'll see to it, sir."

"And one more thing. Make sure you rotate the rack so that six empty missiles are ready to be loaded with those nukes as soon as possible in an emergency situation. I don't want to wait for sixty missiles to roll by if I need a nuke," said the captain.

"Aye, sir," said Telco.

Clement nodded, then left him to his work.

Next Clement checked in with Nobli in the propulsion room.

"Are we ready to go interstellar surfing yet, Mr. Nobli?" said Clement, surprising his engineer, who turned quickly from his station at the antimatter annihilation chamber.

"You should never surprise a man who controls enough power to wipe out a star system," said Nobli, smiling. "Yes, sir, she's ready to go. Xenon drive thrusters and the Ion plasma impellers have been test-fired as well. I think she'll fly like a bumble bee, sir."

Clement frowned at the metaphor. "Uh, I don't know about where you're from, Nobli, but on Ceta bumble bees are kind of slow, lazy fliers," he said. Nobli was a native of Helios, like DeVore had been. The planet had no bees of any kind.

Nobli thought about that a minute. "Maybe I meant humming-bird," he said, shrugging.

Clement had never seen a hummingbird. Story was they hadn't been hardy enough to survive on the Rim worlds, but from what he knew, the analogy was a better match.

"I'll take that then," Clement said, and managed a wave to Middie Tsu, who was across a sea of pipes from the two men, adjusting a valve control as he waved back. Clement looked at his watch. "Just four and a half hours, Hassan, and we're back among the stars."

"Aye, sir. Never thought I'd see the day, but it's good to have you back in uniform. It's where you belong, sir."

Clement looked down at his uniform, not one he had ever expected to wear again. "Don't get sentimental on me, Nobli. I'll have you running like a dog soon enough."

"I bet you will, sir."

Clement just nodded to his friend, then brought up another subject. "Have you done any research on other possible applications for the LEAP drive?"

Nobli looked at him sidelong. "Such as?"

Clement leaned in close to his engineer inside the noisy room. "Such as possible weapons applications? We are, after all, using a lot of energy in the drive."

"That we are, sir. There are some theoretical papers. I've skimmed them."

Clement stepped back. "Well, you'll have about seventeen days to look into it. I'd like you to give me an option before we arrive at Trinity. Something that works, Nobli."

Nobli nodded. "We do have the old forward plasma cannon array from the previous iteration of the *Beauregard*. Nobody uses those anymore. Last I saw it was still intact, but I don't know if the piping could hold that kind of energy output."

Clement nodded. "Well, check it out, and let me know in a couple of days, *after* you have everything LEAP-related running smoothly."

"Will do, sir," said Nobli, and then Clement was gone again.

Captain Clement sat and watched his crew from his command seat on the bridge. Ivan Massif was busy teaching young Middie Adebayor about some navigational principle or other. Mika Ori was at the helm, tinkering with the controls while reading a training manual on her hand pad. Yan's station was empty, as it had been for the last two hours, and Captain Wilcock was taking up the engineering console, watching everything like a curly-haired hawk. As a precaution, Clement had shut off the engineering controls, so mainly Wilcock had to stare at a blank panel, and that was fine with Clement.

Clement looked at his watch again. 1140 hours. Still twenty minutes to go and everything was green to go on his master console. They'd missed their two-hour early ready mark, but that had just given him the excuse to yell at everyone again. He'd just got back from one last sweep of the *Beauregard*'s stations, even stopping too take an inventory of medical supplies with Lieutenant Pomeroy. It had been his third such sweep of the morning.

Finally, he'd had enough.

"Commander Yan to the bridge, please," he said impatiently over the ship-wide com. A few seconds later and he heard her footsteps clanking on the open metal stairs to the bridge.

"I was just down in the galley having a last coffee," she said casually as she keyed in the code to unlock her station.

"I'm glad someone's relaxed," Clement said, then he keyed in the code through his com panel to the Admiralty, and Elara DeVore. "Middie Adebayor, do you have a communications badge?"

"I do, sir," she said after snapping around to him at attention.

"Then get on the engineering console and raise station traffic control."

"Aye, sir," she said, and started making her way to the console, which was occupied by Wilcock.

"Captain Wilcock," said Clement, "I'm afraid you'll have to sit this one out in your cabin."

"But, I have—"

"It's not my fault they made the bridge so small. You should register a complaint with the Admiral when you get back," Clement deadpanned. Wilcock scowled at Clement but reluctantly relinquished the station to Middie Adebayor. The sound of Wilcock's boots clinking down the short stairwell brought a smile to Clement's face.

A second later and Admiral DeVore popped up on the main bridge display.

"I was just about to call in and wish you all good luck," said the Admiral.

Clement smiled at her. "I'm actually just calling to ask for early clearance to depart. We've been ready for over an hour now . . . and frankly, I'm bored," he said, lying.

DeVore laughed. "I wouldn't expect anything else from you,

Clement. Clearance is given. Good luck. We'll see you in about a month."

Clement stood. "Thank you, Admiral," he said, and snapped off a departure salute.

At that DeVore switched off the feed from her end.

Clement turned to his middie. "Do you have Kemmerine Station traffic control on the line, Middie Adebayor?"

"I do, Captain."

"Please inform them we are seeking early clearance from the dock. Fleet Admiral's priority," he said.

Adebayor repeated the same to traffic control and then got a positive beep in return.

"Stations, everyone. Prepare for departure," said Clement.

Yan got on the ship-wide com and repeated Clement's command. Within a minute all the boards showed fresh green lights again.

Clement turned to Mika Ori. "Lieutenant, you may shove off at your convenience," he said.

"Aye, sir," said Ori, then proceeded to turn to her station and cut the *Beauregard*'s moorings, using a tiny burst of the thrusters to move her away from the station. Once the ship was a hundred meters clear of the dock, Ori turned the ship expertly and began to accelerate using the thrusters, the station fading quickly behind her.

"Xenon thrusters making .0005 light, sir," said Ori.

Clement acknowledged and then sat back in his chair for the first time as in-service captain of the *Beauregard* in fifteen years.

"Light up the Ion drive, Lieutenant. Increase speed constant to .025 light. That should give us about three hours to the jump-off point for the Trinity system."

"Aye, sir," said Ori, quickly turning and making adjustments on her console board. They all felt a slight tug at the increase in speed as Ori activated the Ion plasma drive.

Clement turned to Ivan Massif. "What's our course, Navigator?" he asked.

"Generally on course for the Trinity system, sir," replied Massif.

Clement looked at the lanky Russian. "Generally on course?"

Massif shrugged. "It's not like navigating inside 5 Suns Alliance space, sir. Trinity is 11.5 light-years away. We can be off by quite a ways on our final target and still be well within the mission parameters, especially from this distance, sir. You don't want me to fly her right into the Trinity star, do you?"

Clement smiled. "No, Ivan, I don't. But if you don't mind me asking, what will be our dropout point in the system?"

"Based on what the last probe did, we'll be about ten AU out from the outermost planet, and that last planet is only about 0.06 AU from the Trinity star itself, sir," said Massif.

"Six *hundredths* of an AU? How many klicks is that?"

"Just under nine million kilometers, sir," chimed in Yan.

Clement mouthed a sardonic "thank you" without saying anything. "Those planets must be packed in tight," he then commented.

"The three habitable worlds are within 2.5 million kilometers of each other, sir," said Massif.

"Very close, then," said Clement.

"Short orbital years too, sir. Four, six, and nine days, sir," said Massif.

Clement whistled. "Just a fraction of 5 Suns Alliance space. This will be interesting flying, Mika. I hope you're ready," he said, turning to his pilot.

"Always ready, sir," she replied. "But for now it's just the milk run until we get that LEAP drive turned on. I could do it in my sleep, sir."

"I bet you could, Mika." Clement stood and took the short walk around his compact bridge. "Well, we're on our way. The next milestone should be in about three hours when we turn the LEAP engine on. Until then, I'll be in my cabin, monitoring. Call me if you need anything. And Commander Yan, call Captain Wilcock to the bridge to take the con. And tell him not to touch anything."

"Aye, sir," said Yan, smiling, as Clement departed the bridge.

Clement got a knock at his door, not an entry-request chime, mind you, but a real knock, about thirty minutes later. Clement pressed the OPEN button on his desk and the door slid aside. To his surprise it was Yan, bearing a bottle of Argyle whiskey and a pair of drinking glasses. He stood to greet her.

"Why, Commander, this is most unexpected of you. Cutting into my alcohol rations already, I see."

"I felt this was a moment worth celebrating," she said as she sat down in one of his desk chairs. Clement joined her at the table and after popping the bottle, he poured a healthy portion of whiskey into the glasses. She took her glass and raised her hand in a toast. "To Captain Jared Clement, and the crew of the 5SN *Beauregard*," she said.

"To the *Beauregard*." They clinked glasses and then drank, Clement savoring the taste. "Ah, god, that's good," he said, leaning back in his chair and then swiveling slowly back and forth. "I wish they'd outfitted this cabin with a recliner."

"For what? Watching tri-vee or your sports?"

"No, Yan. Just to have a drink in and read a good book."

"We have millions of books in the ship's library."

"True. But reading off a pad isn't as fun as holding a real book in your hands. Plus, there's the thrill of the hunt."

She frowned, looking perplexed. "Hunt? What do you mean?"

"Browsing through shops full of ancient leather-bound books. Finding just the right edition. I find it all very relaxing," he said.

"More relaxing than the whiskey?"

"Much," he said.

She put the cap back on the bottle. "Well, I think that's enough celebrating for one day," she said, then headed for the door. "Congratulations again, Captain," she added. "I'll see you on the bridge."

"On the bridge, Commander," he said, then finished his whiskey ration, savoring the taste.

Clement took over the bridge, relieving Wilcock, whom he exiled back to his quarters, with the *Beauregard* about twenty minutes from the agreed-upon jump coordinates. After running through reports from all his subordinates and doing his pad systems check, he called down to Hassan Nobli in the engine room.

"How's our new baby?" he asked.

"Purring like a kitten, sir, but ready to leap on a moment's notice."

Clement smiled. "Was that a pun, Mr. Nobli?"

"Do I really have to tell you that?"

"No," said Clement, smiling. "We'll be arriving at the LEAP coordinates in about..." Clement trailed off as he checked his watch. "Eighteen minutes. Will you be ready?"

"Most definitely, sir. Will you be coming down to watch?"

"Honestly, I hadn't thought of that," admitted Clement.

"We'll give you a show, I promise. And if anything goes wrong, you'll be one of the first to die," joked Nobli.

Clement laughed. "Here's to hoping nothing goes wrong. I'll see you in a few minutes," he said.

"Aye, sir."

Clement slid out of the captain's couch and nodded to Middie Adebayor at the engineering console. "Raise the Admiral, please, Middie."

"Aye, sir," she said. About thirty seconds later she had DeVore on the line and put her image up on the main bridge display.

After a second or two delay, DeVore smiled. "All ready?" she asked.

"Ready, Admiral," Clement said. "Request permission to activate the LEAP drive and depart 5 Suns Alliance space."

There was that hanging delay again, then DeVore said, "Permission granted, Captain Clement. Good luck."

"Thank you, Admiral. We'll see you sooner than you think."

The local ansible network adjusted for the time delay at that moment and DeVore answered almost immediately. "Oh, I'm sure of that, Captain," she said.

With that Clement saluted and gave Adebayor the cutoff signal. DeVore faded from the screen and was replaced by a ship's system status view. Clement got on the all-ship com.

"Now hear this. All hands prepare for LEAP drive activation. Take all safety precautions. Captain Wilcock to the bridge," he said, then hung up the com. He turned to Yan. "You have the con, Yan."

"But sir, Captain Wilcock is the ranking—"

"Not on my ship, Yan. Now that we're about to leap out of the Admiral's jurisdiction, I make the rules. You have the con at all times in my absence, unless directed otherwise. Wilcock can take your station. I'll be in the engineering room watching Mr. Nobli light this baby up."

"Aye, sir."

And with that Clement was gone, Yan slipping comfortably into his chair.

✧    ✧    ✧

Clement entered the engine room with three minutes to spare. He shook hands with Nobli and his technicians, who numbered three if you included Middie Tsu. The two senior men then entered Nobli's office, which had a full view of the engine apparatus and the console stations.

"You'll want to watch this monitor, sir," said Nobli, pointing to a display at the back of the room. Clement stepped up and examined it. It showed a diagram of the main LEAP drive components, the antimatter accelerator, the positive proton accelerator, the intermix reactor chamber, and the four drive infusers that would create the wave itself.

"I could monitor this from the bridge," complained Clement. "Plus, I have my back to the reactor."

Nobli shrugged. "Sorry about that, sir. But at least if something goes wrong you'll have the knowledge that you'll be annihilated into subatomic particles before you have any chance to gripe about it." Then he turned to his techs. "Take your stations," he ordered. Clement watched as the three young crew members took their stations. One, a woman, was at the antimatter accelerator, the second at the proton accelerator, and Middie Tsu was at the intermix console facing the reactor.

"Isn't this just an automated process?" asked Clement.

Nobli shook his head. "I've been running this engine for six months, Captain. It can be temperamental. Each part of the process has to be carefully monitored and managed."

"Like what, for instance?"

"Like when we just let the software run the system, the engine start can be rocky. We even blew up one of the probes when they opened the intermix chamber too early. I've isolated those problems and we've now got it down to a fine art."

"Which is?"

Nobli never looked up from his board, nonplussed. "You have to let the protons warm up longer than the antimatter particles, by fractions of a second. If you release them too soon, sometimes things go boom. We give ourselves a safe margin, Captain. Don't you worry."

Clement turned to look at Middie Tsu at the intermix console. "Hassan, Tsu has only been on the ship for a day, and you've got him controlling the intermix chamber."

"I've run him through the process, sir; he's good at following orders." That didn't fill Clement with confidence.

Nobli looked at his watch. "Final reports," he called out with one minute on the clock. They all gave their assent to go. "Stand by for LEAP drive initiation on my mark."

Clement waited as Nobli counted down to ten seconds, then he took a deep breath and looked away from the crew and to his assigned monitor.

"Initiate proton accelerator," said Nobli from behind him. The left side of the monitor turned an icy blue. Seven seconds.

"Initiate antimatter accelerator." This time the right side lit up bright yellow. Five seconds.

The wait seemed like forever. Clement forced his attention to stay stuck to his monitor and let Nobli and his crew do their jobs. The last seconds clicked by . . .

"Now, Tsu! Open the reactor chamber!"

The entire board lit up a vibrant green as the energy filled the main chamber and then tracked outward along the four spines of the infusers, encompassing the drive carousel in an instant.

The carousel started spinning on the monitor.

"Confirm readouts," yelled Nobli as the LEAP drive hummed to life.

"Confirmed!" said the excited female tech from her station. "We have positive confirmation of a contained LEAP wave bubble."

"Are we moving yet?" asked Clement, turning away from his monitor.

"Just a second," said Nobli, holding up his hand. Then he smiled, relieved. "We're moving sir, .16 light and accelerating."

"How long—"

"Until we go superluminal? About two minutes at the recommended acceleration rate, sir," he said, not the least bit intimidated about interrupting his captain.

Now Nobli came to Clement's station. The two men watched in silence as the monitor showed steadily increasing levels of power, and steadily increasing speed. Almost dead on two minutes and the ship seemed to shift ever so slightly.

"That's it, sir, we're superluminal. 1.05 light speed!"

"Well done, Nobli," said Clement, shaking his chief engineer's hand, then repeating, "well done," to the three techs as he went and shook each of their hands. Clement started clapping and the rest of them all joined in. "Congratulations to you all. Well done," he said a third time as the com bell chimed.

Clement brought up the signal on his monitor. "Yes, Yan," he said.

"Captain," she replied. "You should come up here and see this. It's . . . spectacular."

"On my way, Yan," he said, then gave a last wave to the propulsion team and scrambled back across the cargo hold and up the gangway to the bridge.

Yan was right. Looking at the forward visual display was like looking at space through a fishbowl. Stars of all colors swept past them as they cruised by, the tiny dots representing passing stars, pulsars, globular clusters, nebula, and even distant galaxies. They all floated past the external camera and then twisted and distended as the *Beauregard* moved through the quantum fluid of distorted space, riding her wave of bent gravity at an ever increasing pace. Clement had to remember to breathe as he watched the sight go by on the bridge's three-dimensional monitor.

Spectacular indeed.

All one could really do was look at the passing starfield and marvel, but even that got repetitive. Mika Ori, for her part, called it "romantic," with a warm, knowing glance directed at her significant other. In a way he found himself envious of the two of them. They had something he had never had, and likely never would. Their obvious love for one another had never waned in the decade-plus he had known them.

Clement ordered the two of them to cross-train all the middies, just in case, and as a way of getting them to focus on something else besides each other.

Then he left the bridge, letting out a heavy sigh as he slowly navigated the hollow metal steps to his cabin, alone.

# ✲ 8 ✲

Three days later and the ship had settled into a routine. There wasn't much to do, and the crew, quite frankly, was getting bored, so Clement shortened duty shifts and let everyone cross-train in any area of service they were interested in, sort of as a hobby. That worked for a short time, but then Yan suggested he try something else to "spice things up."

"What do you mean by that?" he said, staring at his first officer from the opposite side of his office table.

"By 'spice things up' I mean lessening the rules against fraternization among the crew," she said.

"By fraternization, you mean sex?"

"Sexual intimacy, yes. When people get bored they will bend the rules, just for a break in the monotony. My experience has told me that it will happen anyway on long-duration space voyages, and a month or so is plenty of time for bored souls to get into trouble."

Clement leaned away from her. "I see. I confess to not having dealt with this problem before, so I will likely defer to your experience in the matter."

"Well, before it wasn't a problem because you always had Elara DeVore."

He sat back from the table, and spoke with an edge of anger at her implication. "Not in that way, Commander, not while I was captain. And that will not be happening for me on this mission."

She responded without any emotion or acknowledgement of his anger. "So you say, Captain. Nonetheless, you have my recommendation."

"I do, Commander. You're dismissed," he said curtly. He was beginning to wonder if having Yan on this mission was going to be a blessing or a curse—but, he did have to think of the welfare of his crew.

An hour later Clement issued a memo to the crew indicating he was suspending all rules against fraternization, on the condition that any crew "interactions" lead to "no drama" regarding daily work assignments. He tried with his wording of the memo to limit the "interactions" to those of similar rank to prevent any unease among the crew.

Soon it seemed everyone was enjoying their new freedoms, and taking every opportunity to exercise themselves in the bedroom. The new policy seemed to have the desired effect on the morale of the crew, and there were more than a few smiling faces around the ship. For Clement though, he had to console himself with the occasional drink from Yan's stash of whiskey.

The LEAP drive was humming along as usual, and Clement found himself astonished by the rhythmic ease with which the LEAP system performed, creating an antimatter singularity thousands of times per second, then annihilating it with a proton and capturing enough explosive power to bend the fabric of space. It all seemed so easy. *Probably make scientists from earlier centuries roll over in their graves,* he thought.

But this time his stop-in had another purpose, and he dragged Nobli into the small engineer's office in the Propulsion Center. "I think you know what I'm here to talk about," started Clement. "Have you come up with any ideas about converting some of the power the LEAP drive creates to a defensive weapon of some kind? Maybe a shield?"

Nobli smiled as he looked up at Clement from under his circular wire-rimmed glasses. "Oh, a bit of this and that," he said as he fiddled with his pad display, then handed it to Clement. The display showed fully drawn schematics, installation guides, and equipment specs for what Nobli was calling the "Matter Annihilation Device," or just MAD for short.

"What the hell," said Clement as he swept through the drawings. "Don't you have a hobby? Or at least a girlfriend?"

"No to both," said Nobli. "You give me an idea, I can't stop running with it, can't shut my mind down. It's one of my charms. I didn't sleep for three days until I had this all figured out."

"It's impressive," Clement conceded. "But how practical is it? Is this something we could really build?"

"Build? I've already prototyped it. It will work, that's for certain. But you can't fire it while we're using the LEAP drive reactor for propulsion, and we'd have to have a pretty clear line of sight to any ship to be sure of hitting anything."

"You're joking, right?"

Nobli shook his head. "Not in the least. The biggest problem was sheathing against the energy beam to keep it from annihilating *us* in the process of firing. I coated the old plasma-cannon piping with the same nanotube material as the reactor core is made of. Should be more than enough."

"But how would we aim such a weapon?" asked Clement.

"Line of sight? How did you aim the old plasma cannon?"

Clement thought for a second. "Through the helm station. There was a restrictor nozzle on the cannon port that the helmsman could use to aim. It wasn't very effective."

"And the nozzle will be burned off in the first microsecond if you ever light this thing up," said Nobli.

"So . . . you're telling me I have the most powerful weapon in the known universe but I can't aim it at anything?"

"True, but you did say this was only for emergencies. If that's the case, I recommend you personally take over firing control of the MAD, and you do the aiming yourself. And you'd better make sure you're damn close to your target when you fire on it."

Clement rubbed at his eyes. "What's the estimated range of this thing?" he asked.

Nobli looked at him with a very serious look on his face. "Somewhere between one klick and eternity," he said.

Clement took that as Nobli's usual sarcasm. "What about enemy shielding? Will it penetrate gravity shields?"

Nobli leaned back, a look of astonishment at his boneheaded commander on his face. "Captain, you're annihilating tens of thousands of micro-universes a second. I can't think of a goddamned thing in the universe that could stop that."

"How close?"

"What?"

Clement was frustrated. "How close is too close to fire this thing?"

"A thousand kilometers?"

"C'mon, Nobli, you said I had to get close. How close?"

Nobli looked down at the floor. "The destructive radius is probably close to one hundred klicks, maybe one hundred fifty. It's hard to say without test-firing it. You'll have to use your best judgment. And . . ."

"And what?"

"And . . . there's a chance that this weapon may not detonate in any traditional way, like ordinary or even nuclear ordnance. The beam could . . . just keep going."

Now Clement was confused. "Going? To where?"

Nobli just shrugged. "Anywhere. That's why I recommend you use your own best judgment before firing it."

"And that's what I don't want to do," Clement said, exasperated. "I want you to craft me a mechanism that tracks, aims, *and* fires. How soon until you can hook this thing up?"

Nobli scrambled around the floor of his office for a few seconds and then pulled out what looked like normal plumbing and pipes and held it out to Clement. "I told you I'd already prototyped it."

Clement held it in his hands, it was light to the touch, almost fragile. "You're sure this is—"

"Damn sure, Captain," said Nobli. "That long pipe hooks right into the plasma tube in the floor. The top vents into the reactor." Clement handed it back to his engineer. "But as I said, I suggest we don't try and install it until we arrive in the Trinity system and we're in normal space."

"Understood," said Clement. "Make it your first priority to hook this up when we shut down the reactor. And make me some kind of app control for firing it that I can use from my command console."

Nobli sighed. "Captain, I'm not a programmer," he protested.

"And that's why I want you to build the firing control for me. You'll keep it simple, and that's what I want."

"But, Captain—"

"Did that sound like a request, Engineer?"

Nobli sat on the edge of his swivel chair, staring at his commanding officer over the top of his wire frames. That was as close as he ever got to complaining. "Understood, sir," he said.

"Thanks, Hassan." With that Clement sauntered off to finish his rounds, unsure if his ship was safer or not.

With one more full day before arriving at the Trinity system, Clement and his team had one last round of entertainment planned. Middie Telco had set up a safe shooting range on the cargo deck as instructed by his captain, and there had been a shooting tournament almost every night since they'd gone under the LEAP drive. Clement had won his share, but with only one more day to go everything was on the line.

The rules were simple, fire live rounds into targets, highest score wins. So far about 42 out of 50 had been the average to take a win, but this night felt different. Everyone was pumped up to win the final round.

Many of the crew had already tried their hands at the target; the high score on the board when Clement showed up was a 39 from Telco. Not bad, but not impossible to beat either.

The command crew was the last up, plus Lieutenant Pomeroy, the medic who had been doing some final prep for landfall at Trinity. Clement watched as Captain Wilcock took his rounds, scoring 32 out of 50. Wilcock always seemed to underperform somehow, no matter what the task. Nobli was staying out of the competition so next up was Ivan Massif. The lanky navigator was a good shot, but he was streaky. He hit his first seven shots but then missed three in a row. He ended up with a 37. Mika Ori came next and despite her diminutive figure she was a great shot and hit 43. Yan gave it her best but hand weapons were not her forte and she settled for 37 out of 50. Then it was down to two, himself and Pomeroy.

She was a tough-looking tech, probably Marine-trained from what Clement could tell, brown hair pulled back in a tight ponytail and she had that look of efficiency about her. Clement was sure he wasn't going to catch a break from her tonight. She came to him with a coin in her hand. "Flip you for it. Winner gets last shot." There was an "Ooo" of the challenge from the crowd of ten watching the contest.

"You're on," said Clement.

"Call it in the air." Pomeroy flipped the coin.

"Tails," called Clement. She caught the coin and flipped it over on to the back of her hand, then lifted her palm.

It was heads. The last shooter almost always had an advantage, knowing what score they had to beat. Clement went to the assortment of cobra pistols and tested each one for weight and balance, then loaded a ten clip of kinetic rounds and primed the first shot. He took to the stage inside the firing range. It was all black. The holographic targets would come up at random locations; you had to fire your rounds at the target and then reload four more times and get your shots off, all within sixty seconds.

The first target lit up. Clement raised his pistol and fired with expert precision. All ten shots lit up the target. After the reload he missed one each on the second and third rounds, and two on the fourth. The last round came up and he tracked the target, fully concentrating until he emptied his clip.

46 out of 50.

Pomeroy took that all in stride. She loaded up and entered the chamber before turning back to her captain.

"What does the winner get?" she challenged. Clement thought about that for a moment.

"Loser buys the first round at the first tiki bar we find on Trinity," he said. Everyone laughed at that, and Pomeroy smiled. "Loser buys a full round for the crew at The Battered Hull."

"Done," she said. As she turned back the first target lit up and she started firing. She didn't miss any in the first two clips, one early in the third, then another in the fourth. Clement held his breath. He was nothing if not competitive, and he was, after all, the captain. A miss in the middle of the last clip gave him hope. Then the final bell sounded. Her minute was up.

47.

The crowd cheered as she came up and shook his hand. Clement couldn't help but smile.

"Well done," he said. "I owe you a drink."

"Yes you do, sir, and I'm going to hold you to it!" she said. "At Trinity?"

"At Trinity," he replied. "If we don't find that tiki bar, we'll build one ourselves."

Everyone was at their stations and prepped with twenty minutes to go to shut down of the LEAP drive. The bridge was quiet and everyone was ready, if not a bit tense. Clement ran through his command displays, noting the new icon for using the LEAP reactor as a weapon that Nobli had uploaded, then decided he wanted verbal reports from his people.

"Ivan, time for shut down of the LEAP drive?" he asked.

"Eighteen minutes now, sir," reported Massif.

"And what will happen when we exit quantum-fluid space?"

Massif turned to his captain. "The bubble will slowly dissipate. Of course, we'll lose speed rapidly when we hit normal space again, cruise for about an hour at near-superluminal speeds. Then the inertial dampeners will slowly take away our momentum during that time until we reach a manageable cruising speed. In fact, we've already been slowly decelerating for the last forty-eight hours; current speed is 1.12 light."

"And what if I want to slow us faster than that, to optimize our drift toward a planet, or maybe change direction toward an interesting object?"

Massif nodded to Mika Ori. She turned from her station then.

"We can use the thrust reversers," she said. "Of course, that will put g-force pressure on us, but nothing we shouldn't be able to handle. If there is an 'interesting object' in our path, we can use a variety of slingshot maneuvers to get where we're going, but the charts the unmanned probes made show nothing of significant mass in the area where we'll be dropping out of quantum space."

"And where is that, exactly?"

"There's nothing exact in all this, Captain, but the best guess is about 10.25 AU out from the primary star. That's approximately where the probes have come in."

Mika was always focused when on duty, and that's something Clement liked about her.

"Then what's the best guess time-wise to the first planet in the system?"

"About eight hours, sir. Our speed coming out of the fluid will be about .925 light, and it's hard to maneuver at that speed, but depending on how good the navigator is . . . " She trailed off, smirking at her husband.

"What will a 1.5 g break buy me?"

Ori did a quick calculation on her pad. "We can cut that to about four hours, sir, give or take a quarter hour depending on our exact position, if we properly reorient the ship toward a particular destination," she said, directing the barb at her husband again. Ivan smiled this time but said nothing.

"And the length of the burn?"

"Twenty-two minutes by my calculations, sir," she said, without looking back to her pad. She had already figured it out in her head.

"Thank you, Mika. Let's plan for that."

"Aye, sir."

"Middie Adebayor," he said to his systems officer, "once we drop in on the Trinity system proper I want you to start a full-scan protocol on the planets, starting with Alphus, Bellus, and Camus," he ordered.

"Are you expecting communications, Captain?" asked Adebayor.

"No, but it is standard procedure for any ship entering a potential battlefield."

"Are you expecting a battle, sir?" asked Adebayor, again.

Yan cut in here. "You won't last long on this bridge if you question all of your captain's orders, Middie. That's my job. Yours is to do what your captain requests."

"Yes, ma'am," replied Adebayor. "But if I need clarification—"

"You don't in this case, Middie," said Yan, stepping out from behind her station. "Now I suggest you stick to your board and follow your orders."

"Yes, ma'am," said Adebayor again, and glued her eyes to her board, appropriately chastened. Yan came and stood beside Clement, who then called down to the propulsion room.

"Nobli here," came the reply. Clement looked up to the timer on the main screen display.

"Shut down the LEAP drive fourteen minutes from my mark, Mr. Nobli . . ." He looked down at his personal watch instead of the ship's clock, "Mark," Clement said.

"Aye, sir," acknowledged Nobli.

Clement shut off the com to propulsion and switched to Middie Telco in the weapons bay. Telco acknowledged.

"Store everything for the transition, Middie. We'll be running at 1.5 *g* deceleration for about four hours. After that, I want those missiles back up and ready, understood?"

"Completely sir. We'll be fully operational well before then, sir. 1.5 *g* isn't that much of a load."

"Spoken like a young man," replied Clement. "I'll hold you to that. And inform Captain Wilcock that he's to release the atomic warheads to you upon your request. I want us locked and loaded the whole way in, Middie."

"Aye, sir."

Clement turned to his first officer. "Commander Yan, call all hands to stations, prep for deceleration to exit LEAP space."

"Aye, sir," she replied, then she got on the ship-wide com and ordered everyone to take their deceleration stations.

The next few minutes rushed by as systems reports continued to come in. When the time mark finally came, Clement called down and gave Nobli the order to cut the LEAP drive at his discretion. The forward viewer showed the bending of space steadily decreasing until the flow of stars clarified and resumed a more normal appearance, or rather, as Clement thought, a much more mundane one. Nobli called up just as they all felt the tug of the g-force deceleration, in toward planet T-7, the outermost world in the Trinity system with a high-content methane-based atmosphere.

"Point nine two five light speed as predicted, sir," said Mika. "We're decelerating toward planet T-7, estimated time of arrival at target four hours, thirteen minutes, sir."

"Excellent work, everyone. What's our path inward from there?"

Ivan Massif had that calculation. "Based on our current trajectory and the alignment of the planets we can use T-7 to cut our speed through aero-breaking, then swing in toward T-5, or Camus as they call it, break again, and that should put us at the fourth planet, Bellus, in about sixteen hours' time, sir. Our speed will be sufficiently low to be captured gravitationally by the planet, if the probe's reports on her mass is correct."

"Best get to reviewing all the reports from the probes and verifying the data against real measurables. I wouldn't want to skip past one of the new worlds and end up having to claw ourselves back using thrusters," said Clement.

"Aye, sir."

"Plot and execute," ordered Clement. Then he looked around his bridge, proud of his crew and excited for what the next part of the journey would entail.

# ✷ 9 ✷

Two hours into the *Beauregard*'s deceleration toward T-7, the first sign of trouble appeared when Middie Adebayor called Yan over to her station.

"Something wrong, Middie?" asked Yan.

"I'm not sure yet," said Adebayor. "I've been scanning for radio signals as the captain ordered, and so far I've just picked up the normal background signals from each of the bodies in the system. But I'm also picking up an anomalous signal that's *not* from the planets or the star, and it appears to be *behind* us, ma'am."

"You mean farther out?"

"Yes, ma'am. About six hundred AU, ma'am."

"That's quite a ways out, especially for a system as compact as this one. Is it moving?"

Adebayor looked at her instruments. "Yes, in our same general direction at about .15 light, ma'am, closely matching our own speed."

Yan thought for a moment about what to do next. "I'm going to take this up with the captain," she finally said and started to walk away.

"Do you want me to deploy the radio telescope array?" Adebayor asked as Yan moved off.

"Not yet," replied the second-in-command without turning around. "We'd just have to roll it back in for the aero-braking maneuver anyway."

Yan made her way down the five honeycombed metal steps to the command crew cabins and knocked on Clement's door. He responded with a positive chime and Yan made her way into his cabin.

"Business or pleasure?" said Clement, not looking up from his many technical systems pads.

"Business," replied Yan, taking his barb in stride. "Middie Adebayor has detected a radio-emitting signal about six hundred AU behind us."

This got Clement's attention. "Behind us? Is it moving?"

Yan nodded. "At about .15 light."

"That's pretty fast for a comet, and we can certainly rule out a planetoid or a spherical body with an atmosphere."

"I agree, sir."

Clement ran some calculations on one of his pads. "That puts the object about two weeks behind us, if it's making the same vector as we are," he said.

"Closer to thirteen days," Yan replied. Clement gave her an annoyed look. Yan sighed. "Sorry, I was brought up by a mathematician. The object's vector is roughly the same as ours."

Clement stood. "Do you think it's following us?"

Yan shook her head. "I could be wrong, but they would have had to know our arrival point and time in advance, and I doubt that's common knowledge, if it's a vessel," she said.

"Size?"

"Unable to tell at this distance. Middie Adebayor wants to pull out the radio array and get a better look at it."

Clement leaned on the edge of his desk. "It could be a natural object of some kind."

"Or it could be a ship."

"Noted, Commander. My advice is that we maintain our course and speed, continue through our aero-breaking maneuvers, then deploy the array once we've established orbit over . . . what's the planet's name?"

"Bellus. Alphus, Bellus, Camus. A, B, C," she said.

Clement gave her a glare of annoyance. "We'll deploy the radio telescope array once we arrive at Bellus. We'll continue our planned survey from orbit while Middie Adebayor gets us some pictures. Further action will be determined at that time," he said. "Comments?"

Yan went to attention. "Your advice seems sound, Captain."

"Thank you, Commander." Clement looked at his watch. "The way I make it, officer's dinner is at 1700. Aero-breaking at T-7 is at 1930 hours."

"I'll have the ship ready, Captain," said Yan. Then she turned and left the cabin without looking back.

Clement picked up one of his pads and switched the display to monitor Adebayor's station. The radio signal showed up as an amber blip on a red background. He put the pad back down, and started to worry.

Clement was on the bridge deck at 1900, a full thirty minutes ahead of the braking maneuver.

Yan hadn't rejoined the bridge crew yet, but Ivan Massif and Mika Ori were both at their stations, and Middie Adebayor was handling the engineering console. Hassan Nobli was in the propulsion room and had refused to move away from his equipment. Captain Wilcock was at Yan's station but wasn't talking much, which suited Clement.

As he waited for Yan he patiently ran through ship's systems checks, checking off each one as he went. A shadow came over him then and surprisingly when he looked up, it wasn't Yan but Adebayor who stood over his station, blocking the light from the other consoles.

"Can I help you, Middie?" Clement said.

She cleared her throat before speaking. "Pardon for interrupting, sir," she started.

"Don't apologize for doing your duty, Middie. I assume this is something important?"

"Yes, sir. I believe so, sir." She hesitated as he looked at her expectantly. "Could you come to my station, sir?" Clement nodded and exited his command couch to take the few steps to port to the engineering console. Adebayor showed him her screen. "I've been tracking the anomaly, sir, and it's hard to track without the radio array, but it seems to me that the anomaly has changed course."

"Changed course?" said Clement, obviously disturbed by the news.

"Yes, sir. It appears to be on a vector now for the inner habitable world, Alphus, sir."

Clement looked at her projected course for the object. It was indeed on a course for Alphus.

"When did this course change happen?" demanded Clement.

"I first detected it about twenty minutes ago, sir."

"Twenty minutes? Why didn't you notify me immediately?"

She cleared her throat again. "You were unavailable in your cabin, sir. And I needed that time to verify that my observations were correct, sir," she said.

"Wait here," he said, then went back to his console and called Yan to the bridge. She arrived a few seconds later, swapping positions with Wilcock, who left the bridge.

"What's up?" she asked.

Clement led her to the engineering console and had Adebayor repeat her report to Yan.

"We have another ship then, and under intelligent control," Yan said.

"It seems so," replied Clement. He hesitated only a second before calling the entire command crew to the officer's galley.

Once inside the galley the command crew, all those on the bridge except Adebayor, were joined by Nobli and Wilcock. Clement cleared his throat before beginning. His explanation was to the point; there was another ship in the Trinity system.

"The question, gentlemen, is what we do about it. The thing is on a course for the inner planet, Alphus, while we are on a course for T-7 to pull off an aero-braking maneuver that will put us in orbit around Bellus. It seems to me that we have an obligation to investigate this object. Is it human? Is it one of ours—or perhaps it's even from Earth? Opinions," he said.

Ivan Massif spoke first. "It could be alien. And that would change everything." The fact was that in more than three hundred fifty years of sub-light interstellar space travel and colonization, no evidence of an alien civilization had ever been discovered, until possibly now. There were protocols for such things, but quite frankly Clement hadn't taken the time to review them, or even consider First Contact as a possibility. He realized now that he probably should have. This was, after all, the first superluminal human space mission in history.

"This is not an equipped First Contact mission," said Yan. "Our job is to survey the three habitable planets in this system and assess them for immediate habitation."

Nobli shrugged that off. "Equipped or not for First Contact, we are here, and so are they. I think we need to know who or what we're dealing with," he said.

Next Mika Ori piped up. "To proceed on to our target while they stay in orbit around Alphus would seem a waste. We should find out who and what they are, and find out now."

Clement turned to Wilcock for his opinion. "Captain?"

"I think we should complete our mission as scheduled, and report back to our superiors as ordered," he said in his whiny voice. It made Clement cringe involuntarily. It was also the exact answer Clement expected from a staff officer.

"In the three-plus centuries that humankind has been sending out ships into interstellar space, the 5 Suns are the only colonies that we know of that have ever been established. We don't know of any others, and we haven't had contact from Earth in almost three centuries. The possibility that this could be an alien probe is something we can't ignore. Further, the possibility that it could be an Earth-colony ship is also worth exploring." He looked around the table, and there was no dissent.

"Middie Adebayor wants to deploy the radio telescope to get a better look," said Clement.

"You can't do that while we're aero-braking, which by the way is only ten minutes away now," said Nobli.

"I'm aware of that. My thinking is that we need to find out what this thing is, as soon as possible?" Clement turned to Mika. "Can we adjust our aero-breaking around Trinity-7 and use the effect to slingshot ourselves on to an intercept course with the anomaly?"

She slowly nodded her head. "We can, but you're asking me to calculate some pretty fine maneuvering in just a few minutes."

"Then you better get to it," said Clement, nodding toward the bridge. She left quickly.

"I'd better go plot that course," said Ivan, and followed her. Clement acknowledged silently with another nod, then turned to the rest of the crew.

"Stations for aero-braking, everyone. We're going to find out what this thing is, and what we might need to do about it," he said.

"So that's your final decision?" said Wilcock in a demanding tone.

Clement stood up, much taller than the diminutive captain. "It is, Captain Wilcock. Now since you're not needed on the bridge, I suggest you ride out the aero-braking in your cabin," he said, then walked away.

Yan gave Wilcock an annoyed look, then followed her commanding officer to the bridge.

"All stations report clear for aero-braking maneuver, sir," called Yan from her station.

Clement acknowledged and then looked down to his command board. All was green. His bridge crew was strapped in and ready.

"It's your call, Mika," he said out loud.

"Aye, sir, acknowledge I have the wheel. Aero-braking will commence in thirty seconds and should last about seven minutes in duration, pulling 5.5 gravities. Once clear of Trinity-7's atmosphere we will engage in a two-minute, thirty-second Ion plasma burst at three *g*s, which should allow us to intercept the unknown well before it reaches the inner planetary ring, if the navigator's course vectors are correct," she said, needling her lover's ego.

"They are," snapped back Massif. Clement gave a quick chuckle at that.

"My ship is yours, Pilot," he said to Ori.

On the mark Ori went on the ship-wide com and called out the beginning of the aero-braking cycle. It was rougher than Clement remembered from his old days in the Rim Confederation Navy, but as Ori had reminded them over the com, T-7 had a "bumpy" upper atmosphere. After seven full minutes of grinding and rattling the *Beauregard* was once again in open space and free floated for a few precious seconds, the crew weightless with the artificial gravity turned off. It was thirty seconds of bliss until Ori hit the thrusters, pushing the ship again on its new vector toward the unknown bogey.

After the two and a half minutes of thruster burn at three *g*s was up, Ori pronounced them on course for intercept of the mystery object. Clement ordered the artificial one *g* restored and everyone gave a sigh of relief as they were released from their acceleration couches.

Clement quickly ordered Adebayor to deploy the radio telescope array. "How long until we can get a good picture?" he asked of the middie.

"Ninety minutes for deployment and calibration, sir," she said.

"Then get to it." At that he ordered Yan back to his cabin for a conference.

"What do you think this thing is?" he asked her, almost before the door to his cabin had shut.

"It's hard to say, but my best guess is that it's an Ark ship," said Yan.

"Which means someone has previously surveyed this system and is so confident of its habitability that they sent a ship out a long time ago."

"Fifty years, at least. If it's a colony mission, yes, sir."

"But DeVore said this system was only explored a few months ago when they developed the LEAP drive. Whoever sent *that* ship, if it's in fact a colony vessel, sent it out decades ago. If it was the 5 Suns Alliance, they would have had to send it out a very long time ago, given the limits of faster-than-light travel. It's possible they could have observed this star system through some other means, and sent a covert colony ship back then."

"If that's the case then I would be curious as to the timing of our mission. The chances of us both arriving in-system at the same time by chance seems small," replied Yan.

"Agreed. It's quite possible that DeVore knew we'd find this ship when we arrived. It may even be the real reason for our mission," said Clement.

Yan nodded. "I have to admit with what I know of the Fleet Admiral that is at least a possibility. She's well known around the Alliance Navy for keeping information close at hand and she's got a reputation for springing surprises, especially ones that are to her advantage."

This time it was Clement's turn to nod agreement. "The question is why would she keep it from us? Even from her hand-chosen executive officer? I can see why she'd want me in command of this mission, *if* she believes this is a possibly hostile vessel."

Yan shook her head. "I don't follow you."

Clement crossed his arms, thinking out loud. "I'm disposable, Yan, and so is my crew. We're all rebels with no real value to the 5SA. This prototype is an old, reclaimed Rim Confederation gunship. Almost everything on this mission is expendable."

"Including me," said Yan. That realization hit her hard. "What about Captain Wilcock?"

"He could be working for her. We have to take precautions for that eventuality."

Now it was Yan's turn to be pensive. She paced back and forth in the cabin a couple of times, thinking. Finally, she said, "What's the point of all this, Clement? I mean, why lie to us?"

He shrugged. "To get us all on board for the mission. If we knew how potentially dangerous it was, would any of us have signed on? I don't think so. No, I think Fleet Admiral DeVore knew what this mission was really all about. She made up a romantic story about a prototype mission to test a revolutionary new technology and we all bought it. Our real mission was always to encounter and confront this Ark ship, which means it must have come from somewhere else."

"Earth?"

"That's most likely. The problem is we have no idea what Earth is like now, or rather, what it was like when this ship was launched. I suspect that the Admiral has her ideas about this Ark, and they're not good. If I can trust of what I know about Elara DeVore at all, I know her habits and work patterns, and I know she always has a backup plan. I highly doubt we are the only ship in the 5 Suns Navy that has the LEAP drive. And I'd bet my last whiskey that they're on their way here, right now. We're the bait, Yan. DeVore will find out all she needs to know about this colony ship from what happens to us."

"That's not the Fleet Admiral I thought I knew."

"And that's not the Elara DeVore that I know, or knew. She played me perfectly."

Both of them stood silently for a moment.

"What if this is, in fact, First Contact?" said Yan.

"I think it's unlikely this is an alien vessel. But then the question becomes, how did the Earthmen discover the Trinity system?"

Yan shrugged. "The same way we did, I suppose. Long-term probes, perhaps launched decades in the past. This system is a lot closer to Earth than the 5 Suns Alliance is."

"Or they have LEAP technology, or something similar."

"I'd bet dollars to doughnuts that ship is sub-light powered. We'd pick up some kind of radiant energy signature if it had FTL capabilities, I'm guessing," said Yan.

Clement nodded agreement. "That's a good guess, I think. But, what if it is aliens?"

Yan eyed him. "Then you were right to bring atomic weapons on board."

Clement shuffled uncomfortably in his seat again, then reached for his desk com.

"Captain Wilcock to my cabin, please," he said into the com, then cut it off before Wilcock could answer. The less interaction he had with the man the better he felt about things. Presently Wilcock buzzed at his door and Clement let him in. "Take a seat," said Clement. Wilcock sat down with the two mission commanders.

"Captain Wilcock," started in Clement, "as I'm sure you know I'm aware that you and Commander Yan have access to the keys and codes for the atomic warheads. I'd like you to load those warheads onto our missiles, please."

Wilcock frowned. "And as you know, Captain Clement, I need a command authorization or an imminent threat to do so. Since my commander is Fleet Admiral DeVore and she's weeks from here even at superluminal speeds, and as there is no imminent threat to the *Beauregard*, I must decline your . . . suggestion," said Wilcock.

Clement nodded but continued. "I understand your stance, Captain. But I do believe the *Beauregard* is under imminent threat. That unknown could be an alien ship, and we could be facing a showdown over the Trinity worlds. I'd much rather go into any contact scenario with my defenses fully prepared. For all we know that ship might attack us the minute we're in their range."

Wilcock shifted in his chair and looked toward Yan. She remained impassive.

"I'm not sure that this situation would require that level of preparedness—"

"Captain Wilcock, have you ever commanded a ship in battle?" interrupted Clement.

"No sir, but—"

"Then trust me on this. Every moment, every second, is crucial in a battle situation. If this *is* a hostile ship, and if it is aliens, they could have weapons so superior to ours that we might only last seconds against them. We need to be as prepared as we can be. Do you understand, Captain?"

Wilcock looked to Yan again, then swallowed hard. "Sir, I mean no disrespect, but—"

"I agree with the Captain," said Yan suddenly. Wilcock looked over at her, then back to the determined Clement. Seeing as he was now outvoted, Wilcock caved.

"Very well, sir. But I will be filing a protest over this in my log."

"That's your choice."

"It will take some time to prepare—"

"Middie Adebayor should be able to give us a look at this thing in an hour and a quarter. I expect you and Yan to have those warheads loaded by that time," said Clement.

"Aye, sir," said Wilcock, reluctantly.

Clement turned to Yan, who was already pulling out her activation key from around her neck.

"We'll report back within the hour," she said.

"Good," replied Clement, then watched them both leave his cabin, headed for the missile room.

Yan watched as Captain Wilcock opened the locker containing the atomic warheads by entering the release code. The doors to the locker opened automatically and he carefully pulled the first warhead, a stainless steel cylinder about thirty centimeters in length with three electronic leads and a small digital display panel, out of the locker and handed it to Middie Telco, who was in charge of loading it into the first missile. Telco did so with care, making sure the power leads to the device were secure. He checked again, as he had when they were first brought aboard, that the warhead had sufficient uranium density for use as a weapon. For the second time, Telco got an affirmative reply on his radiometry scanner. He nodded to Yan and Wilcock, and they began the process of arming the warhead by loading in their key codes from their random-number generators. Once both codes were locked into the arming panels, each of them in turn inserted their physical keys into the consoles and turned them to arm the warheads.

"First warhead armed," said Yan.

"First warhead armed," confirmed Wilcock. He then nodded to Telco, who activated the loader, and a second missile, sans warhead, slid into the loading catapult, pushing the first missile into firing position.

"Arming second warhead," said Wilcock.

When they had repeated the process six times and the missiles with the atomic warheads were loaded and locked down, Yan called to Clement to confirm.

"Get back up here stat," said Clement. "Middie Adebayor says she thinks she can get a signal in a few minutes."

"Aye, sir," said Yan, who then turned to Telco. "Keep this room locked down under guard, Middie. No one in or out of here unless it's your relief."

"Aye, sir," said Telco. Then Yan nodded and headed for the bridge. Wilcock, for his part, was already gone.

They all squeezed into the cramped bridge, even Nobli and Captain Wilcock, to see the first images Adebayor was getting from the radio telescope array. Clement tried to be patient, his ship on a general intercept course with the unknown, but clearly artificial, object.

"I've got the first image Captain," said Adebayor. Clement merely nodded for her to put it up on the main screen display. A black background started to paint with a blotchy image of red, yellow, and green. What it showed was clear, a cylindrical-shaped object.

"I'd say artificiality is confirmed," said Yan.

"I agree," replied Clement.

"First Contact with an alien race?" said Yan.

Clement contemplated that possibility. "If it is, then we have to assume they have at least an equal technology to our own, if not likely superior."

"But from what we can tell, they don't have LEAP technology, or something similar."

"Then we need more answers. XO, please note the date and time of our first sighting of this vessel in the log. We could be living in a historic moment, and what we do next could affect more than one civilization. And please record all further interactions with this vessel. Perhaps it will be valuable to historians, some day."

"Aye, sir," said Yan, returning to her console to activate the log recorder.

Clement turned to the middie. "What telemetry can you give me on the object?"

"Coming in now, sir," said Adebayor. "Length, precisely six

kilometers. Circumference, .05 kilometers. Speed continues to deplete to .012 light. Engine appears to be an electromagnetic particle drive geared for constant acceleration and deceleration. Vector unchanged toward the inner habitable planet, Alphus, sir."

"Are those hull measurements approximate?" asked Clement.

"Negative, sir," replied the middie. "Those measures are as exact as we can make them."

"Then it's one of ours. Human," stated Clement.

"How can you be sure?" questioned Yan, returning from her console.

"Six kilometers long by a .05 klick circumference? I'd bet my last dime on it. Kilometers are how humans measure things, Yan. And an Ion particle EM drive is exactly the kind of technology that was used to send ships out to the 5 Suns Alliance stars, four centuries ago."

"How do you know that?" He smiled at her.

"High school history, Commander," he said with a shrug. "The *Mayflower* was a one-hundred-foot English merchant sailing ship with three masts."

"What's a *Mayflower*?" said Yan, looking confused.

Clement smiled. "Later," he said, then turned to his navigator. "Mika, at our speed and theirs, can we intercept them?"

Lieutenant Ori looked at her display console. "Aye, sir, in about nine hours we should be able to match course and speed without too much trouble. Their deceleration is constant now."

"Then let's do it." Clement turned to Hassan Nobli. "Prep the shuttle, Nobli. We're going to be heading over there."

"Do you think that's wise?" replied the engineer.

Clement shook his head. "Wise? No. Necessary? Yes," said Clement, then he got up and headed for his cabin, the crew scrambling to their stations in his wake.

# ✳10✳

The unknown was close enough now for standard visual observation. It was a simple cylinder, but immensely long at six kilometers. If there were human colonists on board, there were a lot of them. The fact that it was constructed using a human measuring standard, however, almost certainly indicated a human origin. That was some small comfort, at least. The question at hand, though, was who had built it, and for what intent.

The Ark ship (as Clement was now convinced that it was, whether he was willing to share that with the crew or not) had a general silver-gray color with black caps at either end, with no discernable exterior features to distinguish it. It looked more like a great torpedo or missile than a colonization ship. Ark ships usually ran with large solar panels to power the interior environment for the passengers. Usually. It was possible this particular ship carried its crew in a deep sleep, however, powered by a nuclear fusion reactor, thus not requiring the typical level of active environmental systems.

"We'll be able to match her course and speed exactly, sir, if you give me another few minutes," said Mika Ori at the helm.

"Do it," replied Clement, then looked around the room before hitting the ship-wide com. "Attention, crew of the *Beauregard*," he said. "In a few minutes, we'll be in intercept position of the unknown. At that time, I will be taking over an expeditionary team in our only shuttle, leaving Commander Yan at the con. For this mission I will be needing a team of specialists to do an evaluation of whatever that ship is and what's on it. Therefore, I have selected the following crew to join me: Middie Daniel, Captain Wilcock, Middie Telco, and Medical Technician Pomeroy. Engineer Nobli will stay aboard with Commander Yan on the *Beauregard* to monitor our progress via visual com link. The rest of you are to be at your stations on high alert. We have to be ready to exit this area at high speed if necessary. So man your stations, do your jobs. I trust you. Clement out," he said as he shut down the com. Yan approached him then.

"Is it wise to go yourself?" she said.

"Always," replied Clement. "I never pass off what should be my responsibility. And I know you think you should lead the mission, but I want you here in case there's trouble."

She looked chagrined. "But why take Wilcock, and the two middies?"

Clement smiled. "Can you think of anyone on this ship more expendable than Wilcock? And Daniel hasn't had much to do. Telco and Pomeroy I trust with a cobra rifle. So that's that," he said.

Yan nodded, but she wasn't happy. "Understood, sir."

Twenty minutes later, after confirmation from Mika Ori of their match to the unknown for course and speed, Clement was in the prep room with his team pulling on an EVA suit. Middie Telco came through, already suited but without his helmet on yet, and delivered weapons to each of the shuttle crew—standard cobra pistols for the suit side holsters and the key to one of the cobra rifles, preloaded—that were already on the shuttle. Clement watched with disdain as Wilcock attempted to holster his pistol. After the third try Wilcock's finger accidently set off the safety and Clement rushed over and grabbed him hard by the wrist to stop him from burning off his leg.

"Didn't you get any goddamn basic training?" said Clement as he pulled the pistol from Wilcock's hand, reset the safety, and then put it in the holster himself.

"I did, sir," Wilcock protested. "I know how to use a weapon."

Clement just stared at him, then donned his helmet and sealed up his EVA suit.

"Everybody on board. When we get over there I want everyone to use their rifle as the main weapon of defense with the pistol as a secondary," he said.

"Are we expecting trouble, sir?" said the annoying Wilcock.

"Not necessarily, Captain, but we always prepare for it. Now all aboard."

With that the techs that had helped them prep vacated the cargo hold and the shuttle was positioned for launch. Once the room was cleared and the environment evacuated, Clement took to the pilot's seat with Pomeroy, who had a shuttle pilot's accreditation, next to him. The others gathered in the back and strapped in. Clement signaled up to Yan for launch clearance, which was given. The cargo bay doors opened and Clement fired up the engine, hitting the gas hard as everyone slid back into their passenger seats. He leaned over to Pomeroy and joked, "Just making sure they're awake back there." She smiled.

The crossing was uneventful and Clement swung the shuttle into a close track to the unknown, heading down her length slowly. Clement tested his com link.

"Nobli, Yan, what do you make of that hull?" he asked. There was a pause, then Nobli came on the line.

"I'd say you're looking at reinforced regolith with a shiny coat of sealant on it, sir. The old Ark ships were designed this way, to keep things like meteors and other objects from destroying the ship in flight."

"What's regolith?" asked Pomeroy.

"It's solar system material from moons and asteroids, rocks and dirt, some metals. In advanced Ark design, they used a thick layer of it over an internal hull to protect the ships as they moved through the interstellar void. Common practice back in the Exodus days. Not surprised to see it here," said Nobli. At that Clement switched to the shuttle's com line to his crew.

"We're looking for anything that resembles a docking bay or external air lock," said Clement over the com. "Don't be afraid to go to the portside windows and have a look out." It was Middie Daniel who called in what looked to be an external air lock one third of the way down the length of the cylinder.

"Good eyes, Daniel," said Clement over the com.

"Thank you, sir," replied the middie, happy to be contributing.

"It sure doesn't look like a match for our docking mechanism," observed Pomeroy. Clement eyed the hatch. It was round. The shuttle's was rectangular, like the shape of a doorway, big enough for a human to pass through. Hopefully, the round shape of the Ark's door wasn't an indication of the crew's shape. That could indicate a nonhuman design.

"What do we do?" asked Pomeroy. Clement thought about that

as he pulled the shuttle in close, matching course and speed with the unknown and the hatch.

"Middie Telco," Clement called over the com.

"Aye, sir," replied the eager young man.

"Vent the air lock to vacuum and prepare a tether, and four C-7 charges. We'll need to blow that hatch."

"Yes, sir!"

"And you'll be the one to set the charges," said Clement as he came down from the pilot's nest to the shuttle cabin.

"Aye, sir," Telco said, trying to stay calm, and quickly went about his business. Daniel helped him get tethered up and Wilcock handed him the four charges. Clement wanted someone else to handle the explosives, anyone, but he just bit his lip as Wilcock managed to get the job done correctly without destroying the shuttle.

"Could blowing the hatch be seen as an attack by us on them?" came Yan's voice over the com. Clement paused for a moment before responding.

"That is a consideration, Commander. But . . . looking down the full length of this ship I don't see any other such opening, so unless you're suggesting we knock on the door . . . "

"Understood, Captain," replied Yan, then cleared the channel.

A few seconds later and Telco entered the air lock, shutting the door behind him as he vented the chamber to space. Clement and the others watched as he used maneuvering jet bursts to cross the threshold of open space to the unknown's hatch, trailing the tether all the way. Telco set the charges expertly at twelve, three, six, and nine o'clock, then quickly jetted back to the shuttle. Once he was back inside and the air lock was sealed, Clement turned to Lieutenant Pomeroy.

"Take the controls and give us some distance, at least five hundred meters," he said. Pomeroy did as instructed. Then Clement turned to Telco. "Um, Telco, I almost forgot, did it look like there was any way in?"

"You know I was so busy setting the charges . . . "

"So, nobody looked for an air lock control?" asked Wilcock.

"Well, I guess our arrival will be a surprise, then," quipped Clement.

"Six hundred fifty meters, sir," called Pomeroy from her station. Clement acknowledged.

"Everyone lock down their EVA suits." There was a round of affirmatives.

"Vent the cabin pressure please, Pomeroy," ordered the Captain. They waited as the small shuttle quickly drained of environment. Then Clement turned to Telco.

"You have the controls, Middie," said Clement, giving the excited young man a chance to shine by handing him a remote detonator. "Detonate when ready."

Telco calmly counted down from five, then lit up the explosives. After a flurry of cloudy gas escaping from the unknown, the area quickly cleared to reveal a fairly round gash in its side. Pomeroy maneuvered the shuttle in close again, then they loaded up their cobra rifles and proceeded over in an orderly manner, Telco taking the lead and acting as an anchor while the others made the tethered crossing.

They were in what appeared to be a long, twisting drain shaft of some kind which required them to crouch as they went. Telco took the lead, cobra rifle in hand, followed by Pomeroy, Clement, Daniel, and Wilcock, the least valuable member of the crew as Clement saw it, taking up the rear.

"What do you make of this shaft, Pomeroy?" asked Clement of the medic.

"Well, I'm no expert, but this appears to be a passageway designed to expel a specific cargo, something that fits the spherical shape of this tube. There are rails to speed up the process."

"Any guesses on what that cargo might be?"

"Not at the moment, sir."

They proceeded about thirty meters more until the passageway turned and came out at what appeared to be a maintenance room. The room had a doorway, with a locking mechanism. The door itself looked human-sized, if that meant anything. Clement fired up the com back to Nobli and Yan aboard the *Beauregard*.

"Hassan, can you see this?" said Clement. "We're in some kind of maintenance room. There's no gravity but there is a door lock."

"Can I see the door mechanism?" asked Nobli through the now scratchy com line. Clement moved up to the door and put his body camera close to a lit panel. There were red, amber, and green buttons on the left of the panel and a series of characters on the right, none of which Clement could read. The red light was lit.

"What do you make of it?" said Clement.

"Well, some of the characters look like Chinese," said Nobli. "But I can't read them."

"It's not Chinese," said Yan through the com. "It's Imperial Korean."

"And how do you know *that*?" asked Clement.

"I studied the history of the old Korean Empire on Earth, mid-twenty-first century. They took over almost everything in the Asia-Pacific region at that time. That looks like a more advanced form than I studied, probably mixed in with some traditional Chinese characters," said Yan.

"Can you read it?" asked Clement.

"I'll try . . ." They all waited impatiently as Yan stayed silent for at least thirty seconds. Finally, she said: "I think the red light is a warning indicator that the room is in vacuum. It's telling you . . . it's telling you that if you open the door decompression could occur. There's also another indicator . . . Do you see that blue bar just below the main console?"

"On the side here?"

"Yes, that's it. Press that bar."

Clement ordered everyone to get close to him before he pressed it, then hit the button on Yan's advice. A large bulkhead-type door slid down fast behind them, cutting off their exit through the tube as the room started normalizing atmosphere. The colors on the door panel lit up from red to amber to green.

"Pomeroy?"

"Atmosphere is breathable, sir. Outside temp is just over 14 C, sir. Not tropical but breathable," she said.

"Everyone keep their helmets on. We're not through this yet," warned Clement to his party. "Yan, in your opinion is it safe to go through this door?"

"Safe? That's relative, sir. You're there. You came for a reason, and that reason is to discover what's beyond that door, correct?"

"Correct. Um, how do you suggest we proceed?"

Yan laughed. "You might try pressing the green button," she said. Clement looked to Pomeroy, who nodded, then pressed the button.

The door opened to a dark and misty chamber, almost like a fog, and dimly lit. It was packed floor to ceiling with round capsules that were roughly man-sized, hanging from the ceiling. The capsules went on in multiple rows in both directions from where they stood, disappearing into the fog in the distance.

"So, this is eerie," cracked Pomeroy. Clement ignored her.

"Boots," said Clement, ordering everyone to activate their magnetic boots. There were bits of paper floating around the room, indicating a low- or zero-g environment. The team started slowly walking, Clement ordering them in farther. As they passed the individual capsules there were no windows discernible, no way to look in, and nothing moved on them except the occasional blinking monitor light.

"Opinions?" he asked as they looked around the room, taking their first exploratory steps.

"It's something you might expect on an Ark ship with the crew in a deep freeze. There must be hundreds of these things," said Pomeroy. "Maybe more."

"Colonists, then?"

"Perhaps," came Nobli's voice over the com. "How big is that room?"

"Big enough we can't see the walls," said Clement. "Let's reconnoiter. Pomeroy with me. The rest of you take the far side of the room," he said, pointing to his right from the door. "And look for a way out of this room." There was a round of quiet "Aye, sir's" to that.

As they proceeded there were more and more rows of the capsules, and Clement was not prepared to crack one open and find out what was inside. He called to Telco with the other group. "Status?" he asked.

"No change, sir. Just lots and lots of these capsules. I'd say there are definitely people inside, human or otherwise, in stasis, sir," replied Telco.

"Agreed, Telco. Now if we just knew *who* they were." Clement checked his arm monitor. He set it for a counting procedure, and scanned up and down the rows with an amber light pulse. After a few seconds it came back with an estimate. "Monitor guesses there are more than four thousand of these capsules in here," he said.

"Brigade strength," piped in Daniel. That was smart.

"I wish you hadn't said that, Middie," said Clement. "All right, everyone proceed forward until we locate the far wall. Let's find a way out of here." As they walked slowly through the environmental mist Clement brought Yan in for a consultation over the private com.

"If each of these capsules has a single soldier in it . . . " He trailed off.

"Why are you assuming they're soldiers and not colonists?" replied Yan.

"Nothing about this ship indicates colonization, Yan. It seems strictly military in function, to me anyway."

"Assuming that's true, I'd say that those capsules are designed for use on a habitable world. That tunnel you blew your way into was probably for deploying the capsules to the surface."

"From space?" Clement said, a bit incredulous.

"They probably have thrusters for braking and landing on a lower-gravity world like Alphus. Remember, it's only about 0.66 *g* of Earth gravity."

"Okay . . . "

Yan continued. "The capsules likely contain everything they'd need, weapons, rations, equipment and the like. Just ready to be deployed."

"And the . . . passengers?"

"Likely not revived until the capsule was deposited on the target world."

This made Clement uncomfortable. "So you're leaning toward this being a military mission as well?"

Yan hesitated. "You've got to see the rest of the ship first before I could draw that conclusion."

"Thank you, Yan," he said, then cut the line. Now he was worried.

Middie Daniel found the outer door, complete with the same key that they had found in the maintenance room. Clement called over to Yan to get a reading of the commands, but it was just general information, no instructions. There was a key panel, though with Arabic numerals on it, the problem being that they didn't have the key code, or even a guess as to how to figure it out.

"Can't we just blast it?" said Telco.

"I see subtlety isn't your strong point, Middie. Other, more helpful suggestions?" Clement asked the expeditionary team.

"Your cobra pistol has an electromagnetic-pulse setting," said Nobli over the com from the *Beauregard* almost immediately.

"A what?" replied Clement.

"A small EM-pulse generator. It's a defensive setting, for when you might want to disable local enemy mobile communications and the like," replied Nobli.

"I had no idea," said Clement. Soon all five of the expeditionary team were playing with their cobra pistols to find the setting. Clement looked up and decided he had to put a stop to this fiddling or risk an accident. "Enough," he said, reaching out and putting his hand over Telco's pistol. They all stopped. "Someone volunteer."

"I'll do it," said Daniel, beating Telco to the punch to volunteer for once. Clement nodded.

"Gotta spread the love around, I guess. All right, Daniel, you get the assignment. Everyone else holster their pistols." Clement watched as they all did as ordered except Wilcock, who fumbled to get his pistol holstered again. Once that process was over without incident, Clement took Daniel's cobra pistol and, following Nobli's instructions, set the pistol for a short range EM pulse before handing it back to the middie.

"How far back do we have to be for this?" Clement asked Nobli.

"Three meters should do it. But Mr. Daniel should have the anti-pulse mode on his suit activated."

Clement let out an exasperated sigh. "And how do we do that?"

Nobli explained the process and Clement ordered everyone in the crew to do the same, then take their distance from Daniel. Once they were set, Clement gave the middie an order to proceed at his discretion.

Daniel stood half a meter from the door and pointed the pistol at the door lock, then counted down from five as Telco had done, then fired the pistol. There was a flash of blinding white light, and after his eyes cleared Clement could see the door mechanism had gone dark, as well as several monitor panels on the near wall. The rest of the room hummed on quietly, dim lights glowing in the near dark mist.

They all rushed up to the doorway to see the results of Daniel's handiwork. The locking mechanism was dead, and the door was slightly ajar. "It must have activated the door-opening sequence just before the circuits burned out," said Clement. Then he turned to his young crew members. "Well don't just stand there, Middies, get the damn thing open." He and Wilcock and Pomeroy stepped back while the two middies struggled with the door for a few minutes. At some point they must have hit a release mechanism as the door eventually slid open quickly.

Clement led his expeditionary team, cobra rifles drawn, into the dark. The hallway they were in was even dimmer than the capsule chamber, but minus the mist. That was a plus. They used their EVA suit lights to scan as they walked. The hallway was long and empty, with curved walls, and there were entry doors every few dozen meters on both the top and bottom of the hallway with no deference to gravity, or "up" and "down." Like being inside a can of peas.

"Split up again," ordered Clement. "Wilcock, you take the two middies that way"—he pointed back down the hallway they had just come up—"Pomeroy and I will go upstream. Report whatever you find." Then he looked down at his watch. "Rendezvous back here in thirty minutes. We don't want to overstay our welcome," he said.

Wilcock checked his watch and then led the two middies away while he and Pomeroy made their way to the nearest doorway, across the hall and up the wall from the capsule chamber. Clement called in a request to Nobli for a better way to enter and exit each room, which, surprisingly, Nobli provided. It turned out a negative EM pulse would clear the door codes without damaging the key. Pomeroy tried it on the near door, reset the key code randomly, and the door slid open. Before Clement let her go in he sent the procedure to Wilcock via the com for the second group to use. There was, however, increasing static interference in both their internal and external communications. That worried Clement.

He and Pomeroy stepped inside the chamber and found it nearly identical with the one they had entered originally. It was full of more capsules, and not much else. The same was repeated twice more before they entered the third chamber down from their original entry door.

The door opened into complete darkness. Even with both of their helmet lights on, the room had a deep, dark feeling and a coldness to it. Frankly, to Clement, it was downright creepy.

"I found a console," said Pomeroy. Clement went to her and looked at the panel, dimly lit from her suit light. "These look like environmental controls, and this should be power," she said, pointing to a glowing blue LED icon with an unreadable symbol on it. "Do we light it up?" she asked Clement.

"Hold on," he said, then tried to raise Wilcock and the middies. He couldn't connect with them. "Must be the walls in here," he said.

"They could be reinforced against unauthorized communications," posited Pomeroy.

"One question then, why would you do that if this were a civilian colony ship?" Pomeroy shrugged.

"There may be only one way to find that out," she said.

Clement looked at the panel with the power icon on it, and nodded.

Pomeroy pressed the button.

The panel started to light up slowly, activating systems in a seemingly pre-planned order. Eventually overhead lights came on from a single glowing light panel bolted to the ceiling.

A chamber below them started to light up. Clearly they were in a control room, high above what lay in the massive central chamber below. They went to the window and looked down.

There was a large collection of ships in what looked like an aircraft carrier bay. Some seemed sized for a small number of occupants, others were significantly larger.

"Attack ships," said Pomeroy, "Three-man light attack clippers, I'd bet."

"Dozens of them," replied Clement. "And those larger ships could be destroyers with ten to twenty in the crew." All of them were starting to receive power through the activation system they had just lit up.

Clement grabbed Pomeroy by the arm and quickly dragged her out of the room, not bothering to shut the door behind them. They "ran" as best they could in low gravity with their grav boots on, heading back the way they had come. Clement called to Wilcock on his com.

"Wilcock! Get back to the maintenance room. We're getting out of here," he said, a bit more frantically than he would have liked.

"Already on our way, sir," Wilcock replied through heavy static. "We found tons of military equipment in several chambers, and more capsules."

Clement stopped in his tracks. "What kind of equipment?"

"Armored vehicles. Mortars. Fixed gun emplacements and the like. Enough for a full division, or more."

"Shit!" said Clement, and started moving again. "Get to the maintenance room as fast as you can!"

"Aye, sir."

He and Pomeroy continued their "run" as best they could. Within a minute's time, Wilcock and the two middies were straight ahead of them at about two hundred meters, already at the door to the capsule chamber and maintenance room when the first shot was fired from behind Clement's shoulder. A bright red energy blast hit Middie Daniel in the gut and he fell. Clement whipped around and pulled his cobra rifle, quickly returning fire with kinetic tracer rounds.

"Unlock your boots! Go zero-g! Now!" he ordered.

Pomeroy did as ordered, pushing off the hallway wall and propelling herself toward Wilcock and the two middies. Telco was pulling Daniel inside the capsule chamber. Clement turned back and saw six soldiers in full EVA gear slowly coming at him, rifles drawn, in battle crouches. He unlocked his boots and then fired a volley of suppressing kinetic rounds at the soldiers, who scattered. The resultant force from his shots propelled Clement down the hallway at a fast clip. It was one way to hasten his departure, but a dangerous one. He kept shooting, and the soldiers kept scrambling, but he was going way too fast now . . .

The big arms of Middie Telco wrapped around him and both men hit the wall and then skidded down the hallway about ten meters before Telco's boot grips stopped them. Clement switched his magnetic boot controls back on and they both made for the capsule room door with Pomeroy and Wilcock supplying the suppressing fire for their retreat. Once at the door Telco pushed Clement through the threshold. On the ground was Middie Daniel's body, a hole burned clean through his abdomen.

"He's dead, sir," said Telco.

"He is, Middie. Let's get out of here," he ordered his remaining crew into full retreat, and they went back through the capsule chamber to the maintenance room, locking the door behind them. Telco had carried Middie Daniel's body over his shoulder. Clement opened the maintenance room door using the blue button again, then fired his cobra pistol in plasma mode to melt the control panel in place. He ordered his crew out of the deployment tube and they quickly tethered their way back to the shuttle. The crossing took longer than Clement wanted, Telco being slowed by carrying Daniel's body, and he worried about enemy soldiers shooting at them the whole time. Finally, they got back home and got the shuttle underway, moving away from the Ark ship and toward the *Beauregard* as fast as Clement could make the shuttle go.

Once they were clear and moving at an acceptable rate of speed, Clement turned the controls over to Pomeroy and went back to check on his crew. Daniel's body was laid out on the shuttle floor. Telco looked down on his friend.

"Those were soldiers, sir. And that ship. I didn't see anything that wasn't military grade," Telco said.

"We also saw a dedication plaque," said Wilcock. "If I read it right, the ship is called the *Li Shimen*, after a famous general of some kind."

Clement looked to Telco. "Middie Telco, when we get back aboard the *Beauregard*, get our missile tubes loaded with the nukes. We may need them all if we're going to escape this situation. And don't delay, you get me, Middie?" Clement turned to Wilcock. "You're with him."

"Understood," said Wilcock. "The warheads are already armed, sir."

"What about Daniel, sir?" Telco asked, looking at his dead friend's body. Clement shook his head.

"Leave it, son. There's no time."

"But—"

"The ship comes first, Middie. That's an order."

"Aye, sir."

Clement looked to Wilcock. "Give him whatever help he needs, Captain."

Wilcock nodded and exchanged a knowing glance with Clement. The middie needed to be kept busy.

Clement nodded back to Wilcock, hoping he could trust him, then went back to the shuttle pilot's nest.

"Time to the *Beauregard*?" he asked Pomeroy.

"Eight minutes, sir," she replied.

"Get me Yan on the com."

Pomeroy hooked up the com channel so he could raise his first officer on the link by switching to a private channel. "We have trouble coming, Yan. Prep the ship for battle, and fire up the Ion plasma drive," he said.

"What's happened? Our com link was cut off," said Yan.

Clement held his tongue for just a second, contemplating his next words.

"This is no colony ship, Yan. It's one hundred percent military, and unfortunately our presence there woke them up. They'll be coming. For us."

"Military? As in navy?"

"As in, invasion force. My guess is this is an Earth Ark, sent here to claim these planets before the 5 Suns Alliance can. And we're stuck right in the middle of that squabble," Clement said.

"She betrayed us?"

"She set us up, Yan, like we talked about in my cabin. It's going to be up to us to survive on our own now."

"I can't believe it, I can't believe—"

"Believe it, Yan. There's no time for tears over lost loves. We'll be on board in five minutes, Commander. Have my ship ready to fight or run when I get there," finished Clement.

"Aye, sir, I will," said Yan.

And with that Clement shut off the com line.

# ✳11✳

They were still two minutes out from the *Beauregard*'s cargo deck when the first signs of trouble came. Light attack clippers, the three-man-style ships he and Pomeroy had seen activated in the ship's hold, came swarming out of the Ark. As near as Clement could tell they were in triangle formations, which was a standard tactic for LACs. The biggest problem, though, was that there were *a lot* of triangles.

"Estimate of the number of LACs, Pomeroy?" Clement said.

"At least sixty," she replied.

"We probably saw five times that number on the Ark."

"Then these are likely only the first group of teams to come out of hydro sleep."

Clement nodded agreement. "They have way too much firepower for this shuttle," he said, then called up Yan again. "Yan, I need my ship moving the moment we're down on the cargo deck."

"Understood, sir. Based on my observations so far those LACs warm up slow, especially after fifty years in hydro suspension. Likely the crews aren't very much 'with it' either. I know I'd be groggy after sleeping half a century," she said.

"We can't make any assumptions, Commander, just preparations. Get those nukes loaded and ready to fire, and set all of our conventional missiles to proximity detonation. There's too many LACs to ensure we can get them all with individual missiles."

"Understood, sir. See you in thirty seconds," replied Yan. Clement looked down at his watch, just to confirm.

"Take us in, Pomeroy," he said.

They landed hard and fast and Clement immediately made for the bridge, only pausing to let the air pressure between the cargo deck and the air lock equalize. He swept onto his bridge still in his

EVA suit and took the center seat from Yan. She had immediately started the *Beauregard* on an escape path using the Ion plasma drive, but the old girl still took time to accelerate, and those LACs were closing to firing range. He got immediately on the com to Telco in the forward missile room.

"What's the status of my nukes, Middie?" he demanded.

"Locked and loaded in the tubes, sir," said Telco.

"Captain, we may want to wait on the nukes as a last resort, not a first option." This came from Yan.

Clement scanned his tactical screen, which identified the sixty incoming LACs, and it didn't look like they were coming to negotiate.

"Middie, load the main tubes with conventional missiles first, proximity warhead settings. Keep the nukes on standby, but I want them ready when I need them, Telco, or you'll be scrubbing the bathrooms all the way home," said Clement.

"Understood, Captain," replied Telco.

Clement looked to Yan. "You could have made that suggestion earlier," he said.

"I know, but—"

"No time, Yan," Clement said as he waved her off. He stood and started peeling off his EVA suit while giving orders at the same time. "Ivan, plot us a course that will take us toward Bellus. If that Ark wants to chase us they'll have to break off their original course to follow us. That could save us some time. What do you think, Mika?"

She turned from the pilot's seat, thinking for a second, then pulled up her plasma screen and made some calculations. "A day, maybe two if they parallel us. But they could also choose to use Alphus as a slingshot without a course change. If they do that, it might be less," she said.

"Why so little time?" asked Clement.

Ori canted her head a bit, looking at him. "This system is really packed. The planets are very close together compared to the 5 Suns, or even the Rim system, and thus easier to get to."

Clement nodded as he finished removing his EVA suit and tossed it aside, then sat back down at the captain's console. "We need another option," he said. He checked the tactical board, which showed the Earth Ark LACs were within eight minutes of firing range. He called down to Nobli. "Hassan, can we use the LEAP drive inside the system?"

"Well, yeah, you can use it anywhere. You just have to be aware it can cause collateral damage," replied Nobli.

"At this point that might be to our advantage. Can we *navigate* with it?"

"You mean use it as the main drive? I don't know. It was designed to get you from star system to star system, not planet to planet, which is a pinpoint target. Where did you want to go?"

"Bellus," he said.

"Jesus, Jared, that's a big ask. The calculations would take—"

"Five minutes, Hassan. I want your best guess to Ivan by that time. And make sure the drive is warm. We could need it at any time."

"Impossible to do, Captain. But of course if that's an order . . ."

"It is."

"Understood, sir."

Clement cut the line and then turned to Yan at the XO's console. "Battle status, XO."

"They're faster than us now, sir. They'll reach firing range on us in seven minutes, thirty seconds," said Yan.

"Engage the static field, and load up the first volley of missiles, Commander."

"Aye, sir," said Yan, scrambling over her board. The static field was designed to protect the ship from micrometeorites or small kinetic weapons like ball bearings, which could tear a ship to pieces if it was going the right speed.

"Prepare to fire on my mark."

Yan looked up at him. "Sir," she said, acknowledging her readiness.

The LACs were closing on the *Beauregard* and Clement had precious few seconds left to make his decisions. He called down to Nobli one last time.

"Do you have my calculation?" Clement demanded.

"I do, sir," replied Nobli. "It's rough, but a 0.085 second application of the LEAP drive should be enough to get us clear of the battlefield and propel us in the general direction of Bellus. I uploaded the calc to Ivan and he has the new control app."

"Very good, engineer. One more thing."

"There always is."

"The control app for the MAD weapon."

Nobli stayed silent for a moment, then said, "Already uploaded to your command console, sir."

Clement looked to his board and confirmed it was there.

"Do you intend to use it, sir?"

"Only in an emergency. Will it hinder our ability to use the LEAP drive for our escape?"

"Well, I don't recommend using them at the same time. That might rip a hole in *our* universe, or explode the whole damn thing. Just remember when you use the MAD it acts like a bypass valve. Once you activate it the power will flow out of the ship until you give the stop command, then the valve will turn off automatically. Like flipping a dead man switch."

"So I could use it as a weapon, then use the LEAP drive right after?" asked Clement.

"Theoretically, yes, sir."

"Thank you, Nobli." Clement looked down and activated the MAD control app. It lit up green on his console, then went to amber as he put it on standby.

"Yan, best guess to enemy firing range?"

She shrugged. "Any second now, Captain," Yan replied. Mika Ori turned quickly from her pilot's console.

"Incoming missiles, Captain," she reported.

"Sound the alarm. Evade and distract," Clement ordered. Claxons went off throughout the ship as Ori accelerated the *Beauregard* using the Xenon thrusters on top of the Ion plasma drive to evade the incoming missiles. She also activated her defensive countermeasures at the same time. Clement watched as the initial barrage of a dozen missiles were easily distracted by the *Beauregard*'s defenses, exploding harmlessly in the jungle of chaff well away from her hull.

"Initial barrage ineffective, sir," reported Ori. "It appears their weapons use simple heat-seeking targeting. Good thing we warm up our countermeasures. Easily handled by our defenses, sir."

"So far, Mika. But I bet our friends learn quickly." He turned to Ivan Massif. "Ivan, program in our escape route to Bellus using a 0.085 second burst from the LEAP drive. I want to be ready to bug out as quickly as possible."

"Already done, sir," said Massif. It was the navigator who would control the LEAP burst from his navigation position.

"Shall we return fire, sir?" asked Yan in a rather urgent tone. "They're prepping another volley."

Clement shook his head. "Not yet, Yan. Let's see what our friends do next."

A few seconds later and the fleet of LACs answered with a second, and then a third barrage of twelve missiles each. Ori turned the *Beauregard* this way and that, swaying as the missiles approached. Clement didn't have to call for countermeasures this time. Mika knew her job.

The missile groups had been fired seconds apart, in a crisscrossing pattern to counter the *Beauregard*'s defenses. The first batch fell prey to the countermeasures again, but the second was more effective, with three of the missiles acquiring a targeting ping on *Beauregard*.

"Defensive missiles, Yan," ordered Clement. Without a word Yan launched six conventional missiles to intercept the incoming enemy fire. All three enemy missiles were taken out at a range of five kilometers from the *Beauregard*.

"Reload conventional missiles," Yan called down to Telco in the missile room. Then she turned to Clement. "Five klicks isn't much of a safety margin," she said.

Clement nodded. "Agreed. Mika, how fast are they closing on us?"

Without turning she replied, "That five-kilometer cushion will be gone in two minutes, sir."

Clement hit his com. "Missile room, this is the captain. Belay that last missile command. Load two of the nuclear warhead missiles into the launchers. I repeat, load two nukes into launchers. Commander Yan will be down with her activation key."

"Aye, sir," said Telco, a bit of quaver apparent in his voice, even over the com.

Clement looked to Yan. "Go," he said with a nod. "Get Wilcock. I'll fire the missiles from here." She went.

Clement turned to Massif at the navigation station. "Ivan, prepare to activate the LEAP drive on the course Engineer Nobli gave you on my order."

"Sir," snapped Massif in acknowledgement.

Clement waited as the light attack clipper fleet closed again on the *Beauregard*. He got a green light confirming the nuclear missiles were locked and loaded. Yan came back to her station presently.

Then the LACs launched their next missile volley.

"Incoming! Thirty seconds!" declared Ori from her station. Clement didn't have to order the evasive countermeasures.

Five groups of twelve missiles launched in volleys one second apart, streaming in toward the *Beauregard* in a weave pattern that would be impossible to avoid. They were going to get their target, one way or another. Clement activated the MAD weapon and held his finger over the firing button, but he still had one more card to play.

"Commander Yan, are the nukes ready to fire?" he said over the com.

"Aye, sir," Yan replied.

"On my mark. Countdown please."

"Twenty seconds."

"Hold."

"Fifteen seconds."

"Hold."

"Ten—"

"Fire!"

The ship shook as the nukes rolled out of the launch tubes and accelerated at hyper-Mach speeds, far outpacing the incoming missiles. They all watched on the main tactical display as the nukes closed to proximity range of the enemy missiles in seconds, then detonated.

Nothing.

"Insufficient detonation, Captain!" exclaimed Yan over the com. "Nukes did not explode!"

Clement looked to the incoming countdown clock, which was at 0:03 . . .

"Ivan—" he said.

Then the universe shifted around him.

# 12

Massif hadn't waited for Clement to give the order. He had engaged the LEAP drive and the *Beauregard* had slipped from normal space into its quantum-fluid bubble for a period of 0.086 seconds before automatically shutting down. In that time the *Beauregard* had traveled an indeterminate amount of distance and scrambled most of the crew's brains. Clement felt his mind returning to normal slowly, like pieces of a jigsaw puzzle coming together. He looked out on his dimly lit bridge as his crew struggled to regain their wits.

"Thank you, Ivan," he croaked out before clearing his throat and sitting up higher in his command chair. All the main systems on the bridge had blinked out and were rebooting.

"You're welcome, sir," said Massif.

"Mika . . . " He had to clear his throat again, then, "Where are we?"

"Uncertain, Captain," the pilot said from her station, her hand quivering on the controls and her voice weak. Clement could see she had been shaken by the LEAP transit. "My main tracking console is knocked out, but the underlying telemetry says we're still in the Trinity system."

"In the neighborhood, then?"

She turned, a wan smile on her face. "In the neighborhood, yes, sir." Then she ran her hands over her console more certainly as systems began to come back online. "I think I can get us a visual, if that would help, sir."

Clement nodded. "As good as anything, Lieutenant," he said. With that the main display screen lit up. It showed a blue-green mass in sunlight looming over them, but half the planet was eclipsed in darkness.

"Jesus Christ! Is that Bellus?" said Clement.

"I think so, sir. We were on a general heading for her, but I didn't think we'd be this close," said Massif.

Just then Yan returned to her station. "Systems coming back online, sir. We're just slightly less than eighteen thousand kilometers from Bellus, sir," she said.

Clement got on his com to Hassan Nobli. "That was quite a calculation, Engineer. Another tenth of a second and we'd have been in the mantle of the planet."

"You said you wanted my best guess, sir. You got what you asked for," replied Nobli.

"I did indeed. Thank you, Nobli."

"My pleasure, sir."

Clement shut off the com and then turned to Yan. "What happened with my nukes?" he asked in a demanding tone.

"I've already done a quick analysis, sir. The yield . . . the yield was insufficient for a fission explosion, sir," she said.

"Insufficient? You mean they were duds?"

Yan nodded. "Essentially, sir."

Clement slammed his fist on the arm of his command couch. "I thought we verified the nuclear yields back at Kemmerine Station?"

"We did, sir. My only conclusion is that the warheads had insufficient plutonium mass for detonation, and that some kind of masking agent was used to deceive us," she said.

Clement sat back in his command chair, his face flushing red with anger. "In other words, we were sabotaged by Admiral DeVore."

"It appears so, sir."

Clement leaned forward in his couch, clasping his hands together, speaking softly so that only she could hear. "We've been outsmarted by Elara DeVore for the last time, Yan," he said through tight lips. He felt like someone had just cut open his body and let his guts fall to the floor. "This betrayal . . ." he started, "this betrayal is absolute, Yan. And it's not the first time."

"What do you mean?"

"I mean I now know who betrayed me at the Battle of Argyle Station. Elara DeVore. That's how she was able to advance through the ranks of the 5 Suns Navy so fast. She sold us out, all of her crewmates and friends onboard the *Beauregard*, for her own advancement."

Yan hesitated. His words were filled with anger and resentment. She could almost feel his pain. But . . .

"That was a different war, Clement. It's over now. Now we have to focus on this ship, this crew, and how to save them," she said.

He finally exhaled and took in a deep breath. "I can't deny that I want to crawl inside one of those whiskey bottles, Yan. Forever."

"You can't," she replied. "This ship needs you. Hell, *I* need you. The over-promoted rich girl from New Hong Kong. You're the only person who can make this work, Clement. We all need you."

Clement sat back, thinking. "If she was willing to go this far, she had to have an accomplice on board, someone to back her plan up."

Yan nodded. "Wilcock," she said.

Clement bolted from his seat. "Get your sidearm, Commander. Mika, get us into a higher, stable orbit over Bellus and maintain." He looked to Adebayor and Massif. "The two of you are to go to the armory and bring back one sidearm and one cobra rifle for each of you. When you return, seal the bridge and only open it on my personal orders. Understood?"

"Yes, sir," came the chorus reply.

"Mika, seal the bridge while they're gone, and only open it for them when they return."

"Will do, sir," she said.

Clement grabbed his cobra pistol from his discarded EVA suit and primed it, then looked to Yan. "Ready?" he asked.

"Ready, sir," she said with a nod, loaded pistol in her hand.

Then the two of them headed off the bridge and down the gangway, toward the forward missile room at a dead run.

"You know I could be working for Admiral DeVore as well," said Yan as they ran to the forward missile room.

"You could be," admitted Clement. "But if you are then now would be a good time for you to put a cobra round in my back."

Yan reached out and stopped him. "You know that's not going to happen," she said. He looked at her, his face not giving away any emotion one way or another.

"I hope that's true, Yan. If I'm wrong about you then this whole mission is a suicide run, and every life on this ship is forfeit."

"It is true, sir," she said. "I'm loyal to you."

"Good," he said, again without commitment, then, with a nod of his head, "let's go get our traitor."

They picked up their pace, weapons drawn.

When they entered the missile room, two decks down and directly below the bridge, Captain Wilcock had his cobra pistol to the back of Middie Telco's head. Yan and Clement stood in the doorway, their sidearms laser-targeted on Wilcock's forehead.

"Traitor," said Clement, his aim not wavering. "What did you do to the warheads?"

Wilcock looked at him with disdain, but chose to answer. "Depleted uranium casings. Fooled all of you into thinking you had a fully functional nuke," said Wilcock as he shifted to put Telco's head between him and their targeting laser sights.

"That action could have killed us all. Those LACs had us dead to rights."

"I was ordered to sacrifice my life for this mission, if that was required," replied Wilcock, emotionless.

"Ordered by Fleet Admiral DeVore."

"Of course. Now enough of this. Let me through to the shuttle or Middie Telco here will get a softball-sized hole in his head."

Clement shook his head negative. "That's not happening," he stated flatly.

"This isn't a negotiation, *Captain*." He said the last word with open anger. "You've got five seconds to step out of the way."

Clement exchanged a glance with Yan. She took one step to the right.

"Keep moving," demanded Wilcock. Yan took another step, followed by Clement yielding the door opening. "More!" he said as he moved with Telco toward the yawning hatchway. Yan took two more steps, Clement one, and then Wilcock pushed Telco toward them and ran for the door, slamming the hatch behind him as the three of them tried to untangle themselves.

Yan ran to the door. "Sealed," she said. Clement waved her aside and raised his pistol at the door lock from barely a meter away.

"Jesus!" exclaimed Yan as she and Telco dove for cover. Clement fired at the lock mechanism, blowing the door clean off its hinges and into the hallway, then scrambled through the hatch and started running after Wilcock. He slid down the metal stairwell rails, barely touching the stairs with his feet as he ran. When he made it to the cargo hold Wilcock was ahead of him, running for the open shuttle door. He had one shot from almost 10 meters away with a close-range weapon.

He didn't hesitate. The kinetic cobra round hit Wilcock in his outstretched left hand just as he was reaching for the shuttle stair railing, bits of metal and flesh splattering against the shuttle's hull. Wilcock fell in a sprawl off the shuttle steps and onto the deck. Instinctively he reached for his wounded hand with his free one and his pistol went skittering away. He howled in pain as Clement raced across the deck and then went into a slide, kicking Wilcock's discarded pistol under the shuttle. Seconds later Yan and Telco arrived, along with Pomeroy and a slew of the rest of the crew. Wilcock was still howling like a schoolgirl, holding his shattered left hand.

"Take charge of our prisoner, Mr. Telco," Clement said, then turned to Pomeroy, "Get him patched up, with as minimal medical supplies as possible, no pain meds, and then throw him in the brig."

"Uh, we don't have a brig, sir," said Telco.

Clement looked around the deck. "Well, we used to. Put him in the shuttle air lock then and attach him to a tether until we decide what to do with him."

"Aye, sir," said Telco as he and Pomeroy hauled the whining traitor off the deck.

Clement looked at Yan. "My cabin, five minutes," he said. She nodded as Clement stormed off.

Clement stopped at the bridge to give the all-clear and then ordered Massif, Ori, and Adebayor to begin a survey of the light side of the tidal-locked Bellus.

"What are we looking for?" asked Massif.

"Any place to set down. We may have to hide for a while. And get a bead on that Ark ship. I want to know where they're heading."

"Aye, sir," came the responses, and then Clement made for his cabin. When he opened the door, Yan was already inside.

"That was too goddamned close," she said as he entered.

"No kidding. That bastard Wilcock. Worthless piece of shit."

"You're forgetting Admiral DeVore."

Clement shook his head. "No, I'm not. But we can't deal with her out here. We can deal with Wilcock, though," he said. They both sat down, facing each other. Clement leaned forward.

"This is my fault, Yan. DeVore thought I would drink my way through this trip. She was counting on me *not* being the man I used to be. She expected I would be the lout I've been on Argyle Station for the last nine years since my war parole ended. She thought she knew what I would do. Well, I didn't disappoint her. I am that man. She played me easily enough. And to think I even slept with her on Kemmerine," he finished, shaking his head in disgrace.

Yan opened her mouth to talk but said nothing for a moment, then, "I disagree, Captain. You foiled her plans. We should all be dead by now, but you've saved us. You are not that man on Argyle Station. I know she's had you under observation for at least the last year, probably more than that. You were the perfect patsy, but you beat her. We're all still alive."

Now it was Clement's turn to stay quiet. After another minute he spoke again, changing the subject.

"I've no time to waste on Captain Wilcock right now. We have a military Earth Ark ship bearing down on us with a hundred times our firepower. We have no nukes to defend ourselves, and an Admiral back home who has deceived us and sacrificed us to the wolves for her own selfish reasons, and I'm just trying to figure out what to do next."

"About which part?"

Clement looked at her. "First things first. Wilcock, I guess. I'm having a hard time trying to avoid my first impulse," he said.

"Which is?"

"His actions warrant execution," he said. Yan went quiet and pensive at that. "You don't agree?" Clement prompted.

"I do agree."

Now it was Clement's turn to get quiet again as he thought about things. Finally, he stood up, his decision made, and Yan stood with him. "Call all ship's personnel to the loading dock in twenty minutes, save for Mika and Ivan."

"Yes, sir," said Yan. The two stood together as she looked at him, hoping for more, but he stayed resolved. With nothing more to say, she left the room to inform the crew. Once he was alone, Clement went to his cabinet and poured himself a glass of the Argyle whiskey. He drank it quickly, in one shot, to steel his resolve. He'd killed many enemies on the field of battle, but this was the first time he'd considered executing a man, even if he was a traitor.

Clement looked at the bottle again, and all it represented. He'd crawled in and out of a bottle like that a dozen times since the war, always wondering what had become of his friends, but never allowed to know what became of them by the rules of his war parole. Well, now he had found out. Elara DeVore was the one who betrayed them, no, *him*, at the Battle of Argyle Station. He wondered if delivering him to the 5 Suns Navy had been part of the deal she had obviously cut with them to betray the Rim. In any case, it had undoubtedly led to her decade-plus rise in the 5 Suns Navy, all the way to Fleet Admiral. Like he'd said to Yan, Elara DeVore always had a backup plan.

He looked at the bottle, longing for another hit, if nothing else just to numb the pain of his memories of DeVore, and of being her lover. He'd been through a lot in his life, but he had never felt betrayal like he felt it now. That's what DeVore had robbed him of, his ability to trust *anyone* from now on.

He turned away from the bottle, focusing on his tactical pad but not really looking at it. Captain Wilcock had no doubt been deceived by DeVore just as he had, but Wilcock had willingly put the entire crew in mortal danger, he'd committed treason, and mutiny. In Clement's mind, there was no real choice. Wilcock had to die. Regrettably, he was merely a pawn standing in for the person who was the true villain here, the one who should be standing for execution. In that moment, he silently vowed he would bring Elara DeVore to justice. Then he stood, and spoke out loud in his empty cabin.

"You'll be the first person I've ever executed, Captain Wilcock," he said quietly to himself, "but probably not the last." Then he put the bottle away and left his cabin, heading for the loading dock.

Captain Wilcock was sealed in the shuttle air lock, facing the largest exterior door on the *Beauregard*. His injured hand was crudely wrapped and he winced in obvious pain, missing at least two fingers from his left hand. *It would be cruel to extend that pain,* thought Clement.

Most of the crew were now gathered around in a disorganized

group, and Yan was the last to arrive with Lieutenant Pomeroy. Clement wasn't happy. He stood on the gantry landing, looking down on his crew.

"Commander Yan," he called out.

She snapped to attention and stepped forward, looking up at him from the deck. "Sir."

"Organize this rabble," he ordered. She did. Within a few seconds the crew had organized itself into three rows of five and two of four, by rank, with only Wilcock, Clement, Yan, the deceased Middie Daniel, plus Ori and Massif (who were busy running the ship) missing from their ranks. Clement signaled to Telco to activate the com so that Wilcock could hear the conversation from inside the air lock, but not reply or be heard by the crew. Once that task was complete, Clement started in.

"We are here to enact punishment on a traitor, Captain Craig Wilcock, who deceived this ship and her crew by placing nonexplosive nuclear warheads into our defensive armament, thus endangering the entire crew aboard the *Beauregard* during the attack by the Earth Ark ship. I have debated those actions, along with his placing Middie Telco in peril by holding him hostage with a cobra pistol to the head, and his attempt to steal our only shuttle to escape justice. I believe Captain Wilcock was working with Fleet Admiral DeVore of the 5 Suns Alliance Navy, another traitor, to use this ship as a test to seek out the power of the Earth Ark ship we encountered. This ship and her crew were no doubt considered an acceptable expense by the 5 Suns Navy, or at least by Admiral DeVore herself. Neither I nor *any* of my crew were informed of this except for Captain Wilcock, who clearly had an escape plan in place if this ship was destroyed by a superior force. As captain of this ship I cannot condone, forgive, nor commute the penalties for Captain Wilcock's actions. I therefore sentence the traitor, Craig Wilcock, to capital punishment by evacuation into the vacuum of space, as prescribed in the 5 Suns Alliance Navy Code of Military Justice."

The crew was dead silent at this. Clement could hear Wilcock banging on the air lock door, a quiet thudding sound as he realized his final fate was at hand.

"This ship, her crew, and this mission have been betrayed by the Captain, the Admiral and the 5 Suns Navy. It is now up to each of you to decide where your loyalties lie. We are now a crew without a nation, a ship without a flag. We cannot trust the 5 Suns Navy, which commissioned this ship, nor the Fleet Admiral. Each of us, therefore, must decide our fate from this point forward. As my last order as the captain of this 5 Suns Alliance Navy vessel, I order the execution of Captain Wilcock and will carry it out myself. From that point onward your decisions to follow my orders will be completely voluntary. I leave that decision to each of you."

Clement stepped down from the gantry to the cargo deck and walked to the air lock door. Wilcock was in a panic, beating the door with both his hands, leaving a bloody stain on the window from his injury. The pain in his face as he faced the terror of his own demise was obvious, but Clement reminded himself of Wilcock's cowardice, of his betrayal, of the people on the *Beauregard* he could have killed. He knew it should be Elara DeVore in that air lock, but she wasn't here, and Wilcock had done enough to warrant this punishment on his own. He wondered if he could do the same thing to DeVore as he was doing to Wilcock. He decided at this point, he could, to both of them.

He activated the outer door controls. The interior alarms went off as Wilcock panicked even more, looking for any way out. Clement pressed the release button.

The doors parted and Wilcock was quickly sucked out by decompression, his body dangling about ten meters outside the air lock, still tethered to the ship, spinning and writhing in cold space. He flailed his limbs as he spun around, out of control, with nothing to grasp on to but his last breath. In seconds it was over, his body rigid and lifeless. Mercifully Clement detached the tether, allowing him to float away toward Bellus, where his body would burn up in the atmosphere. Clement closed the outer doors and activated the atmosphere controls, flooding the air lock with environment again, then turned back to his crew.

"All hands, return to stations. Command crew will meet in the officer's galley in thirty minutes to discuss our next actions. Dismissed," he said, then walked straight past Yan and back up the gangway, heading toward his quarters.

Clement shut the officer's galley doors as the last of his command crew squeezed into the small space. Present were Yan, Nobli, Ori,

Massif, and Lieutenant Pomeroy, who Clement had specifically invited. He'd left Adebayor to manage the ship now that Mika had put it in a stable orbit around Bellus, and they were only a few meters from the bridge at any rate.

"To business then," said Clement. "We're alone in an unknown star system, we've been betrayed by our commanders and are undoubtedly considered expendable by the 5 Suns Alliance Navy, and most especially Fleet Admiral DeVore. Are there any objections to my declaration that the *Beauregard* currently flies no flag, and that the decisions we make to survive are ours, and ours alone?" No one in the room said a word.

"Your silence is considered acceptance of our new standard. I will note in the log that we all took this stand of our own volition. From this point on, I propose that we adopt the 5 Suns Alliance military code as a temporary makeweight from which to conduct our onboard affairs. We are not pirates. Please state any objections now." Again, there were none. "Good. Now that that business is complete, I need reports on the condition of the ship, our tactical status, and a review of the data we have compiled on Bellus." He turned to his right. "Commander Yan?"

"The ship is running smoothly on all systems. We have forty-eight conventional warhead missiles remaining at our disposal, although it is uncertain how effective they would be against the Ark ship. On a tactical basis, the Ark ship remains in a deep-dive course inward toward Alphus. From their current approach they could either do a burn to establish a stable orbit around the planet, or accelerate and use it as a slingshot to change their course back out toward Bellus, and us."

"We won't survive another encounter with that Ark ship, especially if we have to fight them with conventional weapons," said Clement.

"Is there another option? I mean, besides conventional weapons?" It was Mika Ori, the former fighter pilot, asking the question.

Clement exchanged a brief glance with Nobli. "No other options that I'm prepared to discuss at this time."

"But shouldn't—" started in Yan.

Clement cut her off. "Not at this time, *Commander*," he said firmly, then turned to Ivan Massif. "What have your surveys of Bellus turned up, Navigator?"

"We've made six orbits of the planet, sir. Our initial survey results have been ... surprising."

"Such as?"

"We've identified abundant fresh water on the planet sir, above the ground. The planet is tidally locked to the Trinity star, with the same side facing the star constantly, and conditions are remarkably stable throughout the biosphere. There are high mountains in both the extreme north and south that receive regular snowfall and produce a near-constant melt that proceeds toward the equator of the planet through deep river valleys, where they collect in numerous freshwater lakes and seas. Surface temperatures throughout eighty percent of the planet average twenty-four degrees Celsius, with very rare variations. Vegetation is pervasive and there appears to be a lot of potential for animal life. There is also a large saltwater sea near the equator of the planet that could provide the seeds for ocean-based lifeforms."

Clement nodded. "Sounds like a paradise."

"There is one other issue, sir." This came from Pomeroy. Clement nodded for her to continue. "When I was conducting a survey for bioforms, I discovered signs of ... more advanced life on the planet, sir."

"Advanced? Say what you mean, Lieutenant," demanded Clement.

"I would say, sir," she said hesitantly, "that these bioforms were organized in such a way as to be almost immediately recognizable as organized communities, sir."

"You mean some kind of, uh ... intelligent communities?"

"Yes, sir. Things like simple artificial canals to serve the communities, potential crop fields, things of that nature. Sir."

"So there's some kind of potentially intelligent life on Bellus?"

"I would say so, sir," Pomeroy said.

Clement unconsciously rubbed at his chin. "Perhaps there've been missions to this system before. Could they be military bases left by previous Ark missions? Either from Earth or potentially from the 5 Suns?" he asked.

Pomeroy frowned slightly as she considered his question. "It seems unlikely that these are military settlements, sir. They aren't giving off any indications of advanced technology. They look more like primitive settlements, sir."

Clement leaned back in his chair. "So we have a mystery. We'll have to take all of this into consideration should we go down to the surface. For now, let's continue our surveys and not jump to any conclusions."

"Aye, sir."

"One other thing, Lieutenant. As of right now I'm giving you a field promotion to Lieutenant Commander. This will become official once we decide whatever fleet we'll end up serving in." There was a chuckle at that around the room. He turned to Yan.

"I also want you to promote the middies to full ensigns. They've all earned it," he said.

"Understood, sir," Yan replied.

Clement turned to Nobli. "Status of the LEAP drive, Chief?"

"Ready to use at any time, sir," he said.

"So we can escape whenever we want; we just have nowhere to go."

"Exactly, sir."

Clement nodded. "Keep her ready, Chief. We may need to bug out of here at any time." He leaned forward then, addressing the entire room. "Continue with your surveys. As a precaution I want us to look for a safe place to set down, hopefully away from these communities, or whatever they might be. Mika, that will be your job. Ivan, I want you to let me know when and if that Earth Ark changes course or speed. If they use Alphus to slingshot toward us, we may have to find cover, and fast. Keep all the other systems at optimal. Be prepared for anything. Remember, we've been betrayed by the 5 Suns Alliance, and the Earthers are to be considered hostile until further notice. Dismissed," he said.

As the room emptied, Yan stayed behind for a private word.

"What about those 'communities' on the surface of Bellus?" she asked.

He considered her question for a moment. "Despite what Pomeroy says, I have to believe they're military. If they are, we may be stuck between a rock and a hard place. I'll need options, Yan. That's where you come in."

"That *is* my job, sir," she said.

He nodded. "Then I'll leave you to it."

She left without another word. After a few seconds Clement followed her to his bridge, and an unknown destiny.

# ✵13✵

Twelve hours later, after a full cycle of sleep and refreshment, Clement found himself back on the *Beauregard*'s bridge, staring intently at the input from the long-range radio telescope on the main wall display. All of the primary bridge crew were watching the image of the Earth Ark as it bore down on Alphus, the innermost habitable planet of the seven worlds that composed the Trinity system.

The tactical display showed the Ark as it decelerated into the gravity well of Alphus. If she was planning on making for Bellus to pursue the *Beauregard*, she would have to make her turn and accelerate by skipping off of Alphus' atmosphere and then firing her main engines in a five-gravity burst to change course. If, however, she intended to stay on her original course to orbit Alphus and deploy her forces there, she would have to make a much smoother turn and continue to decelerate until she had established a steady orbit over the planet.

The bridge was tense and quiet. "Distance of the Ark ship to Alphus, Navigator," Clement asked.

"One hundred fifty thousand kilometers and closing, sir. At this pace she'll touch the atmosphere in twelve minutes, then she'll pass behind the planet and out of our line of sight. After about four minutes she should reappear on the other side of the planet, then either keep to an elliptical orbit and continue decelerating, or fire her mains and accelerate toward us," said Massif.

"How difficult a maneuver is this, Mika?" Clement asked of his pilot.

She shrugged. "I've never done it with anything remotely that size, sir, but my guess is they have a programmed autopilot carrying out the burn. They also have the gravity well of Alphus to help them, and although she's not as massive as Bellus or Camus, if I was betting on it, I'd say they can pull it off."

Clement nodded and turned to Yan. "Ship's status?"

"Ready for anything, sir. Locked down and prepared for any order you give."

"And if we have to go to ground?"

"We have a spot in the northern hemisphere at the convergence of three river valleys that we can set the *Beauregard* down on, about twelve klicks from the nearest of those settlements, sir."

"Thank you, Yan," he said, then turned his attention back to the display. The crew waited in silence, with Massif giving occasional updates. Finally, there was a glint of light as the Ark started her pass to the far side of Alphus.

"Atmospheric contact confirmed," said Massif. "They'll be out of viewing range for the next four minutes."

Clement fidgeted in his couch, which he was finding increasingly uncomfortable as time went by.

"Is it raise or call?" said Yan absently.

Clement looked at her, surprised by the poker reference, then turned back to the screen. They'd know soon enough.

There was another flash of light as the Ark ship came around the far edge of Alphus right on schedule, then the screen lit up with a bright flash of light that temporarily blinded the screen sensors. There could be little doubt now as to their intent. They'd fired their engines while they were still inside Alphus' atmosphere.

"How long until they get here, Ivan?" asked a disappointed Clement.

"Nine hours, twenty-seven minutes," said the *Beauregard*'s tall navigator.

Clement stood up and looked around his bridge. "Then we have half that long to get this ship down to a safe haven on Bellus," he said, then looked down at his watch. "Commencing now."

The next few hours Clement and Yan were a flurry of motion, validating landing procedures, surveying the landing site, prepping the ship for atmospheric travel. The *Beauregard* was never really made for operating in an atmosphere, but she always had the capability as a backup to staying space-borne. Clement had only ever landed her twice in her Rim Confederation Navy days, once on an asteroid to hide from 5 Suns Alliance hunter-killers that were pursuing her during the War of the 5 Suns, and once on a desperate resupply mission on Ceta near the end of the war. But this was a different *Beauregard* from the ship he had commanded, as Clement was well aware. Doing anything like a landing maneuver was going to be a completely new experience for everyone. He was with Mika Ori, looking at her proposed landing site.

"Will this area provide us enough cover?" said Clement.

"From what? Atomic missiles? Light attack drones? Pterodactyls?" she replied.

"Observation," he snapped back at her. "Can we find enough ground cover to hide the ship from military observation cameras, drone flybys, and the like?"

Her pretty face twisted a bit as she thought about the new problem her captain was presenting her. "We wanted to land here," she said, pointing to a peninsula between two of the rivers. "But there isn't any ground cover, at least not enough to cover a two-thousand-ton spacecraft. If we went inland another five klicks though, there is a river delta with a flat rocky sandbar closer to the mountains. If we come down there we'll have ready access to a large amount of vegetation that's taller than the ship herself. Knocking down some random trees could provide us with enough cover so we'd look like a natural formation from space. But if a drone got close, say within five hundred meters, we'd be dead meat."

"I'm more concerned with whether a sandbar could hold the weight of the ship. What about this clearing here?" said Clement, pointing to a smaller area another kilometer inland.

Mika pursed her lips as she was thinking. "It's a much tighter fit," she stated.

Clement looked up, catching her eyes as he smiled. "That's why I hired the best pilot in the fleet," he said.

She sighed and looked at the chart again. "This is what you want, isn't it? Make my job tougher."

"I just want the ship to be as safe as it can be, and I *know* you can fit us in there."

"Like thread through the eye of a needle, sir," she said.

He smiled wider. "I knew you wouldn't let me down."

With that he left Ori to calculate the breaking maneuvers while he made his way down to see his chief engineer. Nobli looked up from behind his wire-rimmed glasses and crinkled his nose at Clement as he came in.

"I've got plenty to do here to get my LEAP drive secured for a planet-side landing, Captain, so I hope this isn't some kind of pep talk."

"It's not," said Clement, "rest assured."

The two men eyeballed each other, each waiting for the other to go first. Finally Clement spoke.

"Can we protect the LEAP drive components from damage as we touch down?" he asked his engineer.

Nobli shrugged, a noncommittal gesture. "Probably," Nobli said. "If we can keep her level, and the landing legs deploy properly, and about nine thousand other things don't happen."

"Because if they do we'll be stranded here with broken wheels and no way to drive home?"

"Close enough," said the engineer. "What you're doing isn't easy, Captain."

"I know that," snapped Clement, wiping sweat from his brow. It had been a stressful day, and it wasn't close to over. "If we shut down the LEAP drive, let it go completely cold, how long will it take to restart?"

Nobli leaned back, then scribbled some calculations on a sheet of paper as Clement looked on, worried. Nobli looked up then.

"About .26 seconds," he said.

Clement let out a relieved sigh. "Remind me never to hire you again," he said.

Nobli laughed.

"You've forgotten about my sardonic sense of humor?"

"I never knew you had one." Nobli looked at his captain again. "Just don't let your hotshot pilot ruin my engine, and we'll get along fine," he said.

"I take it the thrusters can get us airborne in a hurry?"

"Absolutely. The mass of Bellus is slightly less than two-thirds of Earth, so escaping should be easy enough. Firing up the LEAP drive is no problem, *once* we're in space, and we have someplace to go."

Both men knew what the next question was.

"And the weapon?" asked Clement.

"Again, you'll have it when you need it, Captain. But we both know it's never been fired, and using it that way is only theoretical."

"Then let's pray we never have to use it," Clement said on his way back out the door.

With five hours to go until the Earth Ark had to make her initial fire to establish orbit around Bellus, Clement and his bridge crew were ready to descend to the surface. After verbally running an all-systems check with his crew and ordering all unnecessary (for the landing) personnel to their bunks to strap in, Clement turned his ship over to Mika Ori.

"Take her down, Pilot. And don't break her," he said.

"Aye, Captain," said Mika. Clement lay back deep in his safety couch while the pilot took over, activating the ship-wide com to address the full crew. "Course nominal on descent. Speed also nominal for this maneuver. Atmospheric insertion will occur in one minute, six seconds." Clement tried not to count off the seconds, leaving the calculating to the ship's timer. "We'll make one full orbit while we pass from the dark side of Bellus around to the light side a second time. By then our deceleration should be complete enough for me to fire the braking thrusters and take operational control of our flight."

"Will we be visible to the Earth Ark if we use the atmosphere to brake?" asked Clement.

Ori muted the com to reply to her captain. "The first twenty seconds we'll be visible, but it will be against the light side of Bellus. After that we'll pass behind the event horizon to the dark side and they won't be able to track us. When we come around again our speed should be sufficiently slowed so that we won't be visible to even their best cameras, if we've guessed at their level of technology correctly."

*If,* thought Clement. *He hated that word.* He said nothing more as Ori guided the *Beauregard* into the upper atmosphere of Bellus. Suddenly he wanted a drink of the Argyle whiskey badly. He suppressed the impulse, with difficulty.

When she hit the atmosphere bubble the external monitors started to flare to life, showing views of reentry plasma as the technical displays lit up with valuable data and telemetry.

"Let me know when we're out of sight of the Ark," said Clement. The next few seconds were hell for him, not knowing if the enemy could see his ship lighting up like a flare in the daylight.

Seconds later, Ori spoke to the entire crew again as the ship started to shake. "It's going to get a little rough for the next forty-five seconds or so, then it should calm down," she said reassuringly. Clement glanced to his right to look at Yan. Her eyes were closed and she had a death grip on the arms of her safety couch, holding on for dear life as the ship shook ever more violently. He looked down at his own hands then and realized he was in a similar posture, and he forced himself to relax.

The bridge crew of the *Beauregard* rode out the remaining seconds in agony, then savored the pause as the ship stopped shaking and resumed a more peaceful ride.

"You have a thirty-second respite," came Ori's voice over the com. "Then I'll fire the rockets again and we'll make the majority of our final descent on the dark side." Clement swallowed, wondering again why he hadn't taken a hard drink before they started this process, then switched on his monitor to a visual view of the dark side of Bellus.

Since the planet was tidal-locked to its nearby red dwarf star (only 4.25 million kilometers away), the light side was always facing the star, and the dark side always facing away. While the light side received nearly seventy percent of standard luminosity (measured by Earth standard, of course), the dark side, technically, would receive none. But as Clement could see, there was some light, no doubt a reflection of the luminosity of the third habitable world in the Trinity system, Camus, and perhaps even the sixth planet, a larger world with a greenish, clouded atmosphere only 0.017 AU distant. What could be made out was a rocky terrain, with mountains and floes of ice all bathed in a deep ruby glow. It was a place worth exploring someday, *but not just now*, Clement reminded himself.

Presently the *Beauregard* slid deeper into Bellus' atmosphere and Ori fired the thrusters, pushing the ship lower. This time the burn seemed to last interminable minutes, the g-forces tugging at the crew while they braked and decelerated. By the time they came around the event horizon again and into the light side, the burn had ended and the gravity relented. Clement looked up to see Ori piloting his ship from her console.

"Braking maneuvers complete," she said over the com. "The ship is under my active control. We're at five thousand meters and dropping quickly. Estimate nine minutes to landing sight."

"Can they see us?" asked Clement.

"Doubtful," said Ori over the private com, "unless they have far better sensing equipment than they should have."

"Let's hope for that," replied Clement, then sat upright in his couch. The rest of the bridge crew followed suit with their captain. Clement glanced at Yan, whose eyes were red and watery, but she smiled wanly back at him without saying anything. He realized he was covered in sweat inside his navy fatigues, as likely was the rest of the crew.

Clement sat in silence as Ori guided the ship skillfully over a ridge of mountains and what looked to be green, junglelike vegetation, though Clement had only ever seen a jungle in education videos. Ceta, where he grew up, was a sparse and brown world, exactly the opposite of the Trinity worlds. Finally, as they broke through the cloud barrier, Clement could see their proposed landing sight, a land of three rivers converging in dappled orange sunlight. One of the tributaries fed into the main river via a spectacular waterfall. It was beautiful. "Do you have our landing sight, Mika?" said Clement.

"I do, sir. Setting her down won't be problem, sir, and there's plenty of cover. I could even put the *Beauregard* under that waterfall, if there's a big enough cave behind it."

"Not necessary, Pilot," he said, smiling. "Our original intended landing site will do just fine." And with that they all watched as Ori skillfully dropped the *Beauregard* from a hover mode, extending her landing legs and placing her right where her captain wanted her, in a clearing surrounded by trees. She landed and settled with a bump, Ori giving the final call of her narration.

"*Beauregard* is down. I repeat, *Beauregard* is down. Welcome to paradise, everyone."

At that Clement got up from his couch and started giving orders over the com. "Lieutenant Pomeroy, I want one last atmospheric check and virus scan. Middie Telco, correct that, Ensign Telco, organize a team and get some of those trees knocked down to provide us more cover, then deploy the shuttle, we might need her. Commander Yan"—he turned to his second-in-command—"prep an observation drone and get her ready to launch in one hour. I want to keep an eye on our friends up there," Clement said, pointing to the ceiling.

"Aye, sir," replied Yan, looking better every minute from the ordeal of landing. Then Clement looked around his bridge, as it came to life with activity.

The *Beauregard* was down.

# ☀**14**☀

An hour later and the *Beauregard* had her air cover, a high atmosphere drone with an exceptional high-definition camera. The first pictures showed the Earth Ark making steady progress to its insertion point for orbit around Bellus. Clement got his team moving quickly, prepping the shuttle in case it was needed, and to his surprise, Ensign Telco was readying another vehicle.

"What is that?" he asked of Telco, pointing to a large structure the ensign was building out of what looked like empty missile casings.

"A pontoon boat," said Telco.

"A what?"

"It's a boat that sort of glides over the water. We have them all over on Metairie," he said.

"Where did you get it?"

Telco puffed out his chest a bit. "I made it, sir."

"You . . . made it. Out of what?"

"Everything was on board, sir. I remembered from reading the manifest before we arrived in-system. I used spare missile casings for pontoons, used weapons crates to build the carriage, and Mr. Nobli supplied me with a spare pylon motor from the LEAP drive stores for the engine. I thought it could come in handy in case we went planet-side," he finished.

"That it could," said Clement. "How long until you can have it in the water?"

"Any time, sir. She's ready now."

"Capacity?"

Telco looked at his creation. "I can configure her for six, sir, if you want to include weapons and provisions."

"I do, Ensign. Keep her undercover for now, at least until the Ark ship makes her first pass. We might have use for her to get upriver after that."

"Will do, sir. And sir, she'll have a much lower heat profile than the shuttle, sir. Almost negligible."

Clement smiled at the ensign's youthful enthusiasm. "Carry on, Ensign," he said as Yan came up to him. They started walking back to the *Beauregard* together.

"You're not thinking of actually using that thing, are you?" she asked.

"It's an option, Commander. I do want to get upriver and see those settlements."

"Before or after the Ark ship passes?"

"After," Clement said, looking up to the twilight sky. "How much time do we have?"

"Mika says about two and a half hours."

"Let's get her battened down, and call back our drone."

"Yes, sir," she replied.

A look of concern crossed his face then, and he did his best to hide it from Yan.

The crew waited in the cargo hold for the Ark ship to pass. It was tense, and very quiet. Yan held up a finger to indicate the Ark would be right on top of them now. Every light, every system that could be shut down, was. Nobli had estimated that with the brush covering the *Beauregard* and the passing hours since she had gone cold that there was only a ten percent chance she'd be detected from space. But that surely wasn't the Ark ship's only means of detecting enemies, especially if she was a war ship.

Ten minutes after the Ark ship passed over their position, Clement ordered Telco to deploy his pontoon boat. Then he gathered with his command crew.

"We're going upriver to check out those settlements. It's about fifteen kilometers from here. How fast can your new boat go without creating a ruckus?" he said to Telco.

"At a safe speed of say, twenty klicks an hour, probably get there in about forty-five to fifty minutes," he said.

"Go fire her up," said Clement, nodding toward the boat. "We'll be there in five minutes."

Yan stepped up. "So who else gets to go on your little expedition?" she asked.

"Logically, you should stay behind and run the camp, but I know you want to go and frankly I could use your expertise. Mika and Ivan, I'll take you as well, since you both have some, uh, directional expertise."

"In other words, so we don't get lost," said Mika, teasing.

Clement smiled and nodded. "And lastly I want a field medic, so Lieutenant Pomeroy is in." He looked to his engineer.

"Oh, great," said Nobli sarcastically. "Just what I always wanted. My own command."

"Look, you're the best I have at organization. I want you to keep everybody busy setting up camp, establishing work shifts, and all of that. And keep the lights on minimum, just in case."

"Aye, sir," said Nobli, ever reluctant.

"Since this planet is tidal-locked to the star, it should never get either too light or too dark. Planets may pass between Bellus and the Trinity star from time to time. Remember this system has very tight orbits. Use that to your advantage, work at random times, keep energy expenditures to a minimum. Plan for that Ark to pass every . . . " he looked to Mika.

"Thirty-three minutes," she finished.

Clement nodded. "And no damn campfires," he said.

"Aye, sir," came Nobli's reply. Clement waved his crew toward the pontoon boat, then held back for a second.

"And Nobli, if they find you, if you've got incoming enemies, get the ship out of here. Even all the way back to Kemmerine if you have to. Understood?"

Nobli nodded reluctantly. "Understood, sir."

With that Clement made for the boat, where the crew had assembled and Ensign Telco had the engine rumbling quietly. He got on and helped push off into the gentle running waters of the river, the engine humming as they accelerated toward the settlement camp, and the unknown.

Thirty minutes in and five kilometers from the settlement Clement ordered Telco to slow the boat down. They'd seen precious little in the way of fauna, but Telco did spot some very terrestrial-looking river fish along the way. There was little in the way of insect life, with the banks of the river mostly inhabited by a mixture of tall grasses in green, purple and yellow. There were occasional breaks in the grass canopy but what glimpses they got of the river lowlands showed a mostly empty landscape of open meadows or stands of tropical-looking trees. Three klicks from the site of the settlement Clement ordered the boat to the shore and they started hiking inland. Mika peeled away her uniform jacket and tied it around her waist.

"God, fresh, humid, moist air again. I'd forgotten what a luxury it was," she said.

"It's beautiful here," agreed her husband as he walked up and put his arm around her.

"Let's stay focused," Clement said to the group. "Our objective is to observe these people and see what their function is, and identify if they're even human. We'll split up into pairs, spread ourselves out, and observe. Make for the settlement from three different directions, and stay in touch via your ear coms." Clement held his up so they could see it and then placed it in his ear.

Clement stayed the central course toward the settlement with Yan, while Mika and Ivan went to the right, with Telco and Pomeroy flanking left.

"It *is* beautiful here," Yan said as they made their way across the flat, grassy ground together in the dappled sunlight of Bellus. It was like pictures of the autumn season on the core planets that he had seen in school, only here, it had that golden-red glow all the time.

"Let's not get distracted," said Clement.

She responded by taking his hand as they walked. "Don't you ever enjoy a moment of peace and quiet?"

"Not when I'm exploring an unknown world filled with unknown people for the first time," he retorted, but he didn't pull his hand away. "For all we know they could think humans are delicious."

"Well, if you eat the right parts, I suppose that they are."

He shook his head in frustration at her. "You make my job very difficult, Yan," he said. She just smiled as they walked.

Presently they found themselves on softer ground. There were tall stalks of plant life ahead of them that had seemingly arranged themselves in a rough but orderly way. Clement stopped and kicked at the ground. It showed signs of having been recently turned.

"This is a crop field," he said, pushing his way through the plant stalks.

"How can you be sure?" asked Yan.

"I grew up on an agrarian planet, remember?"

He grabbed one of the stalks and pulled it toward him. It looked familiar. He ripped open a husk and it revealed the treasure inside. He showed it to Yan.

"This is corn," she said. "A hybrid I don't recognize, but undoubtedly corn."

Clement tapped his earpiece and got on his com. "We've found crops," he said. "Looks like an Earth-type corn. I'm afraid we have to assume that these camps were either from an earlier colonization, or from a military operation of some kind. Raise your awareness, and make sure your sidearms are loaded." The others all reported the same type of findings back, with crops like pumpkin, cabbage, and cauliflower. This definitely seemed like an Earth-seeded colony.

When Clement emerged from the cornfield, he made his way to Yan, who was staring at an amber glow of light a few hundred yards in the distance. "Yan, what are you—"

"Shhh—" she said, finger to her mouth. "Listen." She took him by the hand again.

In the distance, Clement could hear what amounted to the gentle splashing of water, and something else. The sound of what appeared to be a woman's voice.

She was singing.

They crawled to within about ten meters of what was clearly a water pond, hiding themselves in the tall grass. An amber glow came from the water, some form of bioluminescence it seemed, which lit up the pond around its edges. The singing was louder here, a lilting, content, and even evocative high sound. It was almost like the voice was in a state of harmony with the bioluminescent life-forms. They glowed brighter and warmer with each rising of her song.

Clement and Yan cleared some of the grass, to get a glimpse of what was making such a beautiful noise.

"There," Yan pointed. Across the small pond a creature was standing in the water, halfway immersed in the amber glow. It had long gray or white hair, a skin tone that matched the amber of the water, and it was playing as it sang, gently splashing the water. Then it turned to face them, looking around as if it had heard a noise.

It didn't take a genius to figure out they were staring at a woman, a humanoid woman. Two rounded and very feminine breasts danced buoyantly in the light as she resumed her playing and singing. Her rib cage was positioned exactly as a human woman's would be. She had two long arms, two legs, shoulders, and even a belly button. Her pubis was covered in the same fine white hair as was on her head. She frolicked in the water, diving in and then popping back up, swimming back and forth from side to side.

"Do you think—" started Clement, whispering, before Yan covered his mouth with her hand.

The creature stopped for a moment, looking in their direction as if it heard something again. They both hid, trying not to be detected. After a moment, the singing and splashing of the water resumed again. Clement looked to Yan and then leaned in to whisper in her ear, even quieter than before.

"That's a woman," he said. And she was, a beautiful, youthful, and very human-looking woman. Yan just nodded as he pulled back and they resumed observing her.

She played for a few more minutes and then decided to lie down on a sandy beach on the far side of the pond. They watched as she ran her hands through her long, wet hair, then she settled back on her elbows. After a few minutes of this, she lay down completely flat. They watched as a hand slid down her body, to her pubis, and she began a gentle rubbing of the area.

"No!" whispered Yan. This time Clement covered *her* mouth. They watched her together, the two of them moving closer together with each passing second, as the woman slowly pleasured herself, reaching her climax within a few short minutes.

As she lay basking in the afterglow, a new rustling came from the tall grass. A male emerged, the same amber skin, the same white-colored hair. She rose and greeted him with a passionate kiss, wrapping her arms around his neck. After a moment of kissing and rising passion, they ran into the pond to play together, hand in hand. "Well," whispered Yan, "They do make them handsome here on this world."

"You mean they make them hung," he whispered back. Yan smiled playfully at Clement, then reached out to him.

"No need for embarrassment," she said. She slid closer to him, and he looked at her. She was beautiful, and what was going on in the pond was epically romantic. They continued to watch together as the couple engaged in flagrant and unabashed lovemaking, with her straddling him as he entered her, holding her just above the water line of the pond, her hands on his shoulders.

Several minutes passed as the couple engaged in a rousing session of sex play, including multiple positions and vigorous exertion on both their parts. When the moment of climax came they embraced each other, then slowly slid back into the water together. The amber glitter of the bioluminescence in the pool seemed drawn to them and they slowly rolled together in the afterglow.

"It's bliss," whispered Yan, holding Clement as close as he would let her. After a few more minutes of kissing, the couple left the pond together, hand in hand, chattering in a peculiar language as they walked off into the distance.

Clement looked to Yan and she leaned in and kissed him hard before he could stop her, and frankly, he didn't want to. He was aroused to the point of wanting to just let go with her, but he stopped himself.

"Not an option, Commander," he said. "You know that."

She blew out a hard breath of frustration and rolled onto her back, looking up at the stars. "Now I understand why you drink," she said. He was about to respond when they were both surprised by the flushed faces of Ivan Massif and Mika Ori looking down on them.

"Did you see that?" exclaimed Mika in a whispered voice. Both Clement and Yan scrambled to their feet. Mika and Ivan both had the warm glow of sex about them. They had clearly experienced the same inspiration as the couple and had acted on it. Who was he kidding? They always acted on it.

"We did," answered Clement, running his free hand through his hair. "Obviously."

"I see you two were inspired by the . . . display," commented Yan as she tidied up her tunic.

"How could you not be?" said Mika, smiling from ear to ear. "Weren't you?"

Clement shook his head. "Command protocol, and all that," he said.

"I can't believe you let that get in the way," teased Mika.

"As if you two need any excuse," said Clement, looking around, hoping to change the subject. "Where are Telco and Pomeroy?"

"Busy, if they were watching," joked Mika.

"I doubt that. Pomeroy prefers women," Clement said, then hit his com to call them. There was no answer for several minutes until Pomeroy came on, quite breathlessly.

"We'll be with you . . . in a few minutes," she said, then cut the line.

"Apparently she's had a change of heart," said Yan impishly. Clement just looked perplexed. When the two finally appeared they both looked as though they'd had a hot and heavy encounter. Clement ordered Telco to raise the ship and get a report, and he walked off to do so, while the rest of them interrogated Pomeroy.

"Um, that's not . . . like you, typically, is it?" started Clement.

"No, it's not," agreed Pomeroy. "I've played with Telco before, but with another woman present. I do have a theory though. That bioluminescent organism, it appeared to have an effect on our randy couple, and on me," she said. "I mean, I'm not normally attracted to men, but I couldn't keep my hands off Telco. Permission to take a sample, sir?"

"Of?" replied Clement, smirking.

Pomeroy sighed. "The bioluminescence, of course," she said.

"Granted," replied Clement. Pomeroy stormed off to the pond.

At Telco's return he reported back that everything was normal at the ship. This gave Clement free reign to explore further.

"So what do we do next?" asked Yan. Clement nodded as Pomeroy returned with her water samples.

"We go on," he said. "And follow our randy friends to their home."

"And then?" asked Yan. Clement shrugged his shoulders, looking around at his crew of intrepid explorers.

"We make contact."

# ✵ 15 ✵

Twenty minutes later and they were looking down on a large camp of rounded huts made of wood and dried straw. There was a path that led into the center of the camp where a bonfire burned in a pit with several people gathered around it. Men, women, and children dressed in simple clothing chattered around the fire in their language, eating, drinking, and socializing. The rounded huts went off into the distance, as did multiple pathways, and there were many other bonfires burning off in the distance.

Clement signaled his troupe to the ground with a silent hand gesture. He whispered to his team to keep their chances of being exposed to a minimum. "Observations," he said, looking from each one of his team to other. Pomeroy spoke first, quietly.

"This is clearly a simple culture. They don't seem to want for much in terms of food, fresh water, and the like. They obviously learned at some point how to cultivate crops, and the near-constant climate gives them no great challenges to overcome. The food is always plentiful, the water always flows . . ." She trailed off.

"In other words, no upward pressure on their society to move forward?" observed Clement.

Pomeroy nodded. "No need for innovation, no need to evolve, no new discoveries to kick them in the butt to move their culture upwards."

"Sounds like paradise," said Yan.

"If you're a type B personality," commented Clement.

"This lack of innovation may be bred into them over many generations," offered Pomeroy.

Clement turned to Telco, looking for a different perspective. "What do you see, Ensign?"

Telco looked around for a moment. "Looks like a stable society. No obvious predators. And the people seem happy," he said.

"Observe. Estimate the population," ordered Clement.

Telco took a few seconds to look around them. "I'd estimate around fifty of the huts. Seven to eight people per structure, so say population of this village would be around three hundred fifty."

Clement shook his head. "Look again." The closest bonfire had fifteen to twenty people around it with five huts nearby. There were several young couples going in and out of each hut, children running about from hut to hut, people moving around at a frequent pace. "I'd say more like ten to twelve people per hut, multiple families in each, or at least multiple sex partners. My best guess would be that we have a population of at least five hundred."

Telco nodded. "I see it now, sir," he acknowledged.

Anthropology lesson over, Clement turned to Ivan Massif. "Thoughts, Navigator?"

Massif pointed to the sky. "See that dark object?" They all looked skyward. There were affirmative grunts all around. "That's the next planet in, Alphus. My guess is it will partially obscure the Trinity star in about twenty hours. That will create a significant twilight at that time. The two inner planets also provide a nighttime obscurity on a regular, periodic schedule. I can calculate it when we get back."

"So it will get dark? Or darker," stated Yan.

"As close to dark as it gets here. Remember, all these planets are tidal-locked to the star, the same face toward the sun at all times. But with the planets so close together, I'm sure there are multiple occultations happening all the time. That would be an opportune time to return and observe, and perhaps introduce ourselves."

Clement agreed. "Let's come back at that time and evaluate what we have here," he said.

"But we're here now," said Yan.

"And we can come back," replied Clement. "I think this trip has been, uh, eventful as it is. Let's take what we have and get back to our ship. Agreed?"

They all nodded.

"Any chance of stopping by that pond one more time on the way back?" said Mika, impishly.

"You're insatiable," said Clement, shaking his head as he stood, then signaled his team to move out.

They were halfway back to the pontoon boat when Nobli called in his alert. They'd picked up a drone on the scanners, heading their way.

"Lock the ship down, we'll be back as soon as we can get there," ordered Clement. Nobli acknowledged and Clement ordered his team to double-time back to the boat. Once aboard they shoved off quickly and headed downriver, but Clement ordered Telco to slow to half speed. Metal objects moving at speed could easily be picked up by a sophisticated drone, and Clement had to assume the Earth Ark builders had sophisticated military equipment.

The ride was tense as Nobli called in periodic updates. The drone ended up passing about thirty klicks south of their location, but if it were using an overlapping orbit to try and detect the *Beauregard*, it would move farther north in latitude on the next pass, and depending on the size of the overlap, it *could* detect the ship on the next pass.

"We have to take precautions," he said to Yan after he ordered Telco to push the boat to full speed.

"What about action against the drone? Can we take it out?" she asked.

"That could give away both our presence and our position."

"Could?" Clement shrugged.

"It would be a risk," Nobli said.

"What about using our own drone to take it out before it gets near the ship?"

Clement looked at her. "They probably have more than one, so we would just end up without a drone. It would put us at a disadvantage," he said in a dismissive tone. Clement was a man who had been in many battles. Yan clearly was not, and as much as he liked her, the gap in their combat experience was still vast. Yan gave him a sour look.

"I'm just trying to be helpful," she said.

"I understand," said Clement, then turned his attention back to the progress of the boat.

They arrived back at the *Beauregard* a few minutes later. Clement ordered his crew to prep for discovery by the drone on its next pass, which would be in thirty-two minutes.

"What are your orders, Captain?" said Nobli, thankfully relinquishing command back to his friend.

Clement took Nobli to the side. "If we shut down the *Beauregard*, went completely dark, what are the odds that drone would detect the ship?"

"I'd say less than fifty-fifty, but if we went completely cold it could take us up to three hours to refire the ship," the engineer said.

"Understood. But right now I'd take those odds over being discovered by that Earth Ark and her troops. And there's another complication. We discovered natives. They appear human, or at least humanoid," Clement said.

An astonished look crossed Nobli's face. "Natives? Human natives? You mean colonists, don't you?"

Clement shook his head. "I'm not so sure unless they were biologically modified for this planet in some way. We need to know more. I'm thinking that we should abandon the ship temporarily, and perhaps mix in with them, to study them some more. What do you think?"

"I think this mission has gone seriously off-kilter," said Nobli.

"Can't disagree with you there. Give me a number. How long to go cold?"

"If I shut down everything, maybe two hours before the ship's radiation signatures would dissipate to background levels."

"That's close enough for me."

At that Clement brought the entire crew together in the clearing outside the ship. "The Earth Ark drone will pass over us in"—he looked down at his watch—"twenty-eight minutes. I'm ordering Engineer Nobli to shut down the *Beauregard* completely, to go cold, essentially. That will aid us in avoiding detection, but it's no guarantee. It will take approximately two hours for the ship to go completely cold, and we will require up to three hours to refire her and get her back into action once we return. So, there is a risk if we are attacked. My plan is for us to spread out into small groups of three to four individuals, and, using the natural wood and brush from the planet, light small fires to make it appear as though we are a small settlement of natives. Don't use any devices that would burn hotter than a natural fire. This should distract from any residual heat signatures the ship will be emitting and hopefully the drone will just pass us by. Once the drone has passed we'll begin the journey to the native encampment and try to contact the natives there. If they are friendly, we should be able to mix in with them and keep ourselves safe for a while."

"To what end?" questioned Yan. "I mean, what's our ultimate goal here?"

Clement looked to his first officer. "To keep the Earth Ark from detecting us and to determine what their mission in the Trinity system really is, then to try and counter it," he said.

"What about getting home?" asked Ensign Adebayor from the crowd.

"Getting home is our ultimate consideration," said Clement. "Survival is our immediate one. Since we are no longer under the protection of the flag of the 5 Suns Alliance Navy, we have to assume they will consider us as hostile as well. It seems likely that the navy, or rather, Fleet Admiral DeVore, never intended us to survive our first contact with the Earth Ark, which they surely knew we would encounter. So the question now is, what exactly is 'home' for us at this moment?"

"That's a question for another day," cut in Yan. Clement was thankful for her assistance in swaying the crew.

"Any further questions?" Clement stared down the crew, looking at each member, trying to detect dissent. He found none. "Then let's get started." He checked his watch again. "We now have twenty-five minutes. Form small groups, spread out and light fires, but be sure not to use anything that would give off an artificial heat signature. We want that drone to think of us just like the natives, not a sophisticated navy crew. Go!" he commanded, then raised his voice. "And be sure and take firearms, personal rations for three days, and any equipment that might come in handy in assessing the natives, as long as it carries a low energy signature." he said. And with that they all scattered.

With seven minutes to go Nobli sealed up the *Beauregard* and then was off with his group. Clement, Yan, Pomeroy, and Telco made a foursome and started away from the ship on the near bank of the river. Telco had covered the pontoon boat under shrubs and grasses.

Clement observed small fires burning bright against the dimming sky as one of the two inner planets of the Trinity system was partially obscuring the star, making for a brief twilight effect. He sat down around the campfire next to Yan.

Telco for his part was following Pomeroy around like a puppy dog, no doubt enamored by her after their brief solo affair at the pond. Pomeroy seemed indifferent to his presence as she was no doubt returning to her previous preferences for female companionship, now free of the aphrodisiac effects of the pond bioluminescence. But she kept the young ensign busy with small tasks like collecting wood for the fire while she set up some of her biological-testing equipment.

Yan sat silently next to Clement as he tried to track the Earth Ark drone with conventional field glasses. He had a pair with him that had been a memento of his father's time in the 5 Suns Alliance service and he'd grabbed them on his way out of the ship. Any powered glasses could have no doubt been detected by the passing drone.

"She should have passed over by now," he said, "but I didn't see her."

"Perhaps you're not as good with those as you thought," Yan said.

Clement dropped the glasses and looked at her. "I used to track communications satellites with these, home back on Ceta, when I was a kid. They're good enough. And any drone moving on a straight-line course should be detectable with the naked eye, let alone an assisted one," he said, then returned to his tracking. The "night" sky of Bellus was clear enough and dark enough that detection should have been possible, unless the drone was specifically designed for stealth, which a military one might be.

"There she is!" said Clement, pointing at the sky, picking up the drone and tracking her across the starfield. "She's moving fast and she's low, maybe fifteen hundred meters or less. She may not detect us at all," he said. Presently he handed Yan the glasses and directed her where to look.

"I see her," said Yan. "Can she even detect us at that speed?"

"She can probably detect the fires, but I doubt she'd be able to take a count of our personnel. We'll probably just show up as a series of heat-signature blobs unless they really enhance the images. That could take hours of work, assuming they have similar technology to ours, and I doubt they'd bother if there's nothing anomalous on the scans. Her vector should take her well north of us on the next pass. We should be safe, for now."

Yan handed him back the glasses as he tracked the drone until she disappeared over the horizon. Clement got on the com system and declared the all-clear and for his team of twenty-two souls to re-form.

"Telco, Pomeroy, Yan and I will head up the river to the settlement in the pontoon boat and make first contact with the natives. Ivan and Mika can direct the rest of you to the camp. That will give us about five hours to smooth things over with the natives before you arrive. Be aware of your surroundings at all times and don't take any chances. This planet seems like a paradise, with no large predators of any kind, but be on alert. Again, small groups would be best; spread out and then gather at the observation point above the settlement and wait for instructions from one of us. Good luck, and we'll see you at the camp," he said.

With that the four of them loaded the pontoon boat with the equipment Pomeroy had brought from the ship, started the motor and shoved off for the settlement. A few minutes in and the twilight sky was glowing amber.

"This is almost romantic," Yan said, leaning into him with her body. Clement nodded, but he didn't encourage her to come closer.

"Almost," he said, looking to the sky.

"Almost."

# ☆16☆

They stowed the boat and covered it near the same riverbank they had landed on the first time and made their way back toward the settlement camp. It was darker than before due to the occlusion of the inner planets, and walking was slower this time around. They arrived at the pond once again and Pomeroy stopped to take some additional samples of the water. The bioluminescence was even brighter than before and bathed them all in its amber glow. Clement detected a scent he hadn't before, sweet and aromatic, and it created a taste in his mouth, almost like vanilla. He noticed Yan lingering near him, touching his skin at every opportunity. He found himself aroused by her mere presence, but he fought off any baser thoughts and tried to focus on the mission at hand. It was difficult.

As they departed from the pond to head to the settlement he took Pomeroy aside.

"This bioluminescence, it has an airborne component, doesn't it?" he asked.

"Yes, I think so. I'll have to conduct some more tests, but I'm pretty sure it's got an aphrodisiac quality to it," she replied.

"No doubt about that. Plus, I smelled a vanilla scent, even tasted it in my mouth." She nodded.

"I did as well. And Ensign Telco's biceps were looking pretty tempting to me again," she joked.

"I wonder if that could be natural?"

"You mean my attraction to Telco? Unlikely."

Clement shook his head. "No, I meant the bioluminescent aphrodisiac," he deadpanned.

"Oh. I don't know," she admitted. "I'll need time to set up my equipment to come to any conclusions, but it certainly is a convenient coincidence if you wanted people to be fruitful and multiply."

"Well, I hope we can get you that time when we reach the settlement."

"Aye, sir," she said as they walked on.

A few minutes later they gathered on the outskirts of the settlement camp, looking down on the communal fire from a nearby hillside. Things had gone quiet coincident with the occultation of the Trinity star. It was noticeably darker, and it seemed many of the tribe must have been sleeping. Clement looked at his team.

"Yan and I will go in first and see how they greet us. You two will follow once I give the signal. Stay out in the open but out of the camp until I signal you in. We won't know how they will react to strangers until, well, until we know. If anything goes wrong . . . "

"Understood, sir," said Pomeroy, tapping her sidearm cobra pistol. Clement nodded and took Yan by the hand, trying to look as friendly as possible, as they made their way toward the dwindling bonfire at the center of the first group of huts.

"Trying to start something, sir?" Yan teased.

Clement shook his head. "I think you know my stance on that by now, Commander. Just trying to look as friendly as possible to meet the natives."

As they approached the camp there were only three people in a rough circle around the fire, which was attended by an older woman with distinctly gray hair and a couple of young children, a boy and a girl, perhaps only five standard years old or so. The woman had loose-fitting clothing that appeared to be woven covering her body. When she saw Clement and Yan approaching she stood up and chattered something to the children, then raised her voice slightly. People began to stir in the huts at the sound of her voice. Clement and Yan came right up to the fire as she stared at them approaching her, still holding hands. They stood there, smiling, as adults and children of various ages started coming out of the huts. The looks on their faces were ones of astonishment and curiosity. They talked amongst themselves, looking and pointing fingers at the two strangers.

"Their language . . . " started Yan, "I can almost make out . . . it sounds similar to Old Imperial Korean, like the twenty-second-century language we found on the Ark."

"Can you talk to them?"

"I'll try," said Yan. She stepped forward, toward the bonfire, and said words Clement didn't understand to them. There were surprised looks, then a few laughs.

"What did you say?" asked Clement.

"I tried to say that we are friends, and asked if they would welcome us. Obviously, I got something wrong."

"Try again."

Yan turned to them again and spoke. This time there were nods and more smiles.

"I told them there were about twenty of us coming, and could they accommodate us," she said.

A young woman stepped forward and spoke to Yan in their language. "What did she say?" asked Clement.

"I think . . . she wants to know if we're the ones who were watching her at the pond," Yan said. "I guess we weren't as quiet as we thought."

"I guess not. Tell her it was you and I. Be honest," Clement said.

Yan spoke again, and the girl laughed, then turned to the gathering crowd and spoke to them, and then they all laughed. She turned back to Yan and said something else.

"She wants to know if we enjoyed watching them," said Yan, turning to Clement with a smirk on her face. Clement just shrugged; he couldn't keep himself from smiling, embarrassed they had been found out. Yan stated a positive response, and the crowd laughed again. Then the woman came forward and gave Yan a hug.

"Ask them if we are welcome. Tell them we are here to learn about their people," said Clement.

Yan, still in the girl's arms, asked her question. There were nods and welcome grunts all around. The girl pulled away from Yan, who was quickly surrounded by people touching her dark hair and coveralls, and came to Clement. She hugged him and then kissed him on the cheek, leading him by the hand back to the gathering crowd around the fire.

Fifteen minutes later they were sitting around the fire eating berries, some sort of baked cake and fruits. Yan was conversing with the girl, whom Clement decided to call Mary. Clement had used his com to call in Pomeroy and Telco, and had relayed the friendliness of the natives to the rest of his approaching crew.

Communication was slow as Yan was the only one with the necessary language skills. Pomeroy had set up her equipment and was busy running tests, taking DNA swab samples from willing natives. Ensign Telco was very popular with the ladies, who seemed enamored with his dark hair and large, broad shoulders. He was taller than most of the males at six foot four. The men seemed to average about six one, the women were tall at five nine or five ten. There was a general uniformity of looks as well: the amber-toned skin, light hair, and they were almost all, both male and female, good-looking and well proportioned. Clement had his suspicions about these people and their origins, but he was willing to wait on Pomeroy's test results before expressing them. And one other oddity was that they had no proper names, at least not that Yan could figure out.

Within a few hours the rest of the crew arrived and Clement had them spread out among the settlement, to make friends and learn what they could. Mary, for her part, stayed with him and Yan almost exclusively, inviting others over when Yan had a question she could not answer.

After a few hours of questioning a picture of the settlers was beginning to form. They referred to themselves as the descendants of the "First Landers." It was unclear what this meant, and they had very little concept of numbers, but Clement and Yan suspected that the First Landers were the original group of colonists who had come to Bellus from "somewhere else," probably Earth, they surmised. It appeared as though the original colony had failed and the survivors had spread out until they occupied a large portion of the fruitful plain they lived on. They also were told of the "Hill Place," where the original colony had either been or had a base. Clement determined they would make a trek to the Hill Place in due time, if it could be found.

As one of the inner worlds occulted the Trinity star again and things began to get darker, the crowd quieted down and returned to their huts to sleep or conduct other activities, taking many of their new companions from the *Beauregard* with them. Mary, however, took Yan by the hand and started with her out of the camp, toward the pond.

"Going somewhere together?" asked Clement mischievously.

Yan turned back, smirking. "Oh," she said, "are you jealous?"

Clement looked at Mary, and her barely-there clothing. "Very," he said. "These people seem to have a remarkably open sexuality."

"So I've noticed." Yan turned back and spoke to Mary, who chattered back at her, smiling. "She said you can come along, if you'd like," said Yan. Clement looked to Yan and the beautiful Mary.

"I don't want to be the third wheel—" he was interrupted by Mary's chattering again. Yan said something back to her, and the conversation went on like that, back and forth for a few moments.

"I think she feels sorry for you."

Clement hung his head. "I feel sorry for me too." He waved them on, then turned toward one of the beds in an empty hut. "Good night, Commander."

"I want you to know this is only for anthropological research," Yan said as he walked away.

"Of course it is," he said. Then Mary giggled, and the two women sauntered off together.

When Clement awoke he was still alone in the hut and it was "day," or what passed for daytime, outside. He rose and went to the communal food tray and ate. Eventually Yan turned up.

"You're awake," she said. "I guess you wouldn't have been much fun last night. You needed the rest, hmm?" He looked at his watch.

"I slept a standard eight hours," he said.

"Well, that's not standard for them. Mary was awake after three hours, as soon as it got lighter. I managed another two after that. I'm guessing this constant light-and-dark cycle plays hell with their circadian rhythms," she replied.

Clement gave her a quizzical look. "It doesn't seem to affect them. They seem to rest when they want to," he said.

"Yes." Yan looked up at the gentle salmon-colored sky. "Maybe this is Paradise," she said.

"Could be. Um, does Paradise have a latrine?" Yan smiled and pointed behind the row of huts.

"That way," she said.

Clement nodded. "When I get back I want to form a team and find this 'Hill Place.'"

"We'll be here, Captain," she said, smiling again.

After concluding his business, Clement called his team together and picked himself, Yan, Mary, Pomeroy, and Telco to go to the Hill Place. Mary assured them (through Yan) that she could find it. Pomeroy loaded up Telco with her technical equipment and Clement added a penetrating sonic radar–mapping kit. The young ensign took it all in stride.

On the way up, Pomeroy informed him of her initial test results.

"As you may have suspected, they are absolutely human in every way, but they seem to have been specifically adapted to this world, down to the melanin in their skin and the size of their eyes to adjust to the slightly darker sun," she said.

"Are they clones?" Clement asked.

Pomeroy shook her head no. "More likely . . . genetically engineered specifically for this world," she said.

"A eugenics program?" Pomeroy responded with a shrug.

"I'm no history expert, but it does seem to be in line with what Yan tells me about this ancient Korean empire on Earth."

Clement thought on that for a moment, then:

"What do you think the purpose was in putting them here? If we assume this planet, and perhaps the others, Alphus and Camus, were seeded with human life, what was the intended outcome?" he asked.

Pomeroy got a frown on her face. "I can only conclude they were put here as an advance population, a workforce of some kind."

Clement nodded. "Slaves?" he questioned. "But why such a long gap between the original seeding and the arrival of an overlord force? According to what Mary said last night they have been here for many generations."

"Could be lots of reasons. War back home, technological setback, a natural disaster on Earth. We just don't know. But it seems likely the people here were abandoned for at least a couple of centuries."

"Until now."

"Until now," she agreed.

"And now the masters have come back to claim their property, and the only thing that stands in their way, is us," said Clement, pointing at his chest.

"For the moment," replied Pomeroy. Clement thanked her and then caught up with Yan and Mary, who were busy chatting as they held hands, walking up the trail together.

"Can you ask her how much farther it is to the Hill Place?" said Clement. Yan chattered to Mary and Mary responded with a shrug.

"She said 'a bit more distance,' if that helps?"

Clement shook his head. "It does not."

By Clement's watch it took another thirty minutes of crisscrossing switchbacks before they reached a flat mountain plain. Another ten minutes after that and they finally reached the Hill Place.

What they found was an abandoned bunker of stone and concrete with a glass dome that had collapsed over years of decay. The bunker sat on a high rock ledge, looking out over the fertile valley below. Clement led the team to an overlook where he used his field glasses to survey the terrain below. It was low, flat land broken only by rivers and the occasional dot of light representing the odd settlement or two. Presently he handed the glasses to Telco. "What do you make of that plain, Ensign?"

Telco scanned the valley from left to right. "I'd say it's about one hundred fifty klicks across, sir. I count about a dozen settlements of various sizes, but there are probably more."

"Estimated population?" Telco put the glasses down and turned to his commander.

"Judging by the size of our camp, I'd estimate up to fifteen thousand, sir," he said.

Clement nodded approval at Telco's assessment and then proceeded inside the bunker with the rest of the team. The ruin was essentially empty, with very little in the way of equipment or any kind of recognizable technology. He ordered Yan and Pomeroy to spread out while he and Telco explored what seemed to be the main nerve center of the base. After thirty minutes of fruitless searching, he called them both back.

"Anything?" he asked.

"I found what appeared to be a space for a possible birthing center, a large refrigeration chamber, and the like. Beyond that . . ." She trailed off.

"Yan?"

"What looked like probable barracks for about thirty people. I suspect this was originally a camp for scientists. Probably where the original colony was set up. I'd speculate that as the population grew they were eventually sent down into the valley to live. This base was probably evacuated once it became clear that a follow-up mission wasn't forthcoming," she said.

"They couldn't survive up here—no place for growing crops and the like. Once they ran out of rations they had no choice but to join the populace on the valley floor. Eventually, the succeeding generations likely forgot what their original mission even was," speculated Clement.

"That does fit with what Mary has told me of their legends surrounding this place."

Clement looked at the three women, then turned to Telco. "Get me that sonic-mapping kit," he said to the young ensign. Telco responded quickly by unpacking the device and assembling it, then powered it up and handed it to Clement. Yan sent the ensign out to keep watch on the valley below while the adults continued their survey. Mary followed Telco back outside, apparently uninterested in what they were doing in the lab.

Clement turned the device around the room. It showed nothing but rock and concrete, except for one wall. "What do you make of this, Pomeroy?" he asked his science tech.

She came over and he handed her the bulky device. She scanned the wall at eye level, then took a few steps toward the wall. "I see a doorway, sir, covered up by the concrete." Then she pointed the device to the floor. "I can definitely make out a stairway leading down, sir, but the range of this device is only about ten meters."

"Down to where?" asked Yan.

Clement came up and confirmed Pomeroy's reading, then changed the mode of the device to deep-penetrating radar and handed it back to her.

"Try it now," he said.

Pomeroy looked down again, then let out a soft gasp of surprise. "Jesus, sir! There's all kinds of superstructure here, likely metal, beneath us, up the hill—Christ, it's all around us like latticework, sir!"

Clement nodded. It was what he had expected to find. He had Pomeroy give the device to Yan for a third view.

"This is an arcology," she confirmed. "An engineered structure."

"Pomeroy, how high is this 'hill'?" asked Clement.

"My measurements from the camp were twelve hundred meters, sir, almost precisely," she said.

"And this laboratory?"

"Three hundred fifty meters up, sir."

Clement nodded his head. "This entire hill, this mountain, is artificial."

"But to what purpose?" asked Yan.

"That's to be determined, Commander. One thing is sure, though: Earth did not have the technology to build this kind of structure back when the 5 Suns colonies were founded four centuries ago." He instructed Pomeroy to record the scans she was making and save all the telemetry for further analysis.

As Pomeroy was finishing her scans Clement was about to give further orders when he heard Telco calling them from the ledge. They scrambled out together.

"Something going on at the far side of the valley, sir," he said, handing Clement the field glasses. Clement looked to where Telco had pointed. There was a flashing of light and the distant crackle of ordnance, with smoke rising from the ground. Clement looked to the red-sunset sky. Streaks of yellow could be seen heading for the ground, descending through the thick, warm atmosphere.

"What is it?" asked Yan.

Clement scanned the sky. Dozens of ships were descending now. "Beachhead. They're landing," he said. "Ensign Telco, you and Lieutenant Pomeroy will stay here and man this observation post until relieved. I want details on the scale of this landing. Commander Yan and the native and I will return to the camp and began prepping the people for evacuation. Stay sharp, both of you, and be prepared to make for the ship at a moment's notice."

"Aye, sir," they both responded.

He handed the glasses back to Telco.

"Do you think they'll come here, sir?" asked Pomeroy.

"I hope not. But we have to be prepared. Do your duty. Keep track of the amount of force they're bringing to bear. I'll be in touch by com at the first opportunity after we assess the people's ability to evacuate."

Yan looked to Mary. "They may not even understand the concept of an attack. They've lived in peace and harmony for generations," she said.

"Then you'll have to help them understand," he replied, then took her by the arm as they moved out, Mary trailing a few steps behind them.

"How can I do that? They don't understand complex concepts like war, or even a ship from space," Yan said.

"We have to protect them any way we can, Yan. This is not merely a landing by the Earth Ark forces, it's an invasion," he said. Then he let her go, and they started swiftly back down the mountainside.

# ✹17✹

Telco called in and reported that landings had occurred near three of the larger native settlements in the valley, but he couldn't be sure what the size and scope of the invasion force was, or what the Earth Ark troops were doing with the people. Clement had his suspicions.

Once back in camp Clement ordered Yan to work with Mary to address the people and warn them of what would no doubt be an impending attack. Most of the natives in the camp just looked confused by what they were told. Explaining things the settlers had no concept of was proving difficult. After a few minutes of watching and observing and feeling useless, Clement took Nobli aside.

"Hassan, what's the possibility of getting our drone up to surveil the Earth Ark forces? Find out what they're up to?"

"Well, none at the moment, sir. We'll have to get back to the ship and fire her auxiliary power unit up before we can activate the drone. And even then I'd recommend a high-altitude surveillance. It would lessen the chances that the drone would be picked up by the enemy. If they're engaged in rounding these people up and putting them to work as slave labor, I doubt they'll be paying much attention to the sky."

"But they still know that we're in the system somewhere, and they'll be keeping an eye out for us. I want to get a technical team together ASAP and get back to the ship and warm her up. We may have to leave the planet at a moment's notice. Take Adebayor, Mika, and Ivan with you; they could come in handy if we have to leave in a hurry. I'll send the technical personnel back as well, and any natives that will heed our warning. Prepare some space for them in the cargo bay. We may have some passengers," said Clement.

"Aye, sir."

With that Clement went to find Yan and Mary. The conversations with the native people were difficult, as they simply had no understanding of what an attack from space was. They were a peaceful people, with no needs or wants, and the concept was just completely foreign to them. Telco's last report indicated that three camps had been assaulted but further incursions seemed to have stopped for the moment. The Earth Ark crew appeared to be consolidating their positions before advancing, but Clement had little doubt that they would. He ordered Telco and Pomeroy to come back down from the Hill Place and prep the pontoon boat for an evacuation.

Within two hours most of the crew was gone on their way back to the *Beauregard* and only Mary seemed willing to go with them from the natives, and that seemed to be mostly related to her attachment to Yan. He ordered the last of his people to the pontoon boat, but told Yan to tell Mary to stay behind with her people. The native girl seemed disappointed, but she gave Yan a very sensual kiss goodbye and then made off for her camp.

Telco and Pomeroy arrived presently and with that they made for the pontoon boat and loaded up. They headed back to the ship as fast as the boat would go. Clement, for his part, could only be concerned about the native people he had left behind. They were complete innocents, and they would be no match for the Earth Ark troops, when and if they came.

Once back in camp at the *Beauregard* Clement ordered the boat to be abandoned, except for the engine, in case they returned and wanted to use it again. Telco wasn't happy at leaving his innovation behind, but started working on removing the engine immediately.

Nobli got the APU working and refired the drone, sending it up to a high orbit, then set its course for a pass over the three settlements the Earth Ark forces had attacked. They waited for reconnaissance photos to be downloaded from the drone. Nobli handed him the first one and Clement placed it down on a light table. It was not promising.

The settlements had been completely destroyed, likely by Directed Energy Weapons from space by the pattern of the burn marks. There was a single fenced-in area that stood as a prison yard, and Clement estimated close to two thousand potential slave workers were inside the barriers.

"Preparing the prisoners for work camps," said Clement. Nobli nodded.

Yan sighed. "Is this their destiny now?"

"Not if I can help it," said Clement. "These areas here and here"—he pointed to a group of large equipment stacks—"they look like heavy-drilling equipment, possibly for oil and mining operations."

"We know where they're going to get their workforce," said Nobli, irritated. "How do we stop them?"

"First, we get this ship powered up. Then we get her back in the air, and take it from there," responded Clement. He looked to his engineer. "How long?"

Nobli checked his watch. "Forty-five minutes estimated to operational status, sir. But then I'd like to run readiness checks, especially on the, uh, weapons system," he said.

"No time," replied Clement. "Every second we're on the ground our heat signature gives us away as an artificial object, a potential target. Get her up and running, and you have my release to cut any corners you like. While we're on the ground here we're sitting ducks."

"Aye, sir," said Nobli.

Clement looked to Yan. "We may be in for a rough ride. I want the whole bridge crew ready in half an hour, Commander," he said, returning to the formal use of her rank to indicate his seriousness with the situation.

"Understood, Captain," she said, then hesitated. "Are you ever going to talk to me about the new weapon you have devised?"

Clement shook his head. "Not now, Commander," he said, then walked away from her.

Thirty-two minutes later and the bridge crew was assembled with Yan at her station, Mika and Ivan at helm and navigation, and Ensign Adebayor at the engineering station. Clement took his command couch and called down on the com to Ensign Telco in the missile room.

"Prep conventional ordnance, Ensign," he said. "But don't load the launch tubes. I don't want us going down with our belly full up with live warheads."

"Understood, sir," replied Telco. "Conventional missiles will be ready on your order, sir, but not until."

Satisfied, Clement called down to his engineer to check on the drive and his new weapon.

"All drives are humming, sir. I can give you Xenon thrusters, the main Ion plasma drive, or the LEAP drive at your discretion, Captain. We can really go at any time now," said Nobli.

"And the weapon?" said Clement, quietly.

"Same status as the engines, sir."

"Confirmed, Engineer," he said, then signed off. He hit the ship-wide com. "All stations, prepare for launch. I say again, prepare for launch. Be advised the ship may come under attack at any time. Be ready. That is all," he stated. He turned to Yan. "Final report, Exec."

"My board is green, Captain," said Yan. Clement turned to Mika Ori at the helm.

"Take us up, Pilot," he ordered.

"Aye, sir," she replied, then started the launch process. She took the ship nearly straight up using the thrusters, then activated the Ion plasma once they cleared the atmosphere. Seven minutes later they were in a high orbit, nearly twenty-five hundred kilometers, where hopefully they'd be looking down on their enemies.

"Ensign Adebayor, your task is to find and identify the Earth Ark location," Clement ordered. Adebayor acknowledged and began her scan. "Navigator, maintain high orbit over the planet. I want us to have the high ground in any conflict."

"Aye, sir," said Massif.

Mika Ori put the ship in motion, taking a longitudinal path that would put them over the slave encampments in sixteen minutes.

"Report, Ensign," he demanded of Adebayor after a few minutes of silence.

"No indication of the Earth Ark in orbit over Bellus, sir. No trace gasses, no propellant expended. I can't find anything, sir," she said.

Clement looked to Yan.

"Has she moved on?"

"Possible," Yan replied. "Leave just enough muscle here to do the job, then return to their initial objective."

"Which was Alphus if I recall. But why? Bellus has everything, resource-wise, that they could want. Slave labor, water, ample food stocks, minerals, energy sources... Alphus is a rougher environment, with only a strip of land at the edges of the habitable zone fit for colonization."

"Something else must have come up."

"Like what?" He turned to Adebayor again. "Expand your search away from Bellus, Ensign. Find me that Ark ship."

"Aye, sir," Adebayor said, and started manipulating her displays. "Permission to use the radio telescope?"

"Granted," he said. The ship moved on with silence among the bridge crew, all busy doing their duties. It was Yan who announced the first signs of trouble.

"Forward scans from the drone are picking up blips over the settlements, Captain. By displacement they look like the light attack clippers, and..." she hesitated, "three larger displacement vessels in stationary orbits, Captain."

"Let me see them," Clement ordered. The tactical screen lit up with a description and cross section of the three unidentified vessels. They were about three times the size of the *Beauregard*, and they were emitting alarming radiation signals.

"Light cruisers by displacement, and they have nukes," said Clement, a worried tone in his voice. "How many LACs, Yan?"

"Twenty clippers, sir. And three large transport ships."

"Those will be for the ground troops for the initial occupation. Have they seen us yet?"

"No change in their status, sir," reported Yan.

"Full stop, Mika. Recall the drone. What's our distance to the flotilla?"

"Seven minutes, sir," said Yan.

"Ensign Adebayor, anything on the Earth Ark?"

"Nothing yet, sir."

"All right, they don't know we're here and so we have the advantage, for now." He went to the com and called down to Nobli. "I need you in the galley, Engineer." Nobli acknowledged. He followed that with a call down to Telco to join them. "Yan, Mika, to the galley please. Ivan, you and Adebayor maintain status here. Let me know immediately if anything changes."

"You don't want me in the war conference?" asked Ivan in his Russian accent. He seemed offended.

Clement had no time for his feelings. "This concerns the pilot, not the navigator, Ivan. I need you to stay on top of things here, and plot us an escape course, just in case things go wrong. I need my senior officers on one page," he said.

"Understood, sir," said Massif, reluctantly. Mika squeezed his arm as she slipped by, following Yan and Clement off the bridge and down the six steps to the galley deck.

Once they were all settled Clement started in immediately. "We're facing three light cruisers that have about three times our total conventional weapons displacement each and an additional twenty light attack clippers. Combined, their flotilla probably has anywhere from eight to ten times our ordnance to deliver, plus those cruisers have nukes and we don't. The transport ships probably have Directed Energy Weapons for ground support but I doubt they have missiles, so they're immaterial to a space battle. The Earth Ark appears to have bugged out for the moment. I need a strategy, one that will work for this confrontation. What's our conventional missile count, Ensign Telco?"

"We have forty-eight conventional missiles left, sir," said Telco. "I don't know if that's enough to take out this flotilla."

"It's not," said Clement flatly. He turned to his exec. "Opinion, Commander Yan?"

"It seems to me we have to deal with those cruisers first, then the LACs. The cruisers have tactical nukes, so getting them off the battlefield seems like our first priority."

"Agreed. Engineer Nobli? Any ideas on how we make that happen?"

"The MAD weapon," said Nobli. "It seems our only option."

"A weapon we've never fired, and that we don't even know if it will work?"

"You asked for my best option, Captain. I've just given it to you," Nobli said, then adjusted his wire-rimmed glasses and looked away.

"What is the MAD weapon?" asked Mika.

Clement became pensive, but he answered anyway. There was a time for everything to be revealed, and it seemed this was it. "Matter Annihilation Device, MAD. Essentially a sort of universal death ray. It will annihilate matter at a molecular level. We end up channeling the energy from the LEAP drive reactor into a particle beam. There's a shut-off valve that will end the stream, and we fire it through the old cobra cannon pipelines that have been treated with a carbon-nanotube coating. But essentially, it's a line-of-sight weapon, and not suitable for tactical targeting. Kind of like swatting a wasp with a sledgehammer. If you hit it, the target is done. If you miss..." He trailed off.

"Jesus Christ," said Yan. "Did DeVore give you this thing?"

Clement shook his head. "No. Engineer Nobli worked out the specs and built the piping for it on the outward leg. Essentially, it's a one-of-a-kind prototype, just like this ship."

"And let me guess, it's never been tested?" said Mika.

"Correct."

"So if it misfires, or blows up..."

"You can pretty much say goodbye to a large section of this solar system," said Clement. "But I see it as the only possibility for our success in this scenario, Pilot." He finished.

"Are you expecting me to target this weapon?" she asked.

Clement shook his head. "No Mika, I wouldn't lay that responsibility on you. I will target the weapon. I only need you to fly us into the enemy formation. My hope is we only have to fire it once and we can hopefully get all three cruisers before they target us. Understood?"

"Yes, sir. But they will see us coming. With that much time it will be difficult to get the ship into a prime firing position," she said.

"I understand that, Mika." Clement turned back to his engineer. "We need the element of surprise, Hassan. We can't get it using conventional means. That flotilla will cut us up before we get a chance to fire."

"So you're asking me if we can use 'unconventional' means?" Nobli asked.

Clement nodded. "Can we use the LEAP drive like we did before, to jump a short distance through normal space, and then appear right in front of our targets, convert the drive to the MAD weapon, and take out the three cruisers?"

"You're insane," said Nobli, dead serious. "It would be easier to find the Earth Ark and take it out than to do this to free a few thousand captives. The scale of the MAD weapon keeps us from close, tactical warfare. It's a weapon of mass destruction, like using a sledgehammer for swatting wasps, as you said. You're asking the impossible, Captain."

"I do, Engineer," replied Clement. "That's why I brought you along. I expect a plan presented to me on the bridge in thirty minutes, and I want you all to stay here until you have it." Then he stood and walked away, heading down to the technical labs.

He found Lieutenant Pomeroy in the sick bay.

"You didn't invite me to your little soiree," she said.

"It's a small room," he snapped back, deflecting her fake hurt feelings.

"I have something important to share with you," she said.

"Is it about the upcoming battle?"

"No . . ." She hesitated. "Not exactly."

He held up his hand. "Then it can wait. I know I've asked you for a lot of things that are out of your usual range of skills on this mission—"

"You have," she said, cutting in. He looked at her. She was plain-faced, rail thin and lean, with her dark hair pulled tightly back into a ponytail. She wasn't the kind of woman to be trifled with, he decided.

"What I need from you now is an estimate of how many of the natives might be killed if we take out that flotilla. There could be hundreds of troops on the ground already, based on the size of those transport ships. And if they decide they are vulnerable to attack from above . . ."

"Would they slaughter their captives? Unlikely, in my opinion. That's their workforce. But if they think we're going to attack them from the high ground, they could panic, depending on how well trained and disciplined they are," she said.

"From what I've seen I'm going to assume they are disciplined, experienced troops."

"Then I would say, don't threaten them. Take out the flotilla but leave them alone."

"Let them keep the captives?"

She nodded. "For now, yes, sir. The units on the ground we observed from the Hill Place looked fairly sophisticated, with equipment and armored vehicles. I say leave them alone, then make your way to deal with the Earth Ark, and whatever that problem may entail."

"And come back to free the natives later?"

She looked pensive. "If we survive the encounter with the Earth Ark, yes, sir."

Clement nodded. "I suppose it's irrelevant to ask how ill prepared we might be for a mass-casualty event?"

"Not irrelevant, sir, but the answer is clearly that we aren't. Anything much more than weapons burns or a skinned knee is going to be beyond our medical scope," she replied in a matter-of-fact tone.

"Understood. One more question. Those transport ships, they have no heavy armaments but they do have DEW weapons."

"'DEW' weapons, sir?" she asked, inquisitive.

"Directed Energy Weapons. To be used from space on a specific target. Do you think you and Ensign Telco could take the shuttle over and use that kind of weapon to free the settlers? Take down the fence lines and such? At least give them a chance to escape?" Clement asked.

"We can surely try sir, *if* those transports are empty."

"I'm willing to bet at least one of them is, Lieutenant. Draw up a contingency plan. We may need to use it, and read in Telco on the mission specs."

"Aye, sir."

Clement nodded again and started to walk away when Pomeroy grabbed him by the arm. He turned back to her.

"Lieutenant?"

"That 'something important' I mentioned before?"

Clement exhaled heavily but nodded for her to continue.

"I'm no biologist, and certainly not a DNA specialist of any kind, but I do have an abnormal finding about the settlers that I think you should know about, sir," Pomeroy said.

"The science can wait," he said, and started to turn away again.

She stopped him a second time. "Not this science, sir," she said. He gave her his full attention now, sensing this was important. "I ran a DNA test on Mary while we were on the planet, sir. It was an exact match for a DNA sample I pulled from a settler burial mound, from a bone on one of the lowest layers. Just out of interest, I ran a carbon dating test on the ancient bone fragment, sir. The test was anomalous, so I ran it two more times."

"How anomalous?"

"Sir, the date came back the same on all three tests. The bone fragment was aged at over four hundred years."

Clement's brow furrowed. "I don't understand. Four hundred years is an impossible number. There were no colonization missions from Earth until a couple of centuries ago," he said.

"So we assumed. Sir, I'm no expert, but even I can see that these people were *designed* for this planet, by someone."

Clement did some quick math in his head. "So either someone on Earth had FTL technology far earlier than has been let on, or some unknown power back in the day had extensive knowledge of this system and sent pre-designed people here on a generation ship."

"Exactly."

"That's something we'll have to ponder on another day, Lieutenant. Right now I have bigger problems, like three nuclear-armed cruisers orbiting the planet," finished Clement, and then he was gone.

"Yes, sir," said Pomeroy to Clement's retreating back.

Clement was back on the bridge a minute later, waiting on the attack strategy from his team. He took in a deep breath, thinking about the information he had just received from Pomeroy, but it couldn't change his resolve. It was an issue for another day.

Presently the team returned to the bridge with their attack plan. They gathered at Yan's station. Clement motioned for Ivan Massif to join them. It was Nobli who started the presentation.

"Based on our previous short jump, by using a .000086 second microburst from the LEAP drive we can move the ship approximately twenty thousand kilometers from our current location to another position in space. The navigator, however, will have to keep us on the same plane of the ecliptic relative to the planet, or we could end up passing through the enemy vessels, which would be very bad for obvious reasons. We need clear space on a specific plane to make the maneuver. I will be able to program the LEAP drive burst to occur on your command, through the MAD application on your console. I'll need about five minutes to complete that update," Nobli stated.

Clement turned to his navigator. "Ivan, can you do this?"

Massif nodded. "Aye, sir. I can plot and lock our course so that we are clear of the enemy flotilla when we make our move." Clement acknowledged that with a nod in return and then Mika Ori took over the briefing.

"We'll need to move the ship within their range of vision so they can see us and start to make their move. If they come at us with the clippers first then our maneuver will place us behind the cruisers, which should give us clear shots at them. However, if they lead with the cruisers and then we pop up behind them, we'll have to fight our way through all the clippers, and that could take away our advantage of surprise and leave us exposed to their nukes. So no matter how it plays out, we'll have to be nimble, quick, and decisive," she said.

"Agreed. We only have one shot at this, people, let's make it work to our advantage. One more thing, I've ordered Lieutenant Pomeroy and Middie Telco on a separate mission with the shuttle, once the shooting stops, to take over one of their transports. They appear to have DEW weapons on board and I'm betting at least one of them is empty based on the number of troops we observed on the ground. I'm proposing that we take one of the transports and then use the DEW weapons to free the natives and at least give them a chance to escape captivity. Once we finish this operation we'll be off to hunt the Earth Ark, and the natives will be on their own," said Clement.

"Natives? You mean settlers?" quizzed Yan.

Clement gave her a brief glance of disapproval, indicating he didn't want to pursue this course of conversation. "I want to give them a fighting chance, Commander, until, or if, we can return," he said. She noted his change of tone on the subject. Clement called to the only other person on the bridge.

"Ensign Adebayor, please report on the Earth Ark," he ordered.

Adebayor turned to the group. "No physical sighting as of yet, sir. But I have picked up trace elements of their drive emissions. They appear to be heading outward from the inner system, on a course toward the third inhabitable world, Camus. I'd say they have half a day's head start on us, sir," she said.

"Thank you, Ensign, keep tracking until you find her." Adebayor acknowledged and returned to her scanning console. Clement turned his attention back to his tactical group.

"All the more reason we need to start moving this plan along. Can we be ready in fifteen minutes?"

"I can," said Nobli. The others nodded assent.

"Very well, so ordered." Clement looked up at the ship's clock and used the console controls to set the timer. "Fifteen minutes from my mark...mark." He turned to Ori. "Mika, I want you to take us toward the flotilla, but take us slowly. We want plenty of time for them to see us and then reveal their strategy, clear?"

"Clear, sir," she replied, then the group broke up to their stations.

The waiting was interminable for Clement. Yan left the bridge and then returned after coordinating the shuttle mission with Pomeroy and Telco. Nobli took almost the full fifteen minutes to program the LEAP drive jump app. Clement then changed his mind and had Nobli load it onto Massif's console.

"I'll just give the order, Ivan. I want you to carry it out," he said. It was a change of heart, but the local LEAP jumps were the navigator's job anyway. Firing the MAD weapon, however, was a larger moral choice and one he wanted to reserve for himself.

As the clock ran out on their prep Clement gave the order to Mika Ori to move the ship closer to the flotilla, following Massif's pre-designated course.

"Slow but sure, Mika," he said.

"Estimate three minutes until they spot us, sir," she replied.

"Keep a clear pathway for us to jump, Pilot," he reiterated.

"As you say, sir," she said with a wry smile, noting her captain's obvious nervousness at the situation.

The flotilla quickly picked up on their movements and started breaking into attack formations. The light attack clippers formed into three groups, each group protecting one of the cruisers. Two of the groups, containing seven clippers each, broke off and began accelerating toward the *Beauregard*, while a third group with six clippers held back near the transports, no doubt protecting the command cruiser of the flotilla.

"That's not what we planned for," said Clement. "Time to rethink our strategy."

"Instructions, sir?" asked Ori.

He pondered the situation for a moment, then came to a quick decision. "Pick the nearest subgroup that maintains our line of sight for the LEAP jump and make for them." He hit the com button to the missile room. "Ensign Telco, load all missile tubes."

"Missile tubes loading, aye, sir," came the response.

Clement waited while the tubes loaded up and his board went to green, one by one, then switched his attention to the tactical display as Mika maneuvered the ship closer to the nearest battle group.

"How long—" he started.

"Thirty seconds to firing range of our missiles," interrupted Ori, all business. The clippers were now placing themselves between the *Beauregard* and the first enemy cruiser. Clement decided to put the hammer down early. He looked down at his console again. All green on the missile tubes. He glanced over at Mika, who was watching her range clock countdown to under five seconds. When the clock hit zero Clement used his console to fire the missiles, then he turned to Ori.

"Accelerate us toward that cruiser, Mika. I want us inside the detonation range of their nukes so they can't use them without destroying themselves."

"That range would be about twenty kilometers, sir," said Mika, manipulating her controls at the captain's order. Clement felt the tug of gravity as the ship accelerated at a rapid rate toward the cruiser and its tiny flotilla. The clippers scattered as the *Beauregard*'s missiles homed in on them. The first missiles detonated and destroyed two of the clippers. Three more scattered and avoided direct hits but still took damage from the collective blasts. The last pair of clippers ran from the scene, circling back to protect their cruiser.

"Take us right at the cruiser Mika," said Clement. "Accelerate to 1.5 *g*s." He hit the com to contact Telco again. "Have you got my missiles reloaded, Ensign?" he asked.

"Aye, sir," replied Telco. "You may fire at will."

Clement turned to Yan. "Target the cruiser with all six missiles, Commander," he ordered.

"Aye, sir," she acknowledged with a grave look on her face.

Clement turned quickly back to Mika Ori at the navigation console. "Distance to the cruiser," he demanded.

"Twelve hundred kilometers," she replied.

"How long—"

"Three minutes twenty seconds to optimal range," she replied.

"That's a lot of time to prep and fire a nuke," Yan commented.

Clement turned back to his executive officer. "Then let's give them something else to deal with," he said. "Firing all missiles."

Yan nodded in reply. "Missiles away, sir," she said.

Clement watched on his tactical screen as the six missiles left the *Beauregard*'s launch bay, heading directly for the cruiser. They would arrive at their target much sooner than the *Beauregard* could.

The *Beauregard* screamed past the five damaged and destroyed clippers, still accelerating and closing on the main cruiser. The second cruiser group was in turn closing on the *Beauregard* but was still out of their effective missile range. The two functional clippers from the first cruiser's flotilla desperately attempted to get between the *Beauregard*'s missiles and their cruiser. They fired Directed Energy Weapons and antimissile torpedoes into the path of the oncoming ordnance, but it was too little and too late. One of the clippers got caught in the detection path of one of the *Beauregard*'s oncoming missiles and it veered off, attracted by the clipper's engine heat signature. The resulting explosion was spectacular. This caused the Earth cruiser to change course away from the debris field of the clipper. She also had to decelerate, which only put her more and more into the *Beauregard*'s sights.

Two more of the *Beauregard*'s missiles veered off and struck the last undamaged clipper defending the Earth cruiser, totally destroying her. The cruiser was now hopelessly out of position, her midships exposed to the *Beauregard*'s final three conventional missiles. They hit her broadside and she went up in a sparkling explosion as her interior compartments were exposed to the vacuum of space, venting both oxygen and fuel, not to mention her personnel. She was at least crippled; at worst she was doomed and spinning now down toward the atmosphere of Bellus. But she still had an unfired nuclear missile and that made her a danger, especially to the settlers below.

"Bring us about, Pilot," said Clement. "Pursuit course."

"Sir?" asked Mika, questioning.

"She has an unfired nuke, Pilot, and we have to take her out before she hits the planet," he explained.

Mika acknowledged without a word and started the process of turning the ship toward the falling cruiser.

"Sir," warned Massif. "That will take us out of range for our LEAP jump."

Clement was nonplussed. "Then you'll have to recalculate from our expected intercept position for the cruiser, Ivan." Massif nodded, even though he was clearly unhappy. Clement knew his people and how well they did their jobs, even if they complained about it.

The ship and the crew strained against the new g-forces in play to intercept the falling cruiser. After two minutes Ori got the ship in line to fire and the acceleration rate reduced back to 1 *g*.

"In range to fire, Captain," said Ori. "But we're dangerously close to her detonation range."

Clement said nothing to that as his tactical screen showed him the same info. He called down to Ensign Telco. "Load one missile, Ensign. Once she's fired I want you to reload all the tubes, all six of them, understood?"

"Yes, sir," said Telco. "Your missile will be ready to fire in ten seconds."

Clement turned back to Yan again. "Target her remaining fuel, Commander, or what you think may be her missile bays. Prepare to fire on my command."

Yan acknowledged as Clement watched the tactical screen, waiting for the green light from Telco. Once he got it he didn't hesitate for a second, but took command.

"Firing!" he said. The missile was away, screaming toward the crippled cruiser.

"Get us out of here, Pilot!" ordered Clement.

The ship veered away at high acceleration again, pulling almost three *g*s, bearing loosely on the course that Navigator Massif had laid out for her. Clement switched the tactical screen to reverse angle as he watched the *Beauregard*'s missile close on the Earth cruiser. The resulting explosion totally destroyed the cruiser and a secondary explosion, a nuclear fireball, consumed everything within twenty kilometers around the cruiser, including one of the damaged clippers that was trying to rally back to its mother ship. The remaining two damaged clippers ran from the field of battle as quickly as they could. Once the *Beauregard* was back on Massif's preferred course Clement ordered Ori to decelerate the ship. The second incoming battle group was still a good ten thousand kilometers out, but closing. The command cruiser was still a quarter of the way around the circumference of Bellus, out of range for the moment, so they thought.

After demanding status from his crew and getting the reports, Clement moved on to the next phase of his plan. They gathered around Yan's console and he brought in Nobli and Telco through the com.

"We have eighteen minutes before that second battlegroup can engage us. Our goal, though, is to take out the command cruiser, and she's nineteen thousand klicks from us. This is where we have to use the LEAP drive to get us behind the Earth command cruiser battlegroup. If we have to fight that second battle group I don't think their commander will allow us to use the same tactics on them as we used on the first group. The element of surprise that the LEAP drive gives us is essential. If this doesn't work, I don't see any way we can fight off two Earth cruiser battlegroups, especially with nukes, at the same time. Now, are we all convinced that this plan *can* work?" he said. Clement looked first to Massif.

"We have a pathway to a location behind the command cruiser group, sir, using the LEAP drive," he said, looking up to the ship's clock. "And by my mark we have about eight minutes to execute that maneuver."

"Can we be ready in eight minutes, Hassan?" said Clement through the com.

"We're ready now," replied Nobli. "Ensign Tsu has the drive warm and ready."

Clement nodded. "We'll bring the ship to full stop," Clement said to Ori. She nodded. "Ensign Telco," he said through the com, "I want my full complement of six missiles ready to fire on my command once we complete the LEAP jump."

"Ready now, sir, as you ordered," said Telco.

Finally, he turned to Yan. "You'll fire the missiles on my order, Commander. Make sure we target the command cruiser's critical systems."

"Aye, sir," said Yan.

Clement looked down to his watch. "We go in three minutes," he said, "and may the gods of the multiverse be with us."

☼　☼　☼

Clement ordered everyone on the bridge crew to strap in for the leap. Lieutenant Ori brought the ship to full stop. Commander Yan dutifully reported on the closing speed of the second cruiser group. Clement glanced at his watch, ignoring the ship's clock out of habit, noting there was less than twenty seconds until the LEAP jump, so the second Earth cruiser group wouldn't be able to get within firing range of his ship. He noted the green lights on his board from both Ensign Telco and engineer Nobli. "You have command of my ship, Navigator," he said to Massif.

Massif went on the ship-wide com and counted down from ten. At zero, the universe shifted again.

The momentary disorientation followed, but Clement soon regained his bearings and demanded reports. Yan updated the tactical screen and it showed them just what they wanted to see. They were approximately seventy-five hundred kilometers behind the command cruiser tactical group, who were facing away from them, or rather, were facing toward where they *had* been only a few short seconds ago.

"Accelerate the ship, Pilot. I want that cruiser in range before they know where we are."

"Two minutes at 3.5 gs, Captain," Ori said.

"Acceptable," replied Clement, "but I want an escape course executed as soon as our missiles are away."

"Already plotted by the navigator and locked into my console," said Ori with a snarky smile to her captain as she hit the acceleration boost. Clement was pressed hard into his command couch. "One minute fifty-four seconds to firing range."

Clement's foot tapped the deck nervously as he watched their progress. "Do they see us yet?" he asked Yan at the 1:30 mark.

"Uncertain . . . wait. The six light attack clippers are starting to scramble. I'd say they've seen us, sir."

"Status of the command cruiser?" he asked.

"She's trying to accelerate away from us. But not very fast by our standards," said Yan.

"Mika—"

"Going to 3.75 g, sir," she said, interrupting him. Clement felt the press of weight on his chest, sinking him farther into his couch. He waited as long as his patience would let before asking for an update.

"Time to firing range, Pilot?"

"Forty-three seconds, sir, unless she's got some surprise we don't know about yet."

Clement leaned back deeper into his couch, praying there were no surprises.

Right on time (according to Ori's calculations) they reached missile-firing range. The command cruiser's evasive maneuvers had only gained them a few seconds as the *Beauregard* closed. The clippers, while more nimble than the cruiser, were still trying to turn and face the *Beauregard*. For all intents and purposes, it looked to Clement like he had them dead to rights. But he knew the battlefield could be a cruel mistress . . .

"Sir!" It was Yan, obviously alarmed.

"Commander?" demanded Clement.

"There's no nuke signature on that command cruiser, sir. She must have—"

"Offloaded the nuke to one of her clippers!" finished Clement. "Mika—"

"Moving us away from the battlefield, sir. Nuke detected on one of the clippers! She's closing!"

"How far?"

"Three thousand klicks and closing fast! Forty-eight seconds to contact!"

"Missiles?"

"Not at this range and speed, Captain," said Yan. "They're too close. Our missiles will never even start pinging."

Clement turned anxiously to his navigator. "Ivan, can we jump again?"

"Nothing calculated, sir. It would take at least three minutes for me to plot anything safe."

"What about unsafe?"

"At this range, we'd likely end up inside Bellus, sir."

"Time, Pilot?"

"Thirty-one seconds until we'll be in the destructive range of their nuke, Captain," said Ori.

Clement reached down to his com. "Nobli, prepare the MAD weapon," he said, not waiting for a reply. Then he flipped to another channel. "Ensign Telco, are my missile tubes loaded?"

"Aye, sir," came Telco's voice through the com line.

Clement cut the line and turned to his XO. "Commander Yan, target the command cruiser with a full volley of conventional missiles, and fire," he ordered.

She looked confused. "But sir, the nuke—"

"Follow my orders, Commander!" he roared.

She did. "Missiles away," Yan said.

"Time," demanded the captain.

"Eighteen seconds!" said Ori.

Clement looked down at the MAD weapon icon. It was all green and ready to fire. He looked up to his tactical screen, which showed the clippers coming straight at the *Beauregard* in a tight delta formation, almost like an arrowhead. *Suicide run*, he thought. He tracked and locked on them, and didn't hesitate.

He fired the MAD weapon.

Blinding white light seared out of the *Beauregard*, disintegrating the clipper formation in an instant. The beam kept going, out to a range where Ensign Adebayor could no longer track it, dissipating slightly as it left their tracking range. It would eventually be harmless, but for the purposes of space combat, its range was virtually unlimited.

They all watched in silence as the 6 conventional missiles the *Beauregard* had launched struck the command cruiser, exploding hard against its hull. The ship quickly nosedived into the atmosphere of Bellus, fatally crippled, and began burning up. The last cruiser and clipper flotilla was now retreating from the battlefield at close to three gravities.

Clement ordered Telco and Pomeroy to take the shuttle to one of the transports to carry out their mission. Then he left the bridge, heading for his cabin, and locking the door behind him.

# ✳ **18** ✳

It was thirty minutes before Clement emerged again. He had left a mostly empty bottle of Argyle Scotch on the table behind him. As he walked along the short metal grid and up the steps to his bridge he contemplated the situation. They'd narrowly averted destruction by the clipper's suicide run, and now he knew the fanatical nature of his enemies. He took his seat back on the bridge and looked to Yan.

"Status of the shuttle mission?" he demanded. Yan cleared her throat before reporting.

"Lieutenant Pomeroy reports that they have taken one of the troop carriers without incident and activated their Directed Energy Weapons. Awaiting your orders, sir," she said.

Clement nodded.

"Pipe me through," he said.

Yan hesitated as the rest of the bridge crew turned their heads to look in the general direction of their captain, but none had the bravery to make eye contact with him. Yan left her station and approached her commander. "Sir, I have a concern—"

"You mean 'we,' don't you, Commander?" said Clement, eyeing his bridge team one by one. He stood. "All eyes on me," he ordered.

Mika, Ivan, and Adebayor turned to face their commander.

"If you're wondering, yes, I've had a drink. In fact, more than one. Seeing the true nature of what human beings will do to other humans has shaken my faith in humanity, but it has not altered my resolve. I may be a man who has had too much alcohol in a single sitting in the past, but I am not at that point now. I am in full command of my capabilities, and clear in my decisions to resolve this conflict. The Earth Ark forces will do anything, sacrifice anything, and anyone, in order to fulfill their dreams of conquest. I will not stand idly by while those dreams crush innocent people, especially the innocents on the planet below us. I fought a war against the 5 Suns Navy for these same reasons, and no, I won't let go of these people and will do anything in my power to protect them, and us." He took in a deep breath. "Now pipe in the captured transport, Commander," he ordered, turning to Yan. Yan reached over to her console, pressed an icon, and nodded to Clement.

"Lieutenant Pomeroy," Clement said. All eyes on the bridge were still on him. "Report your status."

"The transport is ours, sir. All of them have been abandoned by the enemy, sir," came Pomeroy's scratchy voice through the com.

"That means all their troops and equipment are either on the surface of Bellus already or they have evacuated to one of the cruisers," replied Clement.

"That is our assumption, sir. We are in geostationary orbit over the work camp now, sir. Our estimate is approximately twelve hundred troops holding approximately three thousand prisoners. They appear to have a dozen armored vehicles on the surface, sir, and a lot of industrial equipment. I would expect mining operations to begin at any time," Pomeroy concluded.

"Ensign Telco," said Clement, "status of enemy weapons systems aboard the transport."

Telco came on the line. "Their Directed Energy Weapons are operational and can be precision-targeted, sir. They left the lights on for us. Only waiting on your orders, Captain."

Clement nodded. "Target their armored vehicles first, Ensign. Then take out the perimeter fencing and allow the prisoners to escape to any forest area closest to the fences."

"What if there are infantry units in those areas?" interjected Pomeroy. As ranking officer aboard the transport she was technically in command of the mission.

"Then eliminate any nearby infantry units," ordered Clement. There was a pause.

"Please clarify last order," came Pomeroy's voice over the com.

Clement didn't hesitate. "Use the weapons at your disposal to eliminate any infantry units that would be in a position to hinder the escape of, or bring harm to, the native prisoners," said Clement. "Is my order clear?"

Again there was a pause, then a quiet, "Yes, sir," from Pomeroy.

Clement continued. "From there, destroy the mining tunnels and any heavy equipment in the camp. Scatter the remaining enemy forces. Once the mission is complete I want you back in the shuttle and back aboard the *Beauregard* ASAP. Are all of my orders understood?"

"Yes, sir," came Pomeroy's reply.

Then Clement gave the cutoff signal to Yan.

"Ensign Adebayor, bring up the camp location on the tactical board and throw it to the main display," he said. She did as ordered and a red-tinted tactical overview of the camp came up on the main board. Information bubbles quickly identified the prisoners, the electrified camp-border fencing, enemy armor, and troop units. They had to wait only a few seconds before the first flashes of DEW light from the transport struck the armored vehicles north of the prison yard. Every few seconds there followed another strike until the armored units encircling the camp were all burning. There was a long hesitation, nearly a minute, until the next burst of DEW fire hit two units on the northern perimeter. They could see individual troops scrambling for cover as the units were devastated by the attacks from their own weapons. The prisoners fled away from the onslaught as the transport's weapons turned to take out the perimeter fencing. It collapsed and burned like kindling. Realizing their chance, the native prisoners finally made a break for the open land, quickly emptying the prison yard as they fled north and into the forest.

The DEW bombardment was sporadic after that, taking out tactical units, five to six men at a time, if they chose to pursue the prisoners. Those who fled in other directions, away from the flood of escaping prisoners, were left untouched. The troops quickly got the message, and began flooding away from the prisoners. Regrettably, many of the troops fled to the mine shafts for cover, not knowing they had just made themselves targets of the next phase of the attack. Again, after what seemed to Clement to be a long hesitation, the DEW attacks turned to the mine shafts. They collapsed as the ground above was vaporized by six-thousand-degree Kelvin heat. Even reinforced metal or carbon-nanotube-coated materials would be vaporized. The mine shafts would become a crematorium. Once again, the attack abated, and then resumed, finally destroying the large stacks of mining equipment. Pomeroy had followed his orders to the letter.

There was no call of confirmation, just a readjustment of the transport's course toward the *Beauregard*. Soon the *Beauregard's* shuttle emerged from the transport, heading home.

Clement shut down his station and turned to Yan. "Do we have missiles loaded?"

Yan looked to her board. "Negative, sir."

Clement called down to his engineer. "Mr. Nobli, send Ensign Tsu up to the missile room and have him load all six missile bays."

"Is he qualified for that?" replied Nobli.

"He is now," said Clement. "Tell him to get his ass up there."

"Yes, sir," replied Nobli, then shut off the line.

Clement turned to his pilot. "Once the shuttle is back on board secure the ship for acceleration. Best possible speed to that last cruiser group, Lieutenant Ori," he said.

"We're going to pursue?" she asked.

"No," replied Clement, shaking his head for emphasis. "We are going to intercept before they go to ground. Ensign Adebayor, reapply yourself to finding that Earth Ark. I want to know where the big game is hiding."

"Aye, sir," she replied.

Clement turned to Yan. "Destroy the empty transports, but leave the one Pomeroy and Telco occupied. We may need it again. And notify me five minutes before we accelerate. Up to five *g*s is authorized. I will be in my cabin. Orders understood, Commander?"

"Understood, sir," she said. Then Clement left the bridge, and everyone was silent behind him.

Yan tapped on his door twenty minutes later.

"Come in," he called.

She entered, noted the empty bottle on the table, and Clement, reclined in his club chair. She absently looked at her watch.

"Five minutes to acceleration. Mika says she might be able to get us to 5.5 *g*s. That would put us twenty-eight minutes away from the last cruiser battle group," she said.

"Thank you, Commander," he replied, staring at the ceiling.

Yan shuffled a bit, unsure what to say next.

Clement stepped in. "If you want to know my condition, Commander, it is as I stated on the bridge, fully capable of carrying out my duties. Regardless of what that empty bottle of scotch may imply," he said, then looked up to her. "Please sit down." She did, taking a seat at the conference table. Clement pulled his recliner up to a sitting position. "You want to know why I did what I did?" he asked.

She shook her head. "No, I understand your decisions. What I want to know is how *you* feel about them, and ask why we are pursuing a retreating enemy."

He hesitated, then: "After the last war I swore I would never take a life again unless it served some military purpose. But these Earth troops..." He trailed off. She waited. "They're much more than just military units. These people are conquerors. Slavers. Genocidal. Fanatics. They don't fight for a reason or a creed or a purpose, they only fight because they are ordered to. And we have to stop them. If we don't, who else will?"

"That's a question you know I don't have the answer to," she said. "So you want to pursue the last cruiser battle group, and then what?"

"That cruiser still has a nuke. We do not. It is a threat to every native settler on the planet and to this ship. And although I don't fancy myself as the defender of the meek, any chance those people have of peaceful self-determination cannot be left to an enemy that has a weapon that could wipe them out in a single flash of light. We will destroy that cruiser, and its weapon," he said.

Yan had a ready response. "There are some who said that you were indeed a crusader during the War of the Five Suns. A man who did everything he could to defend the meek and vulnerable. Are you sure that you're not re-fighting that war here?" Her words cut him hard, and he was thankful he'd drained the scotch, to numb his nerves, and his anger.

"That war was unwinnable from the beginning. Most of us knew that. But the Five Suns Congress left us no choice. The Rim planets were starving; that's why we fought. Here, the settlers have all they need to live, and much, much more. That should be protected for their benefit, as should their right to determine how their vast wealth is used. This is not a revolution, Commander. We're defending the innocent."

Yan nodded. "I understand," she said, then hesitated. "And I agree with you. I will follow your orders, Captain, and I will not question them again." Then she came across the room and kissed him on the cheek. "And now this ship needs its captain on the bridge." She extended her hand and he took it, then pulled himself up and walked past her, opening his cabin door and heading for the bridge.

The 5.5 *g* acceleration was uncomfortable, especially as the acceleration couches weren't really designed for battle speeds. They tracked the final cruiser group, which had been escaping at just under three *g*s and had obviously not expected such a hot pursuit by the *Beauregard*. They appeared to be building up speed slowly for an escape-velocity burn, possibly to the inner planet of Alphus, a habitable planet but much less hospitable than Bellus, and the original target of the Earth Ark before they had changed direction to come to Bellus.

"Time to intercept with that battle group?" Clement demanded from his couch, laying as he was in a reclined position. The tactical board glowed red, projected in the air above him.

"Twenty-four minutes at this speed, Captain," replied Mika Ori, with more than a bit of strain in her voice.

"How much longer . . ."

"Six more minutes, for the burn . . . Captain. They . . . are trying to accelerate . . . to reach an escape-velocity . . . burn . . . but . . . we will catch them . . . on the dark side of the planet . . . before they can burn . . . to Alphus."

Clement reminded himself how small Ori was, and how much the strain of high-gravity acceleration must be on her. It hurt him just to talk, let alone give orders.

He gritted out the final six minutes, until Ori's speed reduction to 2.5 *g*s felt like a vacation on a warm beach somewhere. The crew's couches all slowly resumed a more normal upright attitude as the g-forces steadily ablated back toward a normal one *g*. Clement decided that a twenty-six-minute burn at 5.5 gravities was about his limit. He knew he would be sore once his body fully absorbed the stress. They hit 1 *g* deceleration just eight minutes from the cruiser group.

The light attack clippers had formed a double formation, with three clippers in a triangle pointed toward the *Beauregard* and the other four spaced strategically in a flat line protecting their mother cruiser. It was apparent from this formation that it only mattered to their commanders if the cruiser escaped, not the clippers or their crews. Clement studied the formation. The three forward ships were clearly the sacrificial lambs, and he surmised they would make the first move, likely an aggressive one. The second group of four were much more likely to provide the counterattack to whatever move the *Beauregard* made. Though they were heavily outgunned, with just fighter-style conventional missiles and low-energy cobra weapons, they could provide enough stings, like a swarm of wasps, to damage the *Beauregard* and slow her down. Her static shields would protect her from most of the clipper's ordnance, but a lucky shot could prove damaging to their effort, and any necessary repairs would put them at a major disadvantage.

Clement decided to do what he did best and follow his own battle philosophy: the best defense is a good offense.

"Time to the battlefield, Pilot," he demanded.

"Six minutes to the triangle formation, Captain. Eight to the flat back four, and eleven to the cruiser," she said.

"How long until the cruiser can reach an escape vector to Alphus, Navigator?"

"Twenty-two minutes until she can reach her minimum burn vector, sir. After that we'll have precious little time to intercept her," said Massif.

"So it's a very tight schedule." He looked to Yan. "Let's act before they do. Prep three missiles for that triangle group, Commander," he said. She looked a bit puzzled, but complied, then looked at the clock.

"Remind the captain we are still three minutes from firing range on that group, sir," she said.

"Noted, Commander," he replied. "Pilot, change course to intercept those three clippers. Navigator, factor in a thirty-degree variation in their course, toward us. As soon as that maneuver is completed, put us back on the course for the main group of four clippers. Calculate how much time that will cost us."

"Already calculated," said Ori. She knew her captain. "Three minutes adjustment time, sir."

Clement called down to the missile room. "Ensign Telco, you and Ensign Tsu are responsible for the loading of my missiles. Whatever we fire, I want replaced immediately. Let me know when we get below ten in supply."

"Aye, sir," came Telco's prompt response.

At this Yan came up to him. "You're anticipating their attack?"

Clement smiled. "No, Commander, I'm guessing."

"A hunch?" she replied.

He shook his head. "I call it intuition."

"Let's hope yours is better than mine," she replied, and returned to her station.

Mika Ori turned around to give Yan a look of confidence and a nod. She knew Clement well, and how often his intuition had been proven right over the years.

"At your command, sir," said Ori.

Clement nodded. "Execute," he said.

Once again they were pushed back in their couches as the *Beauregard* changed course toward the group of three clippers, and away from the retreating cruiser battle group at 1.5 $gs$. Because of the distance between them the clippers could have changed course already, and the light of the maneuver simply hadn't caught up with their tactical screens yet. Clement had calculated when they would have had to make their move to make a curving strafing run, a time that had passed ninety seconds before. He guessed when their move would have to appear on his tactical screens for him to be right. Otherwise, he had just given up three minutes of pursuit time on the main Earth cruiser on a bad guess. He looked at his watch as the seconds ticked by.

By his count they made their break three seconds late, but it was within the acceptable limits of his calculation. His missiles would pursue and detect, then pick up on the clipper's heat and electronic signatures. He looked to Yan.

"Missiles loaded?"

"Ready to fire, Captain," she said.

"At your will, Commander," he said confidently. She nodded and the tactical board showed three missiles away. "High in confidence, Commander?" he said to her. She smiled at him.

"No reason to waste ordnance, sir," she replied.

"Pilot?"

"Adjusting our course now, sir, back to the pursuit of the cruiser battle group," said Ori. "We'll pull 1.75 $gs$ for two minutes, sir."

He sank back into the couch again, watching the three missiles closing in on the three-clipper group. They would have seen the launch by now, and perhaps tried an escape maneuver, but it was far too late already. He watched in satisfaction as the three missiles hunted down and destroyed each of their targets with a satisfying burst of light. Briefly, he thought of the nine men or women who had just died, but quickly pushed it out of his mind. In battle, there could only be allies and enemies, and he had no allies in the Trinity system.

"Back on our pursuit course for the cruiser battle group," reported Ori.

Clement called down to the missile room. "Ensign Telco, how many missiles do I have left?" he said.

"Twenty-seven, sir," came Telco's reply. "Six in the launch tubes and twenty-one in reserve."

"Not enough," he muttered, mostly to himself. Yan overheard him.

"So you're saying we need more missiles? Your solution to every problem?" she said, with a slight smirk.

"True," he replied. "Time to the cruiser group, pilot?" he asked Ori.

"Three minutes to firing range on the back four clippers, sir. Seven minutes until the cruiser is in range," she replied.

He looked at his tactical board. Those clippers knew they had to be sacrificial lambs for the cruiser, so their crews must know they were already given up for dead by the cruiser's commander. He simulated a strategy on his board, counted his missiles again, then called down to the missile room. This time he got Ensign Tsu.

"Ensign, de-rack two of my missiles," Clement ordered. There was a pause before the reply.

"Confirm, sir, you only want four missiles in the launch rack?" replied Tsu.

"Those are my orders, Ensign," he said, then cut the line. A few seconds later and the missile-room icon on his board went from amber to green. His missiles were loaded.

"Why only four, sir?" Yan asked.

Clement looked at her. "Intuition again, Commander. Target the Earth cruiser with our four missiles," he ordered. Yan looked puzzled. Mika Ori turned from her station.

"Sir, we're still a minute out from firing range on those clippers, and another five minutes before we're in range of the cruiser. Sir," she added the last with emphasis.

Clement looked to both women. "I'm fully capable of watching a clock. Now, target the Earth cruiser with our four missiles. That's an order," he said.

Ori turned back to her station while Yan programmed in the coordinates of the cruiser. The conventional missiles would fall well short of their target.

"Ready, Captain," she finally said. "Cruiser is targeted."

"Time to the clippers, Pilot?" said Clement.

"Nineteen seconds," Ori replied. When they got within the last ten seconds she counted down to zero.

Clement turned to Yan. "Fire missiles," he ordered calmly.

They all watched on the tactical display as the missiles streaked out of their launch tubes and began arcing well away from the clippers, on a vector for the cruiser.

"They won't reach the cruiser," said Yan. As they watched in silence, suddenly the four clippers started moving, burning fuel in a high-acceleration maneuver. Within seconds, all four missiles impacted the remaining clippers, completely destroying them. The bridge was silent.

"How did you know?" said Yan. All eyes on the bridge looked to their captain for an answer.

"Those clippers were given up for dead by the cruiser commander. They knew facing us was suicide. I guessed they would follow their orders to the letter, and try and intercept any missiles targeting the main cruiser. I was right. It's what fanatics always do," he said.

"But our missiles were no danger to the cruiser. They don't have the range," said Yan.

Clement shrugged casually. "But they don't know that, Yan. I counted on their fanaticism overpowering their logic. If they'd calculated the burn rate of our missiles they would have seen that they were no threat. They'd still be alive, and I would be out four missiles," he said.

"Intuition, again?" Yan asked, giving him a look that indicated she was impressed.

"If you like, or experience. Now, how long until we reach actual firing range on that cruiser?"

"Three more minutes, Captain," said Ori.

Clement sat back in his couch and contemplated his next move.

The Earth cruiser had started evasive maneuvers at almost the same time as the last of its escort clippers had been destroyed. It was certain she would have multiple countermeasures available to her, including kinetic weapons (basically, small ball bearings or other material shot into a missile's path), chaff to distract, and possibly even drones that would simulate the cruiser's telltale signatures for heat and electronics. In Clement's experience, often hunting a single ship rather than attacking a battle group could be the more difficult proposition. With a single ship it was down to the particulars of a hull's design capabilities, and their captain's willingness to use those capabilities. Clement contemplated each factor as he formulated a strategy that would use minimal amounts of his remaining missiles. He had twenty-three left.

They entered firing range with the Earth cruiser still eleven minutes from her escape-burn vector for Alphus. Those would be very long minutes for the cruiser's captain. Clement decided he needed more information. He turned to his navigator.

"Mr. Massif," he started.

Massif turned to face his captain. "Aye, sir."

"Can you calculate the maximum course variability that cruiser can execute that will still allow them to reach their escape-burn point in the minimum amount of time?"

"If you give me a minute, sir," he replied.

"You have two," said Clement as the navigator pivoted back to his station to do the calculations. "Lieutenant Ori, no matter what course changes that cruiser makes I want us to stay within the maximum firing range of her at all times. That means stay on her tail, even if we lose some ground, as long as we maintain a firing lock on her."

"Yes, sir," said Ori. At this Yan approached his station.

"Why don't we fire now? We're in range," she said.

"We have twenty-three missiles left, Commander. I don't want to use all of them taking out this cruiser."

"You're planning on holding back, for going after the Earth Ark?"

"Do we have a choice?"

Yan contemplated him a minute, then said, "I suppose not," and quietly returned to her station.

Clement's thoughts turned back to his present battle tactics. "Mika, can that cruiser fire her nuke at us?" he asked.

Ori turned. "As far as I can tell, not from its current orientation. It seems to be a simple design, weapons in the front, propulsion in the back. Plus, I would bet her main focus right now is running her engines as hard as she can," she said.

"What's our time factor?"

"She's ten minutes from being able to make her escape burn, and we're seven minutes behind her. But she's pushing three *g*s now, which seems to be her max, and we're steadily losing momentum to Bellus' gravity and magnetic fields, and thus, time," Ori said.

Clement turned back to Ori's husband. "Do you have my calculations, Ivan?" he demanded.

"I do, sir." He threw his screen to the main tactical display. "She can only move within about a three-kilometer range and stay on her primary vector for the escape burn to Alphus," he stated. The screen showed the cruiser's maximum maneuvering range in relation to her escape-burn path.

"That's pretty wide for a conventional missile," commented Yan.

"I agree," Clement replied. "If only we had more information on her missile countermeasures." Yan smiled as Clement's face lit up with a slight smile. Then he stood.

"Course, Pilot?"

"Locked in on her, sir," said Ori.

"Time to burn range?"

"Nine minutes, sixteen seconds," replied Massif.

He turned to Yan. "Missile status?"

"All green on my board, Captain. Six missiles at your disposal," she replied.

"Prepare to fire one missile on my order," Clement said.

"Just one?" quizzed Yan.

"One," he repeated.

She complied. "Single missile ready, sir. Locked on target for the Earth cruiser."

"Fire," he said.

Yan launched the missile. It arced out toward the cruiser,

accelerating at hypersonic speed. The cruiser probably had less than thirty seconds to respond before impact. Clement studied the enemy ship closely. She lurched starboard in a "Crazy Eddie" maneuver, trying to escape the incoming missile, releasing chaff and drones as well. The missile turned to follow the cruiser, and then impacted into a cloud of kinetic chaff which caused her to explode.

"Detonation half a kilometer from the cruiser, Captain. Enough to rough her up but not much else," reported Ori.

Clement stepped forward to Massif's station and started marking it up, laying plot lines across the screen with his digital pen. He turned to Massif.

"From what I saw, this is her maximum operational variance. Any more and she'll lose her track on her escape burn, which is her best chance of survival."

"She is starting to pull away from us, still burning her acceleration thrusters," interjected Ori.

"Yes, but we can still counter with another high-$g$ burn and catch her. Her captain knows his best chance to escape is right now. We will eventually catch him," said Clement. "Do you agree with my assessment, Ivan?"

"Unless he has something else up his sleeve, I'd say you have it to about seventy-five percent, sir," he said.

Clement went back to his station and started typing in coordinates into his tactical screen, then threw them over to Yan's station.

"Three missiles, Commander. On my mark and on those vectors," he said.

"Ready," she said a few seconds later.

"Fire."

The three missiles streaked out of the *Beauregard*'s missile tubes, two from the port launcher and one from starboard. They converged on the three courses. Clement waited as they closed on the cruiser, second by second. The cruiser captain tried the "Crazy Eddie" jump to the same side, starboard, as the first time, spewing out her chaff and counter measures.

One missile exploded into the kinetic chaff. The second picked up a decoy drone and exploded a kilometer from the cruiser. The third missile bored straight on, hitting the cruiser directly in her main propulsion unit. The resulting explosion was impressive, but not a kill shot. This ship, most likely the flotilla command ship, was built stronger than her predecessors. She tried desperately to use maneuvering thrusters to keep her from diving into the planet's atmosphere, but dive she did. Before they hit the upper atmosphere of Bellus, more than two dozen escape pods were birthed out of her as she dropped, a falling hulk, from the sky. They tracked the pods, twenty-six in all, as they fell to the surface on the dark side of the planet. Survival for very long in that environment seemed unlikely, and Clement pitied the survivors, but had no empathy for their plight. They would have destroyed his ship and his crew without a second thought.

They watched together in silence as the empty cruiser, save possibly her captain, entered Bellus' atmosphere and began burning. To their surprise much of the cruiser made it to the surface before it exploded in a nuclear fireball. Clement hoped the dark side was indeed an empty wasteland, as they had surmised.

He sat back in his command chair, called down to Nobli and Telco and Tsu, thanking them for their work. Then he turned to Ensign Adebayor at the science station.

"Please tell me you have a course on the Earth Ark, Ensign?"

She smiled, her teeth bright white against her dark African face. "I do, sir. Estimate we can catch her in three days, if she stayed true to her original vector," Adebayor replied.

He nodded, then looked around the bridge at his crew. "Well done today, all of you. Mika, set us in a stable orbit around Bellus for the time being. Everyone take eight hours rest. Then we go to find out where that Earth Ark went, and that may be our biggest challenge yet," he said.

There was a chorus of "Aye, sir" and then Clement was off to his cabin, laying down, and finding sleep the moment his head hit the pillow.

# ☆19☆

Yan knocked on his stateroom door six hours later. It wasn't a perfect rest, but it was enough. He opened the door and let her in.

"I take it you want to chat," he said, making his way to his regular chair while she sat at the table again. He poured them both some water and they drank.

"I'll get right to the point," Yan said. "There is some questioning among the crew of our pursuit of the Earth Ark. Many think we have been through a harrowing time and fought battles we were never intended to fight. Remember, we had a small crew to begin with and we've lost two—"

"We didn't 'lose' Wilcock," he interrupted, "I executed him."

Yan paused before continuing. "Agreed, sir. But we are down on personnel and most of the crew is not military trained. They're techs and scientists and geo survey specialists. If you hadn't picked up those four middies—"

"Yes, but I did," he said, interrupting again. "because I knew we might need some military muscle. What's your point, commander?"

"My point is this is not a gunship, regardless of what this hull used to do in the War of the 5 Suns. It is a prototype FTL ship sent on a science mission to test a revolutionary drive, survey three planets for possible colonization, and then return. Instead we have been involved in several military altercations and it appears you want to involve us in more. Many of the crew want to go home, to their husbands, wives and families, not fight another battle against a far superior enemy," she said.

Clement contemplated her points. They were all well taken. He had a decision to make.

"And the fact that I will likely be arrested when I return to

211

Kemmerine Station, and be tried as a traitor—do they think I'm delaying our return because of that?" he asked.

"Some do. Most just want us to go home. We're overdue as it is, so it's likely DeVore will send an unmanned probe to find out what happened to us soon, if not already."

"And the fact that many of them will likely be interrogated and possibly charged with treason for following my orders when we get back to Kemmerine Station?"

"I don't believe that's a strong consideration, sir. They're focused on getting home in one piece." Clement refilled their water glasses and drank again while he thought.

"And what about you, Commander? Where do you stand? Do we find out what that Earth Ark is up to? Or do we turn tail and run home?" he said.

"My heart says we should leave and come back with more force—"

"If we're not court-martialed. And *if* we can trust Admiral DeVore, which I don't believe we can," he replied.

Yan's frustration peaked and she stood up to face him. "If you'd let me finish . . . " she said. He nodded. "My heart says we should cut our losses, but my head knows by the time we get back Trinity may be in the hands of the Earth Ark forces, forever. And that's not the kind of future I want to leave for the natives, let alone the long-term consequences for the worlds of the 5 Suns. These natives are a good and sweet people, and we need to give them every chance to live their lives as they choose."

At that Clement stood. "One more thing I need to know, Commander. If I choose to continue pursuit of the Earth Ark, will you be with me and follow my orders?" he said.

She stared at him from across the room.

"I will, Captain. I will follow your orders whatever decision you make, whether I agree with that decision or not," she said.

He looked back at her, studying her eyes. Her gaze was steady and unwavering. In that moment he had never been more attracted to her. She was becoming a fine officer, but she was also an extraordinary woman.

"Tell the crew I will address them in the cargo bay in five minutes," he said. She nodded, and then left his cabin. Clement went to his sink and washed up, then wiped his face. His next choice would be decisive, and possibly seal the fate of the *Beauregard* and her crew. He was ready.

He left his cabin, heading for the cargo bay.

The crew had gathered as he came down the gantry stairs, stopping on the metal landing about ten feet up, overlooking them. Yan stood next to him. The other bridge crew would listen in on the ship-wide com. He looked down at the assembled crew, looked at their faces, seeing them not as *his* crew, but as men and women who had been exemplary in their loyalty and performance under great duress and personal sacrifice.

He took a deep breath in before beginning.

"Loyal crew of the *Beauregard*. Commander Yan has done her duty and brought your concerns to my attention. I understand the desire to return home. It has been a long and difficult mission, and not one that you had expected this when you volunteered. I never intended this to become a military mission, but clearly Admiral DeVore did, as she sought out an experienced military captain to command it. I ask you to consider once more the fact that some of us, most likely me, will face charges when we return to 5 Suns Alliance space. I cannot tell you that has not crossed my mind. But I will say that it has not affected my decision-making. I believe we have made the right choices both for our own survival and for the natives we encountered on Bellus. I desire for them to live free, not as slaves to some heartless empire back on Earth that has most likely passed into history already."

He paused.

"My decision to pursue the Earth Ark is to determine her intent. She may be, for all we know, prepping to exit this system and return home. But the point is, we don't know. And I think it is vital that we find out why she left Bellus, and what her intent is, whether in this system, or some other. I have ordered a pursuit course to find out what her intentions are, whether we can do anything about it, or if retreat is our best option. I will not attack that ship without further provocation, and I do not want more battle. I had enough of that in the War of the 5 Suns.

"So each of you has a decision to make. Will you stay loyal to me and give me the two or three days I need to catch the Earth Ark and determine her intentions, or will you demand of me that we return home now, and leave this system and her people to an unknown fate? And one last point, although this is not a democracy, and I am not bound to your decision, I will follow what you decide, regardless of the personal cost to me."

He looked down over the faces of his crew. Seventeen people stared up at him, and besides Nobli, Pomeroy, Tsu and Telco, he didn't really know any of them. He had left his fate to these people.

"Please let me know your desires by either leaving the deck if you wish to return to Kemmerine, or staying for thirty more seconds if you wish to see out the mission of locating the Earth Ark and determining her intentions." He held out his hands. "If you wish to return home, you may leave the deck now," he said.

Two techs quickly departed, and others moved around or shuffled their feet, but they all stayed focused on their captain. Yan watched the time on her watch and then dropped it to her side to indicate the thirty seconds was up. Clement looked to his crew and smiled.

"Thank you for putting your trust in me," he said, then went up the stairs to his bridge. Behind him, he heard Yan's voice call out:

"Ship's company, dismissed!"

He smiled.

Once on the bridge he took an informal poll of Mika, Ivan, and Adebayor. They were all with him. Yan followed him in and took her station.

"Orders, Captain?" she said.

Clement turned to Ensign Adebayor. "Ensign . . . I have to confess I've forgotten your first name?" he said.

"It's Kayla, sir," she replied with a smile.

"Kayla, what do you have for me on the Earth Ark?"

"Nothing visual, I'm afraid, sir. She's out of range of our telescope and scanners. But I do have a track for her based on her Ion plasma propulsion emissions. She made first for Camus—the third habitable world and fifth in the system—made multiple orbits there, then left a track as she accelerated away toward a course that would take her between the two gas planets in the outer part of the system."

"Could that track put her on a vector to escape the system? Do we know if she left any forces on Camus?" Clement asked.

"She is not on an escape vector as far as my analysis shows," cut in Ivan Massif. "From what I can tell she is heading for a Lagrange point between the two gas planets. The two planets are very close together, the outer one being .015 AU from the larger, inner planet," said Massif.

"And how far is the inner gas planet from Camus?" asked Clement.

"0.008 AU, Captain."

"And how far are we here at Bellus from Camus?"

"0.09 AU, sir."

Clement crossed his arms, thinking. "Add it up for me, Ivan. How much time to each destination?"

"Given the relative positions of the planets—and they do orbit at differing speeds despite their close proximity—I make it sixteen hours to Camus with a 1.25 $g$ burn, sir," said Massif.

"What if we made it a 1.5 $g$ burn?" he asked.

Mika Ori chimed in here. "I was thinking of the comfort of the crew, sir, but at 1.5 $g$ we could cut that to twelve hours."

Clement didn't hesitate. "Let's do it at 1.5 $g$. How long will the burn have to be to get to Camus in twelve hours?"

"I'd like to make one more full orbit after this one, sir, to pick up some momentum. The navigator and I will set the vector to Camus, but I'd like to go closer to Bellus to take advantage of her gravity to sling shot us, sir. I make it twenty-eight minutes until our burn, then another nineteen minutes for the 1.5 $g$ burn, sir," Ori said.

"And then at least two orbits of Camus once we arrive to verify whether the Earth Ark left any forces there," said Clement, rubbing his chin as he thought.

"Thirty-nine minutes to make an orbit of Camus, sir," said Ori without Clement even asking.

The captain looked up to Massif.

"Once we establish a vector to the Lagrange point, another twelve-minute burn at 1.5 $g$ to get us out there to .045 AU, sir. Nine hours estimated travel time," finished Massif.

"That's assuming she's still out there," Clement said. It all added up to about twenty-six hours of maneuvering.

He turned back to Adebayor. "Good work, Ensign Kayla. I'll be needing long-range scans of Camus well before our arrival to see if they left us any surprises," Clement said.

"Yes, sir," she replied enthusiastically.

He turned to Yan. "Inform the crew of our schedule, Commander. Everyone can ride the burn out in their couches if they like. It looks like the best time to get some rest will be during the twelve-hour flight time to Camus. I want to make sure we have at least two of you on the bridge at all times. Oh, and Mika and Ivan, I know how much you like, uh, spending your time off together, but I'll need one of you on the bridge at all times, for safety's sake."

The *Beauregard*'s pilot gave him a mock pout and then turned back to her station.

Massif just shrugged his shoulders. "Of course, sir," he said.

"Ensign Kayla," Clement said to Adebayor, "you're relived for the next six hours unless called."

"Aye, sir," she said.

He turned to Ori. "Mika, once the burns are completed I want you in your quarters as well for six hours. You can relieve your husband at that point. Same for you, Yan, six hours down time, beginning immediately," Clement ordered.

"And what about you, Captain?" Yan asked.

"You can relieve me at the end of your rest period. I can't promise I'll sleep during that time, but I'll try," replied Clement. "In the meantime I'll stay on my bridge. I like it here," he said. Yan and Adebayor started to exit the bridge, Adebayor yawning as she departed.

Yan lingered for a second, then whispered to Clement, "I'll have Pomeroy issue you a five-hour-timed sleep pill," she said.

"You know I hate those things," he whispered back.

"As your exec, I'm not giving you a choice, Captain," she finished, then left for her quarters.

Two hours after the burn and acceleration and well into the rest shifts, Clement took a break, leaving Massif alone on the bridge to relieve himself for a few minutes. As he went down the six metal steps to the command cabins, he saw motion at the end of the hall. He had given Lieutenant Pomeroy Captain Wilcock's old stateroom, and he was surprised to see the back end of Ensign Telco departing her cabin. He watched as they kissed goodbye at the doorway, and Telco left without noticing him in the hall, heading back down the gantry steps to the missile room. Pomeroy, for her part, did see him, and came up to him as if to give an explanation. Clement attempted to wave her off with both hands.

"No explanation needed, Lieutenant," he said in a low, almost whispered, voice.

She kept coming anyway.

"You deserve to know what's happening on your ship, sir," she said in an equally low voice. Clement put his hands behind his back, attentive, but saying nothing.

"Since the sex pond incident on Bellus, sir, Ensign Telco has developed a sort of youthful attachment to me," she said.

"Anyone can see *that*, Lieutenant," replied Clement with a slight smile.

"I have tried repeatedly to discourage him, as you know where my preferences lie in regards to . . . intimate relations," she said.

"Of course."

"Well the fact is this crew is mostly men and the other women frankly either don't share my interests or they just don't fancy me. So I finally gave in to Ensign Telco's affections. He's a very likeable kid, sir. And I'm sure he's learning a lot," she said.

Clement smiled broader. "And that's all to his benefit," he said. Pomeroy looked at him, then looked away. "Just don't let him get too attached," Clement warned.

She nodded. "Duly noted. I just wanted you to know, sir," she said.

"Thank you, Lieutenant. Carry on." She smiled and nodded again, then headed back to her cabin.

Clement returned to the bridge. "Ivan," he said to his navigator, "I think it's time you had a brief break. Everything is on automatic pilot and I can certainly handle any emergencies from here for a few minutes."

"That's very kind of you, sir," said Massif.

Clement looked down at his console before he spoke again. "I was thinking fifteen minutes, perhaps even twenty, if you think that would be . . . enough time?"

"I do, sir. Twenty minutes should be more than enough. Sir," Massif said, smiling broadly at his captain's generosity. He quickly transferred full control to Clement's console and then rushed down the stairs to his cabin.

Clement shook his head and smiled.

Yan did indeed force him to take the five-hour sleeping pill, and he happily slept, waking on time to clean up and get back to his bridge, which was once again fully manned. He sat down in his seat and pulled his console closer to him. He checked his status board and saw all green on the ship's systems. He pushed the console aside. "Reports," he said loudly. His staff turned to face him. He wanted to hear it from them directly, not read it on some com board. "Our position, Lieutenant Ori?"

She turned from her console. Her face was flushed and her hair was slightly mussed from her encounter with her husband, but Clement could tell she was in good spirits. "Decelerating toward the planet Camus, sir. Our vector will put us in an orbit of four hundred sixty-two kilometers above the planet's surface," she said. "The navigator did an excellent job," she said, smiling.

Now Massif turned from his station, also smiling. "Really, sir, the credit goes to the pilot. She executed my instructions and followed my direction perfectly," he said.

"Well, congratulations to you both for an excellent . . . planetary insertion. Carry on," Clement said. Yan giggled audibly at that. Clement stood and quickly changed the subject from orbital mechanics.

"Ensign Adebayor, can you report on the course and speed of the Earth Ark?"

Adebayor stood up from her station to address her captain. "Tracing the propulsion track of the Earth Ark I can now say with more certainty that they were here approximately forty-eight hours ago. They made three orbits, then used the planet's gravity to accelerate on to the next location, the Lagrange point between the two gas planets," she said.

"Well done, Ensign," the captain said, then addressed the full bridge crew. "We'll make three orbits, as they did, then use the planet's gravity to accelerate away to the Lagrange point. Somewhere in there, we'll hopefully get a line of sight of them in open space. That will be up to you, Ensign," he said, nodding to Adebayor. "Your radio telescope will have to find them."

"Understood, sir," she said.

Clement addressed Ori again. "Take us into orbit, Pilot," he said. "Aye, sir."

"Commander Yan, conduct a survey of the habitable side of Camus, see if it matches up with the unmanned probe's observations. And please look for signs of natives," he said.

"Aye, sir," replied Yan.

It took another forty minutes for the *Beauregard* to achieve a stable orbit over Camus, initially on her permanent dark side. The ship came around quickly to the sun-facing side of the tidal-locked planet. Clement examined the 5 Suns Alliance probe's records on the planet. Camus was approximately fifteen percent larger than her inner neighbor, Bellus, but just as pleasant according to the probe's records. Her mass was 0.68 of standard, but very close to the 0.62 of Bellus. The principal difference in the worlds was that the main land mass of Camus was in a ring around a large central saltwater ocean, which made it look like an eyeball planet. Several islands, some that almost qualified as minor continents, dotted the ocean. The planet was warm and inviting, and seemed just as bright a prospect for colonization as her two sister worlds.

By the time they made their way to the light side of Camus her large central ocean was a gleaming blue, even in the dim red light of her tiny Trinity sun. Yan's scans showed Camus had a high oxygen content, higher even than Bellus, with an average planetary temperature of 20.5 Celsius from nearly pole to pole. Not quite as warm as Bellus, but still quite comfortable, and a positively blissful twenty-four Celsius at the equator, where a convenient string of nine large islands/small continents dotted the ocean. The band of central warmth that ran diagonally across the planet was nearly thirty-seven hundred kilometers wide, and the large islands were all comfortably ensconced in that region, both north and south of her equatorial line.

"Good design," muttered Clement as he read Yan's report. She heard him, and came to his station.

"There is something else," she said, with some trepidation.

"Something you didn't put it in your report? Why not?"

"Because I'm not sure of the scans. Each of those islands showed . . . anomalies."

Clement shifted in his chair. "Define 'anomalies,' Commander."

"I can't be certain, but each of those islands had mountains that were ... highly regular in shape and height. Geometrically regular. Like ... " She trailed off and looked away, almost as if she were unable to say it.

"Say it, Commander."

"Like ... pyramids, sir."

"Pyramids? As in ... constructed objects? Why wouldn't the previous probes have picked them up?"

"The automated probes were only designed for basic evaluation and survey, not for detailed exploration, sir. Also, the pyramids are offset in such a way as to appear to be a bit more natural. They could have easily escaped the probe's analysis. Sir, these pyramids, their scale is off the charts. Kilometers high. If they are constructs, no technology known to humanity could have built them," Yan said.

"What would their purpose be?"

"That I certainly can't say. But it is a mystery, one worth exploring further, in my opinion."

Clement thought about that. It was quite possible that DeVore had learned about these pyramids from the previous probe's telemetry, and he surmised that could be another reason why she wanted control of this system so badly. Possible alien technology ...

"Lieutenant Ori," he said. "Can we adjust our orbit on the next pass to fly over the equatorial islands and not disrupt our escape vector?"

"Let me check," she replied, looking down on her handheld tablet and running quick calculations. "We can do it, yes, sir. It will take a sixty-second thruster burn on our next dark-side pass"—she looked up at the ship's clock—"in thirteen minutes."

"Do it," Clement said. Then he went to Adebayor's station, trailed by Yan.

"Ensign, we're going to need full observational scans on each of the equatorial islands. There are some mountains there that Commander Yan wants to take a closer look at. She'll pass on the coordinates."

"Aye, sir. What type of scans, Commander?" said Adebayor to Yan.

"Infrared. X-ray. Ground-penetrating radar, if you've got it, and high-resolution color photographs. Can we do all that?" asked Yan.

Adebayor nodded. "We can, sir. However, at our current orbital speed it will be difficult to get all nine islands. How many do you need?"

"A minimum of three, but five would be preferable," replied Yan.

"I can do five, sir. I'll set up an algorithm to optimize the procedure."

"Can you have it ready by our next light-side pass?" the captain asked, looking at his watch. "That's in thirty-six minutes."

"Can do, sir."

"Thank you, Ensign."

Mika Ori executed the thruster maneuver without incident, and they were soon on the light side of Camus again. Adebayor began taking her pictures as Yan monitored them in real-time from her station. Clement watched as a worrying frown came across his first officer's face. He put it down to her concentrating on the data, rather than her displeasure with what she was seeing. It took about fifteen minutes for Adebayor to complete her scans of the five islands Yan needed to make her assessment, and another twenty for Yan to analyze the results before she looked up at her captain.

"I'd like to consult with you in your cabin, Captain," she said in a noncommittal tone.

"Of course," he replied to her, then addressed Ori. "Time to our escape burn, Pilot?"

"From our current position to the initial burn point on the dark side, thirty-eight minutes, Captain," she said, then added: "It will be a 1.50 $g$ burn, for seven minutes, sir."

"Set the ship's clock to count down to that point, Pilot. Navigator, are we still on vector for an escape burn that will take us to the Lagrange point between planets six and seven?"

"We are, sir," replied Massif.

"Prep the crew for the escape burn. Inform them safety couches are not required but they can be used at their discretion," said Clement.

"Aye, sir," said Massif with a nod.

"The commander and I will be in my cabin for the next . . . ten minutes or so?" he said, turning to Yan for confirmation. She nodded. He caught Mika Ori's eye as Yan passed him to go down the steps to his cabin, and she winked at him. He shook his head and mouthed "no," letting Ori know this was ship's business, not playtime.

He entered his cabin and shut the door behind him, joining Yan at his conference table. "You have something to report, Commander?"

"Yes, sir. Sir, those mountains . . . even from the scans that I received, which are not definitive, they are not mountains, sir. They measure almost identical in height, dimensions, square kilometers of their bases, all close enough to identical to make their differences meaningless." She pulled out her tablet and slid it across the table to Clement. "Scroll through the next five photos," she said.

Clement looked at the first one, a high-definition shot of the first island. The "mountain" was covered in greenery, the base surrounded by rich vegetation. Out of the top there was a plume of white vapor emerging. He slid to the next photo, which was at a different angle but showed essentially the same thing, without the plume. The next three photos were also similar, with some minor variations. Two of those photos showed the plumes.

"What am I looking at here, Commander?" he said.

She sat back in her chair as he slid the tablet back to her. "Essentially, Captain, these are *not* natural formations. They are architectural constructs, placed on Camus by some unknown intelligent entities."

"Human?" he asked.

She shook her head. "Unlikely. From what we've seen of Earth technology from the Ark ship they don't seem to have the scale for it. If we assume Earth technology is approximately equal with the level of the 5 Suns Alliance, then this is beyond them. It's certainly beyond us."

"Could this be technology from another Earth colony? One that was established after the 5 Suns Alliance?" he asked. She leaned forward again.

"It's been four centuries since the 5 Suns Alliance colonies were established. Another colony certainly *could* have been established somewhere in another star system, but no one who immigrated from the Sol system ever mentioned it. As far as we know, the 5 Suns Alliance is the only colony Earth ever established. And my guess would be that if another colony *was* founded, they'd have had a very difficult time reaching this level of technology so quickly."

"You keep referring to it as 'technology,' but all I see are very large hills. Artificial, yes, but what are they for?" asked Clement.

"Terraforming," said Yan. "Those plumes you see are a combination of oxygen, nitrogen, carbon dioxide, and trace organic materials. Whoever made these pyramids is clearly engaged in terraforming, and it appears to be an ongoing process. My studies show the ocean depth between the islands to be somewhere between ten and twenty meters. It is my belief that these 'islands' were once part of a single land mass. The ocean levels have risen over time and much of the land mass is now below the waterline."

"How long would a process like that take?"

"My best guess is about five centuries, but I'm no geologist, though we do have one on board. Should I put that question to him?"

"No," said Clement. He looked at the tablet pictures again. "What about—"

"Inhabitants? I have found some indication that they are down there, though obviously in a primitive social state, much like Mary and our friends on Bellus," Yan said.

"Now I can see why Admiral DeVore wants this system so badly. It's a treasure trove of natural resources and advanced technology, whether that technology is human or . . . otherwise. Let's keep this between you and me for now, Yan. We won't be going down to Camus on this trip, that much is certain. I suggest we go back to our bridge and concentrate on our escape burn to the Lagrange point."

"Yes, sir," said Yan, taking back her tablet. Right at that moment Clement's com chimed in. It was Ivan Massif from the bridge.

"Captain, we may have a situation up here," he said, speaking with urgency in his voice.

"We'll be right there."

With that Clement and Yan were up and out of his cabin and heading to the bridge.

"The bogey has been shadowing us for seven minutes now, sir," said Mika Ori.

Clement looked at his tactical display and found a small black dot tracking their every move. "Where did it come from?"

"After using our telemetry to retrace its track, we picked it up on the last pass over the dark side of Camus. My guess is it was on the surface just waiting for us to pass by overhead," replied Massif.

"Yes, but was it left here by the Earth Ark or by . . . someone else?" Clement asked.

"Someone else? Who could that be?" asked Ori.

Clement deflected that question with another. "Can we get a shot of it from one of our scanners or cameras, Ensign Adebayor?"

"Trying now, sir," she replied.

Clement turned back to Ori. "What's her speed?"

"Matching ours exactly, sir," replied Ori.

"Distance?"

"Ten thousand kilometers and holding, sir."

Clement looked up at the ship's clock; still seventeen minutes to the *Beauregard*'s escape burn. He called down to Nobli in the reactor room. "Hassan, how much time would you need to prep the LEAP engine for another in-system jump?" he asked.

"To where?" replied Nobli.

"To the Lagrange point between the two outer gas giants."

Nobli hesitated. "I can warm her now, sir, but I don't recommend we keep making these short jumps as a matter of course. Is it absolutely necessary?"

"I don't know that yet, Engineer," Clement replied.

"Sir," said Nobli over the com, "these short jumps put an awful lot of stress on the reactor casings. You're releasing a tremendous amount of energy in a very short time frame. The reactor was designed to run constantly for long durations, like a thirty-four-day journey. It wasn't designed to be used for microsecond jumps inside star systems, or as a weapon, for that matter."

"I hear you, Engineer," said Clement. "Can I trust you to hold her together two or three more times?"

"I can't guarantee that, sir, in all honesty."

Clement thought about the situation. Nobli's honesty gave him pause. They had a little over fifteen minutes to the escape burn, which would almost certainly place them in a hostile environment. The likelihood he would need the weapon again seemed high, but he couldn't use it on their mysterious pursuer, nor could he use missiles. He'd have to turn the ship for that, and if the bogey attacked, they could get caught in the middle of their turn maneuver.

"Warm the LEAP reactor, Engineer. Coordinate with the navigator on our destination point. We may have to use the LEAP engine to escape the situation we find ourselves in. Prompt me at my command console when she's ready. If we have to make the jump to the Lagrange point, I'll need you to keep the reactor up and running in case we have to use the weapon. Understood?"

"Understood, sir. But if she cracks . . . we could lose the ship. Hell, half the solar system. And there's still the issue of the return trip home."

"Acknowledged, Nobli. Proceed as ordered," Clement said, then signed off. "Ensign Adebayor, do we have an analysis of the bogey yet?"

"Just coming up now, sir," she replied.

"Show me."

The tactical display lit up with a basic outline of a flat-headed cylinder with a protruding end cap. A simple design, with a high-yield atomic thrust cluster in the back. "Radiation scan?"

"Just coming in now, sir," said Yan from her station. "Indications of a two-kiloton warhead attached, sir."

Clement stepped down from his station and looked at the design as it spun on the tactical display in a 3D graphics presentation. "This is a hunter-killer," he said. "An automated weapon designed to be used to hunt targets stealthily until it unleashes its full power on the target. My guess is she can accelerate to overtake us any time she wants. In such a situation, we'd only have seconds to respond. These kinds of weapons were outlawed in the War of the 5 Suns because the use of AI was considered immoral. But our enemies seem to have no such moral compunction against using them." He hurried back to his station. The LEAP engine icon was green, indicating the reactor was warm enough to be put into use, albeit in an increasingly dangerous maneuver.

"Pilot, increase speed to 1.25 $g$," he called. That was the minimum required for their escape burn.

"1.25 $g$, aye, sir."

Clement turned to Yan. "Inform the crew we may be experiencing higher than expected g-force acceleration. Tell them to prep for a possible LEAP jump. Everyone not required to run the reactor to acceleration couches."

"Aye, sir," said Yan, then repeated Clement's instructions on the ship-wide com.

"Report, pilot."

"Bogey has increased speed to 1.25 $g$. Now 1.3 $gs$. Now 1.5. Continuing to accelerate, sir."

"Thrusters to three $gs$, pilot," said Clement, raising his voice.

"Sir, not all the crew has signaled ready," chimed in Yan.

"No time. They'll have to rough it out," Clement responded as Ori hit the thrusters and the weight of three-$g$ acceleration pushed him back in his couch. He watched the tactical display.

"Bogey has increased speed. 3.5 $gs$ and range is closing. Estimate intercept in one hundred forty-one seconds, sir. Bogey speed now 5.25 $gs$ and continuing to accelerate. Should I activate the main burn thruster, sir?" said Ori.

"Negative. Navigator?"

"Vector established for LEAP jump, but not as precise as I'd like," said Massif, struggling against gravity to get the words out.

"Bogey at six $gs$, sir," grunted out Ori. "Seventeeeeeen... seconds... to... inter... cept..."

There was no choice now. With difficulty, he pulled his console close with just seconds to spare...

Clement woke up on the floor below his station. He'd neglected to strap in before the LEAP engine was activated. He wanted to vomit, and retched for a few seconds before his head stopped spinning and he stabilized. Mika Ori ran past him, holding her hand to her mouth as she ran for her cabin. He lifted a heavy hand to grip his couch and dragged himself up to his station. The tactical telemetry showed him his ship was decelerating at a steady rate, 2.5 $gs$, 2.4, and so on. He looked to Yan. She was pale and drawn-looking but at least she'd had the sense to strap in. Mika returned to the bridge in about a minute. Massif gave her a comforting hug.

"Status report," Clement said, his voice cracking. Ori chimed in first.

"Decelerating to one $g$, Captain. We should be there in about three minutes," she said. Clement sat more upright in his couch.

"What's our position, Navigator?"

"We overshot the Lagrange point by 0.000086 AU, sir, about thirteen thousand kilometers. I told you we couldn't be precise."

"Acknowledged. Ensign Adebayor, what's the status of the Earth Ark? Is she at the Lagrange point? Can you find her?"

"Negative, sir. It looks like she pushed on toward the outer gas planet at some point, but her trail is still fresh. Estimate we're less than eight hours behind her," said Adebayor. Clement turned his attention back to Ori.

"Set speed at 1.5 *g* for the duration, Pilot, pursuit course." Ori hesitated a second before replying, as if reluctant to follow her orders. Finally, she gave an "Aye, sir" and complied. A second later Nobli was chiming in on Clement's com.

"Report, Engineer."

"We have a broken reactor, sir," said Nobli with just a trace of resignation in his voice. "I warned you this could happen. Microfractures in the reactor casing, sir. One or a million of those mini anti-matter universes we annihilate every second could have escaped through the cracks. We got lucky, sir."

"Better lucky than dead, Engineer. How long until the reactor can be repaired?" said Clement.

"I'm not sure it can be repaired. It will have to be scrapped and replaced when we get back to Kemmerine, sir."

"We can't get back to Kemmerine in our lifetimes if it can't be repaired. Unacceptable, Engineer. Give me an alternative."

"Oh, I can patch the micro-fissures, if I can find them all, with carbon-fiber nanotubes and the like, but she's forever fractured, and I can't guarantee she won't implode on us if we try to jump like that again. Once she's patched we can likely run her in a steady-state condition for the trip home, but that's about all I can promise you."

"And the weapon?"

"Untenable at this time, Captain," snapped Nobli with a touch of anger in his voice that the captain would even ask such a thing. Clement thought about that, but not for long. He needed his MAD capability.

"Get to work with Ensign Tsu and borrow any techs you need to patch the casing."

"That will take many hours, Captain."

"Understood, Nobli. You have about eight, maybe less. But . . . I may need that reactor to hold on long enough to use the weapon again."

"I don't recommend that," said Nobli flatly.

"Note your protest in the engineer's log. My orders stand. Prep her for use as a weapon, and make sure she has enough left over to get us home," snapped Clement, then he cut the line. Like it or not, this had to work. It *had* too.

Thirty minutes later and Clement was in his cabin, monitoring all the ship's functions. The hunter-killer had vainly tried to catch the *Beauregard* and stayed on her intercept course even after the gunship had made her LEAP jump. Telemetry showed it eventually burned through its fuel supply and would now drift through the Trinity system on the same trajectory for eons, no longer a threat to anyone. He noted its location. They could intercept it on a future mission or destroy it outright. But not now. For now it was just flying in a straight line with no more fuel, drifting alone in space.

Scans along the path of the Earth Ark indicated they were closing in on her, but precisely what she was doing out here at the edge of the Trinity system near two uninhabitable planets was uncertain. It was something he wanted to figure out before they made the LEAP home, rather than leave the system undefended. And, if he was honest, he still wanted to disable or destroy the thing, if possible. It was a risk worth taking, in his eyes.

The knock on his door came from Yan, as expected. What she presented to him, though, was not.

"Most of the crew want to go home, now," she said as she sat across from him at his worktable, her hands clasped together. She was all business. "Rumors have gotten around that the LEAP drive is compromised, but that you still may want to use her as a weapon—"

"Nobli..." started Clement, shaking his head, angry at his engineer. Yan continued talking over her captain.

"It was Ensign Tsu that alerted me, Captain, not Nobli. To continue, most of the crew are now against further conflict. They think you're risking the ship to get revenge."

"Revenge? On whom or what would I be taking this revenge?" Clement demanded. He did not like the tone or direction this conversation was taking.

"The Earthers, for killing Daniel. DeVore. The entire 5 Suns Alliance. There are plenty of conspiracy theories going around." Clement sat back, rocking in his chair briskly as he contemplated her, and the implications of this situation.

"We already *had* a vote, Commander. They agreed to pursue the Earth Ark until its location and purpose could be determined. We are still on that mission. My hope is that the MAD weapon never has to be used again, but we need it for our own protection, just in case we get into a tactically untenable situation. I still intend to take this ship home, but perhaps not on the crew's schedule." He looked at his watch, synchronized with the ship's clock on the bridge. "In less than six hours we should be able to observe the Earth Ark. She has slowed her speed consistent with decelerating to a destination. What the destination is, I don't know. But I intend to find out," he said.

"So you refuse to take us home at this time?"

He nodded. "That's my decision, and I thought it was the crew's as well."

At that Yan got up and went to his cabin door, opening it from the inside. Several crew members, led by Lieutenant Pomeroy, came into the room, some standing outside the doorway, filling the hall. He recognized Telco and Tsu among them, but none of the bridge crew. Pomeroy, Telco and Tsu were armed with cobra pistols.

"So it's to be a mutiny, Yan?" Clement said, standing but staying as cool as he could under the circumstances. "After you swore your allegiance to me more than once? And now it's come to this? I overestimated you, Commander, and you're honesty."

"I have family in the 5 Suns Alliance, Jared, you know that," she said.

"All of us do," added Pomeroy. Yan looked to the deck, then back up at Clement.

"Captain Jared Clement, in the name of the 5 Suns Alliance Navy I am hereby"—she paused here and took a deep breath—"*relieving* you of command of the 5SN gunship *Beauregard* under Article Three, Section 5.1a of the Navy Code of Justice. You will remain in this cabin under confinement to quarters until further notice. When we return to Kemmerine Station you will be turned over to the Naval Military Service for your court-martial to be adjudicated. Do you understand this order?" she said, implying her rank was now higher than his.

"I do," replied Clement. "But may I remind all of you that you swore an oath to follow me, not the 5 Suns Alliance Navy Command, just a few hours ago. All of you will likely stand trial for that action, and whatever justice I receive I'm sure you are likely to receive something similar from the 5SN. So, if you wish to go through with this, just be reminded that the penalty for mutiny under both the 5 Suns Alliance and the old Rim Confederation Code of Justice is death by hanging. If that's what you wish to risk, I can't stop you. But the fact is, that I am far more likely to be lenient with you than Admiral DeVore will be. May I remind you she sabotaged this mission by giving us fake nuclear missiles. She gave this ship, and all of your lives, up as a sacrifice just so she could see what kind of threat this Earth Ark presented. If that is the person you wish to follow now, I won't resist you. But think on this: We have the means and ability to finish off this threat from the Earth Ark, and guarantee this system is free of outside threats to its native peoples. This will give the 5 Suns, and each of your families, a fighting chance to survive for the next hundred years, and beyond. But if we lose this system, we could lose everything, our entire civilization, in our lifetimes. If you wish to follow your current course, then so be it. There's nothing more I can do." At this Clement sat down, resigned to his fate.

A second later, things changed. Ensign Telco pointed his pistol at Tsu and then disarmed him, tossing the weapon to Clement, who caught it and trained it on Pomeroy. The ship's medic also handed her weapon to Telco, who backed up to Clement's side of the room, and the mutineers began slowly raising their hands.

"There will be no mutiny on my watch," said Telco. "The captain's right. I swore loyalty to him and to this mission. And we can't trust Admiral DeVore, that much is for sure."

"Thank you, Mr. Telco," said Clement. "We can't have this on board the *Beauregard*. A mutiny, failed or not, cannot stand. We have to trust each other for this to work." He powered down his cobra pistol and walked over, handing it to Yan. Telco followed his lead, giving his guns back to Tsu and Lieutenant Pomeroy. None of the guns were raised now. Clement hit the com button.

"Engineer Nobli, there are some very concerned people in my cabin who think we should return home to Kemmerine Station immediately. Is that possible?" he said.

"Another few hours of patching the reactor and we could do it, sir," replied Nobli.

"Fine. Another question, Hassan. Since you're the only one on board who can operate the reactor, would you activate it if someone besides me was giving you the order to go back home to Kemmerine?"

"Kemmerine was never my home, sir. Argyle is; you know that. And I will follow no one's orders but yours, sir. You saved my life a dozen times in the Rim Confederation Navy."

"Thank you, Hassan," Clement said, then cut the line and turned back to the would-be mutineers. "I think you would find similar sentiments among the pilot, navigator, and obviously your missile-room tech," he said with a nod toward Telco.

"You stacked the key positions with people loyal to you," said Pomeroy, angry.

"That's what every captain does, Lieutenant," replied Clement. He looked around the room at the faces of his crew. Few of them would meet his gaze. "I understand all of your concerns, believe me. My parents still live on Ceta and the decisions I make here could adversely affect them if I'm wrong. I know you're worried. So am I. But my suggestion is that we all let his situation play itself out, allow me to go forward with our surveillance of the Earth Ark, which will only be for a few hours more. I will allow Commander Yan and Lieutenant Pomeroy to act as advisors to represent the rest of the crew, if they think I am putting the ship in *unnecessary* danger, I will give them the power of the veto over my orders. Are these terms acceptable?"

There were mutters of agreement and some negative grumbling, but ultimately no one spoke up in opposition to the proposal. When things settled down again, he said, "Then let's get back to work, and quite bluntly, forget this incident ever happened."

At this the crowd started to break up. Pomeroy looked to Yan, who could only hang her head in shame. Telco collected the cobra pistols and they all shuffled back to their assignments, leaving him and Yan alone. Yan looked up to face her commander.

"Captain, I wish to . . . take some time to reflect on my recent actions, in my cabin, sir," she said.

"Take all the time you need, Commander," replied Clement. "But don't be too hard on yourself. This mission has been difficult for all of us, and I still need you functioning as my effective XO."

Yan nodded without another word and departed his cabin.

Once Yan was gone Clement thanked Telco and ordered him back to the missile room, and to be sure to lock the weapons lockers. With that Clement went back to his bridge and found Massif, Ori, and Adebayor waiting for him. Both Massif and Ori wore holstered sidearms.

"We were never giving command of this ship to mutineers, Captain. We wanted you to know that," said Massif. Clement nodded.

"Thank you, Ivan." He turned on the ship-wide com and spoke into it in a calm voice.

"All hands return to your stations and resume your assignments. All is well," he said. Then he sat down heavily in his command couch, and sighed.

# ✦ 20 ✦

The next five hours were tense. Yan did not return to the bridge until a few minutes before the radio-telescope scans were projected to sight the Earth Ark. She asked for Clement's permission to take her station, and he granted it, but not without making her linger at the threshold for more than a few seconds. He wasn't happy with her involvement in the mutiny, and he reserved the right to be pissed off about it. Until that point he had thought they had developed an excellent commander/first officer rapport, but now he felt that trust was broken and he admitted to himself that his feelings were hurt, and that was something he had to be conscious of going forward.

He watched as Yan took her station and activated her dark console. Just then Mika Ori unstrapped her holster and pulled her sidearm slightly out, fingering the safety by clicking it off and on several times before returning the weapon to the holster. She never looked at Yan, but the message was clear, and he was sure Yan picked up on the unspoken signal. There would be a price to pay if she undermined her captain again. Unfortunately, Yan decided to speak up about it.

"Are sidearms now standard issue on the bridge, Captain?" she said.

Clement took a deep breath before responding.

"Lieutenant Ori and Lieutenant Commander Massif have my permission to wear a sidearm at all times, as does Ensign Telco. I would prefer the rest of the crew remains unarmed," he said in as calm and even a voice as he could muster. Ori glared at Yan with an angry look on her face, and Clement did nothing to discourage her, sitting with his hands folded across his console. After a tense moment Yan looked down at her board and Ori returned her attention to her console.

"Do we have a bead on the Earth Ark yet, Ensign?" Clement asked Adebayor.

"Long-range scanners should pick up the Ark in another thirty-three minutes, sir," she said.

"Thank you, Ensign. Navigator, range to the intercept point of the Earth Ark?"

"Seven hundred fifty thousand kilometers, sir. Suggest we begin deceleration to slow our approach to any potential battlefield, sir," Massif said. Ori turned and Clement nodded.

"As suggested, Pilot," he said. She turned and began the deceleration process.

"Are we planning on entering a battlefield?" This came from Yan, and was seen as an unwelcome comment from the rest of the bridge crew, including Clement, who swiveled to face her, speaking slowly.

"I have no intent of taking this ship into battle again, Commander. But I do intend to get close enough to that Earth Ark to determine what she's doing out here, and what her future intent is in the Trinity system and toward the natives. When that is done, other courses of action will be considered, including retreating to Kemmerine, but not until. Is that clear?" he said. His anger was apparent to all the bridge crew, including Yan.

"It is clear, sir," was all she managed in reply.

"Good," he said, swiveling back to the main screen. "Feel free to share the same with your colleagues, Commander," he said, meaning of course her fellow failed mutineers.

Clement called down to Adebayor again. "Does the deceleration change your calculation to visual observation of the Earth Ark, Ensign?" he said.

"No, sir," she said, flashing her stunning smile. "I calculated a standard deceleration into my equations, sir."

"And what if I chose a nonstandard deceleration plan, Ensign?" said Ori, challenging the young officer.

The smile faded from Adebayor's face. "Then obviously, ma'am, I would have to recalculate," said Adebayor.

"Hmm . . ." said Ori, then: "Deceleration rate is standard. Carry on, Ensign."

"Yes, ma'am." Clement smiled to himself at the exchange. This crew needed more of that, experienced spacers pushing the young officers to improve. He regretted it would probably not happen on this ill-fated mission.

Thirty-two minutes later they got their first ping.

"Detecting multiple large objects, about where we would expect them to be," reported Adebayor.

"Multiple objects? Are you sure, Ensign?"

Adebayor threw her console display to the main screen. It showed a long cylinder, obviously the Earth Ark, but two more large blobs flanking her.

"Is that the best visual we can do?" Clement said.

"We're still eighty thousand klicks from the Ark, sir, and moving, as are they," said Massif, helping out the young Ensign with an explanation of the poor visual quality.

"I should be able to get higher-definition photography with the radio telescope as we get closer," stated Adebayor.

"Keep it on the main screen, Ensign, and put up a tactical window as well."

"Aye, sir."

Clement watched as the main screen painted a new view about every ten seconds. With each pass, the picture became clearer. Clement went to the ship-wide com.

"All hands, this is the captain. We are now in visual range of the Earth Ark. She is moving slowly; her direction is pointing away from us, but her actions at this time are yet to be determined. As we get closer and the visual definition of the situation becomes more clear, I will update you on our status. Clement out."

The bridge crew watched in silence as the picture continually repainted for several minutes. The tactical display gave no indication of any further identification of the two "blobs" on the Earth Ark's flanks. Things stayed tense and quiet until the *Beauregard* reached the ten-thousand-kilometer mark. The two flanking clouds now had some definition, and Clement ordered Adebayor to enhance her scans on the closest visual blob of data near the Earth Ark.

The scan repainted a few more times before Clement ordered a hold. He pointed at the screen. "That's a flotilla formation," he said. "I'd stake my reputation on it. I can make out individual ships. That one there looks like one of the Earth Ark cruisers. Do you agree, Ivan?"

"I do, sir," he said.

"I can make out the clippers as well," said Mika Ori.

"There's another class of ship—let me see if I can make it out," piped in Yan, trying to contribute.

"Don't bother. Those tubelike objects are hunter-killers," said Clement. A few seconds later and the tactical system alerts went off like wildfire. The numbers came across the screen in rapid succession. Twenty-four of the cruisers. Over sixty light attack clippers and thirty hunter-killers. No doubt the other flanking formation was made up of similar numbers. "By volume and displacement, I'm willing to bet she's deployed her entire battle force in those two formations. Do you agree, Mika?"

The *Beauregard*'s pilot nodded. "I do, sir. The other formation is now coming in with similar numbers. Assuming the rest of her mass area is reserved for ground soldiers and transports, I'd say she's maxed out her space-borne battle capabilities."

"Sir, those two battle groups are accelerating, pulling away from the Ark," said Adebayor, a nervous tone in her voice.

"But pulling away toward what?" said Clement out loud. He sat back down in his couch and studied both the tactical and visual live streams of data.

"I would say this, sir." The voice belonged to Ivan Massif, and he threw his navigational tracker to the main screen.

It showed a distant group of objects with glowing thrusters, their engines burning bright, hurtling toward the Earth Ark's position at high speed. The Ark's attack flotillas were accelerating to meet them.

"We've stumbled onto that battlefield," said Clement.

"But who are they fighting?" asked Yan, looking to Clement. "The terraformers?"

Mika Ori's head snapped around at that comment, but she said nothing.

Clement looked to his first officer, then back to the screen. He stepped forward and spoke loudly enough so that everyone on the bridge could hear him. "No, not terraformers," he said, shaking his head. "But I'm willing to bet my entire bonus that the fleet coming at us is commanded by Admiral Elara DeVore."

The bridge was dead silent at his proclamation, and no one

challenged it. Within a few minutes they had confirmation of the same. The 5 Suns Alliance Navy fleet consisted of three battlecruisers, half of what was based at Kemmerine Station when they had left; and twelve heavy cruisers, sixteen destroyers, and five gunships, which Clement guessed were the remaining hulls from the Rim Confederation fleet, converted to use by the Admiral just as the *Beauregard* had been. They were in a spread wing formation, or "Eagle" as they termed it, much like he had faced many times in the War of the 5 Suns. The flanking pair of battlecruisers were surrounded by formations of four heavy cruisers and five destroyers each, with the central group having the extra sixth destroyer protecting the capital ship. The command battlecruiser, no doubt Admiral DeVore's flagship, was positioned the furthest back in the formation. The five gunships were at the front of the whole fleet, essentially missile-launching platforms spread out evenly in the formation. The battlecruiser groups were designed to move independently if need be, or to be used as a blunt-force hammer if they stayed together.

The Earth forces were aligned in a seemingly haphazard way, with the light cruisers at different, random positions, the hunter-killers moving to the front of the formation, and the clippers mixing in at random throughout the formation. Both fleets were closing fast on each other now.

"I thought we were the only 5 Suns Navy ship that had the LEAP drive. Weren't we supposed to be a prototype?" said Yan.

Clement shook his head. "No, Commander. We were just the bait. Admiral DeVore must have made this plan from the moment one of her automated probes detected the Earth Ark approaching the Trinity system," he responded. "Estimation of the time until the two forces engage on the battlefield," commanded Clement, not caring who answered the question.

It was Mika Ori. "Seven minutes until the 5 Suns Alliance ships reach missile range, sir, but at the rate everyone's moving, they'll crash into each other first and then it will be a free-for-all," she said.

"I wouldn't expect that from Admiral DeVore," Clement replied, relying on his experiences with her in the War of the 5 Suns. "She's usually quite calculated in how she approaches these things." *And many others*, he thought to himself.

"What do we do?" It was Yan asking the question.

"We lay back and watch, then deal with the winner," said Clement. "Bring us to full stop, Pilot."

"Full stop, aye, sir," said Ori.

"What about the Earth Ark itself? She's just laying back," said Yan.

"Keep an eye on her, Commander. And let me know if she starts to move." Yan just nodded, upset at being relegated to side duty, but Clement didn't care. She had made her own bed, now she had to lie in it.

They all watched as the two fleets closed on each other at incredible speeds. Ori had been right. It would be like a jousting match, both "horsemen" taking their best shots, then breaking off the attack and reforming for another run. It was the kind of battle that could only be conducted with large forces, but Clement found it wasteful. Many lives would be lost in the first few minutes, snuffed out in an instant, men and women disintegrated by atomic missiles or torn apart to die in space by kinetic weapons. And then it would get dirty. Ship-to-ship warfare, probably at too close of quarters for atomic weapons. It would devolve to Directed Energy Weapons or short-range conventional missiles, cutting each fleet to pieces, and possibly even boarding parties, invading and slaughtering each other. Clement had seen enough of it in the War of the 5 Suns, and had hoped never to see it again. In that moment, he regretted ever taking this command.

As he expected, Admiral DeVore made the first move. The starboard battlecruiser group broke from the Eagle formation and made a slashing, high-speed run at the corresponding Earth Ark battle group. The central and port 5 Suns battlecruiser groups, the central one being led by DeVore, both broke to the port side of the Earth Ark formation. They quickly regrouped into an attacking cylinder formation, with the battlecruisers enveloped by their heavy cruisers and destroyers. To his surprise, the five converted Rim Confederation gunships went to the front of the larger attacking group and accelerated, dropping some kind of kinetic charges ahead of the attacking fleet.

"What are those? Scatter mines?" asked Ori.

"Looks like it," said Clement. "We don't have any scatter mines on board and we're not even designed to deploy them. Those gunships were probably retrofitted to carry them."

They watched the portside battle formations as the Earth Ark's hunter-killers took the initiative, fifteen of them accelerating at high-g speeds the manned ships couldn't match. They were trying to get under the curtain of descending scatter mines that the gunships had laid down, but it would be a closely run thing. Very close. If the HuKs could get under the mines, they could attack the underbelly of Admiral DeVore's portside battle group.

The scatter mines had a limited mobility programmed into them, and they burned their thrusters trying to reach the hunter-killers. The HuKs kept varying their approaches, trying to create different angles of attack.

The HuKs slammed into the minefield, several of them exploding in nuclear fireballs on contact. The mines were reacting by trying to track the HuKs and get close enough to detonate, but in the end six of the fifteen Earth weapons got through the initial Five Suns fleet line of defense.

Next, DeVore sent her heavy cruisers and destroyers into the fray against the Earth Ark's light cruisers and clippers. Almost immediately two of the HuKs homed in on one of the 5 Suns cruisers and hit it almost simultaneously, with the heavy cruiser going up in a fireball of nuclear fission. DeVore's destroyers and gunships then barraged the remaining HuKs with a copious amount of missiles, conventional ones, designed to create a literal web of explosive power in their paths. This was a tactic Clement had seen before in battles with the 5 Suns Alliance Navy many times. It was a sheer numbers game and the 5SN had the advantage, and whenever they had the advantage, they used it.

The four remaining HuKs weren't smart enough to change course to avoid the web of incoming ordnance. They slammed into the missile barrage, exploding on contact with missiles or disintegrating into shredded metal as their speed itself tore them apart. At this, DeVore's fleet started the long curve back to intercept the remainder of the Earth Ark's forces. There were scattered skirmishes between the Earth light cruisers and DeVore's destroyers, and the Earth ships had the firepower advantage there. But it would take any two Earth cruisers to take on one of the 5 Suns Alliance heavy cruisers, and DeVore had seven of those left in her formation. The clippers, for their part, simply picked out individual targets and hit them with missiles or DEW beams, trying to cut pieces into the larger 5 Suns Alliance ships. A group of the clippers broke away from the main group and pursued the gunships. Privately, Clement hoped the gunships survived, more out of nostalgia for his old Rim Confederation Navy days than anything else, but he showed none of that emotion to his crew.

He switched his attention back to the starboard battle group. They had engaged at a much slower pace than DeVore's main battle group. The Earth hunter-killers had taken a toll on the 5 Suns heavy cruisers and destroyers. There was no doubt that this 5 Suns battle group had a reliable commander, but he or she hadn't had the advantage of the scatter-mine web that had been dropped by the gunships. The commander had endured the heavy punishment of the hunter-killers, taking three of the Earth weapons out with missiles before they could reach their targets. The destroyers and heavy cruisers had taken on the hard task of clearing the field of the remaining HuKs, and one of each of those class of ships had been taken out by the Earth weapons. The group commander had moved his battlecruiser up into the fray, unlike DeVore and her battle group, which had held the two capital ships back. The battlecruiser took hits from two of the surviving HuKs, but seemed none the worse for wear. She had ragged-edged tears in her port side and had no doubt lost crew, but she was actively engaging the Earth force's light cruisers and clippers with her DEW weapons and a flurry of low-yield, high-speed conventional missiles. With the two groups so closely aligned, the use of nuclear weapons would have assured mutual destruction, so for the moment, they weren't being used. Clement wondered if the Earth cruiser commanders had orders to self-destruct in the event of a potential loss. It certainly fit their previous mode of operation, and that made him worry.

He turned his attention back to the gunships that were attempting to get behind DeVore's destroyer line while being pursued by the large flotilla of Earth clippers. One of the fleeing gunships had suffered propulsion damage of some kind, and at least a dozen of the clippers swarmed over her, attacking with their DEW weapons and short-range missiles. She was damaged and listing, and looked to be in serious trouble. The lead gunship commander, however, decelerated and then turned their ship toward the swarms of clippers, engaging in a rear-guard action to allow his fellow gunships to escape beyond DeVore's destroyer line, while also attempting to rescue his wounded sister ship. He fired a barrage of six high-yield missiles, followed ten seconds later by a second volley. The missiles did the trick, taking out almost all of the clippers. The gunship commander pursued the remaining few enemy clippers and took them out with heavy Directed Energy Weapons fire. They were too late to save their sister ship, though. The mortally wounded gunship drifted, spinning rapidly and burning as it vented oxygen, fire, and probably crew into space. The gunship group commander watched from a safe distance as the critically damaged gunship exploded. There was a brief respite as the group commander waded in on the wreckage of its lost sister ship, no doubt searching for escape pods. Clement had been in one of those before and it was no safe haven in the midst of a battle. The command gunship completed a quick search, and finding no survivors, turned and made their way back to DeVore's battle group, which was engaged in a maneuver to put it back onto the main battlefield. Clement wondered what the gunship's captain must have been thinking. He'd been faced with the same situation many times, and it had always hurt to lose comrades.

While the portside battle group commander was simply holding the line against the arrayed Earth forces, Admiral DeVore's starboard group was once again fully engaged in maneuvers against her foes. She hadn't committed either of her battlecruisers as of yet, but he expected her to play that trump card soon, and she didn't disappoint. The secondary battlecruiser jumped into the fray with DEW and high-yield conventional missiles, just a notch below a nuke in their total expended-energy levels. The use of the capital ship looked like it was going to be a decisive one.

The Earth forces responded the only way they could, by committing their ships to ramming their superior opponents. One of the Earth cruisers collided with a 5 Suns Alliance heavy cruiser and then did the unthinkable.

She detonated a nuke, destroying both ships.

"Oh my god," said Mika Ori, her hand going to cover her mouth in horror. Clement was brought back to reality by the shock of seeing the Earth cruiser commit suicide, but he wasn't surprised.

"We can't be moved by what we see," he said to his bridge crew, trying to reassure everyone. "The Earth forces play by a different set of rules than we do. We've seen that already." A second suicide explosion occurred and then a third happened, and the 5 Suns Alliance forces smartly began to pull back from the Earth ships.

For their part, the clippers had taken to ramming the 5 Suns Alliance destroyers, something they were clearly designed to do, then attacking them with boarding parties. Clement saw one of the 5 Suns destroyers go up in flames, most likely from a nonatomic detonation. He doubted the 5 Suns Alliance crew would do such a thing, so it seemed likely that one of the clipper boarding parties had taken the destroyer's missile room and detonated a warhead inside the ship, the resulting chain reaction leading to the fatal explosion. Another 5 Suns Alliance destroyer had six clippers dangling off of it as it listed through the battlefield. He watched as the destroyer turned on a nearby heavy cruiser, both ships flying the 5 Suns flag, and started firing missiles at it. Clearly the Earth forces boarding party had taken control of the destroyer's bridge. A second 5 Suns heavy cruiser broke off from its engagement with two Earth cruisers and swept toward the rogue destroyer, firing missiles and DEW beams as it came. The destroyer, already damaged by the clippers and no doubt taken over by their Earth crews, didn't last long under that barrage, exploding as her engine drives were taken out.

Finally, DeVore got her capital ships into the fray. Both battlecruisers slashed at the Earth force formation from different sides, DEW cannons firing but holding back on missiles. It was a crowded battlefield, and using even conventional missiles at these kinds of ranges could create serious battle damage to friendly forces. Clement wondered if the battlecruisers had something else up their sleeves, and it didn't take long to detect a new development. Streaks of kinetic weapons, like long metal poles, started hitting the remaining Earth forces dead on.

"What are those things?" asked Ori.

"Some kind of nonexplosive kinetic rounds, likely fired by a rail gun of some kind. They look pretty long," he said.

"I make them at almost twenty meters," said Adebayor, surprise in her voice.

"About the height of your average telephone pole," said Clement.

"What's a 'telephone pole'?" asked Yan.

Clement shook his head at Yan's ignorance, but it was to be expected based on her privileged upbringing on Shenghai. "A telephone pole is a wooden pole stuck into the ground that carries elevated power, telecommunications, and information lines to rural houses, farms, and the like," he said.

"I've never heard of such a thing," said Yan, still surprised.

Clement turned to her, speaking without a hint of sympathy in his voice. "If you'd grown up on a Rim planet, like Ceta, or Argyle, or Helios, you'd know what they are. Coming from a privileged colony like Shenghai, I'm not surprised you've never seen one. Only poor colonies have to use them," he said, then turned away from her.

"They're made of some kind of metal alloy," piped in Adebayor. "My scans show that much."

"Most likely titanium and depleted uranium. They've been used in kinetic weapons for literally hundreds of years. Accelerated by a rail gun, their destructive power comes mostly from kinetic energy. You could cut a ship to pieces using one, especially with the penetrating properties of depleted uranium, and they're a lot cheaper than missiles," Clement said.

"It's like a lance from Hell," commented Ori.

"I like that," said Clement, "Hell Lances."

They watched as the two battlecruisers continued to bombard the Earth cruisers and clippers with the Hell Lances, cutting them to pieces with dozens of them with each pass through the battlefield. The destroyers and heavy cruisers swarmed the wounded Earth forces, finishing them off.

On the portside battlefield, things were more even, but the 5 Suns Alliance battlecruiser, obviously freed to use their own Hell Lances, was starting to cut up the Earth light cruisers and clippers. It wasn't a fair fight to begin with, and now Elara DeVore turned her own formation toward the second battlefield.

It would be a slaughter.

They watched for a few minutes more as the Earth ships fought to the bitter end, but DeVore's combined fleet finished them off to the last man, which is probably the way the Earth forces wanted it.

The total 5 Suns Alliance attack fleet reformed around the capital battlecruisers, and Clement did a recount of Admiral DeVore's remaining ships. The three battlecruisers were mostly untouched. There were nine heavy cruisers still left and thirteen destroyers, although ships of both of those groups had taken some serious battle damage, but were still operational. Those plus the four gunships left Devore with twenty-nine operational ships.

"What now?" asked Ori.

"Now, I would assume they will take out the Earth Ark itself," said Clement.

"How?"

"If it was me, I'd just fire long-range nukes and be done with her. But Admiral DeVore may have other plans. Captured technology is valuable technology."

They watched as DeVore sent in the gunships to launch missiles at the Earth Ark. To his surprise the Ark didn't respond to this provocation, and the conventional missiles did only minimal damage to the Ark's reinforced hull. Next, she sent in a formation of three destroyers. They were clearly among the most damaged ships in her fleet, indicating she was not willing to risk her best. That was telling as to her regard for the people that served under her.

Two of the destroyers closed on the Ark. The third destroyer seemed to be having propulsion problems and ended up dropping back several klicks from the other two. In the next few seconds, it would be her saving grace.

The first two destroyers began a bombardment of the Earth Ark with higher-yield missiles and DEW fire. The missiles had more of an effect than the ones launched by the gunships, but it was still fairly insignificant damage against the massive Ark. The directed-energy fire was a difference-maker though. The two destroyers began cutting into the sides of the Ark, exposing ragged gashes of her inner superstructure. In one case, there seemed to be a hit on a troop-containment area, and several bodies began pouring out of a jagged hole into space. Whether they were dead before or after the chamber they were in was exposed to space, Clement couldn't answer.

It was then that the Earth Ark finally responded. A ring of energy formed around the Arks' midsection, and then suddenly a beam of dark orange directed energy lanced out and cut the two destroyers to pieces in a single strike. At this the trailing destroyer turned as quickly as she could and retreated back to the main fleet. The Ark wound up a second DEW beam from her forward section, directing it toward the retreating destroyer, but missed as she maneuvered away at her best possible speed. At that point she was safe and out of range.

"Ivan, how far is the 5 Suns Alliance fleet from the Ark?" asked Clement.

"I make it three hundred kilometers, more or less, sir," he responded. "Right now, except for that retreating destroyer, the whole fleet is at station-keeping."

"So what's her game? Does she attack in an all-out attempt to take the Ark intact? Or does she just nuke it from her safe location?" It was Yan asking the question. Mika Ori answered.

"The Elara DeVore that I knew would plan a strategy, but she would never hold back on anything once she committed to that plan. Once she started, it was all attack, all the time," said Ori.

"But this is a very different Elara DeVore, Mika. She's not the same woman we knew fifteen years ago," said Clement. That created a feeling of regret in his gut; she surely wasn't the woman he had once loved. He had to actively push that thought out of his mind. He turned slightly toward Yan, but not all the way, before asking his next question. "Yan, can you detect any communications between the Ark and the 5 Suns fleet?"

Yan checked her board for a few seconds. "No, sir, nothing. No attempts being made by either side," she said, then added, "It looks like we have a stalemate."

"Perhaps," said Clement. Then: "That Earth Ark has got to be made of hardened regolith. If she is, then she can withstand conventional attack for days," he posited.

"What's regolith?" asked Yan.

Clement responded. "Surface material from a moon or asteroid, likely poured over an inner superstructure then compressed and hardened. Very helpful for avoiding collisions, say with meteors or other foreign objects, in deep space on long-duration space voyages. I'm not surprised they made their Ark out of it. A fifty-year journey leaves a lot of possibility for unwanted collisions."

"If that hull is made of regolith, it will be very hard to penetrate," interjected Ori, "or especially to land a boarding party."

"I suspect that's what the Admiral is thinking about right now," said Clement, then said to Adebayor, "Any sign that either party has noticed us, Ensign?"

The young Ensign shook her head before saying, "Negative, sir. I've detected no incoming scans or attempts at communication, and none of the ships in the 5 Suns Alliance fleet has pinged our IFF beacon."

"We're five thousand klicks from the Earth Ark in this position, so unless they're actively looking for a ship in this area, their odds of finding us without a deep-space scan are minimal," said Massif.

"I suspect they both have all eyes on each other," commented Clement. "So what's the next move?"

"Sir." It was Yan again.

He turned to her, fully this time. "Commander?" said Clement, not hiding his annoyance at her continued interruptions.

She stiffened, facing his glare. "Might I suggest that we have now completed our mission? In fact, I would say we have even surpassed it, knowing that the Earth Ark fleet has been destroyed, she poses no threat to this system. Perhaps, sir, it is time for us to go home," she said.

Clement then pressed an icon on his console before answering.

"Our 5 Suns Alliance mission is complete, I agree with you on that," he started. "But we still have additional interests in this star system, and that would be the natives. And, to be honest with you, I'm not sure leaving this system in the hands of Admiral Elara DeVore and the 5 Suns Alliance fleet is any better than leaving it to the Earth Ark forces."

"So you're refusing my demand that we vacate the battlefield and return home? That *was* part of our agreement to stand down from mutiny."

"I understand that, Commander. What I'm saying is that this ship has a weapon powerful enough to decide the outcome of this battle, and the terms and conditions under which we leave this system. Trading one set of slavers for another is not an option I'm willing to accept."

"You know goddamn well using the MAD weapon again could crack the reactor permanently, stranding us here," snapped Yan.

"Yes, but under those conditions we could go back to Bellus and live among the natives, then hitch a ride home on a 5 Suns Alliance ship when they took over the system. A ride that, I might add, would surely find me enjoying the trip in the brig. No, Commander, I'm not willing to head home to an unknown fate, not when this entire crew could end up facing court-martial. I'm of a mind to stay, and perhaps even help determine the outcome," he said.

"So you're breaking our agreement?" said Yan, demanding an answer.

"I never negotiate with mutineers," he said, turning away from her.

"So you lied?"

Instead of answering, Clement hit the com on his console. "Ensign Telco, is the reactor room secure?"

"Aye, sir," came Telco's reply over the com speakers. "As soon as I got your ping I locked up the missile room and came down to Engineering, just like we talked about," he said. "The room is now locked and I'm armed, sir."

"Good work, Ensign," said Clement. He stood. "Lieutenant Ori, please escort Commander Yan to her quarters and lock her inside."

When Yan turned Ori already had her cobra pistol trained on her. She surrendered without a fight and Ori took her down the six metal steps to the cabin area. Clement hit the com again.

"Telco, you still there?"

"Sir," replied Telco.

"Put Mr. Nobli on."

After a second of shuffling Nobli's gruff voice came over the com. "What do you demand of me now, tyrant?" he said.

Clement smiled, just a little, at that. "Condition of the LEAP reactor?"

"The cracks have been sealed, but she's still fragile."

"Can we use her as a weapon without destroying the ship?"

Nobli paused before answering. "It's a risk, sir. As I said before, opening up a contained system like this for just fractions of a second to make a short jump or fire the weapon would put a great strain on her. She could fracture again, enough so that we couldn't repair her, then we couldn't get home. Or worse, she could break wide open, in which case we'd likely be consumed by an implosion, along with anything within an astronomical unit, give or take."

"That would be the entire solar system, including the star," said Clement. "Any other alternatives?"

"All I can say, sir, is if you're going to use this thing as a weapon, use it for a sustained period; don't turn it on and off quickly. That would allow us to back the thing down slowly, and create much less stress on the reactor casing," Nobli said.

"I hear you," said Clement. "Thank you, Nobli." He shut down the com as Mika Ori returned to the bridge.

"The commander is safely ensconced in her cabin, sir. I even gave her a chance to get some food and tea from the galley, so we don't have to worry about her for quite a while," she said. "The access hatch from the cargo bay is also secure and the rest of the crew have no access to the cabin area, bridge, or critical systems."

"Well done, Ori. The missile room is secure and Telco just locked down the LEAP reactor room. You all did your jobs well," Clement said, then he turned to Adebayor.

"Ensign, these people have been part of my crew for long time. We are loyal to each other in every way. But I want you to know that I do not and would not require you to serve against your will. The actions we take next could be considered capital offenses by the 5 Suns Navy, or they could result in a positive outcome for both us onboard the *Beauregard* and the settlers in this system. If you have any doubts, then you are free to go to the spare cabin and sit this one out," he said.

Adebayor turned to face him directly. "I understand, sir. I've come this far, and I'm committed to the outcome of this mission, so I will give my commitment to you for the duration of this action, however it might come out," she said.

Clement nodded. "You're a very brave young woman, Kayla Adebayor," he said to her. "Also, know that I'm going to wipe the mission tapes from this little adventure before we get home, so when we do get back, you will be under no obligation to me. Your record will be clean."

"Understood, sir. Thank you, sir."

"Carry on," he said, which was the highest compliment he could give her.

"So what do we do next?" asked Massif.

Clement looked back and forth to his small crew. "Pilot, fire the engines and accelerate us toward the Earth Ark at 1.5 *g*s," he said. "Navigator, make sure that our flight path will keep us aligned with the 5 Suns Navy fleet as well."

"Aligned in what way?" Massif asked.

Clement clasped his hands behind his back. "Aligned so that we can fire the weapon at them both, the Ark and the fleet," stated Clement flatly. "We're going to end this battle."

# ✳ 21 ✳

About fifteen minutes into their acceleration burn, they started getting the attention of the 5 Suns Alliance fleet, and presumably, Admiral DeVore. She sent her four converted gunships to intercept the *Beauregard*, essentially outgunning her four to one, in conventional weaponry anyway. Clement ordered no response to the gunships, as they would have to do quite a bit of chasing to catch his ship before she inserted herself into the battlefield at the speed the *Beauregard* was traveling. Clement had a plan, but he wasn't willing to share it with his crew just yet.

When it became obvious the chasing 5 Suns Alliance gunships couldn't complete their intercept of the *Beauregard* before she reached the battle zone, they received an Identification Friend or Foe ping from the main-fleet battlecruiser, and Admiral DeVore. Clement wondered what she must be thinking about his ship still being operational, let alone entering an active battlefield. No doubt she would have expected his ship to have been destroyed by the Earth Ark forces by now.

"Receiving an IFF ping from the 5 Suns Alliance flagship, sir. How do we respond?" asked Adebayor.

"We wait," replied Clement, watching on his tactical screen as his ship drew ever closer to both the Earth Ark and the 5 Suns Alliance ships. The bridge stayed tense and quiet for what seemed like an eternity before the flagship repeated her ping.

"Sir?" asked Adebayor.

"I haven't made up my mind yet, Ensign."

At this both Ori and Massif turned to him.

"Who's side are we on?" asked Ori.

"Our own, Mika. Admiral DeVore has betrayed us and gave us up for dead to the Earth forces. The Earth Ark is here to destroy any enemy and enslave the people in this system. I am opposed to both sides of this conflict," Clement said. "Are the rest of you of the same mind?" He looked around the room.

"We're behind you, whatever decisions you make, sir," said Massif.

"Thank you, Ivan."

Thirty seconds later the third ping came. All eyes were on their captain. Finally, Clement was being forced to make a decision.

"Ignore the ping, Ensign. Admiral DeVore knows damn well who we are. Mika, increase speed to 1.75 *g* and take us to within three hundred kilometers from the Earth Ark, but keep her between us and the 5 Suns Alliance fleet."

"Aye, sir," said Ori, and began her acceleration burn. DeVore's gunships fell farther behind the *Beauregard*, and were now essentially out of the fray for the moment. Clement calculated the decisive moment in this battle would come well before the sister 5 Suns gunships could get within firing range of the *Beauregard*. DeVore seemed to realize this as well, as the gunships abruptly changed course, retreating toward the 5 Suns Alliance fleet while keeping a safe distance from the Earth Ark.

"And now there are three of us on the chessboard," said Clement.

"But they have no idea we have the MAD weapon, sir. Could the 5 Suns Alliance fleet have developed it as well, or something similar?" asked Ori.

"It's possible," admitted Clement, "but not probable. The MAD is a Hassan Nobli special for the moment, and that is our only advantage. How long to our destination, Navigator?"

"I make it seven minutes, including the deceleration," replied Massif.

Those would be seven *very* long minutes.

"We've arrived at the designated position, Captain," reported Ori, "three hundred kilometers from the Earth Ark."

"Indeed we have. Thrusters to full stop," he said, once more scanning his tactical display. "The question is, now what? Who makes the next move?"

They didn't have to wait long for the answer.

The fleet com line lit up for the first time in the entire mission.

"Incoming com from the 5 Suns Alliance flagship, sir—voice only," said Adebayor.

Clement sat forward in his couch. "Bring it up, Ensign." She did as instructed, and a gravelly male voice came over the bridge com line.

"This is the 5 Suns Alliance Navy battlecruiser *Wellington* calling unknown ship. Identify yourself and return our IFF ping or you will be considered an enemy combatant and be subject to attack," it said.

Clement held up his hand to Adebayor, watching the clock tick for a full minute before responding.

"5SN Battlecruiser *Wellington*, you know damn well who we are," he said, then gave Adebayor the cut sign. A full two minutes went by before the *Wellington* responded again with the same message from the same source. This time Clement signaled Adebayor to respond immediately, and she patched him in.

"If you want to know who we are, *Wellington*, ask your flag officer, Admiral DeVore," he said. Mika Ori snickered at this response.

It took almost three minutes for the *Wellington* to respond this time, and when it did, it was a very different voice speaking.

"This is Admiral Elara DeVore of the 5 Suns Alliance Navy battlecruiser *Wellington*. To whom am I speaking? Is that you, Clement?" she said.

"This is Captain Jared Clement of the . . ." He trailed off and looked around the room for suggestions as to what navy they represented, but got no help, so he made a name up on the spot. "Trinity Republic Navy gunship *Beauregard*," he said.

For a few seconds, well beyond the normal broadcast delay, they heard nothing, then:

"We do not recognize the navy you have identified, or the Trinity Republic. With what authority do you speak for this alleged entity?" came DeVore's voice.

"You know damn well who we are, Elara. Quit the bullshit," said Clement. Again there was a long pause before she continued.

"We're pleased to find you alive and well, Captain Clement," said DeVore. "We recognize a 5 Suns Alliance Navy ship with the name *Beauregard*, but not one in the Trinity Navy, or whatever you just called it," she said. "And how many ships do you have in this 'navy' of yours?"

Clement smiled, then spoke into the com. "We are a fleet of one, Admiral." There was a dramatic pause again when the only sounds were the crack and pop of the com line.

"You appear to be outgunned, Captain," she finally said, quietly and with determination in her voice.

"That's what the Earth Ark forces thought too, Admiral," replied Clement. "But we're still here, much to your unpleasant surprise, I'm sure."

Her tone went angry now. "I have no time to dawdle with you, Clement. You're in violation of the 5 Suns Alliance Navy military code. You have disobeyed orders and declared yourself flying the flag of an unknown enemy. You are a traitor. Surrender your vessel now, and stand aside. Otherwise you, and your crew, will be considered as enemy combatants."

"I regret I can do neither of those things, Admiral," said Clement. "In fact, I suggest that you withdraw your fleet from this system, and let us deal with the invading Earth forces." He knew that would stick in her craw. She came back on the line, with a laugh.

"You have *one* ship, Clement! A gunship at that, of which I have four left. You have no nukes aboard because I denied them to you. You were a great ship captain in your day, Jared, but that day is long gone. You will all be considered as enemies and your ship will be destroyed," she said.

"Does that death sentence include your adjutant, Commander Yan?" Clement asked, knowing she would be monitoring communications from her cabin. "She was loyal to you." Again, there was a pause.

"Yan signed up for the risks. Every naval officer does," replied DeVore. "Now stand aside, and we will deal with you later."

"Well, since I don't fly your flag anymore, you won't mind if I watch your next move from right here, do you?" Clement said. This time, she didn't respond, and the com line went silent.

It took a few minutes, but her next move smacked of a bit of desperation as she sent in her two sister battlecruisers toward the Earth Ark. They volleyed missile after missile at her, but the Earth Ark stayed resilient, taking the explosions of conventional weapons as scrapes on her hardened regolith hull. They would have to use nukes to have any chance of penetrating the Ark; but it was clear now that DeVore wanted the Ark intact, to strip her of any valuable tech. Clement intended to deny her that prize.

The battlecruisers accelerated their approach then and started firing Hell Lances at the Ark, dozens of them. These had more impact on the hull, but not enough to be decisive. The Ark fired back with her orange DEW beams, but to little effect. No doubt the battlecruisers had hardened hulls against such weapons, unlike the destroyers, and quite possibly energized defensive fields too. A strong enough energy field could deflect a like type of energy. A gravity-based defensive system could even disperse the incoming wave.

What was now obvious was that DeVore would have to commit most of her fleet to take the Earth vessel. Clement was indecisive about whether he should simply allow her to do that and watch her fleet take severe casualties or get involved himself, and end the battle before it started. DeVore made the final decision for him.

A small flotilla of two heavy cruisers and three destroyers, all superior in firepower to the *Beauregard*, broke away from the main fleet and began making for his position. It was obvious their orders were to destroy the *Beauregard*. Clement couldn't have that. He called down on the com to Nobli.

"Hassan, what's the current status of the LEAP reactor?"

"She's warm and ready, sir, but I'd be much happier if we were tuning her up to head home than to use the MAD weapon," he said honestly. Clement nodded even though Nobli couldn't see him.

"I understand. You said it would be better for the reactor, increase our chances of it staying stable and not cracking again, if instead of a quick microburst of energy we used the weapon wide open, in a constant flow for a lengthier period of time," stated Clement.

"I said something to that effect," said Nobli. "But let's face it, any use of the weapon will be experimental and highly problematic. It's a great risk, Captain."

"Acknowledged. How long?"

"What?" said Nobli.

"How long should I keep the weapon open and firing?" There was a long silence before Nobli answered.

"Uncertain."

"Can you estimate the weapon's range of effectiveness?"

"Again, uncertain, sir. It could be anywhere from one kilometer to the end of the universe. We just don't know."

"So, what your saying is, I won't know how well it works until I fire it, and if I do, I should keep it firing for an unknown period of time?"

"Five seconds at a minimum sir. After that, take whatever time you need. I'll be able to gradually back off the reactor power once you shut down the weapon from your console, sir."

"Keep this channel open, Engineer, and prepare to fire the MAD weapon," finished Clement.

"Aye, sir."

Clement turned to his bridge crew. "How long until DeVore's flotilla gets within range to destroy us?" he asked.

Massif answered. "They're two hundred fifty klicks out, sir, and closing fast. I'd say we have two minutes until we're in range of their nukes, sir."

Clement turned to Ori. "Options, Lieutenant?"

"I'd say none, sir. From what we saw of the Ark's DEW range, it's at least one hundred kilometers. If we go toward her, she'll fry us. At the speed the 5 Suns Alliance ships are closing, we have little to no chance to escape, even if we did a max engine burn. And even at that, the best odds I can give you on escape is fifty-fifty, maybe less," Ori said.

"So it appears we only have one option," stated Clement. "Use the MAD weapon on 5 Suns Alliance Navy ships." He looked to his two compatriots. Mika Ori had always been his conscience on decisions like this, providing her thoughts and advice during the War of the 5 Suns. She and Elara DeVore had often butted heads on what was legitimate strategy and what wasn't.

"I don't see any other viable choice, Captain," she said. He looked to Massif.

"You know I have no love for the 5 Suns Alliance, sir. I say do what we have to do to stay alive," he said.

Clement looked up at the ship's clock, then over to the young Ensign Adebayor. "Ensign?"

"I want to live, sir," was all she had to say. Clement sighed and sat back in his command chair.

"Nobli, arm the MAD weapon," he said into the com.

"Armed," was Nobli's only reply.

Clement called up the tactical screen on the main display. The 5 Suns flotilla was closing. He only had one minute and twenty seconds before they could fire nukes at him and destroy the *Beauregard*. He looked down at the MAD weapon icon on his console. It was green and ready to fire. He aimed the weapon as best he could, sighting the lead heavy cruiser in the middle of the 5 Suns Alliance formation. He took in one last, deep, breath.

And fired.

The white energy of the Matter Annihilation Device surged out of the *Beauregard*'s forward cannon port. It took microseconds to cross the space between his ship and the 5 Suns Alliance flotilla. The lead heavy cruiser simply ceased to exist. The flanking ships on either side were swept up by the beam as Clement moved it back and forth from side to side, manually aiming at the enemy fleet with his fingers on the targeting control. He went past the five-second safety margin and let the beam go on for a ten count before he shut it down. The ships of the 5 Suns Navy flotilla were gone from the universe.

The bridge stayed dead quiet.

"Nobli, report," Clement demanded.

"Weapon successfully fired, sir. System gradually backed down to within safety limits," reported Nobli.

"Can I use it again?"

"I would say yes, Captain. The reactor didn't even flinch at the firing. I think she was glad to expend some energy, finally."

Clement smiled at that. "Have I ever told you that you need a girlfriend, Nobli?"

"Many times, sir," he replied.

Clement turned to his navigator. "Ivan, could you track the range of the weapon?"

"I lost it after ten thousand kilometers, sir. It was simply moving too fast," said Massif.

"Let's hope it dissipates," replied Clement. He looked to Ori. "Pilot, take us toward the Earth Ark, thrusters only," he ordered.

"Aye, sir."

"We didn't start this war, but it's within our power to end it," he said, then he leaned back in his couch to watch his ship close in on its next target.

☼　☼　☼

The 5 Suns Alliance Navy battlecruisers were engaged in a death dance with the Earth Ark. Though the Ark was mostly stationary, it was using maneuvering thrusters to get different angles for its DEW beam weapons, trained now on the two attacking battlecruisers. The battlecruisers for their part were moving in a sweeping spiral motion, attacking from various angles, then adjusting their courses and making another run. The toll they were inflicting was heavy, but they failed to penetrate the regolith layers protecting the hull of the Ark. It was a constant flow of Directed Energy Weapons, missiles (from the battlecruisers—the Ark didn't appear to have any), Hell Lances, and smaller kinetic weapons. No nukes. DeVore wanted the Ark intact, but she didn't know her enemy were fanatics, and they would never let that happen. Clement momentarily mused over the possibility of just sitting back and watching the two forces destroy themselves, but then discarded the idea. He was a man of action.

Ultimately, the 5 Suns Navy barrage was ineffective. Admiral DeVore had to make another move, and Clement knew she knew that. She had undoubtedly seen her flotilla destroyed by the MAD weapon, and she made no more attempts to intercept the *Beauregard*, who for its part was now within one hundred twenty klicks of the Ark and the battlecruiser group, and perilously close to the Ark's DEW weapon range.

Clement ordered full stop and watched as DeVore committed another group of her ships, heavy cruisers and destroyers, to the battlefield.

"Those ships are going to get eaten up by the Ark," said Mika Ori. "They don't have the gravity shields against enemy weapons that the battlecruisers do."

"It's possible that the heavy cruisers have gravity shields," commented Clement. "They're big enough to carry the generators."

"They didn't have them during the War of the 5 Suns," said Massif.

"That was fifteen years ago, Ivan. I don't think Admiral DeVore has been sitting around in regards to military improvements for her fleet," said Clement. Clement had seen designs for energy shielding during the war, but the Rim Confederation simply didn't have the resources, or the ships, to carry such a defensive upgrade because of the size of the field generators. It was possible the 5 Suns Alliance Navy had solved that problem.

Clement watched the tactical screen as the second 5 Suns Navy flotilla committed to the battle. DeVore herself hung back on her battlecruiser with a small defensive group of five destroyers, three heavy cruisers, and the four remaining gunships. Everything else was now committed to the battlefield.

He watched as the battlecruisers cut off their attacks and reformed with the approaching 5 Suns Alliance battle group. The Destroyers, the most vulnerable ships, went first, followed by the heavy cruisers and then the battlecruisers. Again, the weakest ships out front, as cannon fodder. It showed ultimately that their commanding officer didn't care if they lived or died.

The destroyers for their part stayed well out of range of the Ark's DEW weapons, then lobbed a single missile from each ship.

"Those have to be nukes," said Mika Ori.

"Confirmed," said Adebayor from her station. "I'm guessing one-kiloton warheads from their energy signatures."

"Trying to blow a hole in her sides, but not destroy her. They want her tech," said Clement. The Ark lit up its DEW defenses and took out some of the missiles as they came in range, but three got through. They impacted on the hull of the Ark, one forward, one near the middle, and another at the Ark's stern, closest to the *Beauregard.*

"Looks like they're trying to take out her DEW defenses," said Ori.

Clement made no comment. There was a flurry of angry communications between the *Wellington* and the destroyer commanders. It seemed someone was unhappy they hadn't gone closer to the Ark to launch their missiles.

They watched as the heavy cruisers moved up and launched another volley of missiles.

"Ensign?" asked Clement of Adebayor.

"These are carrying a heavier load, Captain. Scans say somewhere between three and five kilotons each."

Clement watched as several of the missiles were taken out by the forward and midships DEW arrays; the rear one near the stern, and closest to the *Beauregard*, appeared to have been knocked out. Still, one missile got through. It was enough. The missile struck home near the midship DEW array. It blew a sizeable hole in the side of the Ark, more than big enough for a boarding party to invade her. She was helpless now, and it was only a matter of time before her crew was annihilated by 5 Suns Alliance Marines, offloaded from the battlecruisers.

They were closing now—no fear of the Earth Ark's defenses. They took out the remaining DEW array with a pinpoint nuclear strike from a destroyer, and she was defenseless. In a matter of minutes the boarding would commence, the slaughter would start, and the battle would be over.

"Do we destroy the Ark before DeVore can get her hands on it?" asked Ori.

"The Ark crew is doomed anyway," said Clement. "If we use the MAD weapon we may be doing them a favor compared to what the 5 Suns Alliance Marines might do to them."

Clement called down to Nobli to warm the MAD weapon again, and a few seconds later he had the green light on his console.

"How close to boarding are those 5 Suns Alliance ships?" Clement asked.

"Estimate three minutes until the heavy cruisers and destroyers reach the hole in the hull and begin boarding her," replied Massif. "The battlecruisers are hanging back."

"In case she chooses to destroy herself," said Clement. The scene was an ugly one, with no good choices. Clement was resigned to his decision. He would have to destroy the Ark to keep it out of DeVore's hands.

"Captain!" the warning came from Adebayor. "I have movement from the rest of the attack fleet."

"Throw it to the screen, Ensign."

The main tactical display was replaced by a scan of the remaining 5 Suns Alliance ships, the destroyers and heavy cruisers that had hung back with the *Wellington*. It didn't take a genius to see what they were doing. The ships had regrouped, and they were making straight for the *Beauregard*.

"Ivan?"

"Seven Minutes until they are within missile range of us, Captain."

Clement did not take that well.

"It appears they learned nothing from their first attack," said Ori.

Clement nodded, thinking of the lives already lost; the lives on board the Earth Ark and the 5 Suns Alliance Navy ships; the lives of the natives back on Bellus; and the fact that Elara DeVore, a woman he once loved, was trying to kill everyone left in his life that he cared about. He made his decision.

"Pilot, turn the ship"—he looked down at his tactical board—"nineteen degrees port."

"Nineteen degrees port, aye, sir," Ori replied. He waited until she had completed her maneuver, then threw the tactical screen back up for all to see. He trained the sight for the MAD weapon on the Earth Ark. From the angle he had he could likely envelop most of the Ark in the first few seconds.

"Engineer, is the MAD weapon ready?"

"You have a green light on your board, Captain," said Nobli in a noncommittal tone.

"Acknowledged. Count me down from five, Pilot," Clement said.

Ori did, and as she reached one, Clement hesitated, only for a moment, and then fired. The Ark disintegrated first, enveloped by the weapon's blinding white energy beam. Clement swept the aiming control across his board, from port to starboard, hitting and disintegrating the two attacking 5 Suns battlecruisers next. The final sweep encompassed the attack group heading for the *Beauregard*, and they were swept from existence, all hands lost in a matter of seconds. The beam carried on into space, and coincidentally took out one of Admiral DeVore's remaining defensive destroyers, quite by accident.

Clement shut down the weapon, then put his head in his hands, rubbed his face, and gave a deep sigh. "Pilot," he said in a quiet voice, "thrusters ahead, full max, close on the remaining 5 Suns Alliance fleet."

"Aye, Captain," replied Ori quietly. She knew what a heavy burden her captain carried with him now.

"Ensign Adebayor," said Clement.

"Sir," she replied.

"Send a text communiqué, to the 5SN *Wellington*, and Admiral DeVore by name. Tell them we are demanding their immediate surrender. No terms offered; no conditions will be considered. Tell them they have five minutes to reply with their unconditional surrender. Tag it with my name and rank, as Captain of the . . . Trinity Republic Navy ship *Beauregard*," he said.

"Aye, sir," she replied, and began crafting the communiqué.

"Will she surrender?" asked Ori. Clement gave a tired, tight smile.

"I hope so," he said. "I've had enough killing for one day."

# ✷ **22** ✷

It was a long five minutes, but eventually Admiral DeVore and the *Wellington* did surrender. In the wake of the overwhelming power of the MAD weapon, it wasn't surprising. Still, he had to plan for all contingencies, seeing as the remaining fleet was still led by DeVore, and he didn't trust her. At all.

Clement ordered all the remaining 5 Suns Alliance Navy ships to disgorge themselves of their weapons, dumping them in a specific area of space, which they did, as far as the *Beauregard* could determine. It was a lot of weaponry, conventional missiles, nukes, warheads, Hell Lances, scatter mines. They all were set adrift in space. Then Clement ordered the 5 Suns Navy ships to move off to a safe distance. He had Telco fire two conventional missiles into the floating pile of ordnance. The resulting series of explosions was both spectacular and rewarding. Clement had disarmed the enemy.

He ordered the 5 Suns fleet to make a course for the innermost habitable planet in the Trinity system, Alphus. Admiral DeVore never made direct contact with them during any of the negotiations.

The trek was a slow one, on thrusters only, with the *Beauregard* trailing the rest of the 5 Suns Navy fleet all the way. Nobli had privately informed Clement that the MAD weapon could likely never be fired again if they were to complete their trip home, and that suited Clement, who swore Nobli to absolute secrecy on the subject. No one needed to know the greatest weapon in the history of humankind couldn't be fired again. Intimidation was the key factor; the weapon's power had already been demonstrated.

At one point, one of DeVore's remaining destroyers started to drift from the preapproved flight path. It was one that had taken a good deal of damage in the battle against the Earth Ark. Nonetheless,

Clement, giving no quarter, ordered a double missile launch, the conventional weapons exploding near enough to the struggling destroyer for her captain to get the message. The ship chugged along, getting back into formation, but under great duress. Clement called on the fleet channel and ordered her to either be towed or abandoned by the 5 Suns Alliance fleet. Presently a heavy cruiser swept into position and put a tow line on her little sister, and further discipline was avoided.

Early on the second day of the voyage inward, Clement ordered Yan released from her cabin, and given free run of the ship again, except for the bridge. For his part he stayed in his cabin, out of the way of the crew, but assuring them at every turn that the fighting was over and they'd be heading home soon.

He was surprised when he heard the knock at his door, his monitor showing Yan standing outside. "Yes, Yan?" he said through the com.

She pressed the com panel outside his cabin to reply. "Permission to enter, Captain?" she said.

He hesitated for a second, then said, "You don't have a weapon, do you?" It was supposed to be a joke, but even Clement wasn't sure if that's how he meant it.

"No, sir."

At that Clement slid open the cabin door and stood to face his former first officer. It was the first time she had been in his cabin since the mutiny. He motioned for her to take a seat at the table across from him.

"Please," he said. She declined with a shake of the head. Clement sat back down.

"What then, Commander?" he said expectantly.

"I don't think I hold that rank anymore, Captain," she said. Vaguely, he felt sorry for her, but he wasn't going to let that affect his decision-making processes.

"I'm not sure it's at all clear who holds what rank in what navy right now, Yan," he said, trying to be comforting in some way, if he could. "You wear the rank of commander in the 5 Suns Alliance Navy, so that is how I will address you. Now, I assume you have something to say to me?"

She straightened and looked straight ahead, but not directly at

Clement. "Sir, I came to apologize. The mutiny action was ill-advised, and I expect to be dealt with as any mutineer would."

Clement held up his hand to stop her. "It was a mistake," he said. "If I put everyone who had a mutinous thought or action on this mission up to the bar of military justice there would be no one left to fly this bird."

"Sir, I—"

"Wait," he interrupted her. "This mission put you and all the others under the strain of choosing between your homeland, your families, and the mission. You didn't choose that. Admiral DeVore made that choice for you when she set us up for destruction at the hands of the Earth Ark. No one on this ship will be referred for judgment by me, in any navy, when we get home. You all did your jobs as best you could and quite frankly, I'm proud of all of you. You're forgiven."

"Sir, if you'll let me finish . . . "

Clement looked at her. Her eyes were red, she had obviously been crying very recently, and she looked disheveled, like she hadn't slept well for several days.

Clement nodded for her to continue.

"I came here to apologize to you as your first officer, sir, but it's more than that . . . " She trailed off again, and now Clement was confused.

"Yan?" he said in a tone that indicated he was trying to reassure her. Now she looked directly at him.

"Sir . . . I'm trying to apologize to you as a woman. I betrayed you, betrayed the relationship and trust we had developed. That meant something to me, and I think to you too. I think I know how you must have felt being betrayed by Elara DeVore, and in many ways, I did the same thing to you. I wouldn't blame you if you hated me. That's what I came here to apologize for. Sir," she finished, and lowered her gaze, head down in submission.

Clement hesitated for a second, then he got up and went to her, put his arms around her as she leaned into his chest, crying softly. He kissed her on the forehead.

"You're forgiven for that as well, Yan," he said. She continued to cry. They stood there for a long time before she composed herself. She nodded at him and then turned to leave.

She got to the door before she turned back and said, "Thank you, Jared." He smiled at her, and she left.

Then he sat down in his chair, and sighed.

After a trip of three days the fleet arrived and made orbit over Alphus, and the cleanup began in earnest. Clement sat on his bridge with his command crew, sans Yan, and watched as the 5 Suns Navy fleet followed his orders.

The crews were evacuating from their ships and heading for the surface of Alphus, one ship at a time. Clement had allowed them enough equipment to set up individual camps up and down the habitable strip of the innermost Earthlike planet of the Trinity system. Alphus was unique in that its sun-facing side was mostly too hot for life to thrive, except for a two-hundred-fifty-kilometer-wide strip of green which encircled the otherwise dry, desert planet just at the edge of its light side. There was a range of high mountains that defined the break between the dark and light sides of the tidal-locked world. These mountains received enough snow to create a constant runoff of fresh water down into the valleys below. The habitable zone of the planet ran the circumference of the planet, north to south, and it created a comfortable ring of life that could be colonized, or in this case, used to exile a crew of undesirables. Clement had no time to investigate the planet, to see if it had the signs of terraforming that her sisters Bellus and Camus had, but he suspected they would find that evidence eventually, along with the possibility of native settlers, as on the other two worlds. The ring of mountains that separated the light side of the planet from the dark side seemed very regular. It could have been the result of thousands of years of consistent tidal-lock pressure from the Trinity star, or something more... artificial... in nature.

Clement made the evacuated crews spread out along the ring, so that they couldn't form communities easily. He wanted them to struggle on their own as much as possible, and certainly not work together with Admiral DeVore. If they were focused on survival, they would be far less likely to cause future trouble.

Once each ship was emptied and the crews relocated to the surface of Alphus, Clement ordered the ships of the 5 Suns Alliance fleet to be scuttled on the dark side. They did so one by one, the only exceptions being the former Rim Confederation Navy gunships. Clement wanted those for himself, eventually, so he had Ivan Massif program them for an automated burn to orbit around Bellus, out of range of any remote control the 5 Suns Alliance fleet survivors may have. After five days of this process, and relocating the crews to camps dotted throughout the habitable ring, it was time to deal with Admiral Elara DeVore, and the battlecruiser *Wellington*.

Clement went to the surface in the *Beauregard*'s shuttle, with ensigns Telco and Tsu aboard for muscle, along with Tanitha Yan. She had a decision to make. After looking over the large camp made by the *Wellington*'s nine hundred fifty crew and verifying for himself that they had proper supplies, access to water, and no weaponry, he went to a high ridge, looking down over the wastelands of Alphus' sprawling desert. He sent orders for Admiral DeVore to join him there. Telco and Tsu stood watch for him, armed, as they waited for the Admiral to arrive. Yan stood off to one side, looking very unsure of herself.

To his surprise, DeVore came alone, without an escort of any kind. Clement waved off the young ensigns to a safe distance, and Yan stepped away so the two commanders could speak alone.

"Admiral," Clement said, with only a slight nod of respect as she came up. They stood side by side on the ridge, not looking at each other, but rather looking out over Alphus' searing wasteland instead.

"Mr. Clement," she replied, not willing to acknowledge his rank in any way.

"Your surrender saved many lives, Admiral," he said, trying to be a bit the gentleman.

"Your betrayal of the 5 Suns Alliance Navy caused many unnecessary deaths, all of them at your hands," she snapped back. That set him off.

"You know damn well it was *you* who betrayed *us*. You never intended for my ship or my crew to survive. You planted a saboteur, deceived us by not giving us real nukes, and never told us we would be facing an incoming enemy force from Earth. Those who were killed died on the field of battle, honorably, with the exception of Captain Wilcock, who was executed by expulsion to vacuum for his treason. You sent flotillas to try and destroy my ship two separate times, but we had a weapon quite superior to anything in your arsenal," he said, pausing before delivering the coup de grace: "Which is why you are my prisoner, and not the other way around."

"We'll figure out how to match your weapon, Clement. And when we do, there will be hell to pay for you and your worlds," DeVore said.

Clement snapped around to face her. "Have you forgotten you come from one of those worlds, Admiral? Have you forgotten why we fought the War of the 5 Suns? Have you forgotten the people of Helios?"

"That's ancient history, Clement. My plans for this star system are far more important than the inevitable death of three Rim planets which have no hope of surviving on their own."

"These plans of yours, they're more important than the rest of the 5 Suns Alliance? I've figured out your plan, Elara. You intended to come here and set up your own little despotic rule, free of the 5 Suns Alliance and any responsibility, all built on the backs of slaves left here hundreds of years ago by forces unknown. You planned to seize and reverse engineer alien technology, or whatever it was that left the terraforming tech on those planets. It's why you were building such a large fleet at Kemmerine, to break away from the 5 Suns Alliance, and claim these worlds as your own," he said.

"Perhaps," she said, then looked away from him.

He eyed her. There was nothing left of his feelings for her. She was an arrogant despot, nothing like the woman he had been in love with so many years ago. He pressed his point to her. "Did you ever think that the terraforming technology on these planets could be used to improve life on the Rim worlds, or was it only to build your personal empire here?"

"It never crossed my mind, Captain. Not even for a second. Those worlds, that war, it's all in the distant past for me. Trinity is the future, and regardless of this situation, my vision for this star system will prevail."

"Your . . . vision?" He was getting angrier now. She still wouldn't look at him.

"Perhaps my original intent was to prevent a cascading failure event from driving the 5 Suns Alliance into barbarism. That doesn't matter now, anyway. The remainder of the fleet at Kemmerine will eventually come looking for us, and we'll be rescued, and then we will take this system."

"Delusional," he said. "Your ships have been most helpful in replenishing the *Beauregard* for our trip back to 5 Suns space, Admiral. And when we get to Kemmerine, with our new weapon, *your* command base will become *our* command base, and the people there will have to decide to join *us*, or leave forever."

"And just who is 'us,' Captain?"

"The Trinity Republic Navy, Admiral. Thanks to you I'll have almost thirty ships waiting for me when I get to Kemmerine, plus science labs, transports, and battleships that can all be equipped with the LEAP drive. We'll move the population willing to immigrate from the poorest planets in the 5 Suns Alliance to the richest ever discovered, where we will live in harmony with ourselves and our native brothers and sisters," he finished.

She turned back to him. "Pie in the sky, Captain."

He took a step toward her. "It's clear you need a demonstration, Admiral. You may want these," Clement said, handing her a pair of light-blocking goggles. She took them reluctantly and put them on. Clement signaled to Telco, who went to his com and communicated an order as they looked out over the empty plain of Alphus' desert.

Slowly, from the sky, a dark shape began to descend, picking up speed and burning brighter with every second as it pierced the atmosphere. It was the *Wellington*, being scuttled in full view of her commanding officer. The ship descended with a haunting slowness of speed, seemingly dragging out its own death for its audience. As the flaming hulk hit the surface there was a blinding flash of the nuclear warhead Clement had ordered left aboard her, lighting up the sky in Alphus' full red-yellow daylight. They all looked away from the brightness; even with the benefit of their protective goggles, it was a strain on the eyes. The light soon faded and Clement removed his glasses. In the desert, many kilometers away, the sight of a mushroom cloud grew in the sky like a fierce storm.

"I will see you hang for this, Clement," DeVore said, dropping her goggles to the ground as if they were useless.

"That's a discussion we can have if you ever get off this rock, Admiral. You and your crew are prisoners of the Trinity Republic Navy, the full force of which I have just invoked on you, your crew, and your ship. You will remain here, surviving if you can on your own resources and what you can find from nature. When I return to this system, I will deal with each of you appropriately."

"Will you execute me, your former lover?" said DeVore, taunting him.

His head snapped around to her, his hand going to his cobra pistol in its holster. "I'd like to do that right now, Admiral. But I've decided that I like the idea of trial and execution by lawful forces better than a swift end for you. Captain Wilcock got lucky. He died in seconds. I want you to ponder your own demise, which is why I'm stranding you on this rock. For now."

"I thought you would have learned your lesson about fighting powers bigger than you in the War of the 5 Suns," DeVore said.

"Clearly not, Admiral, and neither have you, apparently. You're the one who unwittingly gave me the most powerful weapon in the known universe. You're the one who mounted it on a Rim Confederation Navy gunship, and you're the one who put a rebel captain in command of it. Whatever you've reaped from this situation, it's you that's sown it." He started to walk away from her.

"Our scientists on Kemmerine Station will soon develop your weapon too," she said. "It's undoubtedly based on the LEAP drive reactor."

He looked back at her. "Thirty-four days from now those scientists will be *our* scientists, Admiral. I intend to take Kemmerine and make it our base of operations for the migration from the Rim planets to Trinity. And I think the 5 Suns Alliance government will find your little adventure out here to be very illuminating. Do they even know about LEAP technology? I doubt it. Hell, they might even join us against you when they find out the level of your betrayal. Now goodbye, Admiral, and good riddance." Once again he turned to walk away.

"I'm still Elara DeVore, Jared. And whether you believe it or not, I still love you," she said.

He turned back to her for the last time, shaking his head. "The Elara DeVore I loved died a long time ago. You're nothing like the woman I fell in love with, Admiral. I've moved on. I suggest you do too. And by the way, I know you were the one who betrayed the *Beauregard* to the 5 Suns Navy, back in the war. I once swore I'd put a knife in the traitor if I ever found out who it was, and now that I have, I think somehow that being stranded here, your fleet and your dreams of power destroyed, is a much better punishment. You'll have plenty of time to think on your past sins."

At that, he started to walk away, the two ensigns going with him.

"What about me?" called Yan from behind him. Clement stopped to look at her.

"I assumed you'd want to stay with your commanding officer," he said with a nod to DeVore.

Yan shook her head at him. "No, sir, not anymore. Not after what I've seen and heard." She turned to DeVore. "Admiral DeVore, I hereby resign my commission in the 5 Suns Alliance Navy, effective immediately."

"Think about what you're doing, Yan," said DeVore, a clear warning in her tone.

"I have thought about it, Admiral, and my decision is easy. After seeing your true nature I'd prefer to take my chances in an untried fleet with only one ship than to serve another minute under you, and those of your kind. I'll gladly join the Trinity Republic Navy, if Captain Clement here will have me," Yan said.

"I will," Clement said quickly. "But I won't tell you it will be simple, or as easy as leaving the 5 Suns Alliance fleet."

"I'm well aware of that," she said, then ran to catch up with him and the two ensigns.

"I would never have given you command of a ship, Yan. I suspected you were too self-serving, a spoiled rich girl. Then you proved the point for me. And I can now see that my judgment on that was correct," said DeVore, turning away from her.

"Well, at least I have the satisfaction of knowing that my captain will never send me on a one-way mission to die, Admiral. That's more than I can say about most of the poor souls that served under you." And with that Clement and the rest were gone, leaving Fleet Admiral Elara DeVore to stare out at the glowing remnants of her once powerful fleet.

# ✳ **23** ✳

The return trip to Kemmerine station was a bit of a celebration, at least at first. The crew had managed to strip the 5 Suns Alliance ships of the best rations and alcohol they had, including wines, exotic cheeses and meats, brandy, cognac, and many more luxuries. Clement, though, stayed away from the alcohol. He wanted a clear head for the challenges that waited at home. Everyone was imbibing and having fun, relaxed for the first time on their entire voyage.

When they arrived home to 5 Suns Alliance space once again there was renewed hope among the crew, hope that things would now start to get better, for all of the worlds of the 5 Suns Alliance. Their arrival at Kemmerine station was greeted with a full battle alert by the station, but thankfully no ships were scrambled to intercept the *Beauregard*.

Clement hailed them by com and told the command staff of officers running the station of the events in the Trinity system, its riches and bounty, and of his intention to take control of the station in the name of the new Trinity Republic. He also told them of his plan to help the poorest of the people of the 5 Suns Alliance to begin migration there. The officers at Kemmerine were skeptical, until Clement showed them the outcome of the battle for the Trinity worlds and the *Beauregard*'s new weapon via a visual com link. Behind the scenes, Nobli was begging him not to use the MAD weapon again in a demonstration of power. Clement didn't want to, but if the Kemmerine officers resisted . . .

In the end, they didn't. The com evidence and the accompanying telemetry seemed to be enough for the Kemmerine Station managers, in the absence of their commanding officer and the entire expeditionary fleet she had left with. They quickly negotiated terms of armistice with Clement and his mythical Trinity Republic Navy, and allowed for the *Beauregard*'s return. Clement in turn ordered all the ships at the station to stand down and for their crews to depart their ships before he would bring the *Beauregard* in.

A few hours later, Clement docked the *Beauregard* at the station in the same port she had left from, Dock 20, and the first of the crew scrambled off the ship to book trips home to their families as quickly as they could. In the end, all except for the core group of Massif, Ori, Nobli, Yan, and the three surviving ensigns, Telco, Adebayor, and Tsu, stayed aboard with Clement. Pomeroy came to Clement before she left and pledged her future support, if he would allow her a quick trip home to New Paris to see her family, which he accepted.

Eventually they all went aboard the station themselves, locking the ship down and then warning the ranking station officers that the *Beauregard* was set to use the weapon on every ship in the dock if her hull was breached without the proper entry codes and DNA match. It was a bluff, but one the officers were unwilling to call.

Clement dismissed his crew to find quarters before he was escorted, with Yan, to the Admiral's office. He noticed DeVore's name was nowhere to be found on the large oak doors or anywhere else in the office. He swore the station's officers in as temporary attachés to his command, and they readily agreed. It appeared that Admiral DeVore had run a very tight command, with her chosen officers on the inside and any others she disapproved of, regardless of their skills or experience, on the outside.

He and Yan began the long work of inventorying the station's remaining ships, personnel, and supplies. He also ordered the station to full military alert and all nonmilitary personnel off the station immediately. This caused a scramble as civilians had to book passage home, but it was done in a modicum of order, led by the able Commander Yan.

The ship inventory was sparse. DeVore had left the station with twenty-six ships: twelve destroyers, all older models than the ones she had taken to Trinity; ten light cruisers, which were at least twenty years old and likely relics from the War of the 5 Suns; three transports, which could move about three thousand people at a time; and one unfinished modern battlecruiser. All had been retrofitted, or were in the process of being retrofitted, with LEAP reactors, and the battlecruiser had two. Clement ordered the retrofitting work to continue, but he placed priority on getting the large, unnamed battlecruiser ready. They had to order the gravity-shield generators from Shenghai for all ships that were big enough to carry them, those being the older generation light cruisers. It would be weeks before they could be delivered.

Having set things in motion to his desired purpose, Clement agreed to meet with a council of five senior station commanders. All of them had ties to the Kemmerine sector, and none were from the core systems of Colonus A and B, or for that matter even Virginis. Both Kemmerine, with two inhabited planets, and the three Rim worlds were far distant from the central systems and often had different agendas from the main body of the 5 Suns Alliance. They were also poorer planets than the core systems.

Yan sat to Clement's right as his adjutant as he addressed the command council.

"Gentlemen, what we have here is an opportunity unique in human history, a chance to start anew on planets that are rich and bountiful. It is my belief that the people of both the Rim worlds and the Kemmerine sector could benefit greatly from migration to these new worlds. If you read the classified report that I sent you last night, you are aware of Admiral DeVore's plans for populating these new worlds with settlers from both the Rim and Kemmerine sector. Kemmerine is rich enough to survive on its own, especially with trade from the new Trinity planets, but the Rim planets are all failing, and the populations there face starvation if we don't intervene. Hell, it's the reason we fought the War of the 5 Suns in the first place. This migration solves the cascading societal-collapse scenario that Admiral DeVore outlined and that the 5 Suns Alliance government will face within a decade. The development of the LEAP drive opens up new possibilities for trade with the Trinity worlds, so all of the original colonies can begin to flourish again."

The command council seemed convinced by his arguments, if not totally sold on the idea of breaking away from the 5 Suns Alliance central government. An older man named Colonel Gwyneth spoke for the station commanders.

"You may not be aware of this, Captain, but since the war the penalties for treason have been enhanced," he said.

"What can be worse than hanging?" asked Clement, confused.

"They take your assets, and immediate family members can be arrested and held for long periods—years, in fact. So you can see our reluctance to break with the 5 Suns Alliance completely."

"I do see *your* problem, Colonel, but this is not a revolution, it is a migration, an opportunity to save all the 5 Suns Alliance from collapse."

"Yes," said Gwyneth, "but you are declaring your ship as part of the 'Trinity Republic Navy,' which we both know does not exist. I propose a more . . . diffident approach to the 5 Suns government."

Clement sat back, intrigued by this proposal. "I'm listening," he said.

Gwyneth cleared his throat before starting again. "We here on this council, we are old men and women, not youthful like you are."

"I'm forty-four," cut in Clement.

"Yes, but still, a man very much in his prime. We here"—at this his hand swept the room—"are not of a mind to change allegiances at this time in our lives, to upset the apple cart, if you will."

"I'm waiting for you to get to the point."

Gwyneth faced his palms to Clement in a soothing gesture. "We think, sir, that a project of this size, an undertaking of this sort—millions being moved from our star systems to other, unknown, worlds—this is a job for a younger man, one with the vigor and ambition that we, in some ways, lack. We think you would find a receptive audience for your proposals in the Core Alliance Command, if you contacted them."

At that, a gray-haired woman spoke up. "Sir, my name is Commander Gracel. What we are trying to offer you is our support of your mission in the Trinity system, and since the 5 Suns Core Command knew nothing of Admiral DeVore's plans, we believe, with our backing, that you have a very good opportunity to be placed in command of this station, not as a potential adversary, but as its legitimate commander, if you are willing to perform your duties under the 5 Suns Navy flag."

"Are you willing to accept that, Captain?" said Gwyneth. "Come back to the 5 Suns Navy, and share the proposal you have with the Core Command?"

Clement looked to Yan, who stayed stoic, and then smiled. "That

I am, Colonel. That I am. But there is one thing I haven't mentioned about Trinity, and that is the presence of natives," said Clement. There were surprised looks around the conference table.

"Natives?" said Gwyneth. At this Yan cut in.

"A few hundred thousand, combined, likely on all three worlds. We don't know who placed them there, or why, but they are completely human in every way," she said. At this Clement jumped back in to the conversation.

"It is our intention to set aside reserved areas for their society to flourish, to live naturally, as they have for many decades. We believe it should be up to this command, Kemmerine Station, to ensure their peaceful survival."

After another hour of this, going over high-level plans and a proposed schedule, Clement left it to the station commanders to make their decisions. The next morning they told him they would present his proposals to the 5 Suns Alliance Core Command, along with the evidence against Admiral DeVore. Clement decided that was good enough.

It would have to be.

# ☆ 24 ☆

It took a few more weeks for everything to be figured out, but eventually the 5 Suns Alliance government agreed to terms for the migration and placed Clement in charge of the entire Kemmerine and Rim sectors, as a 5 Suns Navy Admiral. Clement had to re-swear his oath, and this time he was frankly glad to take it, for the first time in his life.

In all honesty the 5 Suns government seemed glad to be rid of the problems with the Rim planets, and they voluntarily ceded responsibility for oversight of them to Clement. For his part, Clement agreed to full, free trade with the alliance in exchange for a revenue-sharing agreement of seventeen percent to his station. That would be enough to modernize his fleet and keep the Core Command out of his hair for a very long time.

About a quarter of the station workers and navy personnel opted to leave Kemmerine for home or the Core worlds, but they were quickly replaced by new recruits from the Rim, and others from the two Kemmerine worlds, New Paris and Shenghai. It would be a difficult transition for a new administration at the station, but Clement was confident that would work itself out with time.

The transition was already well underway when the crew of the *Beauregard* gathered at The Battered Hull a month later for a reunion of sorts. Clement and Yan were joined by Massif, Ori, Pomeroy, the three ensigns—whom Clement had promoted again to full lieutenants—and even the mostly socially inept Nobli came by. Yan was at his side in a fresh uniform denoting her new rank of captain.

Admiral Clement led a toast for Lieutenant Daniel, lost on the excursion to the Earth Ark. He made sure all the lieutenants got their new ranks made official, with Daniel's awarded posthumously. He even sent a letter to Daniel's parents personally on 5 Suns Alliance Navy letterhead.

As the party wound down, a rather drunk Yan came up to him and put one arm over his shoulder.

"Would you like to go . . . " Then she seemed to lose her train of thought.

"Go where?"

"I don't know. New Hong Kong. See the sites, take a vacation for once."

It had been a very long time since he'd had a vacation, but: "I'm making plans for the next week or so. You'll have to survive without me for a while."

"What? What could be more important than me?" she slurred, clomping her beer glass down on the heavy wood table, some of the contents sloshing out. Then she got distracted trying to wipe up the table. Clement signaled a bar girl who came over with a wet rag and cleaned up Yan's mess quickly. Yan turned to him again.

"Where?" she said.

"Where what?"

"Where are you going?"

Clement finished his glass of sailor's ale before answering. "I'm going home," he said.

She looked confused. "To Argyle?"

He shook his head. "No, to Ceta. I'm going to try to convince my parents to emigrate to the Trinity system."

"Never been to Ceta," she mumbled. "But why go now? It will be at least six months before the first colonists go out . . . there," she said, pointing to nowhere in particular. She drank again from her glass before Clement pulled it away from her. He grabbed her around the waist and spun her close so that they were facing each other on their bar stools.

"Why can't I come?" she asked.

"Well, for one thing, you're drunk," he replied.

She mock slapped him on the shoulder. "Am not."

"Are."

"Not."

He let that hang in the air between them for a moment. "But, well, if you've never seen Ceta . . . " He trailed off.

"Can I go? Can I? Can I go with you?"

"There's not much to see. No monorails like on Shenghai, just railroads. No big, beautiful oceans or mountains, just salty lakes and a few brown rolling hills. It's a very dull planet."

He was playing with her and she knew it.

"I want to go."

"Why?"

"To be with you, Jared. Your . . . my only real friend," she said, turning away and taking another, much smaller, drink from her ale. He reached up and pushed a hanging bang away from her face.

"Well, having a traveling companion does sound like fun."

"It's settled then. What time are we leaving?"

"The shuttle to Argyle is at 5:00 A.M." She looked down at her watch, which read ten past midnight.

"Better take hangover repressors," she said.

"Good idea. But not just yet. I kinda like you when you're drunk," he said.

"You have a one-track mind," she replied, pointing an accusing finger at him.

"I don't."

"Hmm," she said, wrapping her arms around his neck. "It's time to go, Admiral, sir. We have a busy day tomorrow."

"Yes, we do." Clement looked around the room. The three newly minted lieutenants were sitting together, chattering up a storm. Mika Ori and Massif and Pomeroy were engaged in a deep and meaningful conversation, about what he wasn't sure, but with those three, you never knew.

He took Yan by the hand and led her out of The Battered Hull, but stopped at the door and turned back one last time, looking at his crew. They had all done a hell of a job. And then he noticed something he'd never seen before. Hassan Nobli was waving his hands back and forth, no doubt explaining some complex engineering concept to the bar girl, who sat enraptured at his every word and gesture, laughing and smiling. Then Clement smiled too.

Hell, maybe Nobli would finally get that girlfriend after all.